MILA

REDEMPT

LA
ION 2.0

DEBRA DRIZA

KATHERINE TEGEN BOOKS
An Imprint of HarperCollins Publishers

Katherine Tegen Books is an imprint of HarperCollins Publishers.

MILA 2.0: Redemption
Copyright © 2016 by HarperCollins Publishers
All rights reserved. Printed in the United States of America.
No part of this book may be used or reproduced in any manner
whatsoever without written permission except in the case of brief
quotations embodied in critical articles and reviews. For information
address HarperCollins Children's Books, a division of HarperCollins
Publishers, 195 Broadway, New York, NY 10007.
www.epicreads.com

Library of Congress Control Number: 2014949407
ISBN 978-0-06-209042-3

Typography by Erin Fitzsimmons
16 17 18 19 20   PC/RRDH   10 9 8 7 6 5 4 3 2 1
❖
First Edition

For my mom, who never had a chance to read this book . . .
though I like to think she would have approved

ONE

The mountains, with their soaring peaks and yawning valleys, gave off the illusion of safety. A no-man's-land, blanketed with a layer of white.

I trudged through the snow and wove through the pine trees, which hung the air with their brisk, pungent scent. In the distance, the mountains towered over me; immovable, watchful sentries. By comparison, I felt so small.

I clung to that feeling as tightly as the unlit torch that I clutched in my hand. Insignificant. Unimportant. Unknown. In my mind, those three words translated into one delicious thing: freedom.

I inhaled deeply, embracing the pleasant burn of crisp air and the serenity of untouched scenery. The tiny patches of blue that peeked out behind clouds were translucent and pale. Not a deep blue, but worn.

Faded, like a pair of eyes; full of humor, almost covered by a sweep of messy brown hair.

My synthetic heart accelerated in a combination of yearning and fear.

The wilderness could trick you into thinking you didn't have a past. But even though certain pieces of my recent history were inaccessible for now, some would always stay with me, no matter what.

Like kind, caring, funny Hunter.

Crash.

My head jerked to the right, but I relaxed on the next breath. The noise didn't signify a threat. It was a different, yet equally kind boy, tripping over a snow-covered branch and performing a hop-skip to regain his balance.

"Just pitched my last torch. That'll keep the bears away from the cabin at night," he said, giving his short, sandy hair a shake. His constantly rumpled shirt collar was at odds with his steady, even presence.

Lucas Webb. The reason I was safely hidden away in these mountains.

For the time being, at least.

"I'm still looking for a good place for this one," I said, holding up the top end of my torch.

"What about over there?" Lucas pointed to a patch of ground just a few feet south of us.

"Looks good to me."

As we walked under the outstretched pine branches, a fresh clump of snow shook free, landing on my nose. I brushed it away with my hand. The icy sensation sparked something in a far corner of my mind, like springing a hidden door to a secret compartment.

Without thinking, I set the torch on the ground and squatted, curling my fingers around a handful of snow. It compacted into a tight, frigid ball.

"Sarah! You wouldn't dare. . . . I'm barely hanging on to this thing as it is—AHHH!"

A girl squealed, her long brown hair streaming out of a teal beanie embellished with a leering monster face. Her gloved hands windmilled, and then she toppled backward into a giant heap of snow. Her feet were still connected to the crimson-and-black snowboard.

She sat up on her elbows, laughing. "You'd better run," she warned. "You are so dead."

My hand fluttered to my chest in mock horror.

"Wow, Chloe, violent much? I was just testing out the laws of physics. You know, schoolwork."

"What's wrong?" Lucas's concerned voice snapped me back into the present, and the scene vanished as quickly as it had appeared.

I peered down at my hand and unclenched my knuckles. No snow remained, just a watery mess that oozed down the side of my wrist.

I rose. "Nothing. Just another fragment. From Sarah," I

added when I saw his lips about to form another question.

The irony almost made me laugh. Portions of my recent memory were missing, segments that I was desperate to retrieve. No progress on that front. Meanwhile, my mind had no problem spewing forth old memories from the dead girl whose brain matter I shared.

Welcome to the life of a teenage android.

We walked to the edge of the clearing, where we paused to stake my torch and admire the view. But I couldn't quite find the level of peace I'd had moments before.

Not when Lucas was staring at me again.

He'd been shooting me these long, penetrating glances when he didn't think I'd notice.

Lucas knew better. Noticing was kind of my thing. A little bonus of being a walking, talking computer.

"Everything okay?" I asked, turning to face him.

He gave an awkward shrug and shoved his hands into his pockets.

"Oh, yeah. Very convincing." My tone was teasing, but a chill began to form in my chest.

We were tucked away in the wilderness. No one knew we were here. But that didn't stop me from fretting that our every move was being watched. Somewhere beyond these mountains, General Holland—my sadistic creator— was hunting me down, and he wouldn't stop until I was "terminated." Quinn, Holland's old coworker—who had kidnapped me for her own purposes, held me captive, and then abandoned my unconscious body in the desert—was still out there too. What if she was hoping to finish whatever ill-conceived plan she'd started?

And then there was the person I loved. The person who had forgiven me when I'd lied to him, over and over again. The person who'd given me a second chance, only to find out I wasn't the girl he thought I was. Only to find out I wasn't a real girl at all.

The chill in my chest spread its icy tentacles. I had no idea where Hunter Lowe was right now, or whether or not he was okay. He was fine when I last saw him with his parents at Quinn's secret techno-lair. He was maybe a little shocked to discover they were working with her vigilante group, the Vita Obscura, but still safe. . . .

Except—what if Lucas knew something to the contrary and was scared to tell me?

I stared at the tree line, not bothering to huddle into my jacket. Jackets offered no protection from a chill that was generated by fear. I tried to clear my head, but my sensors kept firing, flooding me with useless information.

Temperature: 37 degrees F.

Windchill: 35 degrees F.

Nearest human threat: 153 ft.

I sighed, unfazed by this so-called threat. Lucas's older brother, Tim, who was probably drinking himself into a stupor in the cabin, was more of a danger to himself than to anyone else.

Lucas watched me from the corner of his eye. "I still haven't figured out where or when the device will detonate, if that's what you're thinking."

Device. Detonate.

My hands flew down to press against my suddenly clenched stomach. To the same spot I'd been examining in disbelief since Lucas had revealed that planted inside of me was a masterfully built, virtually undetectable bomb. No matter how many times I gripped my skin, probed and prodded with my fingers, I couldn't discern anything underneath. Not the ropy twist of wires, not the hard edges of building materials that nature had never intended.

General Holland had done a brilliant job of hiding the fact that I was a disaster waiting to happen. He'd even hidden it from me.

I'd just begun to accept myself as I really was—not really human, but not just a machine either. I might have lacked the typical features associated with living beings, but I still had thoughts, and I could still feel. I could experience shattering sorrow. And love. I'd begun to embrace every strange yet amazing notion of what I was and how I was made, only to have the universe chuck a cosmic wrench at me.

I wasn't just a machine. I was a weapon.

Lucas took one look at my face and flinched. "Sorry to bring it up," he said. "I don't want you to worry. I'm making some headway. I've been logging in remotely to Holland's computer—incognito, of course—to see if I can find anything in his files. I'm researching everything I can about timers on explosives. Some pieces are falling into place."

He hesitated with his hand midway between us before curving it around my shoulder and squeezing. "I won't stop until I find what we need. Okay?"

I wanted his words and touch to reassure me, but neither cracked the surface of my anxiety. Not this time. "Thank you. For everything. I don't know how to repay you, or Tim. It's just . . . if anyone gets hurt because of me, I—"

He bent down so that we were eye to eye. "Remember, there's a two-hour window once it's set to detonate. That is more than enough time to ensure my safety, or anyone else's. Got it?"

I scanned his expression, searching for any evidence he was just saying that to make me feel better.

Direct eye contact: No averting gaze to the left.

Hand position: Not touching own face.

Heart rate: 68 bpm, steady.

Blood pressure: 108/64.

Assessment: Body language and physical measurements inconsistent with lying.

As usual, Lucas was telling the truth. Which meant accepting that he was okay with the risk—even if I wasn't. Logically, I knew he was right. A two-hour window would be plenty of time. But the emotional part of me couldn't be swayed. Deep down, I lived in terror that somehow, I might harm Lucas.

And I'd caused so much collateral damage already.

In my mind, I saw Quinn talking to me about the procedure that would limit my emotions. I saw myself agreeing—anything to shield me from all of my internal pain. Next I was up on the table, waiting for Quinn and Samuel to begin the process. And then, the images stopped. Just like an old movie reel that kept getting stuck in the same exact spot. No matter how hard I tried, I couldn't push past the snag, couldn't see how the movie ended.

"What's wrong?" Lucas asked.

I relaxed my muscles into a natural expression, but not quickly enough.

"Thinking about Quinn?" he pressed. Ugh. Sometimes, he was way too astute for his own good.

"Yes. But everything's still a void after the procedure. Any progress on your end?"

Lucas's eyes lit up. He flexed his fingers in the space between us, as if getting ready to conduct an orchestra. I knew what that meant—I'd seen it before. He performed that funny hand maneuver whenever he was excited about some prospective technological breakthrough.

"What? Did you figure out how to restore the data she erased?"

He grinned. "Not completely, not yet. But I'm close."

My shoulders sagged.

"But soon we can connect your system to my restoration program and give it a try," he said, attuned to my subtle changes in posture.

"Really? When?"

"Maybe tomorrow morning. Can you wait that long?"

"Why can't you just tell me what you do know? We can try and fill in the blanks together," I suggested, hoping that Lucas would agree to play detective with me.

"I don't think it's prudent," he said softly. "I only know bits and pieces from picking up your thoughts and talking to you via remote. I don't have the entire picture, and I don't want to give you misleading information. It will be better if we restore your drive."

It was the same line he'd fed me every time I'd pressed him for more details.

The problem was, I read between the lines. The only reason misleading information would be problematic was if something terrible went down after Quinn and Samuel had hacked into me back at her lab.

"We'll get your memory back. One way or another."

The quiet reassurance in Lucas's voice soothed me. I

might not have fully agreed with his decision, but one thing was for sure—I trusted him completely.

Even though my memory would be useless once the bomb went off.

I fell into step beside him as we headed back to his brother's cabin. My measured, even steps were a contrast to his awkward limp, the result of a congenital foot anomaly that no amount of surgery could completely fix. Not that Lucas was weakened by it at all. He was lean but wiry, stronger than he looked. And mentally, he was about as fierce as they came. Without him, I never would have made it out of General Holland's compound alive, and he'd risked everything to come and rescue me in the desert. Even now, he was here with me at great personal risk. He'd taken medical leave from his job at SMART Ops, but he could only be gone for so long without arousing suspicion.

Any day now, he might have to go back and leave me behind. And if I was being honest with myself, the thought of that terrified me.

"Come on, let's get you where it's warm," he said.

I raised an eyebrow. "Like that really matters."

"Fine, I'm freezing out here. Can we go now?"

I grinned and nudged him with my elbow. As we walked, the brown horizontal lines of a rustic cabin peeked through the trees on our left.

Actual distance: 26.25 ft.

As usual, my android sensors required that I had the precise measurements. Because that information was so crucial when you housed an explosive device inside your body.

We passed the trees and entered the small clearing. The A-frame log cabin sat in the rear, ugly and squat like a beehive that had been smashed by an angry fist into half its normal size. Nothing adorned the walls or windows. The rooftop slouched well below the tree line, and the only way to get here by car was via a precarious, off-road path that you had to search forever to find. The walkway that led to the front of the cabin had been shoveled recently, leaving two short snow walls on either side.

The main door creaked open. A scrawny, pale man stumbled out onto the porch, rubbing his eyes like he'd just woken up. When he saw his little brother coming toward him, his body tensed and his eyes narrowed.

"Jesus, Lucas, make sure the door latches when you go outside. And wear your damn jacket if you don't want to catch pneumonia and die!"

Tim Webb followed that proclamation by chucking a navy blue coat out the door and onto the damp walkway. As usual, his gaze completely avoided me. He rarely spoke to me in more than monosyllables or grunts, making it clear that helping Lucas give me asylum didn't exactly thrill him. But I was fine with him keeping his distance. With his bloodshot eyes, unwashed body, and constant reek of alcohol, Tim was one person I wasn't too eager to get to know.

After a particularly loud grunt, Tim slammed the door behind him. The glass in the windows rattled. Lucas stared at the discarded jacket but didn't move.

"Is there ever a day when he wakes up on the right side of the bed? Just wondering," I said, trying to lighten the mood.

Lucas's attempt at a smile failed, strained creases settling around his eyes. "No. At least, not in all the years I remember living with him in the same house. Not a morning person."

We walked toward the jacket. Tim might be grumpy in the mornings and drink from a flask with disturbing regularity, but he was the reason we had a roof over our heads right now. Except for Lucas, supposedly no one else knew about his retreat up here, deep in the thick of unspoiled Bitterroot land. He'd stepped up to the plate when his brother asked for a big favor, and he didn't even know me. For now, I'd gladly deal with Tim's foul humor if it meant distracting myself from the uneasiness that something—or someone— lurked over my shoulder.

Because that feeling never really went away, not for good. It lingered, haunting me like one of Sarah's memories, like the sound of my name on my mother's lips. Like the vision of Hunter's eyes, staring back at me with hope.

Hope could probably survive on this mountain forever, and maybe I could too. But this bomb inside me, it changed everything. No matter where I went, there was really no such thing as a "safe" place. Safety was just an illusion. Because no matter how well I hid or how fast I ran, I couldn't outrun myself.

Even so, I couldn't help but wonder if I should just slip away quietly into the night. Then the only casualty would be me, right? Not a perfect ending, but better than leaving a path of destruction in my wake.

A jolt of determination pushed back against those thoughts, urging me to fight. Reminding me that I still had so many questions. I knew Holland had already created multiple Milas. Both of my "sisters" had been destroyed, but what if there were more androids, and Holland had subjected them to exactly the same horrors as me? When I boiled everything down to the simplest form, not knowing Holland's master plan was even more terrifying than the bomb inside my gut. What exactly was he after?

Was it possible that Tim knew? I'd caught a flash of anger between him and Lucas when they were together, but I didn't know why. Things had been so overwhelming and chaotic when Lucas and I had first arrived that I hadn't wanted to pump him for information. But I knew that the longer it took to get my memory back and figure out the inner workings of the bomb, the more time our enemy had to regroup.

I needed more information. The sooner, the better.

"You're wondering how Holland knew my brother, aren't you?" Lucas said matter-of-factly as he picked up the jacket without bothering to put it on. I trailed him over to a woodpile. A hatchet leaned against the logs.

Specifically, I was wondering why Holland had called Tim a chickenshit back in DC, but I wasn't about to say that out loud. "Oh. My. God. While we were out in the desert, did you plant a thought-reading chip in my head?"

Lucas responded with a half smile and a quick shrug. He picked up the hatchet, widened his stance, and took a swing. A log cracked, but didn't split completely. He grunted and repeated the motion until the wood separated into two halves.

"Don't need one. Sometimes, you're an open book. Maybe it's a glitch in your subterfuge software."

I snorted. "Or maybe you're a glitch."

His eyes widened, and then he laughed. "But I see that teen-girl programming remains intact."

I stopped short of an eye roll, because, really, no sense in proving him right. "Tim?" I prodded.

"Tim. Right." The smile faded, and his grip tightened on the handle. He hoisted the hatchet over his shoulder, inhaled, and then let it fly again.

Thwack!

The blade hit the log a bit off center, but the blade still dug in, sending wood chips flying.

"So, obviously, you caught that Holland is my relative. Uncle. My mom was his sister."

The hatchet lifted again, then lowered.

Thwack.

Air whooshed from my lungs. Yes, I guess I'd figured that much out, but to hear him say it aloud. . . . That he was related by blood to Holland. It was almost unfathomable.

He rested the ax on the dirt, blade down, brushing at the sweat that already beaded on his forehead. I noticed his center of gravity was more off than usual; he was favoring his bad leg. The way he accepted that less-than-perfect part of himself was something I'd admired from the first time I'd met him.

"You want me to take over?"

Without hesitation, he extended the hatchet to me. "You kidding? I was hoping you'd offer three swings ago. Not exactly my forte," he said, with no trace of embarrassment.

I accepted the tool, and lined up to swing.

Arc: 150 degrees.

Velocity: 90 mph.

Metal hit wood with precision and force, cleaving the log into two perfect halves.

Lucas whistled. "From now on, you're in charge of firewood."

Worked for me. Since angst was in my repertoire of android emotions, bludgeoning the wood provided a satisfying outlet. Even though I'd enjoyed Lucas's company a great deal over the last week and a half, I couldn't imagine living up here permanently without going stir-crazy. Between Holland and the V.O., I'd experienced more than enough confinement in my short lifetime.

I rolled that last word around in my head. Lifetime. Did the fact that I clung to such words mean I still hadn't accepted my not-quite-human reality? I didn't think so. It was just—my reality wasn't exactly black-and-white. A big part of my history enmeshed with Sarah's, and she happened to be a real, live human girl.

I'd spent a long time in the beginning fighting to be one thing or the other: human or android. That had been an exercise in futility.

I was human. I was android. I was neither. I was both. In the long run, what difference did the label make? I was simply . . . me.

Air whistled when I swung the hatchet again.

"Tim is six years older than me. For a long time growing up, he was the golden child. First in his class, star on the soccer team. When I was younger, he was my hero. I wanted to be just like him."

Lucas's voice sounded wistful. I paused, studying his expression. Nostalgic, I finally decided.

"And then what?" I said, when he continued to gaze right through me. I choked down a sudden knot of envy for those good memories he was clearly reliving.

I'd give anything to have an actual childhood to look back on. But at least I had fragments of Sarah's, and that was something.

He busied himself lining up the next chunk of wood for me. "He started to fall apart in college. The usual story—smart, sheltered kid from a smallish town gets a taste of freedom and goes wild."

He stepped away, giving me space to swing.

"Except—our family life, it wasn't exactly the white-picket-fence affair that my parents would have others believe. My dad could be harsh. I don't know, maybe it's because my mom grew up with a brother like Holland—maybe that's just what she was used to. Dad really zeroed in on my brother in a way that he didn't on me. For that, I'll be forever grateful. I'm not saying he's directly responsible for Tim getting involved in drugs, because we always have choices, right? But my brother didn't really learn healthy ways to cope, either."

Choices. We always had choices. How many times had I made the wrong ones in the past? Most recently, I'd allowed Quinn to suppress my emotions . . . or at least, I'd given her permission. Now there was a gap where crucial memories should reside.

I shivered, the shadows in my mind stirring again. Things would improve once Lucas restored the missing pieces. At least then maybe I'd know what had happened to Hunter and his parents. Not to mention Daniel, the man who'd fathered and raised Sarah, and helped my "mother," Nicole, and Holland to create me.

"So, he got into drugs in college?"

"Yeah, only, my parents didn't know it at the time. None of us did. He hid it well, but his grades started slipping. Of course, my dad didn't think to ask why or if anything was wrong. All he did was worry about how it would reflect on him, having a less-than-perfect son. So he told Tim he'd cut his funding off for good unless he enrolled in the military and got his act together."

He paused again, so I halved another log. Overhead, the sun sank in the sky, and the air grew steadily colder.

"I'm guessing that didn't work out so well for him? Holland mentioned helping with a dishonorable discharge."

Lucas shrugged helplessly. "We still don't know exactly what happened, just that Tim went MIA from the army, and Holland covered for him. But Tim was never the same again. He's . . . broken."

Broken? I wasn't sure that was the word I'd use. But Tim did seem jumpy. He startled easily, like the time when I'd entered the kitchen without him knowing. He'd whirled so fast, he'd tripped and dropped a glass. Sometimes he studied me when he thought I wasn't looking. Pulse and blood pressure analysis made it clear that I made him uncomfortable. Was it because he was always drunk?

Or was there something else?

I'd learned never to discount any hint of suspicion, however small. Even though Tim seemed more likely to pass out standing up than do anything to endanger me, he was still on my radar as someone to watch.

I continued to hack wood until we had a sizable pile, watching Lucas out of my peripheral vision. There were only two people I trusted in this world. One of them was right next to me, and the other I hoped was on his way back to California, driving down the Pacific Coast Highway toward the home that he loved, where he could be happy again . . . and free.

Lucas bent to place the halved pieces on the makeshift carrier—a plastic sled attached to a rope—and I helped. Then, we dragged the wood toward the cabin.

As we walked, something occurred to me. "If Holland is your uncle, why do you address him so formally?" I searched my memory and no, not once had I heard Lucas call him anything other than General Holland or Sir.

Lucas snorted. "Are you kidding? Do you think he's the kind of guy who'd be okay going by Uncle? Please. He's all about the power, always has been. What's the point of being a general if you can't lord it over people?"

I nodded. That fit in with everything I knew about Holland. He was power hungry, and he wanted complete control. To him, image was everything, and if you threatened that image, well . . . the consequences could be disastrous.

My mind conjured up an image of Holland's sun-worn face, complete with lifeless gray eyes, and my teeth clenched. Precisely why I'd have to leave this mountain eventually.

I swooped down and grabbed a log, calculating just how much pressure I'd need to use in order to reduce it to a crumble of dust. The lingering image of Holland's face unleashed a cascade of pain and anguish, then a wave of blind rage. For a moment, there was a flicker of memory. *My fingers clutched something cold and metal; a scream almost brought me to my knees.* But before I could capture the flickers in a complete picture, the memory was gone.

I looked down at my hands, which were now covered in brown ash. Bits of splintered wood piled at my feet. Lucas kicked the debris away without so much as a raised brow, like he'd seen me crush a log a million times before.

Lucas was different from anyone I knew.

In his case, different was a good thing.

TWO

When Lucas opened the door to the cabin, a gust of heat hit us like a wall. I recoiled, my mind sucked back into the past once again. I'd barely saved my mom from the fire Holland had engineered back in his underground lab, and then there were the wisps of Sarah's memory. Another fire, blazing through a house in the suburbs. *Billowing smoke, hungry flames. My dad's frantic voice.* A different girl, with a different past . . . whose history lived on in me.

"Mila? You okay?"

I blinked, and the inferno disappeared. Only a small, cheerful fire blazed in the stone fireplace.

"Yeah, I'm fine. It's just . . . fires. They make me a little twitchy sometimes."

Lucas shot me a sympathetic look. "Understandable."

Tim turned from the small stove, where a large stockpot steamed, filling the cabin with the aroma of beef stew. As he stirred, I noticed his hands trembled a little on the spoon. He looked us over briefly and shook his head.

"You two must have a death wish. No flashlights or anything? Once the sun goes down, you can't see shit."

As usual, his hair was unbrushed, his jaw obscured by a scraggly beard, flecked with what appeared to be the remnants of breakfast. His faded jeans and gray flannel were the same he'd worn the last two days. Suddenly, I was glad for the aroma of the stew.

His bloodshot gaze zeroed in on Lucas. "And where's your gun? How many times have I got to tell you? There are plenty of natural predators 'round here. I know, you don't shoot living creatures," he said, when Lucas started to protest, "but you might change your mind if push comes to shove. At the very least, you could fire a warning shot to scare them away. Mountain lions and bears don't much like the sound or smell of gunfire."

"Hey, I'm eating your nonvegetarian meals without complaining, aren't I?" Lucas responded. Tim stared him down and Lucas sighed. "Fine. I'll take a gun. But one of you two had best show me how to use it, so I don't shoot off my good foot."

Tim, apparently satisfied, turned back to the stew. "Don't

know how you escaped hunting weekends with Dad, any-way." That came out as a mumble; I wasn't even sure he intended us to hear.

Lucas shrugged. "Oh, that was easy. He didn't want to risk being bogged down by his special needs," he said matter-of-factly. Then, his lips curved into a wicked smile. "That, and the fact that I endlessly printed up anti-hunting articles off the internet and left them all around the house, in his car . . . taped to the deer heads. I'm pretty sure he was disgusted by my lack of manliness."

Tim grunted, muttering a few words under his breath. Not loudly enough for Lucas to catch them, but loud enough for me.

"Better than the alternative."

I felt a ripple of sympathy for Tim. Hard to believe how very differently the two brothers had turned out. Sud-denly, I was even more thankful for Lucas's solid presence beside me.

We piled the wood by the fireplace before settling into the dated but comfy stuffed chairs. A faint scent of cinna-mon and vanilla lingered in the faded brown fabric.

I noticed Lucas winced a little as he adjusted his position.

"Your leg?" I asked.

"It's healed up fine. Just gets a little stiff sometimes."

I bowed my head, guilt gnawing at me, but then it snapped back up when I heard Lucas say my name.

"Stop worrying, Mila. No regrets," he whispered.

Lucas had taken a bullet back at Holland's lab in a last-ditch effort to buy Mom and me time to escape. He'd risked his life for us, even though he had no reason to. From day one, nothing about me seemed to faze him.

He stood. "I need to check on something. Be right back."

I watched him retreat to the first doorway on the left, where he slept in a room on a tiny twin bed that was surrounded by loads of his computer equipment. I could hear the humming, even from outside.

Tim went to the food cooler and unwrapped a packet of cheese, sniffed it, then shrugged and dumped the contents onto a plate. "Don't take it personal. He always was socially awkward," he said in an overly loud voice, and without a hint of irony.

"I heard that!" Lucas called out from around the corner.

"Whatever," Tim said with a smirk. When he caught me watching him, his jaw tightened and he slunk back over to the stove.

I turned my back and reclined in the chair. Somewhere in the distance, a coyote howled, his forlorn cry ringing through the still night air. An answering call yipped from the opposite direction and a sudden chill crept up my arms.

"They're on the trail of something," Tim mused from the kitchen, almost wistfully.

I pulled a blanket over myself and huddled under it,

trying not to think of my own set of predators.

Tim spoke again, over the sound of silverware clanging into metal camping bowls. "I'm no good at conversations."

Was that an olive branch? Or something else? "That's okay. I'm not either."

"Not true. You and Lucas talk nonstop." He said it casually, but the sounds from the kitchen had silenced.

"Do we?"

Tim didn't know why I was here, actually. In fact, Tim had specifically requested to be spared the details. He was bright enough to realize we were probably hiding and neck-deep in trouble, but he'd made it clear that he wanted no part of it. The less Tim knew, the safer he was, and that was fine with me. He might not make the best company, but he was still Lucas's brother. I didn't want anything bad to happen to him. Especially not because of me.

The clanging started up again. "It's kind of annoying. How close you guys are," he said. "He and I were never like that."

Close. The word rattled around in my head and caused me to shift in the chair. Was that the right word to describe Lucas and me? Yes, we'd been through a lot together, and he was someone I could count on in this ugly mess I called a life. But admitting that out loud seemed wrong, somehow. Like by admitting that Lucas and I were close, I was betraying Hunter, who'd given up so much to be with me.

If only I could contact him. Hear his voice again. Know that he was okay.

Tim cleared his throat with a rough cough. "Grub's almost ready. Go fetch Boy Genius."

"Sure," I said. Even though it had been more command than request. His tone reminded me, suddenly, of Holland's.

I stood and made my way toward Lucas's room, knocking on the door with an "It's me."

"Come in."

I entered and smiled at the sight that greeted me. Lucas had stuffed a lot of equipment into a tiny space. Two open laptops gleamed on top of his desk, while off to the side were three desktop computers, stacked in precarious towers. A full-size monitor fought for space with the laptops, while another one sprawled on the floor near Lucas's feet. Several fancy routers shimmered with green and blue lights, their silver casings lit by the glow of the desk lamp.

Lucas's fingers flew over keys, his eyes roving over the content that popped up on the monitors.

Code, mainly, I realized as I read over his shoulder. Mostly hacked. One IP address in particular caught my eye and I flinched.

He was deep in an attempt to infiltrate SMART Ops— Holland's brainchild. The organization responsible for making me.

"What are you up to?"

"Just following a hunch," he replied.

"Need any help?" I asked, even though I knew how Lucas would respond. He was afraid if I hacked into any covert network using my android functions, I might tip someone off to our whereabouts. He'd cautioned me against using so much as my GPS. For now, anything that could leave behind even a whiff of my IP address was banned . . . until he could figure out a way to cloak my information and keep me from detection.

Lucas continued to bite his lip, ignoring me for a second as he scanned more information. His body practically hummed with intensity in the chair. I smiled when I saw the hair on the right side of his head standing straight up, the result of his fingers raking through when he was deep in thought.

Tim might have meant "Boy Genius" as a dig, but I found nothing insulting about it. Lucas, in his quiet, brainy way, was a force to be reckoned with.

"No, not tonight. I just need to . . . crap!"

A page he'd been looking at vanished. His shoulders slumped for an instant before squaring again. "Oh, no, you don't . . ." he muttered. The tapping resumed.

While I was thankful for all that he was doing on my behalf, I couldn't have felt more helpless if I tried. Here I was, this miracle of technology, yet all I could do was twiddle my thumbs and contemplate the universe and my unbelievable, potentially destructive role in it. I hated feeling sorry for myself, but my emotions once again had free rein since Quinn's program had been reversed.

Which was usually a relief. Just not so much at this exact moment.

"Well, dinner's ready," I said. "Smells like rabbit. Maybe we can strain the meat out and just leave the fur clumps—that still counts as vegetarian, right?"

Lucas was so focused on his work that he barely noticed my lame joke. "Okay, be there in a minute."

"Actually, I think I'm going to wind down upstairs," I said.

"You sure?"

"Yeah, it's been a while since my last sleep cycle. Probably should catch up. Tell Tim my stomach is bothering me again, okay?"

It wasn't a lie. My stomach was definitely bothering me, in the sense that the gut-esque portion of my anatomy felt like it was churning away.

"Will do. Good night," he said with an absent wave.

I closed the door behind me and climbed the stairs to my tiny room in the loft. The twin bed was squished up next to a shabby pine chest of drawers. Stark wooden beams crisscrossed overhead, and a real fur rug took up most of the bare floor. Every time my bare feet touched the soft hair, I couldn't help but wonder how the animal had died. Had the animal known it was being hunted, and run for its life? Or had the hunter startled it? Caught it by surprise?

I hopped onto the bed, vowing to shove the rug in the closet come morning. We'd been here for over a week, and while the respite was desperately needed, I knew from experience just how quickly the peace and calm here could vanish.

Images flickered behind my eyes, remnants of the last scene I remembered from Quinn's.

The examination table.

Quinn's auburn hair flashing as she readied her instruments.

Me, feeling utterly overwhelmed. Agreeing to allow her to hack into my programming and alter my emotions.

And then, emptiness. No matter how many times I replayed my memory, the time period between this moment and the desert was a total blank. I didn't know what concerned me more—the dark, missing hours in my past or the dark possibilities awaiting me in the future?

I shivered and wrapped the blanket more tightly around me, hoping that Lucas would go back into his room after dinner and finish the program that might restore the lost data. Visions of Hunter flashed through my head again, and even though I tried to convince myself that he was fine—his parents were with him, after all—the chill refused to fade.

God, I missed him.

I curled into a ball to warm myself, even though I knew the attempt would fail.

My chills, they didn't originate from the environment.

My chills came from fear.

"Mila? You up and about in there?"

Lucas's soft rap at the door early the next morning was accompanied by a whisper.

"No. I went to Disneyland. I'll be back tomorrow," I whispered back.

The door creaked open, and Lucas's face popped into the crack. His clothing and hair looked tousled, like he'd just rolled out of bed, but that was pretty much how he always looked. Shadows under his eyes hinted at a late night, but his wide smile looked excited.

"Sorry it's so early, but I wanted to do this while Tim was outside, messing around with that broken trap."

He patted his pocket and bounced lightly on his feet. "Can you come to my room?"

I followed him downstairs and through the narrow doorway to his cramped living space. Three empty cups, a crumpled bag of pretzels, and a discarded plate perched on top of his computer tower. A glance at his bed showed the comforter was still folded, and his charger remained discarded on his pillow, in the same spot as last night.

Someone had pulled an all-nighter.

Lucas motioned me into the desk chair. I settled on the

edge and stared up at him, daring to hope. Did all that excitement mean he'd come through on the data-restoring program?

He fiddled with whatever was in his pocket again, noted my curiosity, and removed his hand. "Oh, that's for in a few minutes. But first . . . let's jump-start that memory of yours."

He extended a cord to me, complete with a USB port at one end. "My memory?" I breathed.

"No guarantees it's going to work right away," Lucas cautioned, watching my face fall. "But if it doesn't, I think it will only take a few tweaks, at most."

A phantom pain twinged in my neck, just under my ear, as if I could still feel the burn from the last time I'd plugged in. I stared at the cord, but instead of reaching for it, my hands fisted.

Lucas noted the small motion. "This one shouldn't hurt," he said softly.

"And what about . . . that?" I nodded down toward my stomach. "Is there any chance new programming could set it off or something?"

"No, this software is localized. It will only affect your peripheral neurological area, not your central nervous system," he explained. He didn't rush me, though, or try to force the cord into my hand. Instead, he waited. Patient as always.

Eventually, my fingers curled around the metal end as I

willed my frantic pulse to subside.

It would be okay. Whatever Quinn had erased. I could handle it.

Drawing strength from Lucas's steady presence, I gathered my courage. I used my free hand to push aside the skin just under my ear and reveal the slot. Without giving myself a chance to back down, I plugged the device in.

Hot electricity rushed and crackled from my neck all the way to my brain.

Program LuRecoverM 587$ detected. Run program?

"Go ahead and run the program when you detect it," Lucas said.

With a silent prayer, I obeyed.

As I waited in the chair, back stiff, hands clutching the armrests, I didn't know exactly what to expect. Maybe for random images to start flooding my mind, or possibly one continuous video file to start playing.

Instead, I got a whole lot of nothing.

Green code? Oh, sure. The program showered me with that. Numbers whipped through my head, illuminating a pathway toward an empty storage place for the missing data. I even felt the program dive into that void in my past, watched the shadows begin to shrink. But beyond that . . . nothing else happened.

After all that anticipation, my body wanted to sag into the chair, but I held myself rigid. Calm, I had to remain calm. Once the program finished loading, that's when I'd retrieve the lost memories. I was too impatient, that was all.

"See anything?" Lucas asked.

I gave a quick jerk of my head, not trusting my voice to remain steady.

The last bits of code whizzed into my mind.

Data recovery: Complete.

I waited one heartbeat, two. Then I issued the command: *Retrieve data.*

A promising snap of response; a glimmer as the program opened.

Slam!

Program temporarily unavailable for use.

What?

I reissued the command, only to get the same response.

Program temporarily unavailable for use.

The *bam-bam* hammering in my temples grew louder. I tried again. This time, the response varied:

Program currently unsafe for use.

I slumped and relayed the information to Lucas.

He frowned and scooted to the edge of the bed, but didn't look nearly as perturbed as I expected. Not based on the effort he'd put into this program so far. "I was hoping . . . but I sort of expected . . . hmmm."

"Suspected what?" I said. Snappier than I intended, but his nonanswers were beginning to frustrate me.

"I'm sorry, I know this must be hard for you," he said, instantly making me feel about two inches tall. "Okay, here goes. All three Milas were originally made with some organic material. So . . . I'd have to do a scan to make sure, but I think there might be a chance that the human side of your brain is blocking the program and preventing it from functioning."

"Say what?"

Lucas's lips twitched at the sight of my confusion. "Listen, I took a bunch of psychology classes in college—" When I tried to squelch a laugh, a full-on smile erupted on his face and he held up his hands. "I know, I know! Anyway, I did a lot of reading about people who experienced retrograde memory loss, which is similar to what happened to you. They often recovered their memories, but only when they were ready."

"Ready?"

"You know. Emotionally prepared. It's the mind's way of protecting itself from further trauma."

My body went limp once I digested the ramifications of what he'd just said.

Whatever happened after Quinn's procedure was so awful that the human—no, the Sarah—side of my brain was protecting me. Trying to spare me.

His hand curled over mine, briefly. "It's just a theory, Mila. Maybe I'm wrong. Maybe it's just a glitch in the program that I can fix."

I shook my head. "As much as I hate admitting this, you're rarely ever wrong."

Lucas studied me for a moment before reaching into his pocket. "I have something I think might cheer you up. Or . . . something that will distract you."

I leaned forward, staring at his closed hand.

"I've been looking for more background information on your past, your parents . . . that sort of thing. Maybe that kind of information might trigger something in your, uh, Sarah's, memory. It might calm you down and allow the program to work," he said. "It's taken a long time, because I couldn't afford to leave a trace or alert anyone to my presence. But I did it. I finally hacked my way into an old government storage database, with defunct files on retired personnel and special projects."

I knew that hacking of that kind involved serious risks. "You did all that for me?"

He opened his hand and then pressed the flash drive into my palm.

"This drive contains some emails between Nicole and Daniel. I only read enough to know that they're from after the fire."

Hard to believe I was holding conversations between my pseudoparents, after their daughter died. The daughter I'd thought I was, for a very brief time; the daughter in whose likeness I'd been crafted. Like some kind of living-yet-not-quite-alive monument.

All that packed into the tiny, lightweight rectangle nestled in my palm.

"It will hurt," I whispered, almost to myself. "It always does."

"Emotional pain isn't necessarily a bad thing," Lucas said. "It says that you care, and that you're alive. In my book, those are both big pluses."

"Psych class again, huh?"

"Hey, don't make fun," he chided. "Besides, we both know I'm stubborn and nerdy enough to debate your flawed definition of 'alive' for days."

At that, I smiled. "Now there's an uncontestable fact."

"I'm not going to ask which statement you're talking about. Nerdy or stubborn."

"Wise choice."

He crossed his arms and frowned in mock disapproval. "You know, you really should be nicer to me. I could always sneak up while you're in resting mode and reprogram your wise-ass responses to 'Lucas knows all.'"

A strange, bittersweet pang filled my heart. Not very long ago, I'd had silly exchanges like this with Hunter. For a moment, an echo of his laugh rang in my ears and I imagined his smile, but something forced my mind to stay in the here and now, to focus on Lucas.

Perhaps that was the human side of my brain, trying to protect me.

"No. No, you'd never do anything like that," I finally replied. "It's not in your makeup."

His grin faded, and his expression turned serious. "No. It's not."

As his words dissolved between us, a tiny weight released from my chest. Nudged free by trust.

My expression must have been all sappy and intense, because Lucas cleared his throat and stepped back.

"So, want to check out those files?"

Right. The emails.

Like a pro, I folded back my ear again.

"Lucas! You in there?"

Tim's voice outside the door startled me. Inexcusable. Our time out here in the mountains was apparently dulling my sense of danger. My sensors had picked up Tim's approach, but I hadn't bothered to process the information.

Complacency was a luxury I couldn't afford. Not if I wanted to stay out of Holland's clutches.

Lucas jerked his head toward the memory stick. *"Hide it,"* he mouthed. There couldn't be any trace of what we were really doing here.

I snatched the metal piece away from my neck and concealed it within my fist just as Tim pushed the door open.

His gaze flickered from me, to Lucas, and back again. My android heart reacted to the heightened stress by upping its staccato beat, but he just stood there, frowning. Pink streaks marred the whites of his eyes, and his hair looked matted, as if by sweat. His jaw hadn't seen a razor in several days, and he reeked of wood smoke.

Finally, he grunted. "If you two want to get it on, let me know. I'll vacate the premises for a few minutes. That's all you'll need, right, Luke?"

Then he turned and stomped back toward the living area of the cabin. Lucas's face went fire-engine red and I forced an embarrassed laugh.

"Looks like he's got the wrong idea about us," I said.

"He has the wrong idea about everything." Lucas blew out a long, exasperated breath.

Suddenly, Lucas's room felt a little too intimate.

"Let's go for a walk, okay?" he said.

I practically leapt for the door. As usual, he and I were on the same page. Even though we weren't up to what Tim had so crudely implied, we couldn't risk him figuring out the truth. Tim thought he'd put Holland behind him, but nothing could be further from the truth.

In the main room, we passed Tim slumped in a chair, one arm covering his eyes and the other hand gripping an old bottle of whiskey.

"We're going out to check the snares," Lucas said.

Tim made an inarticulate noise, so we grabbed our jackets off the hooks and headed for the door.

"Got the gun?" Tim called out. Lucas sighed.

"It's daylight, and no one is around for miles. We'll only be gone an hour or so."

"Always plan like you'll be out after nightfall. Truth is, you never know when you'll be back. Or if."

"Cheerful. Thanks for that." But I noticed that Lucas grabbed a gun from the rack and stuck it inside the red backpack that took up permanent residence by the front door. He rummaged around inside. "All right, I see trail mix, jerky, water, matches, thermal blanket . . . We okay to go now, Survivor Man?"

"Funny thing, survival. Even when you think you're prepared, it only takes one mistake for everything to get completely FUBARed," Tim said through a hiccup. His arm rolled down and flopped to his side, then he opened his eyes and smiled. "Happy snaring."

We exited the house, still shrugging into our jackets. "That wasn't creepy at all," I said.

"Not at all. Sunshine and unicorns, that's what he's made of," Lucas said as he shouldered the pack.

"But he makes a good point," I said. Begrudgingly.

"Perhaps."

We trudged forward in silence, listening to the *caw caw* of snarky jays and the rustle-whisper of the wind through bare branches. "Do you ever wonder what made him so . . . bitter?"

Lucas curled a gloved hand around a strap and continued

forward. "Every day," he said, honestly. "Though 'made' is a little bit of a fallacy."

We picked our way to the first trap, due east, carefully snaking around a craggy jut of stone. Jagged lines marked most of the glacier-cut rocks that towered above the tree line. "Why do you say that?"

"Because everyone is responsible for their own moods. I mean, unless you're suffering from a medical condition," he said, adding, "Psych 101 for the win."

We rounded a copse of trees to where the first snare was hidden. Nothing there. I pretended not to notice the relieved slump of Lucas's shoulders when he saw the trap was empty. I liked that he valued life the way he did.

"But you just told me yesterday about your dad. . . ."

Another brisk wind kicked up, and he slid the fleece-lined hood onto his head before turning to me. "Right. And that's all true. I'm not saying his reactions aren't understandable, because they absolutely are. I'm just saying that everyone is responsible for their own reactions. If you run around blaming the world for all your problems, you'll be a victim forever."

I digested that as we headed north, toward the next snare. Was I guilty of that? Of blaming others for my problems? I had to admit, there were times when I'd felt like a victim . . . of Holland, of the military, of Quinn. Even times when I'd felt like a victim of the woman I'd known as Mom. But wasn't that understandable, given the fact that ever since I'd been on the run, virtually everyone I'd known had either taken advantage of me, lied to me, or tried to turn me into some kind of top secret weapon?

There were two exceptions: two boys who hadn't done anything except offer me help and friendship.

One boy had even offered me his heart.

When I studied Lucas's face, I noticed that his cheeks had turned a deeper pink than I'd attribute to wind chafing. "Don't mind me. Everyone says I'm too introspective."

I patted his arm and smiled. "It's okay. That's what I like about you. One of many things."

He turned away and looked off into the distance, but not before I'd noted that his cheeks had taken on an even brighter hue.

"Mind if I go off on my own for a little while?" I asked him, changing the subject. The memory stick practically burned a hole in my pocket. I was incredibly curious about the past, and about the younger versions of Daniel and Nicole. Maybe Lucas was right. Maybe these emails would help unlock the part of Sarah's brain that stopped the data-restoring program from running. Maybe all I had to do was read, and I'd be whole again. Or whole enough, at least, to face something really hard.

If what I remembered didn't tear me apart.

"Of course. Stay close, though."

I nodded before loping off into the trees. I found a fallen log and perched. One finger gently traced the fine line behind my ear, where the secret port resided. While cocooned in a haven of trees and snow and solitude, I pushed the drive into the slot and felt a *click!* as the metal snapped into place.

I braced myself for pain, but as Lucas promised, there was none. Just a warm tingling that grew into a steady surge of power. A heady rush as the neural pathways in my body—both human and robotic—prepared for the inward flow of information.

A flow that I controlled. I'd almost forgotten what it was like, this exhilarating feeling that I was useful and capable. Like I was built for some purpose. Only I still didn't know what it was.

The files blinked into my mind, green and glowing. I no longer needed hand motions to manipulate them, as I had when I'd first discovered my true identity. That way had been clunky and slow, relying on physical movement when my brain processed things so much faster.

Now, I could whip through the files in seconds. I prepared to do just that, when the first couple of salutations registered.

Hey Nicole—

Dear Daniel—

Reality crashed over me, and I froze. These weren't just

files, to be analyzed and discarded at will. These were remnants of my past—or the closest thing to a past I had.

The emails were dated, so I started with the oldest. It was from Daniel, and the moment I recognized his name, an image of the man I'd thought of as my father materialized in my head. Dark hair, stocky but fit build. Penetrating eyes that peered right into you. Expression lines, carved into weathered skin. A man who had lived . . . and lost.

The image changed. *For a fleeting second, I saw him tied to a chair, his eyes urging me to . . . what, exactly? My empty hand twitched around an unknown object.* An iron curtain sliced through my mind and just like that, the memory vanished.

I opened my eyes to see that my arm was extended. Like I'd been reaching for that tree trunk in the distance. I summoned it back to my side. Weird. And not in a good way. I was relieved when a new flashing green light registered.

Activate voice reproduction software?

The prompt blinked behind my eyes, awaiting a response. This was a new one for me, so I hesitated. Then I decided, why not? Accepting myself meant becoming familiar with all of my functionality.

Activate.

The next thing I knew, Daniel's voice filled every crevice inside my head.

"Hey Nicole—"

The deep pitch resonated and stirred more memories, both programmed and real. Thanks to recollections of sitting on his lap at baseball games as a girl, playing cards in our house in Philly, and walking the beach hand in hand, this was the man I thought of as "Father," even before I'd ever met him. Only, those memories belonged to Sarah, his real daughter. I was just the imitation. The multibillion-dollar mutant version he and his wife created from scraps. I never lived any of those moments myself.

Dad—Daniel—had feigned true feelings for me, back when Hunter and I had broken into his house in search of information about my past. But then he'd captured us, handed us over to Quinn, and abandoned us at her lab.

Abandoned. . . .

The word triggered a heaviness across my neck, a leaden dread that something didn't quite add up. I shrugged the feeling off and turned my attention back to the emails.

Voice reproduction: Resume.

Daniel's voice.

"—*I'm sorry this weekend was so rough, for both of us. I won't lie, though. I continue to struggle with this decision.*

"*Sarah wasn't a nameless, faceless number from one of your double-blind experiments. She was our daughter. A miraculous, flesh-and-blood person that we raised together. I understand the part of you that doesn't want her life to be in vain, because a part of me feels the same way. But I wrestle with the realities of what we're considering.*

"Should we be doing this? Is it something we can live with?

"I don't give a damn about what the military thinks, or Holland, for that matter. What I give a damn about is you, and Sarah.

"She's gone, Nicole. You hanging on to her battered body is killing me.

"I know I failed her in the end. I couldn't save her. Hate me all you want, but you have to let her go.

"Come home."

The words washed over me, conjuring those same memories that had plagued me back at the ranch in Clearwater. Hot air, blistering across my skin. Acrid smoke, curling down my throat, choking me. Beams, collapsing all around, trapping me in a living sea of red flames.

Just before I'd lost consciousness, I remembered a glimpse of a man.

My father.

Sarah's father.

Real memories, salvaged from another girl's brain and implanted into mine.

"You didn't let her down," I whispered to the empty clearing. "You did the best you could."

I wish I could have told him how the terror had faded fast, once the smoke inhalation took over. How grogginess had overcome Sarah and eventually her body just gave in.

I wish I could have told him, but now it was too late. . . .

Last I'd heard, Daniel had fled from Quinn's. The sight

of me, his daughter's android replica, had been too much for him to handle. It hurt when she told me; I couldn't lie. The pain still lingered. But now, I understood.

I traced the seams of my jeans with my fingers, trying to distract myself from acknowledging that Lucas's plan was working. Maybe my mind really was slowly unlocking the door to my memory vault. Was I ready to know the secrets that were stored there?

I closed my eyes, inhaled a calming breath full of pine and frost. Anxiety was understandable under these circumstances. Time to focus and move on.

Voice activation: Resume.

With that simple command, Mom's soft, clear voice enveloped me.

"Dear Daniel—

"I know this is hard for you, and if there was some way I could ease your pain, I would in a heartbeat. But I can't even ease my own.

"Yes, our daughter is gone, and sometimes, I wish I'd gone with her. It's in those moments that I know, without a doubt, that we need to ensure her life doesn't end in that fire. Sarah was special—you knew it, I knew it. Even Holland knew it. We'd be doing science a disservice if we didn't take this opportunity. Even worse—we'd be doing Sarah a disservice.

"I'm begging you, please—I need this. I'm not ready to let her go. Maybe that makes me selfish, but I can live with that. What I

can't live without, right now, is a chance to see Sarah's face again, alive.

"If you can't do it for me, think of the others. General Holland says Sarah's contribution might be the first step in helping them, and we can't turn our backs, can we?

"I won't leave her here by herself. You should come, if only to say good-bye. Sarah needs us to make this decision quickly. Her body won't hold out much longer, even on life support.

"This is the right choice. I have to believe that. I am lost without this glimmer of a chance. Please, Dan.

"I miss my baby."

The strong woman I remembered had usually been cool and collected, but these impassioned emails reminded me of the mom who'd urged me to live with her last breaths. The sound of her voice made her feel so real, so close.

For a hopeful, wonderful second, I thought I would open my eyes, and she'd be standing in front of me, her blond hair in that messy ponytail, her eyes a pale, serious blue behind square glasses.

"Mom?" I mouthed into the still air. The whisper of the wind was my only reply.

Of course there was no reply, because she was gone. Forever. All because of Holland. She'd trusted him, and he'd destroyed her.

I rubbed my palms across my damp eyes, drew in a shattered breath. Took a moment to compose myself. So, Mom had wanted to be involved with the MILA project from the very start, but what did she mean by "think of the others" and "Holland says Sarah's contribution could be the first step in helping them"? Whatever he wanted, Holland was perfectly capable of manipulating a grieving parent to get it.

But what did Holland want? Did it have to do anything with the device he'd placed inside of me? Who were these people Nicole thought she was going to help? Did they even exist, or was Holland just feeding her some lie in order to take Sarah away?

I was about to analyze some more files in search of those answers, when a heavy crunch behind the trees registered in the back of my mind.

Lucas?

Footstep analysis: Inaccurate.

Estimated weight: 240 kg.

My head shot up. 240 kilograms? The only thing that might be close to that big was a—

Likely species: Ursus arctos horriblis.

The translation was instant.

Grizzly bear.

THREE

The crunching came from the trees thirty yards south of me. If it followed the same trajectory, the bear would head right for our snare.

But the snare wouldn't do anything to the bear except really piss it off.

All our traps were made to catch small game, and grizzlies didn't qualify.

My mechanical heartbeat quickened as I sprang up from the log, took a fear-fueled step in Lucas's direction, then froze in place, my breaths coming fast and shallow. I felt trapped. I didn't want to draw the bear's attention. But I wanted to be close to Lucas, just in case. I didn't dare call out a warning.

Crunch, crunch . . . SNAP!

The snare sprang shut.

I peered toward the sound, but dense green branches blocked my view, so I listened instead. It was like the entire forest had gone still, holding its collective breath in anticipation of something terrible. Even the jays had stopped squawking.

Following nature's lead, I went statue-still. I couldn't give in to the impulse to move and look for Lucas, not when I was flying blind. I'd be putting us all in danger. I needed more input to formulate a plan, and maybe my android sensors would help.

Wait, I told myself. *Any second now. . . .*

There. The crunch of heavy footfalls cracking through an icy layer of snow. The bear was on the move. But I had no idea where it was going, or where Lucas was. I took a cautious step forward.

Thermographic imaging: Activated.

The snowy landscape disappeared, replaced by an explosion of color. A navy blue background, interspersed with green vertical bars. Trees, I realized.

Just beyond those, another image appeared, one that made my body go numb. A deep orange silhouette so enormous, it could only be one thing.

Image dimensions: 7 ft., 9 in. tall.

The animal was a beast. But the appearance of the much smaller red lump, about ten feet away, made me choke down panic.

Lucas.

He huddled in a ball behind a tree trunk, out of the bear's line of sight . . . for now.

Our trap had startled the bear into rearing up onto his hind legs. His head moved this way and that. Scenting. He knew we were trespassing in his forest.

My pulse pounded in my ears, fueled by a strong dose of programmed adrenaline. The rush caught me off guard. I'd missed it, this desire to act and protect. Part of me wanted to run out and challenge the bear, but I needed to analyze first. I couldn't take unnecessary risks with Lucas's safety. I forced myself not to move.

Probability of targets colliding: 65%.

If I stayed put, there was a small chance the bear wouldn't interpret Lucas's scent as some kind of threat, and would amble off of in search of a more promising meal.

But the overwhelming odds were that it would find him. Pursue him.

My mind zipped through scenarios, like creating a distraction by throwing a rock, or sprinting past the bear and leading it away. Before I could decide, my sensors flashed.

Threat detected.

Engagement: Imminent.

The bear's giant orange thermographic image whirled around, up on his hind legs, like he'd used some kind of superpowers to detect me. Although he didn't roar or make any kind of sound, I could see colored breath puffing from his mouth as though he was panting with excitement. Only two trees stood between him and me.

Crap.

Normal vision mode: Activate.

My sensors warned of the decreasing distance between us.

30 ft. until engagement.

25 ft.

The projected time until confrontation streamed in milliseconds. Should I call for Lucas's help, as my instincts dictated?

Suggested maneuver: Zero motion.

Stay put? I stifled a hysterical giggle.

My android logic insisted I remain reactive, not proactive. My human logic said something else.

Requesting alternate course of action.

With the bear now less than fifteen feet away, the directive remained unchanged.

Refrain from motion until otherwise notified.

I gritted my teeth against the urge to scream. Refrain from motion? Seriously?

Then I saw Lucas stumble forward.

"Hey! Over here!" he shouted, waving his hands overhead.

I stared, frozen to the ground, while my heart spasmed with fear, shock, and something else I couldn't identify in the chaos.

"No," I tried to warn, but the lump in my throat swallowed the word. Lucas waved his arms harder and started to clap his hands.

"Over here, you overgrown slipper!"

"Lucas, stop!"

Too late. The bear whirled and lumbered toward Lucas with more speed than I would have thought possible. I held my breath as Lucas jumped for a branch and hoisted himself into the tree. He scrambled upward, but even as I sprinted toward him, I knew I wouldn't reach them in time.

The bear leapt. His massive paw whipped out and swatted at Lucas's foot. I saw a blur of gray and blue when the sneaker ripped free and arced through the air.

Injury analysis: Possible minor appendage damage.

Risk of major damage: Low.

As that information flashed, I stooped and grabbed a heavy rock. The bear moved, but only to climb atop a three-foot boulder near the tree. Clever. He'd positioned himself with better leverage and access to Lucas.

Attack: Imminent.

Projected target: Abdominal region.

I threw the rock as hard as I could and yelled, just as the bear launched a massive paw at Lucas. He struck and the blow hit Lucas's forehead. Lucas jerked back with a cry, one hand losing its grip on the branch. I watched helplessly as he dangled there, while the rock smacked the bear's head and bounced off. The bear reared back with an outraged roar.

Injury assessment: Negligible.

Desperation flooded me. I'd thrown that rock hard. The blow might've been fatal to a human, yet it barely registered with the grizzly. I scoured the ground. Weapon, where was a real weapon? For what little good it would do. Meanwhile the animal backed off the boulder and turned toward me, panting heavily.

It was almost as if the bear was stunned by the attack. Even in this wilderness, the bear had zero competitors. What kind of creature would be bold enough to challenge it?

Feral brown eyes met mine from a distance of 9.8 feet. My sensors calculated a multitude of strategies while the bear's gaze remained transfixed on me.

He had no idea what he was dealing with.

Lucas held his sleeve to his forehead. Blood trickled from beneath the fabric and down his cheek. If the bear smelled it, he might turn on Lucas again. I watched the bear lift his head, saw his nostrils dilate. I stopped breathing. But the bear didn't turn away. He wasn't scenting Lucas. He was scenting me. Like he was searching for something.

Then it hit me. The bear was searching for the smell of fear.

Emotions triggered chemical reactions, which triggered different scents. Animals could smell those emotions. Did

I even have a fear scent to find? What would happen if I didn't?

I packed away any panic and anxiety and embraced my machine nature.

Heart rate: Reducing to 60 bpm.

Respiratory rate: Minimizing.

I didn't attack. I didn't run. Instead, I stood there as relaxed as possible, not moving an inch. The bear took one hesitant step toward me, then another. He was so close I could smell the fetid-fish reek of his breath, the oily-fur musk of his coat.

If he reared up now and launched a paw, I was toast.

My sensors blazed to life with some choice information:

Target's top vulnerability: Intense sound.

While the bear continued to inspect me, I performed a frantic scan of my android functions. I needed a noise, an obnoxious one that could frighten a bear. Assuming Holland had programmed me with such a thing to begin with.

I was just beginning to despair when I found it.

Select sound effect . . .

Setting octave and volume . . .

Adapting vocal cords . . .

Commence when ready . . .

The noise that erupted from my throat surprised even me. Deep, guttural, and painfully loud. The noise conjured up a demented whale song, reverberating from the bottom of the ocean. From my peripheral vision, I saw Lucas flinch and almost lose his grip.

The bear recoiled, his ears flat. I repeated the sound, stepping forward and waving my arms. The animal shook his head, trying to clear the sound. He turned and took several stumbling steps before pausing to peer over his shoulder at me. I kicked at the ground and bellowed once more. His haunches flinched. Then, with a tiny whine, he lumbered across the clearing and plunged back into the forest.

A thump jerked my attention away from the bear's retreat. Lucas. I turned in time to see him plummet to the ground. I raced to the spot where he sprawled in an ungainly heap, a stream of blood running down from the long scratch on his forehead. He grasped my outstretched hand, his expression dazed. The gun slipped from his other hand, which shook.

"I couldn't . . . I couldn't do it," he said, not meeting my eyes. "Not yet."

"Never mind that, you're bleeding," I said, trying to examine his cut.

He pulled away, fast enough to sting. "No excuses. I should have protected us. I'm so sorry."

My head shake was brisk. "Stop. There's no shame in not inflicting pain or death on a living creature." I knew too well what living creatures could do to one another. Just for now, I was grateful for my android side.

He opened his mouth to protest, but I held up my hand. "Besides, you don't have any experience firing a gun. Chances are, you'd have shot yourself in the good foot."

Some of the tension drained from his face. "There was always that possibility."

"Come on, let's go back to the cabin and get you fixed up."

He looked around, spotted his shoe, and replaced it on his foot. "Great job, by the way. Scaring the grizzly off with that . . . voice," he said, with a bemused smile.

I smiled back. "I can sing something for you while we stitch you up."

His eyes widened before he laughed. "Do you take requests?"

"Sure. Anything for you."

"Gee, thanks," he said. "I'll get back to you on that. And, uh . . . let's maybe not tell Tim about what actually happened. Otherwise, I'll never hear the end of it."

"It'll be our secret."

He met my eyes, and I knew what he was thinking. Just another secret among the many we already shared.

We started south. Lucas's gait was a little unsteadier than usual, but he didn't stumble. I squatted to retrieve the gun from a patch of snow. The metal in my ungloved hand felt cold and slick.

Familiar.

Data Recovery Program: Initiated.

With the sudden zap of a data stream, everything came rushing back.

I saw Daniel first. Tied to a chair. Eyes pleading.

My arm lifted, as of its own accord.

"Mila?" I heard Lucas, but his voice sounded distant. The trees faded from my view, replaced by the inside of a room.

A TV played in the background. Voices.

Holland's. Quinn's.

A familiar numbness flowed through me. Quinn's procedure, it had worked. All those depressing, upsetting emotions, gone. I'd felt . . . nothing. No fear, no love. No pain. Nothing except the bitter, acrid clutch of anger, urging me to follow Quinn's commands.

I remembered staring into Daniel's eyes. *Arm outstretched, finger on the trigger. Getting ready to pull . . .*

But from my memory came Lucas's voice. Calling me back. Encouraging me to think of something powerful.

Whatever you do, just try to feel. . . .

Screams. A woman's—Hunter's mom. I recalled their frantic, terrified pitch, but they hadn't touched me. They'd seemed so inconsequential. Like the screams of a stranger, coming from somewhere far away.

I remembered red words, flashing inside my head.

Security breach detected.

I remembered jerking my hand away at the last possible

moment, making the bullet whiz harmlessly past Daniel's ear.

"I —I tried to shoot Daniel?" I choked.

But there was more. The memories flooded me now, like water through a burst dam.

Hunter, trying to tell me the upgrades had been a mistake. Urgently pressing his lips to mine.

Me, pushing him away when I heard Holland's voice, just as Quinn had planned.

Quinn, leading me to the room where Daniel and Hunter sat bound and gagged, along with Sophia and Peyton, Hunter's parents.

Peyton . . .

I froze on the image of Hunter's stepdad, something dark and ugly churning deep in my gut. Peyton had ambushed us at Daniel's—he'd been working for the Vita Obscura all along. He was the one who'd convinced Hunter to approach me in the first place, back in Clearwater. Supposedly, Hunter hadn't known what his parents were really up to, but at this point, that didn't matter.

The image unfroze and played out in my head. I barely felt able to suck down air. I heard Quinn's voice, droning on about what needed to be done, about government conspiracies. I saw Hunter thrash against his restraints, his eyes wide with dawning horror. I remembered the sensation of lifting my arm, and the smooth, easy feel of the gun in my hand as I aimed at Peyton.

I recalled the slight pressure of my finger on the trigger, and feeling calm and serene when the gun recoiled.

I saw the small red circle that bloomed like a flower in the center of Peyton's forehead. Just before he jerked, his lifeless body slumping into the chair.

Realization was swift as a finger snap, sharp as a rusty spike.

I'd killed Hunter's stepfather.

Murdered him in cold blood.

FOUR

My hand went limp; my legs buckled. My knees hit the ground. I didn't move, even as an icy-wet chill seeped through my jeans and dampened my skin. It wasn't true. It couldn't be. There was no way I could have done such a thing.

The gunshot reverberated through my mind, loud and irrefutable.

"What is it? Are you okay?" Lucas dropped down beside me.

I couldn't form words, or look him in the eye. I couldn't even blink.

All I could do was absorb the impossible ache in my chest, the truth of what I'd done to Peyton. To Hunter. Meeting me had unleashed an avalanche of terror, and one thing was perfectly, utterly clear—the safest place for Hunter was as far away from me as possible.

"Peyton's dead. I shot him," I eventually murmured, with no idea how much time had passed.

I'd taken an innocent, unarmed life—something I never thought I was capable of doing. Yes, I had destroyed Three, my android counterpart, but that was different. She would have killed me first. Hunter's stepfather had been tied up, defenseless. He'd been at my mercy.

My mercy. Right. On that day, my supply had clearly run dry.

"You're going to be all right, Mila. Just breathe," I heard Lucas say.

I could tell by the way he said it. He knew. Maybe not every detail of my missing memories, but he'd known that I'd killed someone. Of course he had. He'd been in my head, communicating remotely through some kind of special transmitter. It was Lucas who had kept me from shooting again. He'd stopped me from murdering Daniel. My own—Sarah's own—father.

"Why didn't you tell me?"

Lucas's fingers slipped from my shoulder. "Damn," he muttered.

Even though he looked so vulnerable with that gash on his forehead, rage flared within my synthetic heart. The feeling was a welcome respite, a chance to push away the helpless gut twist of guilt and replace it with something powerful.

"I trusted you! I thought you were different, but you're just like everyone else. How could you hide that from me?"

Lucas backed away to give me some space. "I understand why you feel betrayed, and I'm sorry. I didn't withhold any information to upset you, I promise. It's just the opposite." He dragged his hands down his face while he gathered his thoughts. "Look, there was so much I didn't know, and it didn't feel right, sharing details with you that weren't fully connected or in a context I could understand. I was afraid letting you in on the fragments I did know would be too confusing."

I didn't need my android features to know he was being honest. And everything he said fit. Lucas evaluated, assessed, but he never intentionally inflicted pain. Every risk he'd taken had been prompted by his desire to help me.

Anger. I'd allowed Quinn to persuade me that other feelings equaled powerlessness, while anger meant control. I'd played right into her trap. Or was it fair to call it a trap?

She'd offered me an opportunity to be just like Three and I'd jumped at the chance. I'd been too wrapped up in my own pain to consider the consequences. In my attempt to escape the role of victim, I'd stepped into the role of monster.

My chin fell to my chest and tears trickled down my

cheeks, one after the other. A saline solution, manufactured to appear human. Which clearly I wasn't. No amount of organic material or borrowed emotion could change the fact that I had lived up to Holland's prime directive.

I was a weapon already—pure and simple.

"Why did you help me? Knowing what I'd done . . ."

"Hey. Hey," Lucas repeated, more firmly the second time. "Look at me."

He waited while I got myself under control. I swallowed a jagged sob and lifted my face. He peered into my eyes, focusing on my anguish.

"Even in the best of situations, good people sometimes make bad choices. Life-altering ones that you can't take back," he began. "In the worst of situations . . . well, you can imagine. Quinn saw a way to exploit your weaknesses."

"So what? I'm not responsible? This is all her fault and I'm off the hook?"

"No, that's not what I'm trying to say," Lucas replied, hands up. He hesitated. "Okay, be honest. Do you blame me for Nicole's death?"

I let out a surprised gasp. "No, of course not. You tried to save us."

"Later, though. Not right away," he countered. "I was the one who helped proctor the tests, right? What if I'd tried to get you two out sooner? What if I'd never agreed to the assignment? Maybe Holland would have had a hard time finding someone else, and that could have bought you time? What if I'm guilty, merely by giving in to him?"

"But you did the best you could," I said. "Holland leveraged your family against you. He didn't leave you much choice."

He studied me intently for a moment, as if waiting. "Exactly."

I glanced away, my eyes damp once again.

"We do the best that we can, Mila. If our choices turn out to have unintended consequences, then next time, we choose better. We grow and learn from our mistakes. And try to treat ourselves kindly along the way. That's what people do."

People. Not machines.

My situation wasn't like his at all. I had known Peyton would die when I pointed the gun at him and released the trigger. I just didn't—or couldn't—care.

My mouth filled with an acrid taste and the ache in my chest expanded. Still, I managed to rise to my feet. The scenery remained the same—snow-covered trees, blue sky peppered with clouds, harsh slices of rock reaching upward. Yet somehow, the serenity had been stripped away.

"Ready to go back?"

Lucas blotted his forehead with his coat sleeve and nodded. I didn't want to keep him from the cabin any longer; he needed to get that cut examined.

It was only a short walk, but when we reached the cabin I felt like we'd been on foot for days. I couldn't stop the stream of memories.

My arm lifting at Quinn's command.

A frightened woman, begging me to stop.

My finger pulling the trigger anyway. Immune to any of the horror reflected at me from the eyes of the captives.

Peyton's head jerking backward before he slumped in his chair.

Hunter's traumatized expression . . .

As Lucas opened the front door, my heart felt like it might explode from the pressure. While before I'd possessed too few emotions, too many flooded me now.

Without a word to Lucas, I spun on my heel and sprinted away from him and the cabin, my arms pumping so hard I feared they might snap off. Lucas's voice called after me, but I tuned it out, focusing instead on how the brisk air smelled of sap and rain.

My boots pounded through the snow as my legs steered me toward the cliffs. The stark, jagged rocks and steep hills would provide my body with distraction. Or punishment.

I pushed myself as hard as I could as I approached the first incline, my sensors warning me of the treacherous terrain ahead. But it was easy to block them out, given the images that kept flashing in front of my eyes.

The higher I ascended, the more the landscape seemed to drift away until nothing remained except me and the stone mountains the glaciers had left behind. Damaged, but seemingly indestructible.

Altitude level: 9000 ft.

Oxygen levels: Dropping.

I could almost taste the thinness of the air up here. I had to press on, keep moving, because if I stopped, I might collapse. I propelled myself upward, savagely clawing my way up through the mountains until an alert triggered my arms and feet to slow.

Warning: Canyon ahead.

Drop-off 5 ft. from current location.

I was close to the edge. The wind was forceful and choppy up here, blowing my hair away from my face. I closed my eyes and just stood there, knowing that there was one thing I could do to redeem myself for what I'd done.

Jump.

My death wouldn't bring Peyton back, of course, but it would be justice, wouldn't it? And a solution to a problem that Lucas was no closer to solving than he was yesterday. If I launched myself off this precipice, the bomb that was inside me would detonate here, far away from civilization.

I wouldn't hurt anyone else.

My feet scooted forward, the tips of my boots just clearing the rock. The wind beat harder against my cheeks. Around me, other cliffs rose toward the sky like aging monoliths, watching silently. A strange melodic hum surrounded me as the air whipped through a stony path.

Another step and there would be nothing. Just air and a feeling of weightlessness until my body hit the bottom of the canyon, thousands of feet below. No worries about the damage I could do. No worries at all.

I thought about Daniel's first email to Nicole. Maybe his instincts were right and I should never have existed in the first place. I pulled out the memory stick that Lucas had given me. Even though I knew there was more vital information on it, something compelled me to chuck it into the vast space below.

The object flew through the air in this beautiful, big arc, and then pitched downward, fluttering on the wind until it was out of sight. My sensors caught on to my intentions.

Distance: 9105 ft.

Chance of mechanical failure on impact: 92%.

Undecided, my arms slowly rose out to my sides, like I was a bird spreading out my wings. In the back of my head, I heard my mom's voice.

If you want to help me, you know what you can do? Live.

A single tear slid down my cheek.

. . . the next time, we choose better . . .

Lucas's words, from not more than an hour ago. Another tear joined the first.

And then my sensors triggered an alert, just a fraction of a second too late.

Environment unstable.

Imminent ground erosion.

The section of rock beneath my feet began to crumble and plummet into the ravine. Survival instinct, programming, something had me shoot out my arm and hook my fingers into a large crack in the cliff. Everything beneath my armpits dangled over the edge.

I could still let go. It would be all over if I just eased my elbow joints and lost my grip.

But my muscles tensed and flexed as my boots scrambled against the cliff, trying to find a slot for better leverage.

I was fighting to stay alive. And it wasn't just some automatic response.

Every awful memory I'd just recalled vanished like the rocks into the ravine, and all I could think about was saving Lucas from that bear. Someone I cared about was in danger and I was able to protect him. That meant something. I meant something. I was capable of horrible things, but I also had the power to do some good in this world. I could still serve a purpose, and that purpose could be to help others. To protect them from people like Holland and even Quinn.

I wouldn't be able to do that if I was splattered all over kingdom come.

My feet found a small pocket of space and my legs were able to push up enough to take some of the pressure off my arms. As my sensors provided me with data, I followed every directive to the letter. Eventually I was flat on my stomach on top of the rock, my fake pulse tearing through my artificial veins.

Recommendation: Seek more stable surroundings.

Return to ground elevation.

As I stood up and brushed myself off, I whispered a good-bye to the mountain and began my descent. My steps became steadier, my footing sturdier, and my mind focused on something besides my past transgressions.

Holland.

He'd convinced Nicole that giving up Sarah to the MILA project was an altruistic act. He'd made her think that it would be saving others.

I knew him well enough to know he was lying. Now, I needed to find out what he was lying about.

In order to protect people from Holland, I needed to go back to the beginning.

To Sarah.

And since I'd thrown away the memory stick, I'd have to retrace her history myself. I owed that much to her. To Daniel and Nicole. I owed that much to whomever else might become a victim of Holland.

And if the bomb triggered somewhere along the way? Well, at least I would go out fighting.

Lucas was waiting outside when I emerged from the trees and into the small clearing. Even from this distance, I could see his shoulders hunched against the cold while he paced back and forth. He checked his watch, raked a hand through his hair, then stared off in the direction of the snares.

My skin prickled with remorse. He'd obviously been very worried, and with good reason. I didn't want to think about what I'd almost done.

"Hey," I called out, breaking into a small jog. When he heard and saw me, his eyes closed and he mouthed something that looked like *"thank god."*

He watched my approach without saying anything, the bandage on his forehead applied so sloppily that it was almost sticking to his eyelid. He must have slapped it on and then come back out here to wait for me until I returned. I was about to apologize, but he didn't give me the chance. He just motioned toward the door and said, "Let's go inside."

We took our boots off and set them along the wall. He pulled his fleece jacket over his head and hung it on the hook before leading me into the sitting room.

And then he let me have it.

"What gives you the right to just run away like that?" he snapped. "I had no idea where you were going or if you were okay. The way you took off, it was like . . ." He stopped, exasperated, and then he flopped down on a chair, putting his head in his hands. "It looked like you weren't planning on coming back," he finally muttered.

Lucas had never been angry with me before and I had no idea what to do or say. "I'm sorry."

"I know," he said, sighing. "But you can't disappear like that. Ever again. We have to stick together. It's the only way . . ."

His voice trailed off and he sighed again, heavier and longer this time. The depth of his concern touched something, deep in my heart.

"The only way to what?"

His hands fell into his lap and he finally looked up at me. "Something happened while you were gone."

"Did you get in a fight with Tim? Is he onto me?"

"No, he went on a supply run after he saw my cut. We're out of iodine," he explained.

"Then what is it?" I asked, a little relieved.

Lucas got up and walked toward his room, nodding for me to follow. Once we got there, he collapsed in front of his computer desk. I sat on the cot where he slept and waited for him to speak.

He cleared his throat, fidgeted with his monitor, and pulled a few screens up. "It's about the explosive device," he said bluntly.

He scrutinized all the open search windows, every one of them filled with information related to bombs.

"Okay, go on."

He slowly turned around, his lips forming a tight, thin

line. "I was able to come up with an algorithm, based on all the research I've done, and was able to use it to analyze fragments of your device's mechanism."

"That's good, though, right?" I said hopefully. "Maybe now we'll be able to figure out how to defuse it."

"I don't know, Mila," Lucas said, his tone grim. "Bombs like these are very hard to defuse."

"How do you know that?"

Lucas spun around and pulled up a rough sketch of the device on one of the monitors, which my sensors were able to translate in seconds.

Object of interest: Destination-locked explosive.
Description: Utilizes sophisticated GPS software and sensors to detonate once in close proximity with a preprogrammed target.
Level of destruction: Anywhere from large-scale to small radiuses, depending on the explosive size.

My hands covered my stomach as it began to knot. "So I'm basically a heat-seeking missile, is that it?"

"No, the bomb is much smarter than that," Lucas said. "It's designed to activate once it reaches a specific area or coordinates. Heat-seeking missiles have guidance systems, sure, but they can go off course, hit things they're not supposed to. The kind you have is mistake-proof."

I got up and stared over Lucas's shoulder, cursing Holland under my breath. "So what's the intended target, then?"

Lucas kicked the leg of the coffee table. "That's just it. The coding on this thing is mystifying. I haven't been able to crack anything that has to do with the destination lock. It could be anything. Or anyone."

Anything. Anyone.

He stood up, his hands placed firmly on his hips. "We know you're safe right here, since you haven't detonated yet. But we have no way of knowing what might happen if you leave the mountain."

"God, Lucas. How about some happy news?" I joked, trying to lighten the mood a little.

He smiled a little. "There is some, actually. The algorithm was able to decipher the device's intensity level, and it looks somewhat localized."

"Meaning I won't take out a whole city if it detonates?"

"More like a few city blocks."

A few city blocks. Enough to kill scores of people. And yet there was this mysterious window of time—a two-hour countdown once the bomb was set to explode. Why the hell had Holland put that fail-safe in place if he'd wanted to do as much damage as possible? And what kind of target was he out to obliterate?

Lucas had done what he could, but the answers were out in the real world, and it was time for me to find them. What was Holland after? If I figured it out, I'd see where this bomb fit in to his plans.

If I stumbled upon the bomb's target, I'd find a way to disappear before it could hurt anyone but me.

"I know you've helped so much already, but I need to ask you one more favor," I said.

"Sure. What is it?"

"Can you help me steal a car?"

Lucas opened his mouth—to say "hell no," I'm sure—but I shut him down before he could go on.

"Look, I can't stay here anymore," I said.

I told him about the things Nicole said in her email to Daniel, how suspicious it sounded to me. Holland was concealing something, but she hadn't realized it. Holland had tricked her.

Lucas listened without interruption, even when I admitted to losing the memory stick in the mountains, which I wasn't entirely sure he believed.

"It's clear that Holland had other people involved with the MILA program, or at least he wanted Nicole to think that," I continued. "Either way, there's something bigger in play here. We both know it, and I have to find out what it is, before Holland makes another move. Or . . ." I couldn't say the alternative out loud, but we both knew: before I blew up.

He looked at the floor. "I get it, I do. But if you give me some more time—"

"No, Lucas," I said firmly. "You don't understand. I

need to do this. I have to do something to make up for . . . everything. It's not about saving me. It's about saving other people. And it can't wait."

Silence. Five seconds, then ten, as he assessed me, his restless fingers rolling at his shirt fabric. "So where do you plan on going?"

An image popped into my head. Nicole and Daniel, sitting around a dinner table in a well-maintained but modest tri-level house. Their daughter cooking something in the kitchen, a surprise for her parents.

"Philadelphia. Where Sarah lived, before all of this happened."

It seemed like as a good a place as any to start.

I waited for Lucas to use his logic or psych-class prowess to talk me out of this, but instead he just went to his closet and grabbed a large duffel bag. "We better get packing, then."

It had never occurred to me that Lucas would want to come along. Having him as my partner made me feel more secure, but I knew I'd also be putting him at risk.

Just like I had with Hunter.

"Lucas, wait. I don't think—"

"You're right, you don't think sometimes," he said, tossing his bag onto the cot. "Mila, you're going to need a backup tech person out there. If you want to remain undetected by Holland, you'll have to disable your GPS settings

76

and probably some other features that might give you away. I can make up the difference with my laptop. And don't forget the cops are still out there on a manhunt, looking for a girl that fits your description. You can't do this alone."

Then he cleared his throat and spoke again.

"I won't let you down like I did in the woods, I promise."

Something tore at my chest. He didn't really think I expected him to protect me from wild animals, did he?

"You could never let me down. Not in a million years."

"So . . . we're doing this together?"

"Together," I said, feeling the warmth of his skin on mine—

And remembering the sound of Hunter's soft breathing as he slept, his body curled up behind me in the still of the night.

FIVE

I had been on the lam with Lucas for no more than two hours, and he was already full of surprises. Before we'd left the cabin, he'd snuck into Tim's room and "borrowed" some things we might need on the road. Tim had only taken cash with him on his supply run, his wallet still stashed in a top dresser drawer. So Lucas nabbed Tim's ID and credit card, putting a wrinkled Post-it on the inside leather flap, with a message.

Sorry. Will explain later. Thanks for letting us stay.

While petty and identity theft had been acceptable to Lucas, he didn't take kindly to my idea of grand theft auto. But thanks to his insanely good bargaining skills, we hadn't needed to commit another crime. As soon as we'd hiked down to the flatlands and reached the first small village, Lucas had found a pawn shop and sold some of his high-tech equipment. Then he'd located a sketchy used-car lot and haggled with a rugged old salesman about the price of a black '92 Chevy Caprice. Within twenty minutes, Lucas had gotten him to agree to a solid grand in exchange for a cash payment. After Lucas had forged Tim's signature to all the paperwork, we were on our way.

I didn't have to lift a finger. In fact, Lucas had advised me to avoid surveillance cameras for now, so I was forced to lurk around street corners and act like a creepy stalker to avoid being seen. But he said it was only temporary. With a few adjustments to my programming, he promised, soon I could go in public with no worries.

I felt reassured by his confidence, and we zoomed onto the Montana highway without incident, but both of us had nerves as taut as guitar strings. My hand was almost plastered to my stomach as I watched the odometer on the Caprice click away. My chest constricted with each fabricated android breath.

"You feeling okay?" asked Lucas.

"Yeah. I'm just . . . I'll be fine."

"Wish I could say the same," he replied, making a nauseated-looking face. "The shocks on this car are terrible. I think I'm getting motion sickness."

I knew he was just trying to distract me. "I have to ask, Mr. Mustang. Why the Caprice? Out of all the crappy cars on the lot?"

"You're going to laugh if I tell you."

"No, I won't."

Lucas shot me a sideways glance. "It's because of psych class."

"Oh, I can't wait to hear this," I said, smiling but not laughing, like I promised.

"For almost a decade, the Caprice was utilized by the police nationwide," he said, his gaze flicking to a sign that placed us near the border of Wyoming. "I figure most state troopers will recognize the make of this vehicle and have a positive psychological response. Thereby becoming less likely to pull us over for speeding. Which we currently are. By a lot."

I sat there, stunned by his brilliance. "Wow. I don't think I ever would have thought of that."

"Don't worry. You're still superior to me, in many ways," Lucas said.

"Well, I am currently at a disadvantage, without my full range of powers. . . ."

"Not for long. Could you check the GPS and see where the next rest stop is?"

Lucas had convinced the car salesman to throw in an ancient TomTom on our sale, since we couldn't use my internal one or Lucas's phone. Too much of a risk of being traced.

I reached over to the dashboard and picked up the GPS, but the screen instantly froze and a mechanical voice repeated a phrase that we'd heard several times already: *"GPS signal lost."*

Dual groans filled the inside of the Caprice. I opened the glove box and reached inside, pulling out a road atlas that Lucas had brought from the cabin. From the driver's seat, Lucas sighed.

"Quit it," I warned, unfolding one of the built-in maps. "I just flipped to the wrong page last time, that's all."

A mistake that had cost us twenty minutes before we'd realized my error.

Once I landed on the correct page, I double-checked our route for any markers indicating interstate rest areas. No wonder everyone had switched to GPS.

"This is so archaic," I muttered, moving my finger along until I found a rest-stop symbol. Using my internal GPS was as easy as breathing for me. I would summon the connection, and just like that, a map unfurled behind my eyes, complete with my own little homing device to lead the way.

"Once I find a way to cloak you, I can normalize all your systems," Lucas said. "You just have to be patient."

"Oh boy."

"What?"

"Patience isn't exactly one of my best qualities," I said.

"Funny, I hadn't noticed that at all," Lucas deadpanned.

I nudged him with my elbow. "There's a rest stop about two miles ahead, Smart Guy."

"Great," he said.

A few minutes later we pulled off the highway and drove down a stretch of road that led to a building that looked like a log cabin. There were two signs out front: one read REST-ROOMS and the other read VENDING MACHINES. Once Lucas parked the Caprice in the lot and shut off the car's engine, he got out and went into the backseat, digging into his duffel bag. He returned with a pair of red-handled scissors.

I said, "Let me guess. I'm about to change my hairstyle?"

"It's the first thing that's about to change," was his cryptic reply.

"Okay, so should I just do it here and use the rearview mirror?" I asked.

Lucas peered around to see how many people were close by. We spied a family in a minivan a few spaces away.

"Let's go inside and see if we can find one of those family bathrooms," he suggested.

I nodded, pulling up the hood of Tim's dirty college sweatshirt and tightening it so that my face wouldn't be visible to any hidden security cameras. We walked swiftly into the building, which was practically empty. To the left of the vending machines, I spotted a family bathroom and we quickly ducked inside.

"I don't mean to rush you, but we should probably—"

"Do this in a hurry? I know. I've been a fugitive for a while, remember?"

Lucas frowned a little as he handed me the scissors, but he didn't say anything else.

I set the scissors on the calcium-stained sink and positioned myself in front of the bathroom mirror, yanking off my sweatshirt. A clog suddenly formed in my throat. Not over the prospective loss of hair. I couldn't care less about that. But over my last haircut, back in a motel room, with Nicole—Mom—wielding the scissors, trying to protect me. That mad race to keep me out of Holland's hands had basically signed her death sentence.

Lucas studied my expression while I gazed in the mirror.

"Want me to give it a try? I gave my mom a haircut a few times," he said.

I glanced at him over my shoulder curiously.

"Agoraphobia," he said simply. "By the time I was thirteen, she could barely leave the house."

"Wow."

I remembered the caged feeling I had at Holland's compound, where I was essentially imprisoned. I wondered if Lucas's mother had felt like that—except, instead of being held captive by another person, she'd been trapped by her own fear. Either way, it couldn't have been an easy experience—for her or Lucas.

"That had to be hard on you," I said, turning back to the mirror. I wished I wasn't so preoccupied with my own problems.

The fact that Lucas had a troubled past only made my admiration grow.

"It was harder on her. I just did what I could to help," he said.

My fingers curled around the scissors, determined to help myself the way Lucas was always helping everyone else.

"We're all flawed, Mila. All of us," Lucas said, his voice so calm and certain. "We muddle through life the best we can, and hopefully learn something about ourselves along the way. Maybe even become better people, if we're lucky."

"I can't imagine you getting any better, though."

Lucas approached me slowly, his image captured in the mirror, right beside mine. His green-gold eyes were bloodshot, but they were still warm. The stubble on his jawline made the angles of his face seem sharper.

"I was about to say the same thing about you."

I stared, transfixed at his reflection, caught up in the ragged pitch of his voice, the raw emotion. The bathroom fan hummed, and beyond that, a stir of voices from behind the door. I wasn't learning anything new about Lucas. I'd known almost from the start what kind of human he was: strong, ethical, compassionate. Why, then, did my artificial

84

heart feel as though it was swelling?

This was Lucas. My friend. But being on the road with him was reminding me of my time with Hunter. Was my memory just playing tricks on me, because I was missing the boy I'd fallen so hard for such a short while ago?

Trusting Lucas was easy. Trusting my own feelings? Not so much.

"So, you ready for this?" he said, breaking the tension.

I nodded and focused on my reflection in the mirror, steeling myself as I held the scissors up. My hair couldn't grow back, so this cut was it. If I made a mistake and left a bald spot, I'd be living with that hint of scalp forever.

Or as long as I survived, anyway.

My fingers closed confidently around the scissors, and I started snipping, locks of hair drifting to the floor in puffy bunches. Lucas grabbed some paper towels and began cleaning up all the trimmings, and once it was all over my neck felt naked. I gazed in the mirror and checked out the results. Tiny wisps framed my face like ebony feathers. My eyes looked huge, my cheekbones defined. The overall effect was pretty waifish, I decided.

Good. Let any foot soldiers that Holland had sent after me, or anyone else who was on my trail, think I was some delicate creature that needed protection. Soon they'd be surprised.

Lucas cleared his throat. His cheeks took on a pink tint.

"You look good," he said finally. Then he checked his watch, his face getting serious. "Now on to phase two."

"Phase two?"

He reached into his pocket and held up a small external drive. "Back at the cabin, I was able to construct some programming software that would manipulate your hardware and help you . . . adapt to your environment."

He paused, like he was unsure of how I'd react.

"Adapt?" I prompted. "What do you mean?"

"Well, the program on this drive can adjust your appearance settings, to whatever suits you," he revealed.

That took a second to sink in. "Appearance settings?" I repeated, thinking about how useful it would be to alter my physical features right now. "So you can change how I look? Beyond my hair, I mean?"

"Not your weight or height or anything, but little modifications, yes," he said, grinning. His hazel eyes went sparkly, and his hands all wavy, the way they did when some techy feat excited him. "We can alter your skin tone, your eye color. Change the shape and contours of your lips, or the shading on your face, which can help alter the look of bone structure."

"Is there anything you can't do?"

"Yes. Tie my shoelaces without using the bunny-ear method."

"So. You can still tie your shoes, you just have to cheat a little."

"I'm not a big fan of shortcuts."

I smiled, reaching out for the external drive. "How does it work?"

"Plug it into the port in your finger and then run the app once it loads," he instructed.

I did as he said, and just as I hooked up to the drive, Lucas went to the door to listen for anyone who might be outside. He nodded when the coast was clear.

Once the program loaded, I studied my reflection in the mirror, taking in one last look at my familiar features.

Open Camo App.

A string of code filled my head and I scrolled through it carefully.

Eyes, lips, skin, contours. It was all there.

"Eyes first," I said aloud, so Lucas could follow along. He took a few steps until he stood behind me. Studying my reflection seriously.

More code, prompting me to alter the color, along a spectrum.

Without thinking, I chose brown first. Five seconds later, my eyes had darkened, going from the color of grass to a deep mahogany. I felt a sharp twinge in my rib cage. Subconsciously, I'd changed my eyes to the exact color of Sarah's.

And of my archrival/android twin, Three.

My reflection was still clear before me, but another image joined it, released from some shadowy corner of my mind.

"You're my, my brown-eyed girl."

"Oh my gosh, Dad, seriously? Not again," I shrieked, swatting at the imaginary microphone he wielded in his hand. I shot Mom an imploring look. "Can't you do something?"

Mom shook her hand, her face stuck in that pretend frown that didn't fool any of us. "I'm sorry, Sarah, but you know how he gets when he watches those reality singing shows." She tsked, but ruined it when her lips twitched.

"Stop that! You're egging him on!" I said, trying to contain my own giggle. Everyone said smart people were the weirdest. Guess my family proved that. Still, I wouldn't change a thing. Most days.

I blinked, and the memory stopped, leaving me shaken. "Brown-Eyed Girl." Once, in a tight spot during one of Holland's tests, I'd been pitted against Three. Seemingly out of nowhere, I'd sung that song.

Now I knew that wasn't exactly true.

"What's wrong?" Lucas asked.

"Another Sarah memory," I said. "I don't think I'm feeling all that brown right now."

After an internal command, my eyes changed pigment again. This time to a dark sapphire blue.

"There. That works. Now, let's see what else we can do."

Another few minutes later, I was still inspecting the results of my pseudo-face-lift. Paler lips changed the entire appearance of my mouth, making it look thinner and less full. My skin tone was now an olive color, my smattering of freckles nowhere to be found. I'd used the contour feature of the program to accentuate cheekbones, elongate my nose, and make my eyes appear a little wider set.

Between that and the new haircut, the results were startling.

"I don't look like me," I said in wonder, tracing my finger along my new cheeks and the flattened curve of my mouth.

Lucas frowned, which worried me.

"What? You don't think it's enough?" I asked him.

He shook his head. "Sorry—no, you're right. It's a lot more drastic of a change than I'd anticipated."

"Why the frown, then? Isn't this a good thing?"

"It's just—" He broke off, swallowing hard. "You're right. It is a good thing."

"But?" I prompted. He was holding something back. I could sense it with both sets of my instincts.

"But, nothing. I was just thinking, I wish that thing could change my looks. Holland is going to catch on to my sick leave eventually and put an APB out on me too," he said. "We should go. We've been in here for close to fifteen minutes. I don't want to get caught."

I took the drive out of my finger port and handed it back to him. Lucas pushed open the door, allowing me to walk through first. "After you," he said.

I had changed on the outside but I still had the opportunity to change on the inside. To learn something and become a better person, like Lucas said a few minutes ago.

Or as close to a person as I could possibly get.

Beyond the Caprice's fly-stained windshield, the city's outline grew more defined. Skyscrapers jutted up like giant, geometric teeth—some rectangular, some pointed. We'd made it to Philadelphia in a little under twenty-nine hours, with me driving ever since we left the rest stop (since I didn't need the sleep), stopping now and then to fuel up. As we careened down 76, my eyes were glued to the scenery that was closing in around us. Recollections from the past were beginning to filter into my head.

"I've seen this before," I murmured to Lucas, who was still half-asleep.

It was nighttime. The city lit up like a fantasyland, full of magic.

"Mommy, look at the lights! Are all cities this beautiful at night?"

From my spot in the backseat, I leaned forward eagerly, pointing at the windshield to the glowing city beyond.

My mom turned to me from the passenger seat, her profile dim in the scant light. "I think Philly is particularly beautiful, but I could be biased."

I giggled. "You use such big words." But even as I

laughed, I realized that she was right. Philly would always be beautiful to me, because Philly was home.

"You okay over there? Looking a little shell-shocked," Lucas said groggily.

"I'm fine. It's just . . . odd, seeing this," I said. The words were completely inadequate to express my experience. How the flare of recognition felt phantom, like something I'd witnessed in a dream.

He nodded again. "Let's talk about what we should do first. Maybe we should start by searching property records near your—near Sarah's old house. That way we can see who's living there now."

Lucas had been able to obtain my parents' old address through his SMART Ops hacking sessions. They hadn't lived in Philly proper, but a northeast suburb called Sherman, which was right next to Bustleton.

Sherman. The first time I'd heard him utter the name, I'd felt an electric snap of recognition. The sensation had faded immediately, but the memory lingered.

Sherman. I turned the town name over in my head. Sherman.

That was the place where Sarah had lived most of her life . . . and where it ended as well.

Mine could end here too. For all Lucas and I knew, Sherman was the target for my destination-locked bomb. But rather than stay in a constant state of panic about where and when it would detonate, I focused on the task at hand—searching for clues that would lead us to unraveling Holland's master plan. I knew he had created deadly weapons—like me. But why?

"That makes sense. I suppose you'll need to research for now, since you haven't figured out how to cloak me yet."

I was surprised at how despondent, almost accusatory, my voice sounded. Lucas had fixed every technological problem he could think of—so why was I whining about not being able to use my android functions? Maybe it was because I'd come to embrace them, even rely on them over the last few weeks. The longer I wasn't able to access my full functionality, the more unsettled I became. It was strange because, for a long time, all I wanted to be was fully human.

But being with Lucas . . . well, it made me think I didn't need to be ashamed of what I truly was. He knew my android side, and he embraced it.

Something Hunter had never quite managed.

"Yes, I'll give it a go. I'm probably faster anyway."

The startled gasp flew out of my mouth before I could stop it. "Very funny."

He chuckled as he pulled out his laptop and flexed his fingers theatrically over the keyboard. "I've upgraded this machine to the nth degree. You might be surprised."

I gripped the steering wheel tightly. "But your method

is so unstable. Look," I said, jerking the car just enough to jostle him and his laptop.

"Hey," he said, clutching it against his lap. "No funny business on the road."

"Sorry, sorry," I said, giggling. "But you don't seriously think you're faster, right?"

He peered at me over his shoulder after tilting back the laptop screen. "You realize that you aren't the newest model, right? And I bet you haven't been keeping up with your updates?"

I blinked. "Updates? What updates?"

He tsked me. "See? Just as I suspected. A computer is only as good as its maintenance." He managed to sound serious, but out of the corner of my eye, I saw his shoulders shake with silent mirth.

Cute.

"I'll show you maintenance," I mumbled, which only made his shoulders shake more. But my grumpy demeanor was contradicted by my growing sense of comfort and ease around Lucas. Us making jokes about my androidness was becoming our little thing, and it didn't make me feel like an outsider. It did the exact opposite. I felt . . . accepted.

Hunter had tried in the end to accept and love me, but whatever chance we had at being together was ruined when I'd . . .

The sound of a gunshot echoed in my ears, threatening

to slice through this moment with Lucas. I fought it off by listening intently to the tapping of his fingers, turning them into a steady calming beat.

As he worked, Lucas would make a small sound once in a while, kind of like a *harrumph*, and when I looked at him, a furrow had formed between his eyebrows. I glanced over his shoulder briefly, keeping my attention mostly on the slowing traffic ahead of us.

Property Records: Sherman, PA

Street?
He typed more, and then a map pulled up.
Zoom.
The street expanded, numerical addresses blinking.

11589 Old Oak Lane.

Number and words. That's all they were. Somehow, though, that particular combination of digits and letters jumped off the screen, drilled through my sternum, and pierced my pump of a heart.

Sarah's address.

My address.

The epicenter of a past life: a normal life, filled with everyday happiness and sorrow. The place where this had all started.

"Not bad," I said, satisfied that I sounded normal, despite the glaring reminder of everything I'd lost, right there on the screen.

He pretended to ignore me, but I caught his quick smile.

```
Current property value: $534,000
Lot square footage: 1950 ft.
Last sale: 119 days prior
Previous owner name: access code needed
```

He paused, fingers on keys, biting his lower lip.

"Do you need help accessing that?"

His lips turned up into a smile. "Think you can do this faster on the laptop than I can?"

"Of course," I said. Sometimes it took a machine to make a machine work.

He gestured to the nearest exit sign. "Pull over and it's all yours."

I accepted the challenge and barreled down the ramp, taking a quick detour. I steered the Caprice toward the first Dunkin' Donuts I saw and parked the car, grabbing the laptop from Lucas.

"Should I go inside and buy a coffee and a cruller? Kill some time while you search?" he asked, raising his eyebrows at me.

"Stay put. This will only take me a few seconds."

All I needed to do was override the access code. I'd just connect with the company's computer server—

Connection. Right. Not going to happen.

I frowned at the screen. I'd always just commanded myself to interface with other computers before. Now I had to try and do this old-school.

"Don't even," I said to Lucas. His bark of laughter turned into a choked cough.

Okay, think. Think. This access code, it was just a temporary stumbling block. If I could issue a data recall and pull up some kind of coding that might act as a trip wire, I could enter it into Lucas's laptop and sidestep the network security.

```
Data recall
Search for programming trip wire
Request for relevant codes
```

Soon I had a multitude of options waiting to choose from, and once I locked on to one, I began typing furiously, cursing when I made a few errors.

"Stupid keyboard," I said.

After a few more missteps, I had the access code overridden. But not in the split second I had been expecting, either.

"There!" I punched the air with my fist.

Lucas didn't say a word, but the way he'd pressed his lips together to avoid laughing gave him away.

"Fine. You're faster on the laptop. For now," I added, handing his laptop back to him.

He graciously didn't acknowledge my defeat. He just took the laptop and began hunting through the information, making sure I could see the screen too. The previous house owner had lived there for five years—long enough that she could have met Sarah—but she'd moved to Washington State. Not exactly easy for us to meet.

Together, we searched through the houses nearest to Sarah's—all rentals and short-term owners until:

Current owner/resident: Margaret Applebaum

According to the records, she'd lived on Sarah's block for thirty-plus years. "This lady seems like our best bet. Should we do a drive-by, see if she's home, and ask her some questions?"

"Sounds good to me," I said.

Finally, he straightened in his seat, stretching his arms overhead and groaning. Then he placed one hand on my knee. "All joking aside, nice bit of teamwork there."

His short hair was flat on one side, sticking out on the other, and his shirt was rumpled. But his gaze was clear and steady as he smiled at me.

Teamwork. Team. Like he considered me an equal.

A flutter rose beneath my ribs, and the place where his hand rested on my leg felt unnaturally warm. I shifted a little behind the wheel of the car. That must have clued him in to my sudden discomfort because he jerked his hand away and cleared his throat, turning back to the laptop like it might save him.

Unsure of what to make of my own reaction, I opened the car door, letting a burst of cold air inside. "So, coffee and a cruller before we go?"

Lucas scratched the back of his head before holding up Tim's credit card. "Sure. Why not?"

SIX

White-and-gray wood. Single story. Elongated porch.

All of the house, wrong, wrong, wrong.

I plastered a moist-feeling palm against the window of the car. There should be a tree, right there. Right outside a second-story balcony. The one Sarah had contemplated using to escape the fire before she realized her parents might be trapped inside.

No mature trees on the lot, anywhere. Only freshly planted fledging ones, their trunks slender and frail.

Like a sudden power surge, reality struck.

The fire. Of course. They'd had to rebuild everything. I'd just expected the house to look the same, the way it had in Sarah's memory . . . but just like Sarah, that house was gone.

Something sank inside of me, a weight that could pin me to the passenger seat forever. This wasn't my home, never had been, and yet I couldn't deny the connection I felt the moment we'd first driven the Caprice through the neighborhood.

Or the relief Lucas and I had felt when my sensors didn't sound an alarm, warning me of a bomb detonation countdown.

"We don't have to do this now. If it's too much," Lucas said, pulling the keys out of the ignition. He'd just parked the car in front of a beautifully kept Tudor a few hundred yards down, so onlookers wouldn't remember it sitting outside Sarah's house.

He didn't say anything else, just sat there while I collected myself. Which was taking much longer than I anticipated. So many of Sarah's memories were being triggered right now, I could barely think. Part of me wondered if this avalanche could be due to what Lucas suggested on the mountain—maybe there was some kind of shift going on with my cellular material.

But what did that mean for me? It would never change who I really was. And wasn't.

"No, I'm not chickening out," I said. "Not after everything we've been through."

Lucas inclined his head. "Before we go in, I just wanted to say—I think you're incredibly brave."

His hand squeeze was part accolade, part encourage-ment. And it worked.

At least for a few seconds.

As we got out and stared up at Margaret Applebaum's house, I remembered when Hunter and I had made a similar stop, back in Tennessee. I'd felt the same sense of anticipa-tion, of hope, that answers might be waiting behind the closed door. Of course, that hope had been tainted by fear. The fear that Hunter would discover who—what—I really was.

This time, at least, I wasn't worried that some skeleton would come tumbling out of the closet.

"Let's hope Maggie doesn't have a granddaughter living with her," I muttered. One who knew judo.

"What's that?"

"Um, nothing. Long story."

No need to burden Lucas needlessly. A snippet of Hunt-er's and my crazy escape from Grady's house played in my head—just missing the armed military helicopter, headed straight for us as we raced away—and my android senses reacted to my increased tension.

High alert?

Yes.

A barrage of information streamed through my head—

Potential human threats in a 100-yard radius: 7.

Weapons analysis: 3 firearms detected.

Aircraft: Boeing 737, 1.6 mi. northwest. Commercial.
Threat level: Low.

It wasn't as much information as I'd be able to get with my full range of capabilities, but still way more than I needed. The data was a welcome distraction from Sarah's recollections of playing tag in the streets and riding her bike along the sidewalk.

I continued to scan our surroundings. Maggie's yard was extremely well tended and tidy, but not that professionally landscaped kind of immaculate. A mower had obviously just hit the lawn, but a bit of brown speckled the green here and there. The white fence that surrounded the property was cheerful, but could use an extra coat of paint.

A pair of sneakers sat to the left of the blue-and-gold welcome mat. White with splashes of orange, small enough that they probably belonged to a woman.

Estimated size: Women's US size 6.5.

A half-empty bag of potting soil was tucked into the corner, along with a small metal trowel. To the right, the porch extended, the edge bordered with a wrought-iron railing. A small metal-and-plastic table with four chairs sat there, with a blooming red plant in the middle.

Lucas was inspecting the porch as well, and nodded toward the plant. "We used to have some of those outside our house when I was growing up. They were my mom's favorites."

A gold Nissan Maxima was parked in the driveway, so I didn't have any reason to believe she wasn't home. Still, my sensors insisted on confirmation.

Human presence: Detected.

We walked up the three steps to the porch together, then I leaned forward, drew on that courage Lucas claimed I had, and rang the bell. We could hear the sound reverberate on the inside, followed by a loud bang and then silence. I sensed rather than saw someone peering at us through the peephole.

After five long, slow seconds, the door cracked open. Through the crevice, we caught a flash of black pants, a white shirt, and a narrowed brown eye beneath a sliver of a denim cap.

"Whatever you're selling, I'm not buying," came the suspicious voice.

Lucas, who stood more directly in her line of sight, cleared his throat. "Hello? Mrs. Applebaum?"

The door didn't budge.

"I knew I should have gotten one of those no soliciting signs," she snapped. "Get off my porch, or I'm calling my neighbor. Who's a retired police officer, by the way."

"We're not here to sell you anything, ma'am. We want to talk with you about Sarah Lusk."

There was an awkward silence as we all stood there motionless. It was almost as though we were expecting Sarah's ghost to materialize.

Then again, Sarah's ghost had been alive from the moment I was created.

"Who are you people?" Mrs. Applebaum finally said. "Is this some kind of cruel prank? Sarah is dead!" The door started to close, but Lucas moved with more speed than I knew he possessed. He managed to stop the slam with the toe of his shoe.

"I'm sorry. We didn't mean to startle you," Lucas said. Then he tilted his head at me. "This is my stepsister Mona. She's Sarah's cousin. If you open the door, I think you'll see the resemblance for yourself."

At first the door didn't move. Then it squeaked while she inched it open farther, wide enough that she could see my entire face. We could also see her for the first time. Mrs. Applebaum was a petite woman in her early seventies, wearing a pair of stretchy black yoga pants and a white zip sweatshirt. Her denim cap was embellished with sequins, a few pieces of gray-streaked brown hair dangling from beneath it. Laugh lines were etched into the skin near her mouth and eyes.

As she sized me up, I waited like a tightly coiled spring. This would be the first real test of my appearance alterations. If Mrs. Applebaum noticed something that spooked her, our conversation would be dead in the water.

Thankfully, though, she seemed to relax, her posture softening at her shoulders. "There is a similarity, yes."

The door opened wider. "Sorry about before. If I get only two solicitors a day, it's a blessing. And sometimes, they don't like to take no for an answer," she said. Then she did something surprising. She reached out and took my hand in hers, patting it gently. "I'm so sorry for your loss. Sarah was such a dear, dear girl."

"Thank you," I said, shifting my weight from foot to foot, hoping that she would invite us in. "We don't want to intrude or anything, but do you think we could talk to you for a few minutes?"

A faint smile formed on her lips. "Of course. Come and have a seat on the porch." She waved us over to the small table. "I'll go fetch us some iced tea."

Maybe this old woman knew something useful.

Mrs. Applebaum bustled back outside holding a tray with three large plastic cups. Ice clinked as she set them in front of us. "Sugar?" she said, nodding at two spoons and a glass container. "I don't have any of that artificial sweetener that's so popular these days, I'm afraid. That stuff is poison, full of toxins. What's wrong with plain old sugar? I like to know where my food comes from, thank you very much."

I took a sip.

Apple cinnamon.

I remembered this flavor.

"Are you trying to bamboozle an old lady?" A Mrs. Applebaum with less gray in her hair peered at me from across this exact same table, fanning a stack of red-and-white playing cards.

I laughed, setting my own cards facedown on the table. Even beneath the shade of the porch, the sun beat down, dampening my bare legs. I took a long chug of the iced tea, the crisp hint of apple sweetened by cinnamon, before pressing the cold glass to my face.

"You like the tea? Sarah drank it when she'd stop by sometimes to play gin."

I drained half the glass to give myself time to recover, conscious of her gaze. "It's great."

"Now, what brings you around these parts?" she said. "Do you live here? No, you couldn't, or I imagine I would have seen you, hanging around with Sarah," she said, answering her own question.

"I'm just visiting. I'm interested in a couple of colleges in the area, and I thought I should stop by Sarah's old house." My chest tightened as I spoke, each word becoming harder to say. "I was shocked to see how different the place is. I hadn't been there in years, but I still remember exactly how it looked, you know?"

Mrs. Applebaum reached across the table and placed her wrinkled hand on my shoulder. "I know. It's hard to face it every day, remembering what happened. Such a tragedy. To lose someone so young." When her eyes began to water, she dabbed at them with a napkin. "I could barely make it through the memorial service. Were you there?"

"We came late, our flight from Seattle was delayed," Lucas blurted out.

My fingers gripped the cup tightly.

"Damn airlines. You can't rely on them to get you anywhere without a big hassle," she said, wiping at her cheeks.

I breathed a sigh of relief. Rack up another save for Lucas.

"I miss that family so much," Mrs. Applebaum went on. "My own kids, they moved halfway across the country, but with Nicole and Dan, I almost felt like they were my own. Though, did you know, my son and his wife and my three precious grandbabies are coming for a visit this Thanksgiving? It's about time. I can't wait. I don't do much cooking anymore, since cooking for yourself isn't much fun. But I am planning a feast! Pumpkin pie, sweet potatoes, creamed spinach, the works!"

Next to her, Lucas nodded, eyes sparkling with genuine interest in her holiday plans. "That sounds great, Mrs. Applebaum. I'm sure your family will have 'a wonderful time."

"Call me Maggie. I never have been one much for formalities," she said.

"Maggie, then." Lucas smiled, easing back in his chair a bit.

Whatever comfort Lucas and I were beginning to feel here, we were on borrowed time. We had a long way to go if we were going to find out what Holland was up to.

I had to cut to the chase.

"I was wondering, could I ask you some questions about the fire?"

Maggie's face clouded over. "I suppose. Although I'm not sure why you'd want to discuss it now, on such a beautiful day."

I glanced over at Lucas, who gave me an encouraging look. So I pressed on.

"I'm sorry. I don't want to dig up awful memories," I said. "But Aunt Nicole and Uncle Daniel. They became estranged from us, once Sarah died. So I really have no clue what actually happened."

"I know what you mean," Maggie replied. "They just vanished from my life too. I wish they'd come by to see me one last time, but I understood. Losing a child like that . . . my word. I can't even imagine."

"So they never talked to you afterward?" I asked.

"Once all the hoopla died down, they were gone," she said. "And the fire was ruled an accident. I read an article in the newspaper, some reporter said something about a lit cigarette." Her lips pressed together tightly.

Lucas piped up. "Did Nicole or Daniel even smoke?" he asked me.

I shook my head. "And Sarah wasn't the type to sneak around with any. She was a total good girl."

Maggie slapped one hand on the table. "Exactly! That's what I told the detectives, too, when they came around to investigate."

Lucas shot me a look. "More than one detective?" That sounded unusual for investigating a fire.

"That's right, though they didn't come at the same time," Maggie explained. "I liked the first one a whole lot better than that second one. He seemed, pardon my pun, like he had a fire lit under him."

Why would two different detectives be sent to cover the same case? I wondered.

"I told the first guy that no one in that family smoked, not a day in their lives," Maggie added. "But I'd seen a man lurking around the house the day of the fire. I figured he might have had something to do with it."

My legs tensed. "You saw a stranger near their house? The day of the fire?"

Holland.

"Um-hum. This creep tried to look like he had business being over there, but something about him was way off." Maggie took a sip of tea and then went on with her story. "When I called out to him and asked what he was doing, he pretended not to hear me, then drove away in a big SUV. I would have jotted down the license plate, but it didn't have one. Just one of those temporary dealership things. Anyway. The first detective seemed very keen on that information,

109

and when he told me he planned to follow up, I believed him." Maggie tried to ward off a grin, but failed. "He had one of those thick mustaches, like Tom Selleck. And when he showed me his badge, I saw photos of his two dogs in his wallet. Showed he had a heart. I liked that."

"What about the second detective?" I asked.

She gave a disgusted snort. "Preoccupied, and disinterested. Oh, he put on a good show, but I can tell when someone is selling me a line of bull."

Lucas stifled a cough with his hand. Like him, I was really hoping that Maggie didn't pick up the fact that we were in the load-of-bull-selling business.

Which made me wonder. Maggie seemed to be exactly what she presented—a kind old lady who felt terrible about Sarah's death—but how did we know that was true? Maybe Holland had told her we might be coming, and paid her handsomely to stall us.

I might be paranoid, but that feeling of apprehension had proven useful in many situations.

So my android sensors performed a discreet survey.

Blood pressure, pulse, body language—all in normal range. No reason to believe she was lying.

Maggie scowled out at the street. "He told me he'd already checked it out, and the stranger was just a serviceman. Checking the pipes, or some such. Rubbish. Never once seen a serviceman wearing jeans and a T-shirt instead of some type of uniform. And where was his company van or truck? Plus, he was twitchy. Kept jerking his head around like he expected someone to bust him at any minute."

Holland, in jeans and a T-shirt? Acting twitchy? Possible, but not likely. Holland was the kind of man who believed his own hype. He'd have no problem explaining his presence, no matter where he was.

Still. "Do you remember anything about what this man looked like? Anything at all?"

Maggie caught her lower lip between her teeth. "I wish I did, but he wore a baseball cap on his head and I never did get a good look at his face. He was tall, though, at least six feet, and plenty scrawny. I remember thinking no one had cooked him a good meal in a long time."

My fingers curled under the edges of the chair. These details definitely didn't match up with Holland. And they weren't much to go on.

"Do you by chance remember either of the detectives' names?" Lucas asked. "I'd love to know if they ever found that guy."

She pursed her lips and frowned. "No, I can't say that I do. But I would imagine you could find all the information in the police reports. As a family member, I'm sure they'd be happy to make you a copy, down at the local station."

I was pretty sure they wouldn't be happy at all, but I just nodded.

Maggie sighed. "I wish that I could see your cousin again. I still miss her. She'd come by on the weekends and keep me company. Made this house feel alive again. Sometimes she'd even bring friends."

"She'd bring friends with her? Really?"

"Well, mostly just one. Chloe Nivens. She and Sarah were practically attached at the hip. They did everything together."

Lucas leaned forward, seemingly excited by this new lead.

Meanwhile, I couldn't move. The instant Maggie uttered that name, my memory sparked.

A girl with long brown hair, laughing and falling back into the snow, still stuck to her snowboard.

Chloe.

When I'd had the memory back at the cabin, I hadn't realized that other girl had been my—I mean, Sarah's—best friend.

"Did you know her at all?" Maggie's question drew me back into the moment. She watched me quizzically from behind her bifocals.

I formed my expression into a false smile.

"No. But Sarah always talked about her. You wouldn't happen to have her number, by chance?" Now that the initial shock had dissipated, some of Lucas's excitement trickled into me. A lead was a lead.

"Chloe's number? Why?"

I searched my mind for a good reason to contact Sarah's friend if I didn't even know her.

But Lucas was quick on his feet again. "She might have some opinions on the schools Mona's looking at. Since she's from this area and everything."

"Not a bad idea. Chloe is very smart. Has a good head on her shoulders," Maggie said before going off on a tangent. "I do think I have her mother's number—Daphne Nivens. Daphne's mom, Opal—that would be Chloe's grandma, god rest her soul—and I used to play gin rummy together. Daphne still checks in on me every now and then, the dear. I hear all about Chloe and her soccer team—she's goalie, you know—their family vacations to go skiing or whatever that newfangled thing is, you know, the skateboard on snow. Seems crazy to me, in the winter, why go somewhere even colder? Arizona, now that's a winter vacation. Anyway, what we were talking about? Oh, right. Daphne's phone number. You want me to find that for you?"

"Yes, that would be great," I said, trying not to let on that her rambling had set off a flood of strange feelings inside me. A powerful emotional connection.

Some deep, hidden part of me remembered what it was like to be her friend.

When Maggie returned from the other room, she held out a pink Post-it note, along with a small business card. "I decided I should check my file folder in the kitchen, where I stash names and numbers. I confess, I'm a bit of a hoarder when it comes to paper—you never know when you might need to call someone. Though I'm nothing like those families on TV. Have you seen that show? Isn't it something else? Those poor people! And that one lady with all those dogs! Now, where was I? Oh, right. So, I got to thinking that I probably wouldn't have thrown away a detective's card, and sure enough, there it was. I wish they had kept him on the case. He seemed like a good egg."

I swallowed hard, barely daring to hope. Talking to this detective could be huge. There seemed reason to believe there was something suspicious about the fire. But why would anyone be targeting Sarah's family?

Even if Maggie was wrong about what she saw, one fact remained. The fire was the unofficial start of the MILA project. Because without Sarah, Holland wouldn't have had the basis for his experiments.

Lucas took the card in his hand and read the name out loud. "Edgar Blythe?"

Maggie nodded. "That's him. A nice-looking man, blond hair, nice brown eyes, though he looked like he could use a good shave. I didn't get the impression he was married—his dress shirt was too wrinkled." Then she suddenly leaned toward Lucas, staring at his forehead with pursed lips. "Before you go, I should get you a new bandage for that cut of yours. It's looking a little . . . gnarly."

Lucas reached up and touched it, a look of embarrassment floating across his face. I was a little mortified too. I hadn't even noticed how old and gray the Band-Aid had become over the last couple days.

"Oh, that's nice of you. Thanks," he said.

Maggie turned to me with a shaking finger. "You two better take care of each other, okay? If it's one thing I've learned, it's that bad things can happen, even to the best of people."

SEVEN

After a promising start, the next hour was a disappointment.

We called both the numbers that Maggie gave us from a pay phone outside the local library. The one on Edgar Blythe's business card was disconnected, and Chloe's mother's cell delivered an automated message that said her mailbox was currently full. I suggested to Lucas that we pick up a burner phone, so that we could at least try Daphne again later, but instead he grabbed his laptop from the Caprice and motioned for me to follow him into the building.

A white-and-blue sign above the sliding glass doors bragged: WHERE DETERMINATION MEETS KNOWLEDGE.

Hopefully that came with a money-back guarantee.

The sliding doors slid open with a *whisk whisk* of moving air. Inside, four middle-aged women juggled toddlers and cell phones while waiting in line to scan their books. A young dad brushed past us toward the exit carrying a beaming little boy who clutched a book about trains. His round baby eyes met mine, and he chortled, releasing the book with one hand to wave.

His innocent little face prompted a new bout of dread, which spilled across my neck and back like a dark, viscous sludge. Beneath the heavy cotton of my sweatshirt, my stomach throbbed.

Could he be in danger? Could this be the place?

I scanned my system for the tiniest hint that another step forward might ignite a storm inside me. But there was nothing, just the sound of my faux heartbeat thumping in my ears. My relief was short-lived when I noticed the security system looming ahead. Did it scan for weapons? If so, we were completely screwed.

Analyzing capabilities . . .

Limited to the detection of registered property

leaving the premises without permission.

Lucas glanced at me and noticed my intense interest in the electronic arch we needed to walk through. Casually, he put his hand on the small of my back and escorted me to the welcome desk, where a librarian was perched on a stool, immersed in her work.

No alarms sounded. But I still felt vulnerable here, in Sarah's town. Even though my appearance had changed, I recognized so many things through Sarah's memories that I felt like everyone could see right through me. And I didn't want to hurt anyone here.

"So I was thinking we could try Blythe's email address, just in case it's operational. If not, there's a chance it's being forwarded to a personal account, which we can try and track down, of course," Lucas said, leading us around some shelving units toward two unoccupied desks in a back corner.

"Good idea," I said. "Maybe in the meantime we could hack into the case files somehow? Like through the police network?"

Lucas dug his laptop out of the bag and popped it open on the desk, making sure the monitor faced the back wall, away from any curious eyes.

I dropped into a chair while Lucas logged on, examining the rest of the library. I noted the number of people in our section—thirteen; the closest escape routes—emergency exit, far left corner, another one through the librarian offices to the right of the front door, worst-case scenario, picture window, ten feet away; and the furnishings, backpacks, and decorations, all in one swift stream.

Across the way, my gaze froze on a poster of two teen girls, reading on a beach. The sign planted in the sand beside them read PENN'S LANDING.

My mind expanded the landscape of the sign, following the beach to a boardwalk. I saw a man, walking hand in hand with a child. A puff of pink cotton candy waved from her other hand.

No, wait. I felt the warm strength of the man's hand, tasted the crunch of spun sugar on my tongue.

A hot wave pulsed through my head, and everything dimmed. The next instant, I saw the man throw his head back and howl with laughter, and then that image fizzled, revealing a blur of others that made my stomach churn.

Blissful emptiness as I held the gun steady, aiming at Peyton's head.

Hunter thrashing against his restraints, his screams muffled by the gag in his mouth.

My finger, releasing the trigger.

And me, feeling nothing . . .

"I just sent a test email to Blythe and it bounced back, so hacking into the police network it is," Lucas said, glancing up at me.

His words plucked me from my self-inflicted horror. I started, but couldn't expel any sound through a suddenly dry mouth.

"What is it?" he asked, his voice concerned. "Are your sensors picking something up?"

"No, I . . ." I swallowed, wet my lips. Tried to decide

what I should tell him. "It's just . . . I need to know if Hunter is okay."

"Right," Lucas said, nodding. "Not knowing must be hard."

Hard? Try unbearable.

"Once we do this case-file search, I can try tracking Hunter's cell phone again," Lucas offered. "I wasn't able to turn anything up at the cabin, but maybe things have changed."

He was just being nice. Odds were we wouldn't be able to locate Hunter, or even Daniel for that matter. Every cell, every chip, every atom of my body froze when I considered the possibility that Hunter was still in danger. He'd only ended up at Quinn's through my subterfuge. If anything happened to him . . .

Then again, if Hunter was fine and we located him, would he speak to me again? And even if he did, what would I say? How could he forgive me? During our last interaction, I'd been a monster.

Inside me, despair warred with hope. Together, maybe, we could all make our way back from the brink of darkness.

"Thanks. I appreciate it," I managed to say, despite the growing lump in my throat.

Lucas nodded and started to *click-click-click* his way into the police database. As I watched his fingers, saw the code flow across the screen, I once again marveled at his skill.

His eyes burned with determination.

In less than ten minutes, he was in.

Case numbers flitted across the screen, and Lucas performed a search.

Sarah Laurent Lusk

Her case number was 4220.

Lucas quickly found the docs associated with her case, numbered one through fifty-four.

Numbers thirty-one and thirty-two were missing. Deleted by an anonymous user. Which might not mean anything at all.

Our heads together, we scanned the existing files, Lucas downloading them onto a flash drive so we could peruse them in a more private location later.

As I read over his shoulder, a phrase in an early report by Edgar Blythe made me freeze.

. . . possibility of arson . . .

Lucas pointed at the line on the screen, making sure I caught it. But I'd already moved on, and a shadow rippled over me. Apparently Blythe had reason to believe this theory. But we weren't going to find out what that reason was . . . because the evidence that suggested arson was located in the two missing files.

A coincidence? That seemed impossible.

I continued to scan files while the shadow thickened into a storm cloud.

"Evidence tampering. It has to be," I said to Lucas.

I slumped in my chair. We needed that information, and the fastest way to retrieve it was if I tapped into the database myself and attempted to reconstruct the files internally. But Lucas still hadn't found a way to fix my security issue, so any internet connection left me vulnerable to detection.

Unless . . .

"This is going to sound like a really weird suggestion," I whispered.

Lucas raised an eyebrow and for some reason, that simple gesture sent a surge of heat into my cheeks.

"What I mean is, if you hook me up to your laptop, the old-fashioned way—"

"You mean, by using a USB?"

I nodded. "Exactly. Would you be able to mask my IP address then?"

"You want to try to reconstruct the files." Lucas nodded. "It could work."

"Well, should we try it?"

"Here, in the library?"

A quick scan revealed a discreet spot for me to hook up to his computer undetected.

Private reading rooms: 4.

Availability: 2.

Reservation required; ID necessary.

"We can sign up for a closed reading room. All you'd need is Tim's ID," I said.

Lucas sat there, considering. "Well, once we connect you, your IP address would be difficult—but not impossible—to trace. I removed all the geolocation information from my laptop and obfuscated the routing information, so you'd be protected. But not for long."

"What are we talking about? Ten minutes?" I asked.

"More like sixty seconds."

"Wow. So generous," I mocked, rolling my shoulders back like I was prepping for battle. To most people, sixty seconds wasn't much time. But in my world, a lot could happen in a fraction of an instant.

The reading room was small, even smaller than my tiny loft at the cabin, and the space was sparsely furnished with a table and two benches. I sat with my back to the door, but the narrow rectangular window in its center had me worried. If we weren't careful, someone could walk by and catch a young computer scientist linking his laptop into the brain of a teenage android. Not your typical study room shenanigans.

Lucas fed a wire into my finger port beneath the table

while I worked on not freaking out and keeping my mind clear of stray thoughts. Wisps of memories threatened to make that difficult, but once I connected to Lucas's laptop and began the mental merge, I drifted into this semitrance, to a land where strings of undecipherable codes formed a language that not only made sense, but was actually a part of me.

Just like Sarah.

"You're fully synched and cloaked, Mila," I heard Lucas say. "Sixty seconds starts . . ." He punched a key on his laptop. "Now."

It only took me three seconds to hack into the database.

Attempt/reconstruct files? *.*

Search original file locations.

Resolve sequence ID.

In less than five seconds, a flood of information poured in, around, through me, but I held my breath when the search stuttered, disrupting the flow of energy.

File reformatted . . . continue recovery attempt?

My bubble of hope burst as if stabbed by a sharp tack. The files had been reformatted. They were probably worthless now.

Continue.

I answered, even though I didn't expect anything to come of it. Four long seconds ticked by before I received a response.

Hexadecimal code recovery: 98.2% undecipherable.

Not especially promising. But still . . .

I extracted the recovered bytes, manipulated them, and eased them into shape, which took longer than I'd wanted— at least fifteen more seconds.

In less than thirty seconds, I'd be unmasked. My whereabouts available to whoever chose to look. But I couldn't stop yet.

A document appeared. Well, only tiny pieces of one. Much of the information was useless—a partial street address for Sarah, a few words about fire containment.

But there was a tiny bit more, and that part made my heart pound.

```
. . . fire pattern and spread consistent
with . . .
```

With what? An accidental fire? Or arson?

A familiar darkness tore through my body, curling my hands into fists and tightening my jaw. Not only might someone have set the fire that had taken Sarah's life, but someone might have tried to cover it up. That fit in with Maggie's story too, about how she felt like the case had been mishandled.

"I got something," I whispered to Lucas.

"Only fifteen more seconds left, Mila," he urged.

I scrolled through the files, noting that many of Blythe's reports were co-signed by a woman. Sonja Lopez. And that, three days after he filed that broken-up report, a new name replaced Edgar Blythe's on the case. Scott Pacelli.

Something slithered down my spine. Three days. Coincidence? Surely not. "Ten . . ." Lucas whispered, starting the final countdown.

Physical evidence: SL11-25, SL11-26, SL11-27, SL11-28.

The numbers continued up to SL11-40.

"Nine . . ."

I loaded them and got more than I bargained for.

"Eight . . ."

Photographs spilled forth. Images of Sarah's house, burned to the ground, charred and blackened almost beyond recognition. Descriptions of mangled objects—a melted family portrait. Fingernail scrapings.

Nothing helpful. And nothing about the possibility of an accelerant, which would prove arson for certain.

"Mila, hurry. Five . . ." The pitch of Lucas's voice deepened.

I double-checked, and then swore. "Three of the physical evidence descriptions are missing," I whispered.

SL11-27, 11-28, and 11-29. Blank.

Before I could dive back in to try to find them, something wrenched free of my finger. For a panicky second, my mind went blank, as empty as those barren files. Then I noticed Lucas dangling the end of disconnected wire.

Thank god he'd disabled the connection. But not before I'd committed every bit of information to my own personal data banks.

"What did you find?" Lucas asked.

I felt the burn of tears behind my eyes. "It's all pointing to a cover-up. I wish we could go to Blythe and get some more answers."

Lucas turned back to his laptop. "Let's just search his name, see what it turns up."

His fingers flew over the keyboard while I watched the screen. I closed the tip of my finger port, but the sizzle of energy remained in my disrupted skin cells.

He pulled up an article from the local paper on the monitor. The headline revealed yet another dead end. Literally.

DETECTIVE DIES IN HIKING ACCIDENT

Forty-nine-year-old police detective Edgar Blythe's body was found at the bottom of a valley on a popular hiking trail. The medical examiner found that a head contusion was the likely culprit, the result of slipping on the trail and hitting his head on a rock. A park official reports that the trail, while usually safe, was treacherous after a prolonged rain, rendering it muddy and slippery.

Lucas pointed at the date. Two days after Blythe logged in his report. The day before Scott Pacelli took over the case.

Was Holland behind all of this somehow, taking one innocent life after another in order to hide his true motives and plans? Or were we going down the wrong road, developing a false conspiracy theory? What did we really have except for shards of information and suspicions from an old woman?

Daniel. He'd always believed something had been off about the fire. But Daniel wasn't reliable—he was grieving over his dead daughter, desperate to find an explanation.

We needed more. Something substantial. A smoking gun. Evidence that would lead us to Holland's schemes, both then and now.

"There's more," Lucas said, pulling up another article. This one detailed how Detective Scott Pacelli had been convicted of drug trafficking in federal court, six months after he'd taken on Sarah's case. He was currently tucked away in a federal prison. "Looks like we won't be able to talk to him either."

I choked down bitterness as another prospective lead slipped through our fingers. But then I realized that maybe it didn't matter.

Sonja Lopez. The woman who co-signed Blythe's reports. I shared the name with Lucas, and he tracked down a recent social-media photo and an address nearby. Sonja was an attractive Hispanic woman, probably in her late fifties. Her brown eyes were as bright as her smile in the picture. From the conference room in the background and the cake with "Congratulations" scrawled across the top, I guessed the picture was taken at her retirement party.

"Shall we pay her a visit?" Lucas snapped his laptop closed.

I could have kissed him for being so eager to help me fit this gigantic puzzle together, under such insane circumstances. I settled for a hug instead.

"Thank you," I mumbled into his shoulder.

At first, his body went rigid. Then Lucas's arms encircled me. His heart pounded against mine for one-two-three beats before he patted my back and retreated.

"I'm sorry, I should have asked first," I said, worried that I'd invaded his space and upset him somehow.

"You don't have to ask first," he said, his gaze settling somewhere beyond my shoulder. "I'm just . . . not used to that kind of affection, that's all."

With a pang, I realized just how much I had to learn about him. He'd let me in to a certain degree—I knew about his family; I'd met his brother; he seemed to want to take down his despicable uncle as much as I did—but clearly there was more beneath the surface. Things he hadn't revealed to me.

At least not yet.

When we walked down the hallway past the other reading rooms, Lucas gave me a playful shoulder nudge, probably to erase any lingering awkwardness.

"I think our next stop should be a fast-food place," he said. "I'd hate for my growling stomach to interfere with our investigation."

"Sure, I could go for a burger and fries," I said, smiling at him.

"It must be nice, being immune to all the health risks associated with trans fats and high fructose corn syrup."

"Yup. One of the many wonderful benefits of being made in a lab," I said, and then winked.

Lucas grinned, and the weirdness vanished. As we made our way toward the lobby, we started talking about how to approach Sonja . . . at least until a bright flash of red behind my eyes made speech and movement impossible.

EIGHT

couldn't even draw a breath. Beneath the stammer of my heart, there was a faint, yet totally foreign pulse of energy, growing stronger with every second I stood frozen in the library hallway. The red behind my eyes flashed in time with the pulse, forming a single synchronized beat.

In my mind, I saw pieces of my body disintegrating in an inferno that took out entire city blocks. Bodies of inno-cent victims splayed across the ground, covered by piles of rubble.

The trigger. It must have activated.

Lucas grabbed my wrist. "Mila? What is it?"

Even if I could speak, I had no idea what to say. If I told him the truth, he'd want to help me get away, and I couldn't risk that. As the hypnotic pulse spread throughout my body—up to my shoulders and down my arms—I thought about how I could ditch him, calling on my sensors to come up with escape routes.

But instead of responding with options, my mind filled with a strange alert that I'd never seen before.

Incoming message.

Before I could determine the type of message or mode of transmission, another alert appeared.

Download commencing.

Hologram projection in 1 minute.

Advise accessing a secure viewing location.

The pulse now funneled directly into my right hand and created an icy numbness. Then the end of my middle finger began emitting blue light.

The truth dawned on me. The detonation trigger hadn't been activated. No, something else was happening, but that realization provided small comfort.

Not when I remembered Three, and how her finger looked, right before—

Lucas positioned himself in front of me. "What's happening?" he whispered, trying not to draw attention.

"Holland." I clasped my hands together in an effort to hide the evidence.

Lucas squeezed my arms. "He tracked you?"

But there was no time to explain. The clock was ticking and I had to find a hideaway before my cover was blown.

Staff-only rooms: 3.

Human targets detected: 7.

Supply rooms: 5.

Human targets detected: 0.

Supply rooms for the win. There was one on the floor below us, next door to the microfiche area, which probably didn't see much traffic these days.

"This way," I said.

Forty-five seconds left until the message was broadcast. We needed to move quickly without looking like two teenage book thieves on the lam. There were people all around us, so we had to balance speed with caution.

We speed-walked toward the nearest stairwell, Lucas limping under the weight of his laptop bag and the worry he must be shouldering, given how little he knew about this latest danger. Once the heavy metal door shut behind us, we bolted down the stairs, Lucas trailing but keeping up the best he could.

With twenty seconds left, we hurried down the hall in search of the supply room. I put my non-numb hand on the doorknob and twisted while my other balled into a fist. The entire thing tingled now, and my finger glowed even brighter. I tried to open the door, but . . .

It was locked.

"Damn it," I said. I could force it open, but then what if the door wouldn't stay closed?

Lucas dug into his back pocket and nabbed his wallet, reaching in and pulling out Tim's credit card. He pushed me aside and jimmied the lock. Once inside, we were safely surrounded by stacks of printer paper and old Xerox machines. Lucas stood by the door, blocking the path in case a librarian suffered a sudden toner emergency.

"What's going on?"

Before I could reply, blue light erupted from my finger, startling the both of us.

Signal: Transmission in progress.

The numbness in my hand descended over the rest of me.

Transmission: Initiate.

The light burst from my finger, like water from a hose, to form a three-dimensional picture. Two figures streamed into existence, only an arm's length away. One of them came into focus. The color and vapor version of Holland looked so real that I could almost feel his gray eyes crawling over me.

"What the hell?" Lucas choked out.

I understood his shock. I'd felt the same way when I saw this happening to Three a few weeks ago. But my feelings— both emotional and physical—were oddly suspended in this moment, and my sensors cued me in as to why.

All properties at maximum capacity.

Diverting energy resources to avoid overload.

"Hello, Mila."

Under normal circumstances, the sound of Holland's

voice would have made me shudder. But nothing about this moment—or my life—was ever normal.

"How is this happening?" Lucas said. "Was he able to locate you through my laptop?"

I wished I knew how to answer him. Three had lied to me. She'd told me I didn't have this capability. Yet here I was, a puppet in Holland's hands once again.

"This won't be quite up to the experience we had last time, I'm afraid," Holland said in his condescending drawl. "Three was wired to transmit live video and sound. But your functionality in this area is very basic. Unfortunate, because that means I won't know what you're up to. I'll just have to make up for that deficit with my message." His smile was slick and satisfied. Triumphant.

For a split second, I felt triumph of my own. It seemed that Holland had been unable to track me, that he remained clueless about his nephew's role in helping his prized creation plot against him. For now. But my relief vanished as quickly as it came, leaving only awareness that Holland could infiltrate my body without my permission.

Violated. Unsafe. Dirty. Those three words drifted through my head . . . ready to pounce once my feelings kicked back in.

"You were probably hoping you wouldn't see me again. At least, not so soon," Holland continued. "But I think you'll be interested in who I have with me."

With a jerk of his computer-generated hand, he grasped the chin of the other mist-and-light figure and yanked until her identity was exposed.

Quinn.

Even the misty holographic image couldn't hide the damage Holland had inflicted on her face. Black and blue circled her eyes, and her nose bent unnaturally to the left, with blood trickling from her nostrils. Divested of her red curls, her shaved head glowed with a pale light. Livid finger marks stood out against the white skin of her throat.

The numbness prevented me from feeling more than a sliver of sympathy for her, or comfort that Holland's hostage wasn't Hunter or Daniel or one of the young members of Quinn's team. But once this transmission was over, I knew my emotions would storm every inch of me.

A thin rope hung from Quinn's neck; Holland grasped and yanked it. Her eyes flew open at the sudden tension before her lids drooped again and her chin fell to her neck.

"Wake. Up," Holland repeated, giving the cord a vicious jerk.

Quinn's startled scream was hoarse, her throat too damaged to muster much volume.

"I'm sure you recognize my former protégé, although I'll admit, she's looking a little worse for the wear."

Holland's drawl betrayed no hint of remorse, no reflection of any feelings he might still harbor for the woman he'd once loved. No sorrow, no anger. Nothing.

"She's been reluctant to share pertinent information about how she was able to modify your programming, and I find I don't have the patience I once had."

Holland's hand reached for something beyond the scope of the hologram, and returned with a deadly looking knife. His eyes never changed expression. He sighed, as though weary of the whole thing.

"I taped this for a reason, because I knew she'd be too stubborn to talk. I wanted to send a message, though. You belong to me, and I will hunt you down. I don't let my property go free. See?"

With one hand, he shoved Quinn's chin up and back. I watched, transfixed and numb, as the knife sparkled in the hologram's lights, almost like the blade was crafted from glitter. Then he made a calm and deliberate motion across her neck. He tossed the knife in the air as the ear-to-ear slash leached a river of blood.

Carotid artery permanently damaged.

Recovery impossible.

Mortality rate: 100%.

"No!" Lucas's gasp echoed through the supply closet while Quinn slid down and disappeared from view.

I hadn't liked Quinn. In fact, I'd hated her for what she'd done to me, and what I did to Peyton under her influence. But that didn't mean that I'd wanted her tortured, or dead at the hands of a madman. A madman who had no qualms harming anyone in order to get to me.

The vision of her pale throat slashed open and streaming red would be embedded in my memory forever. Permanent. Undeletable. And while I couldn't fully experience the terror of what had happened, that respite would end any minute now.

One question pounded a repetitive warning. Who would die next?

Hologram Holland folded his arms, and stared at some vague spot between Lucas and me.

"I'm sure you know about the device by now," he said with no expression. "If you end this little excursion and come back to me, I'd consider disarming it, you know." He glanced down at the floor, at the lump that used to be Quinn. When he looked back up, he was smiling. "Then again, maybe I wouldn't. I can be unpredictable like that."

He pulled something out of his pocket while his soft laugh filled my head like a nightmare.

Then he waved the item so that we'd be sure to get a clear shot.

A small, black handheld remote.

"Maybe I should just save us all some time and start the countdown now."

Lucas choked out "No!" as Holland's finger hovered over the switch. One push, and two hours would be all I had left.

Transmission: Complete.

The blue light vanished, and Holland's image disappeared. Everything around us looked dim and plain, like a gruesome murder had only happened in our overzealous imaginations.

And then the numbness released its grip.

Operating systems normalizing.

Suppressed emotions slammed through me like a swollen river released from a dam. The force buckled my knees, and I sank to the ground. I covered my mouth with both hands to stop the sobs that lodged in my throat.

Another person gone. Another death I couldn't prevent.

Lucas stopped guarding the door and raced to my side. He knelt next to me, but didn't speak. My sensors picked up the elevated speed of his respiration, the stuttered beat of his heart. He had to be battling his own emotions, but he waited, silently, for me to speak first.

I swallowed and parted my lips. Nothing happened. I couldn't form any words. Not when my mind filled with red blood sprays and the crack of gunshots, the scent of sulfur and Sarah's harsh gasps for breath. The sight of Mom's blue eyes, closing forever.

"Mila. We should go." Lucas's voice was soft and coaxing, like he was talking to a wounded animal. I allowed him to lead me out of the room.

I didn't ask him where we were going, because that didn't seem to matter.

It rarely ever did.

★ ★ ★

I sat in the motel room that Lucas had hastily booked and stared at the white wall.

A desk supported my lower arm and hand, which Lucas had arranged palm up. He was hunched over now, playing surgeon.

The last joint of my index finger was peeled back and separated into two pieces while Lucas dug inside with the sharp blade of a pocketknife.

When I flinched, he glanced up from the mess. "I'm sorry, Holland's nasty little surprise is buried deeper than I thought. I'll try not to leave a big mark when I'm done. Deal?"

I didn't bother responding. No mark could ever be as big as the permanent soul stain I'd have from watching Holland sever Quinn's carotid.

He sighed, but didn't say anything, just got back to work with steady hands.

I was thankful for their warmth.

Minutes passed before I heard him ask, "What's this?" Seconds later, his head popped back up. "Good news. I can use this same wiring to install a stealth-mode switch. We'll make it so Holland never tracks you again," he said, before getting back to work.

"Maybe I should just turn myself in," I blurted. The thought had been growing ever since we'd left the library.

One of Lucas's tools clattered to the floor and he muffled a curse. It was so un–Lucas-like that I almost jumped. "Hold that thought," he said, after retrieving his voltameter.

Half an hour later, he was done. My finger sported a new scar, but no hologram projector. Seemed like a fair trade.

Lucas packed his tools into a soft leather pouch and then perched on the bed near me. "Now, why did you say that? About turning yourself in?"

I fiddled with my altered finger. "I'm tired of everyone ending up hurt. Or dead. Even Quinn. I'm sick of the violence. Maybe this whole thing is futile. Running. Trying to figure out his plan."

I shot up off the bed and started pacing. "Who am I kidding? I'm no hero. I can't even save myself," I said, thinking of the box he'd held. His fingertip hovering an inch or so away from the switch. "Maybe the best way I can help save lives is by turning myself over to him."

"Mila," Lucas started. I whirled on him.

"Don't. Just don't. Don't tell me I'm being melodramatic, or that you can't see that just maybe, I'm right. Don't lie to me," I warned. Knowing that my sudden flare-up was only a flimsy cover for a bottomless pit of despair.

He waited me out. When I finished, he patted the bed.

Reluctantly, I sat back down. Then he took my hand in his. "I wasn't going to say that you're being melodramatic. Anyone with a heart would struggle with this."

My jaw dropped. What kind of pep talk was this, anyway? Even Lucas had given up on me, and it was too much to bear. I started to pull away.

"Wait. Please," he said. "Because that's my point. Anyone with a heart. Meaning you."

I stopped edging away. "We both know my heart is fake."

"Says who? How do you define a heart? Because I'm going to tell you how I do." He bridged the gap between us and rested his fingertips on the top left of my rib cage. Feather soft, but solid all the same. "People use the term heart in two ways. To describe the body's anatomical pump, but also their emotional center. Their reservoir for love, and compassion, and all the good things that make some humans amazing."

Beneath his fingers, my android heart fluttered.

"Some people, like my uncle, they don't have that second kind of heart. The most important kind. Even animals have the first type. There's nothing inherently special about that. It's the second type that distinguishes us. Our capacity to love. To feel empathy. To grieve, and to give."

When he paused, a vein throbbed in his temple, and his eyes blazed. As serious as he often was, I'd never seen him quite so intense.

"It's not what we're made of that makes us human. It's our choices and our feelings that do," he said. Slowly and deliberately. "And in that sense, you are a thousand times more human than my uncle will ever be."

Neither of us blinked. I wasn't even sure I could if my life depended on it. Finally, he dropped his hands to the comforter and bowed his head. "Please don't ever say that again."

I continued to sit without moving. Just looking helplessly at the unruly hair on his bent head. Lucas had always made it clear that he appreciated me, but this was something more. This was unwavering faith. A precious gift.

He lifted his head, and his hazel eyes glistened. "Please," he repeated.

I placed a tentative hand on his chest, mimicking his action a moment ago. "I won't say it again. I promise. But only because I believe in your heart."

His eyes burned torchlight bright. So bright that I could feel something in me simmer. Then his lashes swept down, and his gaze fell away from mine. "Then I guess that will have to be enough. For now."

He captured my hand and gave it a final squeeze before rising. "So, are we sticking with the plan to visit Sonja tonight?"

I knew I should be relieved to be back to normal. Better than normal, in some ways, since I knew I would never be visited by another hologram from Holland. Then why did my chest ache with sudden loss? I wouldn't have minded lingering longer with Lucas. But we couldn't waste any more time. Every moment we were in the dark about Holland's plan, he could be hurting people. Killing them. Just like he had killed Quinn. And probably Sarah.

I nodded.

"Good. I'm going to run out and get a few things first. We could use a burner phone, for one. Any requests?"

"I'm good."

When the door clicked shut behind him, I stared up at the ceiling for a long while before flipping on the TV. Cooking show. News. Horrible rock video. Teen romantic drama.

I paused on the last one with a spurt of guilt. I'd been thinking of Hunter less and less. With no way to communicate, he was beginning to slip from my mind.

I looked at my finger, considering. Lucas had said my IP address was now fully cloaked. Maybe I should test it out. Lucas hadn't been able to track Hunter's cell signal, but it couldn't hurt to try again.

Within a minute of trying, I had it. My breathing slowed as I located the telltale blip on the map. Hunter wasn't in San Diego or Clearwater or even Chicago, where I'd last seen him.

Columbus. He was in Columbus, Ohio.

A scant seven hours away.

I rose and paced the room, my thoughts *whir-whir-whir*ing in time to the ancient fan. Why was Hunter in Ohio? Was that where his mom had found a safe house? But how safe could it be if I could track him so easily?

Speaking of tracking so easily . . . if I could do it, then why hadn't Lucas?

The sinister thought wormed its way into my head. Maybe Lucas had. Maybe he had, and lied about it.

I stared at my reflection in the mirror, and my gaze settled on the upper portion of my chest. The left side. I lifted my hand, placing it where Lucas's had been only minutes ago. I closed my eyes and inhaled, feeling my chest swell, and the rhythmic *thump-thump* of my android heart.

My hand fell away, and my eyes opened. I stared at my face, and saw a scared girl. A lonely girl who'd experienced more than her fair share of pain.

Lucas had stood by me through thick and thin. He'd never given me reason to doubt him. I wasn't about to start now.

Returning to my spot on the bed, I flipped until I found a sitcom, and waited for Lucas to return.

NINE

Sonja Lopez's neighborhood wasn't much when compared to the serene suburbs of Sherman. Many of the lawns had been converted to gravel and hardscape, and older model cars dotted the driveways and streets. Very little charm, but the houses and duplexes were tidy for the most part. Practical.

An automatic light clicked on when Lucas and I approached the concrete walkway. My body tensed, the sudden change a reminder that any new place could trigger a death sentence for me and anyone else in a quarter-mile radius. But all was quiet as we walked toward her building. We passed a small patch of grass, where a lone tree grew amidst a clump of sodden wood chips. A cheerful wreath crafted from orange and yellow leaves hung from a scarred and peeling front door, emitting a faint fragrance of sweet mixed with decay.

Lucas stepped onto the porch and the wooden board creaked beneath his shoe. My sensors picked up something unexpected.

Security system.

Video feed.

With a casual turn of my head, I spotted the camera, disguised as part of an outdoor light that shed a sickly glow over the porch. I elbowed Lucas lightly in the ribs to get his attention. When he turned toward me, I pretended to rub my nose.

"Video camera," I whispered.

His eyes widened, mirroring my own surprise.

A security system didn't seem out of place. But a video camera, in this neighborhood?

Weapons scan: 5 firearms within a 50-ft. radius.

Looked like someone was prepared for a break-in. Or an old Western-style shootout.

With Lucas standing so close our shoulders almost touched, I knocked on the door. A gruff response came from behind the door.

"Who's there?"

I slapped what I hoped was a friendly smile on my face and recited our brief story, much as Lucas had at Maggie's. To my surprise, a series of beeps chirped—the alarm, disengaging—followed by the metallic clank of locks being unbolted.

The door eased open, revealing a medium-height, middle-aged woman. Though she had brown skin and a wide forehead like the Sonja in the photo, the similarities were hard to find after that. That Sonja had life in her eyes, and a healthy glow on her round cheeks. Her brown hair had been full and glossy.

The woman who gazed at us looked like a walking skeleton. Sunken cheeks on a face that somehow, despite her deeper skin tone, managed to look chalky. Her clothes hung on her bony frame, and her entire head was covered in a woolen beanie. A short plastic tube jutted from the loose collar of her T-shirt, and when she gestured for us to come in, she grabbed for a metal device with four legs and wheels. She pivoted the walker and shuffled behind it, her gray slippers scraping across the bare, worn floor. We followed her to a cramped seating area with a ratty couch and two chairs.

Seeing her so frail and beat down triggered memories of Quinn. Anger boiled, but I tried to keep it contained. Any whiff of awkwardness or tension could send up a red flag to someone like Sonja, who was trained as a detective. She was sure to observe minute details.

Sonja half sat, half collapsed onto the couch. Not sure what to do, Lucas and I hovered. She shoved the walker out of her way to kick her legs out, flicking her wrist at the chairs. "Sorry, not much on manners these days. Sit."

Lucas took the chair closest to her, but she ignored him. Her attention remained focused on me as I perched on the edge of the other chair.

I prepared to launch back into our spiel, but Sonja beat me to it.

"I knew this day would come," she said, brown eyes unflinching. "I knew someone besides Edgar had to suspect what happened to that little girl. Your cousin."

Finally.

"What did happen to her?" I asked.

Sonja squeezed her eyes shut, the air leeching from her lungs in a gasp. Her cough was a hacking, ravaged sound that made me cringe.

Lucas half rose in his chair, but she waved him back down. "Can I get you something? Water?" he said, once the spell had ended.

"Water won't fix what I've got. Thank you, though." She seemed to notice him for the first time, but she turned her attention back to me. "What happened to her? I wish I knew. But one thing's for sure—someone sure as hell wanted to make sure there weren't any questions."

Her gaze strayed over to the brick fireplace. Several framed photos were neatly arranged, but she only had eyes for one.

A picture of her and Edgar Blythe. She appeared to be in

good health, so it must have been taken several years ago.

"He was a good man, Edgar. A friend, and a damn decent cop. No one will ever convince me that he died in some hiking accident. Bull. For a cop, that man was as cautious as they came. Hated the rain and cold. He'd no more go hiking in a storm than I'd go run a marathon right now."

"So, you think . . . he was killed?" Lucas asked without flinching. He put it right out there.

"Damn right, I do. I didn't want to believe him, you know. Not at first." Her voice softened, like she was recalling good memories. "I told him he was working too hard. That he was talking crazy—who would want to pretend a fire was an accident if it were arson? All his talk of cover-ups. That kind of stuff can end your career."

She glanced at the photo again, and her eyes misted. Reminding us that much more than a man's career had ended over this.

"I asked him to show me what he had, what proof. But he refused. He avoided me like I had the plague. I thought maybe he'd gone off the deep end. Right up until the call came in . . ."

Sonja's chin dropped to her chest. I waited for her to collect herself, guilt tightening like a noose around my neck. This woman was clearly ill, and here I was, asking her to relive one of the worst moments of her life. Part of me thought I should leave her in peace. But I knew I couldn't do that. I needed all the information I could gather. If I knew the truth about the past, I might be able to stop Holland in the future.

When Sonja lifted her head, her eyes gleamed with unshed tears, but her voice was stronger. "All along, he'd been trying to protect me. He let me do some early work with him on the case, but he cut me off. To keep me safe, I think. After he died, I put in for a transfer. I got it immediately. Like maybe someone wanted me gone, I don't know."

She leaned forward and grabbed the handgrips on her walker. "Wait here."

She shuffle-stepped across the room to a tall wooden vase on a pedestal table. She lifted it and unscrewed the bottom with a deft twist. A curled piece of paper slid out. She turned and brought the scrap back to the couch.

"This came in the mail, 'bout a month after Edgar died. Don't know how he did it, or why me. There was a note too, but I destroyed it. He tried to be sly about what he shared, but I figured if I knew what he was saying, someone else might, too."

Another coughing fit overtook her, longer this time.

"Stupid lungs. Just about worthless. Anyway, he told me not to talk if someone came asking questions. Not that I had much to say—he'd never told me much. But now I have nothing to lose. . . ."

I inched forward, hoping there was more to the story than that.

"He said he'd taken on a new filing system. No idea what he meant until I saw the slip of paper he included with the note."

She uncurled her hand and extended the paper to me. I smoothed it out so I could read the words.

The bold black letters jumped off the page.

2240

A case number. Similar to Sarah's, but older.

A spark of realization electrified me.

"He deliberately misfiled the evidence."

"That's what I think, too," Sonja agreed. "I think he knew he was in trouble, but couldn't bring himself to get rid of the evidence. So he hid it, in case someone else might be able to use it in the future."

And here we were. The people from the future. And also from the past.

Lucas rested his elbows on his knees. "That evidence—would it still be at the station?"

She looked at him intently, then shook her head. "Closed cases or dead ends go to the local warehouse for storage."

As Lucas prodded her for info, I assessed her body language and vitals for the fifth time. No hint of lying. Still, there was something else I needed to know.

"Why are you talking about this now? You could have spoken up any time."

Sonja nodded, as though she'd been expecting that question. "I'm not ashamed to admit that I was scared. If they could take out Edgar like that, then I knew nothing would stop them from going after me next." She pointed at her tube. "I've got nothing to be frightened of now. Stage four lung cancer. If they come to kill me, they'd barely be cheating the reaper."

She jutted her chin out, but shivered a little. Lucas rose, grabbing the blanket from the back of the couch and arranging the soft material around her shoulders. He stooped until they were eye level. "Thank you. You have no idea how much it means to us."

I saw him give her hand a gentle squeeze before he straightened. "Do you need anything before we go? Hot tea, something to eat?"

She shooed him away with her hands, but from the softening around her eyes, I could tell she was touched.

"I'm sorry I couldn't do more," she said.

"Don't say that; you've been a huge help," I replied.

Sonja raised a curious eyebrow at me. "Now that you mention it, what am I helping you do exactly?"

I squirmed, realizing she wasn't fully buying our cover story. "Just filling in all the gaps. We've always wondered—"

"Then why is your friend asking where the files are kept?" she interjected, pointing her thumb at Lucas. "You want actual proof. Evidence of a conspiracy. But why?"

Lucas scratched the back of his head and glanced at the floor, so I blurted out a quick response that I hoped would satisfy her. "We're actually private investigators. Hired by Sarah's parents. They want to sue the police and fire departments for mishandling the case."

She cracked out a sharp laugh that turned into a choking cough. "You seriously expect me to believe that?"

"I don't mean to be rude, but it doesn't matter what you believe," Lucas said, gently but firmly. "We have our reasons for needing the documentation and they don't really concern you."

It was strange, hearing Lucas shut Sonja down like that, but he was right to do it. We couldn't give her any more leeway to question us. Not because she was a threat per se, but because trusting anyone with our real motives left us vulnerable.

Sonja didn't seem offended at all.

"I respect that," she said, wiping the corner of her mouth on her sleeve. "But the people who are involved in this won't care what your reasons are either. They'll do anything to make sure you don't get too close to what they're hiding."

I thanked her for her concern as Lucas made his way

toward the door. His hand was on the handle when Sonja called out to us. "Do either of you own a gun?"

Lucas froze in the doorframe. I turned, remembering that we left Tim's weapon back at the cabin. Lucas couldn't even look at it after what had happened with the bear, and after my post-Peyton shock syndrome, I hadn't wanted to touch one again. But none of that changed the fact that we could have used the protection.

"No, we don't," I said.

"Then there's one more thing I can give you before you go," said Sonja, before violently coughing into her fist.

An hour later, Lucas and I were idling outside the police warehouse Sonja had mentioned. From inside the Caprice, we could see that the street leading into the industrial complex was deserted, which was good news for us. But our luck turned when we pulled up to the automatic gate. Locked. Not a surprise, but a disappointment. I didn't want anything to slow us down.

I opened my mind and linked with the signal flowing from the computer that controlled the lock.

Code streamed, in the form of a demand.

Access code required.

I assimilated the code, twisting and forming it into a precise combination of zeros and ones that I needed to communicate with the security system. A back-and-forth, as fluid and easy as a ballet. I led the system through all the intricate steps of the dance before demanding the access code.

One second, two seconds. Three, four—

At 4.54 seconds, the code was mine.

My android brain shot the radio waves back at the sensor, and the gate computer accepted them. A whir and click later, the gate opened, and I drove inside, headlights off.

Night vision: Activated.

The street ahead gleamed before me, tinged in red but perfectly visible. We crept past a line of warehouses until we reached the one on the far right. I slowed and turned at the corner, parking next to a row of Dumpsters. Hopefully the buildings blocked the view of the Caprice from the road, and the Dumpsters would obscure the view from the north end of the complex.

Once the engine was off, the complex fell eerily silent. The only discernable noise came from cars in the distance. I'd take eerie silence over the blare of alarms any day. Especially the internal kind, ones that signaled I'd be blown to bits within two hours.

In my mind's eye, I saw Holland, reaching for the switch.

"You ready for your first adventure as a hardened criminal?" I said, trying to lighten the mood.

Lucas laughed. "I think I already had that when I aided and abetted your escape."

With trembling fingers, I reached under the seat for the

gun that Sonja gave us. Just as my palm grazed the grip, I felt Lucas's hand on my arm.

"You sure we're going to need that?" His voice was soft. Barely audible. I was grateful for bionic hearing.

My fingers curled around the handle. I understood his apprehension. But Sonja's warning about Edgar—that he was killed for seeking the truth—added another layer of danger to our quest. I had to protect Lucas. And I wasn't sure our special abilities were enough, considering how much power Holland wielded.

I placed the gun in my lap and stared down at it, reliving that moment at Quinn's for what seemed like the millionth time. I didn't want anyone else to die.

"This is for worst-case-scenario use only," I said. "And I promise, no fatalities."

Lucas nodded grudgingly, and pulled a ski mask out of his pocket. I did the same. We planned to immobilize the video cameras while we were here, but these masks were an added precaution. The last thing we needed was an APB out on Lucas, too. I chewed my lip. His extended absence from SMART Ops was probably raising suspicions by now. Holland would catch on. It was only a matter of time.

"Mila? The video cameras?" Lucas said, pulling me out of my thoughts.

Right.

Signals from surrounding buildings hovered in my head.

IndustMax Wi-Fi.

JenningsCorp Wi-Fi.

RCHoldings security.

PPD security.

PPD—Philadelphia Police Department. There it was.

The connection streamed between me and their network. Within a few seconds, I located the video-camera server and in a few more seconds, had the server down. Then, I overrode the security alarm in much the same way I had the gate.

I pulled my own knit mask over my head while he grabbed the passenger-door handle. "Remember, we shouldn't stay too long. Fifteen minutes tops."

I nodded, stuffing the gun in the back waistband of my pants, and opened my own door. Walking as quietly as possible, we headed over to the building's side entrance. The alarm was down, but the door was also hand locked by key. I considered shooting at the lock, but the sound would reverberate and signal an intrusion to whomever might be guarding the interior.

I closed my eyes. Then my sensors whirred as they analyzed the properties of the door, providing me with a readout on the thickness, type of hinge, and force necessary to dislodge it.

There wasn't any other choice. Lucas stood back, giving me space. My shoulder hit the wood with a fluid, swift motion. *Crack!* We froze in place when the noise rang out in the still air. Sharp, but not loud enough to draw any attention.

At least, that was what I hoped.

We sidled inside the door and pulled it shut behind us, even though the lock no longer engaged. A small reception area greeted us, with an oversize desk located behind a wall and a barred window. The room was tiny and utilitarian, with paint peeling off the walls and a stained cement floor. Directly through the secured desk area was another door.

After another crunch of snapping metal, we were inside the warehouse itself.

My heart plummeted as soon as we eased open the door. The space was bigger than I'd hoped. Rows upon rows of shelves greeted us, housing objects of all different shapes and sizes. In fact, at first I almost thought we'd made some kind of mistake. I'd been expecting a mass of bland-looking evidence boxes, but instead there was a rainbow of colors here.

"Need a skateboard?" I whispered. They were neatly arranged in little cubbies, their brightly hued wheels and decals cheering the warehouse workers, I imagined.

Lucas spun a wheel with one gloved hand. "Let's try this way," he said, jerking his head to the next row over.

"You take right, I go left?" I said, eying the masses of

evidence with trepidation.

Lucas nodded, and we split up. He went in search of Sarah's actual case file, 4220, while I searched for the one in Blythe's letter: 2440.

I wandered through the first row, which was crammed with items from floor to ceiling. Boxes, all boxes. I was only at 3500, so I kept moving. I rounded the corner and hurried through the next row. And the next.

I was six rows in before the numbers started to get close. 3900, 4100, and there, on the middle shelf. 2440.

With an unsteady hand, I reached for the box, set it on the floor, and removed the lid. Dust flew up, clouding my eyes. On top was a layer of papers all marked with the case number, involving a pyromaniac and property damage.

Wrong fire. I set them aside, barely daring to hope. What if this was a wild-goose chase?

My hands sifted through more papers, my fingers digging downward. My breath hitched when at first, I felt nothing. Just more papers, and cardboard.

No.

But before the first whispers of defeat could take hold, I grazed something slick. Plastic.

The first bag contained a piece of a timer, its wires frayed like an old hem. The second bag held a red bottle, quart-sized. Butane. A popular accelerant. The tags on the evidence marked them as belonging to case 4220. Sarah's case.

My fists closed around the items while the warehouse receded, replaced by a wall of blazing orange. The musty smell of old paper turned into the acrid sear of smoke.

The flames blocked me from going forward. So suffocatingly hot. No air.

My throat constricted in response.

"Sarah?" I staggered to the ground, too weak to stand. Was that Dad's voice, calling out to me . . . or was it a hallucination? Because I suddenly felt so drowsy, my limbs like rubber. If I could rest my head . . . just nap, just for a little while . . .

The memory faded, leaving something hard and cold beneath my head. I opened my eyes and blinked at the barren surroundings from my supine position on the floor. I bolted upright, my synthetic heartbeat in a frenzied state. The girl I'd been—or rather, who I'd been made to re-create—had been murdered. With every minute, I was sure of it. Her fear, her suffering, it was all mine. We were one and the same. I still didn't know why he'd done it, but the man behind the crime was still at large.

I opened the third bag with fingers that still shook. At first, I thought it was empty. Then I caught a glint of something, in the far corner. I pinched the bit of metal between my fingers. Just a fragment; what looked like the remains of a pin. Like something you'd put on your shirt, or your coat, for a bit of bling. The metal was misshapen, and only a hint of color was left on the front. Green, yellow, and blue. I didn't know what the design was supposed to be, but I knew one thing for sure: if Edgar Blythe had hidden it, then he had identified the fragment and determined it was significant.

I returned the timer piece and accelerant to the shelves once I took pictures of them, but I shoved the pin in my pocket. I hurried down the row until I found Lucas, and filled him in with a hushed whisper. Then we quickly made our way toward the door to the reception office, where my exit plan came to a screeching halt.

I threw my arm in front of Lucas to stop him

Human threat detected: 45 ft.

Subject armed.

Weapons scan: .45-caliber pistol.

"Security guard. Turn off the flashlight," I whispered.

Lucas fumbled with the button. The light went off at the same time I heard footsteps on the other side of the door. I spun and pulled Lucas behind me, aware of the *thwack* of my shoes on the concrete as I tried to balance speed with stealth. I veered us down a row of boxes. Lucas stumble-hopped behind me, but didn't complain, even though his human eyes couldn't possibly pick out much in the pitch dark.

Target advancing.

35 ft.

Another metallic clink sounded. My pulse leapt, while the weapon in my waistband grew heavy. We needed to clear the end of the row before the guard entered, or it would all be over. He'd hear us, and I'd be forced to take aim.

Maybe even fire.

I upped our speed, and we reached the row's end just as the door creaked open. I pulled Lucas by the wrist until his back was against the far end of the shelves. We stood there, barely daring to breathe. Something snapped, and then a glow from above the shelves near the entrance.

"Hello? Anyone here? This is security," a deep voice said.

The light moved in time with a heavy set of footsteps, slapping concrete. I cringed. From the way the beam swung, the guard was walking along the wall and peering down aisles.

His current trajectory would lead him directly to us.

My sensors broadcast information as my heart pounded, plying me with information that was preparing me for a fight.

Target statistics:

Gender: Male.

Height: 6 ft., 1 in.

Weight: 205 lbs.

Heart rate: 95 bpm, slightly accelerated.

Footsteps: Slower than average based on weight/ height. Indicates caution.

Weapon: Loaded.

I listened as the measured, even footsteps closed in. Then

the beam of light shot out from the far end of our aisle, just to the left of our heads. I waited, searching for any pause in the guard's gait, any rustle of clothing to hint that he was reaching for a walkie-talkie or weapon. He kept on walking. The beam of light popped out on our right next, then the footsteps continued, away from us, as he peered into each row.

My fingers tightened around Lucas's wrist. In another thirty-three feet, the guard would come to a dead end. That was the moment of truth. My fervent hope was that he would turn around, retrace his steps until he repeated the process on the far side, and retreat back into the office when nothing turned up.

Android sensors counted down the approximate remaining distance, but with only one foot remaining from where my sensors had detected the corner, the footsteps paused.

Silently, I urged the guard to turn and head back toward the door.

One second passed. Then three. The next footstep finally fell, but didn't retreat in the direction the guard had come from. My gaze tracked left, down to the end of the final aisle. To the open area that would reveal us.

The beam of light grew brighter. He was coming.

I brought my mouth near Lucas's ear. "Move."

He grabbed my hand and allowed me to guide him around the corner of the shelves we'd backed up against, one tiptoed step at a time. Praying the guard's footsteps would mask our own.

We took another quiet step, and another. Trapped in a treacherous game of hide-and-seek, one with potentially fatal consequences. All the while, the footsteps behind us grew louder. Raspy breaths caught in my throat. If we were too noisy, we'd be discovered. But if we weren't fast enough, we'd be caught anyway.

I increased my pace, Lucas following, his fingers entwined with mine. Halfway to the exit, then a little past halfway. Hope swelled within me. We were going make it, just barely.

Without warning, Lucas missed a step, his hand yanking my arm downward. I twisted and reached back to steady him, but it was too late. His free arm swung wildly and caught the edge of the shelves.

The thud that rang out sounded deafening. The footsteps on the far end froze. "Hello? Who's there?"

Then the room echoed with the slap of shoes hitting the concrete floor at a run.

Without saying a word, Lucas and I broke into a sprint and raced for the end of the aisle. The flashlight beam hit us way too soon—we still had another fifteen feet to go.

Any second now, the guard would reach for his radio and call for backup. At that point, we'd be seriously screwed. I pushed Lucas ahead of me, urging him to continue running.

When he was two steps ahead, I whirled. I launched myself in the guard's direction. The gun pressed a cold, metallic reminder against my back, and I issued a silent plea to the universe.

Please don't make me use it.

Sure enough, the guard had reached for the radio strapped to his belt. His eyes widened when he spotted me hurtling at him. He fumbled and dropped the device, his hand diving for the pistol holstered around his waist instead.

"Don't move," he said, fingers grabbing the handle and ripping the barrel free.

Target: Located.

Indecision froze me in place. I should draw my weapon. Now, when I could still shoot him in the shoulder, incapacitate him without killing. But shame crashed through me like a tidal wave. An image of Hunter's faded blue eyes flashed in my memory, begging me to hold back. Hunter, who was alive and maybe even on his way somewhere to start the new life he deserved. Without Peyton.

So I ignored the cold pressure in my waistband. Instead my hand whipped out, catching the guard's gun just as he put his finger on the safety. No time for anything else, I utilized my momentum and ducked my head. My skull struck his throat while his gun-free hand dropped the flashlight and snagged my shirt. We flew backward together.

His back hit the concrete floor and I slammed into his

chest. The *oomph* of air forced from his lungs gave me the advantage. I grabbed his gun hand and smashed his wrist hard against the floor. His grip slackened; the gun fell. I slid the gun behind me and out of his range. With a quick punch, his radio was rendered useless.

The guard remained motionless for a moment, clearly dazed. Then he started to struggle. With one hand, I pinned him by the throat.

"Stop fighting me," I snarled, altering my voice until it was deeper than Lucas's.

At the sound, he went completely still, but his heart rate accelerated.

110 bpm, 120 bpm.

Probably terrified I was going to shoot him with his own gun. With my free hand, I dug into my pocket and foraged until my fingers closed around a few thin plastic strips.

Maybe some girls were taught to always carry an emergency lipstick or hair band, but me? Mom taught me never to leave home without zip ties.

The security guard glanced at the ties. His eyes widened, and his right arm swung. His clenched fist struck my jaw. My head whipped left from the force, and I lost my grip on his throat. As I scrambled to regain my balance, Lucas's shoes appeared to my right. He stooped and retrieved the discarded gun, letting the barrel point in the vicinity of the floor near the guard's shoulder.

"Stay down," he said. "Or I'll make you wish you had."

Vocal analysis: Faster speech rate, slight increase in pitch. Probable indicator of fear.

As if to corroborate my sensors, Lucas swiped his damp palm against his thigh. But his gun hand remained steady, giving no hint of the chaos that was surely erupting inside him. Now, if only the guard would cooperate.

After a few seconds that felt like a millennium, the guard slowly raised his hand. "Okay. Take it easy."

I made short work of incapacitating him with the zip ties, binding both his hands and ankles as Lucas kept the gun steady. Once I finished, I didn't waste time. I motioned for Lucas to follow and together, we jogged toward the door.

"Did you get the speakers?" I said when we were only ten feet away. Plenty loud for the guard to hear.

Lucas's forehead furrowed until he picked up my intention. "Not yet—he interrupted me."

At the end of the aisle, Lucas shoved the gun in his waistband and pulled two speakers off the shelves, handing me one. "These will have to do. They're the best and we don't have time for the others now."

Hoping that red herring would be enough to throw the police off our tracks when they investigated, we hurried out the door, through the office, and into the parking lot. The security guard's car sat unattended a few feet away. A quick slash of the tires, and then we hustled on foot to where the

Caprice was hidden, speakers still in tow.

We drove through the gate and exited onto the street, careful not to exceed the speed limit. Once outside the complex, the masks and gloves came off. Instead of driving toward our motel, I wove through the streets in the opposite direction. Lucas didn't question me, just peered blindly into the night with his hands raking through his hair.

"That was a close call," I said.

Silence.

I glanced over and frowned at the ghostlike pallor of his cheeks. "Lucas? Are you all right?"

"I—I'm not sure," he said. He closed his eyes and inhaled a sharp breath through clenched teeth. His Adam's apple bobbed repeatedly. Suddenly, he bolted upright. "Could you pull over? Fast?"

I swerved into an alley located near a liquor store. The moment I put the car in park, his door flew open. He barely had time to lean over before he threw up on the street. My hands clenched the steering wheel and I stared straight ahead, focusing brutally on the acrid taste in my own mouth. Lucas wasn't used to this kind of danger. Yes, he'd saved my mother and me back at SMART Ops, but putting his life on the line like this was different. I thought of his obvious spike in stress when he'd aimed the gun at the guard, and my gut clenched reflexively. That was when he realized he was putting other people's lives at risk, along with his own.

He had to be exhausted. For almost three days, we'd been on the move with almost zero rest. While I could keep going at this pace, Lucas couldn't. Maybe the fact that I could be so open with him had fooled me into thinking that he and I were the same.

Ridiculous, flawed logic on my part. No matter how much he understood me, Lucas was human, through and through. I needed to get him back to the hotel so he could sleep. Everything else would have to wait.

Once he composed himself, Lucas shut the door, using the mask to wipe his mouth.

"Sorry," he said.

"If it makes you feel any better, I've seen worse."

I'd hoped to make him laugh, but his mouth didn't even hint at a smile. "I'm sure you have."

"Thanks for being here," I said as I studied his rigid jaw. If he only knew how much I admired him. He didn't have to put himself in harm's way like that. He didn't even have to be here at all.

That was when his expression finally altered. He shot me a startled look. "Of course. We're a team, remember?"

His posture relaxed, and I felt the tension drain from my neck. A knot in my stomach disappeared. For a crazy moment there, I'd thought that he might call it quits.

"Do you think they'll link the break-in back to Sarah?" I said, trying to steer things back to normal.

"My bet is they'll be going after petty thieves," Lucas said. "That was smart thinking back there. About the speakers."

"Speaking of which." Up ahead, I saw a row of unlocked Dumpsters. No video cameras around. "Should we ditch them here?"

Lucas nodded and we put our gloves back on, tossing the speakers into the Dumpster after we unloaded them from the car. We off-loaded the ski masks about a mile away, in a different set of Dumpsters. The gloves went into an outdoor trash can about a half mile from the last location.

When we got back to the car, Lucas handed me the gun. "This is what I really want to lose. But I don't want to risk someone finding it while digging through the trash." He swallowed, and I thought he might throw up again. "That man, the security guard. He was just doing his job. I'm behind you one hundred percent—more—but we both know I could never shoot."

I took the gun and shoved it under the seat. "I understand." And I did. I knew exactly what taking an innocent life felt like, and the permanent scars it left on you. I didn't want that for Lucas.

Or for me. Not again.

We were quiet on our journey back to the hotel. So much had happened in the last twenty-four hours, I doubted either of us could think straight. I started sifting through the facts in my mind, filing words and images and evidence into compartments in my internal database, but a tap on my shoulder interrupted me. Lucas held up the burner phone he'd bought at the convenience store.

"We have a voice mail," he said, with a lilt in his voice.

My throat tightened. For a fleeting, heart-lifting instant, I thought of Hunter. But I knew there was only one person it could be.

Chloe. Sarah's best friend.

Before we'd visited Sonja, we'd finally gotten in touch with Chloe's mother, Daphne. She had agreed to give our number to her daughter, but there'd been no guarantees she'd call. Now we had another lead to chase. Maybe the final pieces of the Sarah puzzle would finally fall into place.

"Let's give it a listen," I said.

TEN

The next morning called for coffee and pancakes. At least, that's what Chloe had in mind. The message she left was friendly, inviting me out to breakfast at her favorite café, located in a strip mall not too far from where she lived.

While Lucas slept last night, I'd listened to her message several times. The familiar cadence and timbre triggered more than just a feeling of pseudonostalgia. When I closed my eyes, I was actually able to relive happy moments from the past she shared with Sarah: flashes of laughter and play and whispers.

A part of me longed to remain in that state forever. But then the sun came up and it was time to see Chloe face-to-face. She knew Sarah better than anybody. Maybe she had some idea why someone—like Holland—might want to have her killed. But I knew there was a serious danger, that I was preprogrammed to kill Chloe, too. As I approached the café, I swallowed my fear before it consumed me.

A bell chimed as I walked through the door. I froze in the archway, but continued inside when no answering signal stirred the quiet yet deadly device inside me. A bakery display lined the wall on the right, near the cash register. Behind the counter, a machine hissed while a red-shirted worker put the finishing touches on a latte. The aromatic smell of fresh-roasted coffee permeated the entire room. Three college-aged kids sat at a long table in the back, textbooks open next to laptops. Of the ten other tables, only three were taken—the first by a couple, and the second by two women, one with a stroller next to her seat. Normal people on a normal morning. A place I could never fit in.

The third table, squished in a tight corner between the napkin station and the counter, only had space for two chairs. One of them held a young girl. She sat on the edge of the seat and glanced up from her book as soon as I entered.

Her long brown hair was shorter now, cut in a shiny, shoulder-length bob. But her heart-shaped face with the wide-set brown eyes, delicately arched eyebrows, and full lips: that face was the same one from my memory. From Sarah's memory. Today she wore a V-neck coral sweater with skinny jeans and a pair of fleece boots.

She took a sip from a wide coffee cup, slopping a little over the side. As she grabbed for the napkin in her lap, the restaurant seemed to fade away, replaced with a cozy eat-in kitchen.

"I swear, Chloe, you may as well get a lip piercing, because you have a permanent hole in your lip." We sat at the white tiled counter in my house. I reached into the cabinet and tossed her a dish towel.

She dabbed at the brown spot on her yellow sweatshirt before rolling up the dish towel and snapping it at me. "Yeah? Well, you trip a lot. Doesn't mean you need a toe piercing."

"Ewww." We looked at each other before dissolving into giggles.

In real time, present-day Chloe blotted at the spot, gave up, and snuck another peek at me. Hopefully she could see the "family resemblance" Lucas had manufactured for me.

I stepped forward and then hesitated, wondering if I'd made a mistake in asking Lucas to let me do this alone. We had become such a good team and he was quick on his feet during these awkward probing conversations. But Chloe was a little shy around boys, from what I—actually, Sarah—remembered of her. I had been worried that his presence might cause her to clam up.

Lucas wasn't far away if I needed him. But as I drew closer to Chloe, my feelings of doubt and apprehension began to vanish. Instead I was full of longing, like I couldn't wait to reconnect with a long-lost friend.

A wary smile appeared on Chloe's face when she realized I was coming toward her table. She rose from her chair, and gave me a polite wave.

"Mara?"

"Yes, hi. You must be Chloe?"

"That's me," she said, shaking my hand, yet looking me over with curiosity. "You look a little bit like her. Sarah. I was trying to figure out where . . . it's the eye and face shape, I think."

"We always looked a little alike," I said.

I averted my eyes, not wanting her to notice my discomfort. I glanced down at her napkin and saw a quick pen sketch, in blue. A picture of a shaggy dog.

Ink and paper, bold lines depicting me and Chloe, laughing like banshees.

As we sank into our chairs, I remembered that she was a budding artist, someone who saw beauty in all the details that most people never noticed. All of a sudden, the questions I had for her diminished in importance. Now all I wanted to know was how Chloe was doing. Had she displayed any of her artwork at the local gallery? Was she applying to any fine-art programs, like she'd always wanted to? Gone on that museum expedition to Italy and France? Sarah's memories built up so quickly, I was at a loss for words.

Thankfully Chloe spoke first. "I was surprised to get your message from my mom. I don't think Sarah ever mentioned you. Or maybe I'm just not remembering."

"My parents were estranged from Sarah's for quite a while, so it makes sense that you hadn't heard of me," I explained.

"Family drama, I get it," she said. "My parents are separating. Not a friendly breakup either."

"I'm so sorry," I said.

"It's okay," she said. "It's one of the reasons I like to get out of the house these days, so thanks for meeting me for breakfast."

"No problem," I replied.

Behind me, the door opened and the bell chimed again. I gave the new patron a surreptitious glance and scanned for weapons.

No threat detected.

Pancakes and weapon scans. Quite the combo.

So. What would a normal teenager say right now? "How is school this year?" I started, awkwardly.

Chloe studied me over the top of her coffee mug, as if debating whether I was trustworthy. "Ugh. We have to be at school at seven forty-five. That should be criminal. But my art teacher is great. He takes us to Philly all the time. How about you?"

I thought about Clearwater and my days with Kaylee and her crew. It was hard to believe how simple that time was, even though I'd always known, deep down, that something was off about me. Then Hunter had come along. For a while I'd thought he was the answer to my problems, someone to hold on to when I couldn't stop the ground from shifting beneath me.

But that was before I knew what I was. Before he knew what I was.

"I live in the middle of nowhere, so it's pretty boring compared to the city," I said. "And some of the kids are kind of hard to connect with, you know? But I really like to read, so that's a good distraction."

I wanted to know more about Chloe. "How is your mom?" I asked. "Does she still bake those homemade apple pies?"

Her brow furrowed, like she was confused. "Wait, did Sarah mention those? I thought you didn't see each other much."

My pulse quickened when I realized my misstep. "We emailed sometimes. She liked telling me about her friends, especially you," I lied.

Chloe's expression cleared. She grinned like she was delighted to hear that she was important to Sarah.

"My mom is good, but these days the pies are few and far between," she said. "I still miss Nicole and Daniel. When I came over, we used to get in these ridiculous philosophical discussions. They never treated me like a kid. Well, you probably know, even if you didn't get to see them much."

"Yeah, I do," I said, feeling real pain and longing. "Aunt

Nicole could be pretty no-nonsense, but she definitely treated me like an adult." At the end, she'd had no choice. "I always knew I was in trouble when she'd look at me in that one way, over the top of her glasses."

"Oh my god, yes! I loved those glasses. Very nerdy-chic. They looked so good on her. Have you seen her and Daniel at all, since . . . ?"

She stared down at her cup while a tiny fragment of sorrow dislodged from my synthetic heart and dug its shrapnel claws into my throat. I was glad I didn't have to tell her the horrible truth. That Nicole hadn't lasted much longer than Sarah.

"No, not really," I said, with a hard swallow. "They've been mostly keeping to themselves. Which is understandable, given what happened."

"I've wanted to hide out too," Chloe murmured. "Losing Sarah like that, it nearly broke me. I'm an only child so she and I were like . . ."

"Sisters?" I finished.

Chloe swirled the contents of her cup and nodded. Then she looked up at me, her eyes glistening. "Anyway. My mom said you're in town looking at schools and wanted some advice?"

I blew out a breath and braced myself for what I was about to do. I was going to tell Chloe the truth. Sort of. I just hoped that it didn't scare her off.

"That's what I told your mom," I said, hedging a little. "But honestly, that's not why I'm here. I wanted to talk to you about Sarah. I know this might sound strange, but she sent me a couple of weird messages right before the fire." I figured this was a safe enough gamble. "It's always bothered me and I can't seem to shake the feeling like something was wrong. Was anything going on with her?"

I balled my napkin in my lap, wondering if I'd made a mistake by being so direct. But instead of getting up or walking out, Chloe glanced around the café like someone might be listening. She lowered her voice.

"You too?"

Jackpot.

"Ever since she came back from Montford, she'd been acting kind of off," she went on.

The name triggered an unexpected reaction. Like a spider had just crawled across my neck.

"Montford, Montford. Remind me why that name sounds familiar?"

"It's that prep school her parents wanted her to go to, because of that scholarship she got," Chloe explained. "She didn't even last two weeks, though."

"Oh, right. I remember the school, but not the scholarship," I said. Trying to pry without actually prying.

"It was a full ride, and had some fancy name . . . the Waterman? Waterford? Watkins? Watson? Anyway, she told her parents she was homesick, but I don't think that was why she left," Chloe said. "Sarah wouldn't tell me much—just that they did weird things there, that made her feel . . . wrong. I never knew if she was talking about a club, or the teachers, or what. That's what was the strangest thing of all. She wouldn't give me the whole story. And she told me everything, you know?"

Her gaze wandered toward the open window, and the simple motion triggered yet another of Sarah's memories. I could visualize Chloe from a few years ago, gazing off into the distance in the same way over the top of a book, tapping a pen against her lip.

What could prompt Sarah to keep the details of her Montford trip a secret from Chloe, when she told her everything else? Why would anyone lie under those circumstances? Just like that, my mind switched to Hunter, and the many secrets I'd had to keep to preserve his safety. That's when the answer struck me.

Maybe Sarah thought talking would put Chloe in danger.

As I'd learned, sometimes ignorance wasn't just bliss. Sometimes, it was necessary for survival.

"Did Sarah ever tell anyone else, do you think? About what happened at Montford?"

"I don't think so," Chloe said. "I begged her to talk to her parents but she just said it was over. She just wanted to forget about it."

"Did it seem like she'd been hurt or anything?"

She shrugged. "I couldn't say. Maybe. I hope not. It's just—"

"What?"

"Nothing. I guess I wasn't expecting all these questions," Chloe said. "I haven't had to discuss Sarah like this since I spoke with that detective."

I wanted to ask Chloe more about the detective but I didn't want to tip her off that I knew anything about the investigation. With true sympathy, I just said, "That must have been hard."

"It was awful. I was away the weekend of the fire, so I didn't know anything and I couldn't help him at all," she said, her voice breaking. "And I couldn't help Sarah." At least the people who'd gone after Edgar wouldn't be targeting Chloe. She had no idea how lucky she was.

I suggested we order, and she waved a waitress over. While we waited for our food, the conversation shifted into more comfortable territory. As she filled me in on little details of her life, speaking in these long, rushed sentences that I suddenly remembered, I fell in love with Sarah's best friend all over again. When she asked for the check, I wanted to steal it away from the waitress. Just so Chloe would stay a little longer.

But I knew that wouldn't happen: not now, not ever. And I had no right to ask.

"Sorry about this, but I have to go," she said, putting her wallet in her purse. "I have a huge chem test tomorrow and study group is in ten minutes. I need to pull at least a B if I have any hope of improving my average."

She slid out of her chair and I rose. I reached out to shake her hand one last time, but she ignored it and gave me a warm hug instead.

"It was so nice to meet you. Please keep in touch, okay?" she said as she pulled away.

"I'd like that," I said.

The words tasted bitter, especially when her expression brightened. As much as I longed to stay in touch, I knew I would never dare contact Chloe again.

Chloe bit her lip as if considering something, then went ahead and blurted it out. "This might sound weird, but . . . you remind me a little of Sarah. Mannerisms, or, I don't know. Something. When I talked to you, I almost felt like a piece of her was still here." She shook her head, her laugh rueful. "I told you it would sound crazy."

"Not at all," I whispered.

Sarah, me. The same, and yet so utterly different. One alive, one a re-creation. Like Frankenstein's monster.

Her eyes widened as she stared at me, a strange expression crossing her face. For a moment, I thought she had figured it out. That I was Sarah, or what remained of her. A giddy eagerness made me lean forward. She knew. She could tell. And if Sarah's best friend could tell, then maybe that meant—

Chloe smiled briefly, rubbed my arm, and said again, "It was great to meet you." Then she turned and hustled toward the door without looking back.

I slumped back into my chair. I felt so stupid, thinking that there was some kind of connection between us, that even for a moment I could claim Sarah's close friend as my own. But my self-pity gave way to determination when my thoughts turned to Montford.

My heart broke when I thought about how things might have been different if she'd stayed there. Maybe she would have been safe. But why would she abandon it so soon, especially when a full scholarship was on the line?

As soon as I saw Chloe drive away, I left the café and headed to the dollar store where Lucas was waiting. As I walked toward the end of the strip mall, I saw an RV creep past. I followed it with my eyes. I was pretty sure I'd seen it once before, on our way over from the motel. I slowed down to scan its license plate. What if Holland had found us?

Data retrieval . . .

Scanning and storing a stream of images was a useful skill, I had to admit. In a moment, the RV's license plate would appear in my mental log.

Match.

A time stamp on the photo put my initial RV sighting at ten minutes before I met Chloe. As the RV idled at a stoplight, I kept walking toward the store, with the certainty I was under surveillance. Lucas was standing in front of a magazine rack, pretending to read an issue of *Us Weekly*.

"Is that RV still circling the block?" Lucas asked.

Straight to business.

"I just saw it," I said grimly. "When did you notice it?"

"About fifteen minutes after I got here," he replied. "It's passed this way every five minutes or so after that."

"Damn," I breathed.

"There's more," Lucas said, returning the tabloid to the rack. "I caught a quick look at the driver. Looked a little like Daniel."

My mechanical heart skipped a beat. "Daniel Lusk?"

He nodded. "I was going to trace the plates but I left my laptop in the car, and I didn't want to leave here without you."

I didn't know how to react. Of course I was relieved it wasn't Holland, but I was worried, too. Was Daniel watching as friend or as foe? Was he the angry man who'd turned Hunter and me over to Quinn? Or was he Sarah's father? I'd caught glimpses of a sensitive, caring man, just enough to reassure me he had once existed.

Lucas and I exited the store and headed for the Caprice.

Lucas shoved the key in the ignition, but didn't turn the engine over.

"What do you want to do?" he asked. We didn't have long to figure it out.

I formulated a hasty plan. "When we see the RV come around again, pull onto the road in front of him. Cutting him off will get his attention, let him know that we're onto him. Then let's lead him back to that warehouse area we visited last night. See what he does."

Daniel was following us; we had to find out what he wanted. But we'd do it on our own terms.

While we waited, I gave Lucas the abbreviated version of what I'd learned from Chloe. Montford. The Watkins Grant. Sarah's fear and subsequent return home.

When I said Watkins Grant, he frowned. "Why does that sound familiar?"

Before he could figure it out, I spotted the RV, about six blocks away. From that distance, there was too much interference to scan for weapons or other passengers. But I was able to scan the driver's face.

Magnify: 20x.

A familiar set of eyes drilled into my mind.

"You were right. It's Daniel," I said, my voice suddenly hoarse.

Once the RV was in close range, Lucas peeled out of the parking lot and jerked the car right in front of it. The RV

slammed on its brakes before accelerating again and following us, weaving, back to the warehouse area we'd visited
last night.

We passed the nicer section first, where some warehouses
were converted into expensive lofts and restaurants. Beyond
those, seediness remained. And now that Daniel knew we'd
discovered him, we needed a head start. A place to lie in
wait.

I pulled up a traffic map, a blue schema folding out in
front of my eyes, surveying the area around us. I was able to
see all the side streets, storefronts, and stoplights with 100
percent precision.

"In a quarter mile, there will be a gas station on the left.
When we get there, gun it, okay?"

Lucas nodded, and then snapped his fingers. "Wait, I've
got it! Not the Watkins Grant. The Watson Grant. I remember seeing an envelope on Holland's desk. I wouldn't have
remembered, except it was addressed to Cynthia Gordon.
That's my aunt, but Gordon's her maiden name. Holland's
wife."

We didn't have time for this now.

"It said care of the Watson Grant Committee. The font
caught my eye—"

Holy crap. I turned toward him to ask more questions,
but just then we reached the gas station. As instructed, he
slammed his foot on the accelerator and we blew through a

red light. The RV couldn't pursue us through the intersection because of its hulking size.

He raced the Caprice down the road until we reached the turn-in on the left. A deserted driveway, leading to an even more deserted industrial area. The car's tires screeched as he took the corner hard. The rearview mirror showed the RV, now a ways behind but still on our trail.

"That way, toward the back," I said to Lucas, pointing past the first warehouse.

The asphalt here was so uneven that the car bumped and caught some air. He drove us between two dilapidated buildings. We knew the road continued around the back, flanked by Dumpsters overflowing with trash.

"Slow down just a little," I said. Then I opened the door and launched myself onto the asphalt, tucking my arms tight.

Lucas continued around the corner. Once he cleared the other side, he'd stop and pull the door closed before driving back around and partially concealing the car two buildings over. Just enough to hide the fact that I wasn't in the car.

Daniel would go to Lucas first, giving me time to scan and assess and see what we were up against. And if things went south, well—slashed tires in this neighborhood would give us a pretty big head start.

I ducked into the slim space between the Dumpster and

the wall, listening for the RV. On the far end of the building, I heard it rumble into the ancient parking lot. For a moment, I froze, because it sounded like the RV was coming my way. Then it broke for the far end of the lot. Toward Lucas.

Staying close to the wall, I sprinted in the same direction. When I reached the gap between the first building and the second, I peered down the road. Empty. I darted across the opening, then raced along the back wall, my shoes crunching old gravel and debris. Trash fluttered along the bank of mud to my left; to my right, the warehouse looked like it was about to crumble down. A mishmash of offensive smells assaulted me—urine and rotting food.

Before I reached the end of the building, my sensors kicked in.

Human threats detected: 5.

Weapons detected: Tasers, 4 in a 50-ft. radius.

Five people in the RV?

"Lucas," I breathed.

Quinn's battered face appeared in my head. I saw her neck, dripping red blood. I banished the images at once. I might not trust Daniel, but he was no Holland. At least, that's what Sarah's memories kept trying to tell me.

Knowing how many people he'd brought changed my plan, though. I had to get to Lucas, quick. This was looking like some kind of ambush, and if one of us was going to get caught, I wanted it to be me. I could at least try and fight them off on my own.

I hadn't even reached the end of the building when I heard something I shouldn't have. The sound of the RV rumbling back in my direction. How had they known where to look?

The answer dawned on me quickly. The GPS chip that Quinn had supposedly removed. They were still tracking it somehow.

With no hope for escape or evasion, I grabbed two decently large rocks from the mud and took a position near another group of Dumpsters. I'd have to do my best with these makeshift weapons.

The RV swung wide around the corner, blocking the path with its passenger side, and parked. The door opened, then closed. I widened my stance, gripped my rocks, and waited. I also tried scanning for Lucas, but my systems weren't operating normally. When I called upon my sensors, there was this long pause, like I was being put on hold. I hoped that Lucas had found a way to make himself scarce.

A can clattered across the parking lot, just as Daniel rounded the front of the RV. A strange wave of calm descended upon me, propelled my legs forward with a fluid sort of grace. Whatever it took to keep Lucas safe.

Behind the tinted window on the RV, to the left of the side door, another shadow moved. I only caught a glimpse, a blur of a face. Thankfully, a burst of energy cut its way through the delay in my sensor readings, allowing me to get the basics.

Human threat detected.

The door handle turned. I was right out in the open now, but I stood my ground.

Initiate attack mode?

The query lingered behind my eyes, red and blinking.

The door opened.

Attack?

I readied myself to accept, when the first assailant appeared. A beefy young man with pale skin and a walnut of a nose. I knew him even without full control of my android abilities.

Samuel Braggs. One of Quinn's promising cyber-protégés.

Trailing him was a tall girl with blond hair and an angular face. Abby, one of the Vita Obscura members I'd bonded with in Chicago. Back before Quinn had turned me into a brainwashed assassin.

And following her was a boy with floppy hair and pale blue eyes. A boy I had never stopped thinking about since the moment we met.

ELEVEN

There he was. In the flesh. The boy I'd left behind.

The boy whose life I'd ruined.

Hunter.

My legs went wobbly with an electric zing of relief, and then wobblier still with a slow-sludge pour of remorse. Too many feelings, mixing into a dizzying swirl of confusion. Rooting me to the ground below.

But his face, god, his face. The sight alone was worth a thousand prayers.

No matter what, he was safe.

We stood there while the seconds ticked by, locked in some kind of stalemate. No one moving forward. No one moving back. They waited in a tight cluster, as if to draw strength in numbers. My gaze kept returning to one face in particular. Searching for a speck of warmth in the blue eyes.

At first, Hunter looked startled. They all did. It took a second, but then I realized they were reacting to my adjusted facial features. After a minute or so, his expression swept clean, leaving behind a blank stare that settled a few inches to the left of my shoulder.

The boy I loved couldn't bear to look directly at me.

I'd expected this. I'd deserved this. That didn't make it any easier to bear.

And then, the unthinkable happened. Hunter took a step toward me. And another.

Daniel, Samuel, and Abby maintained their positions, but Hunter kept walking, slowly but with purpose. My android sensors remained functional, but my visual focus, it narrowed to a tunnel, turning everything around us into a foggy haze and leaving only Hunter, me, and the dwindling space between us. The experience was surreal, almost like how I felt when my mind relived one of Sarah's memories. Like this moment had already happened to someone else and I was just watching it play back like a movie.

15 ft.

10 ft.

5 ft.

Hunter stopped. Hands in pockets, wary, as if searching for something. Behind him, I noticed the others doing the same.

As we finally locked eyes, I was transported back to Clearwater. Hunter in the hallway, flashing me his crooked grin and brushing his hair off his face. Reading his manga on my bench, outside in the school's courtyard. His glow of excitement as we'd snuck an illicit ride on a Ferris wheel in a deserted amusement park. His lips, closing in on mine . . .

Longing was a sharp twist inside me, a sear of pleasure-pain like the lung-bursting stab after a hard sprint. Did he feel it, too? I lifted my hands, reaching for his. If I could just touch him, and reignite that connection, everything else might fall away.

Reality crashed over me, though, ice water on bare flesh. Hunter would never accept me after what I'd done to his family. There was no coming back from that. Unless we believed in miracles.

"Mila?"

His voice was faint. Like he didn't want to say my name out loud.

"Hi, Hunter."

I cringed at the way I sounded. Casual, like we'd just run into each other at the mall. He couldn't see the *ping-ping-ping* of my nerves as I scrutinized every inch of him.

Scanning . . .

No gait abnormalities detected.

Limb and body positioning consistent with normal function.

Jeans: Estimate one size too large.

Projected weight loss: 7 lbs.

Hair: ¾ in. regrowth from most recent trim.

I exhaled. He was okay. Tired and a little thinner, but healthy.

Safe.

"Are you all right?" he said. "When you disappeared with Quinn, we were really worried something bad had happened to you."

Each word came out of his mouth in this very even monotone, like he'd been rehearsing. Suddenly I was aware of our surroundings again. We were in an alley. A bunch of Taser-armed people had purposefully tracked me down.

Yes, I was in love with Hunter. Yes, I was desperate to make him see that I was sorry for what I'd done and that I was worth holding on to. But could I ever trust him like I trusted Lucas?

I didn't know where my partner was, but I knew he had my back.

"I'm fine. I was worried about you too," I finally answered. "What are you doing here?"

He shot a look over his shoulder. Daniel kept his hand in his pocket. So did Samuel. Hunter turned back, shifted his weight from foot to foot, and took a stiff step toward me. Then another.

Human threat detected.

My sensors screamed red alert, but I overrode that command, determined to let this play out.

When Hunter opened his arms, all warnings faded away. I would trust him with my life. With everything.

My hands curled around his waist, grabbing his shirt while I pressed my face against his chest, his familiar scent invoking a pungent surge of relief and sorrow.

"I'm so sorry," I choked out against the cotton of his shirt. My eyes swam. I willed the arms around me to tighten, to pull me closer. Instead they held me loosely while I listened to the thud of his heart.

I wanted to say a million things to him. To shout my joy that he was here, whole and unhurt. To ask him how and why he'd hooked up with Daniel and the others. To tell him how I'd missed him.

I pushed myself away, just a little, so that I could meet his eyes. Tears trailed down my cheeks, wet and warm.

His gaze narrowed on those, his finger whisper-sweeping one damp cheek. I had a flash of Lucas doing the same thing, back at Holland's lab, in wonder that an android would cry.

He froze. With hands that weren't harsh but weren't gentle either, Hunter gripped my shoulders and pushed me away, like he'd never meant to hug me in the first place, much less touch my tears.

He turned to the group, who waited in silence. "I think she's safe. At least for now."

Without another look at me, he slinked back to join them.

"Can I ditch this now?" Samuel asked, waving his Taser at Daniel.

Daniel grunted, gave a jerk of his head. "Keep it. We've only observed her behavior for a short time. We need to make sure before we let our guard down."

Hunter's greeting. His embrace.

He'd been acting, in an attempt to see if I was still a threat.

His posture now, with the rigid set of his shoulders, his grim mouth, the evasive eyes—that said it all. I could apologize a thousand times but he would never hear it. He didn't care about me. He only cared about the next people I might harm. They must have come here to determine that—for now—I was not a threat. Did they know about the bomb? I wondered. Even without a bomb, they knew I could be deadly. They'd seen it.

"Where's Lucas?" I said.

"He's inside." Daniel jerked his head at Samuel, who walked to the RV door.

Lucas—the other human I'd detected. Now their captive?

Storm clouds gathered behind my eyes, filling my skull with rising pressure.

"Send him out," I demanded, already moving toward Samuel.

Daniel lifted his hands in an attempt to calm me. "He

can't come out right now—" he started, but the squeal of the opening door cut him off.

It revealed Lucas inside. Unmoving. Bound and duct-taped within an inch of his life.

The storm clouds exploded, and I snapped.

Target: Located.

The next instant, I flew toward the door, my fingers locking around Samuel's arm. With a burst of force, I threw him over my shoulder and he hit the ground in a crash that echoed through deserted parking lot. I wanted to check on Lucas, but my anger burned bright, urging me to turn and bring down Daniel next.

I whirled, setting my sights on Lucas's captor before launching myself at him.

The electric pulse of a Taser crackled through my sensors, grounding me before I could ever reach my destination. It didn't come from Daniel, though, because as I fell, I saw his hand still fumbling for the Taser in his pocket. No, this shot had originated elsewhere.

I hit the asphalt hard. Paralyzed and useless, my head lolled to the side.

Warning: Systems—

Syste—

Sy—

My last image was a blurred kaleidoscope of Hunter's athletic shoes; my last sound, his voice saying, "Got her!"

Then I floated into nothing as my system entered the dead space of shutdown.

System rebooting.

Once the reboot initiated, my return to awareness was quick. No gradual easing into the waters; more like stripping down and diving headfirst.

I sat on the hard dirt, my feet bound and my hands secured behind me to a huge tree. The stone circle of a fire pit sat in the middle of a clearing to my left, with a picnic table a few feet back.

Peeking through the dense cover of trees and foliage, I could just make out the RV in the distance.

We were at a campground.

I returned to look at the objects I'd skipped in my initial assessment. Five camp chairs in greens and blues, arranged around the fire pit. And sitting in one, just to my right, was Hunter.

"Got her."

His last words surfaced in my brain. "You Tased me," I said.

"You were attacking us," came his flat reply. Blue eyes met mine in a stalemate.

I looked around, but didn't see anyone else. "Where's Lucas?"

"He's safe. He was fine when you freaked, too. Just tied up—in case."

"In case what?"

"In case you attacked us like you did back at Quinn's," he said, dragging the pointed end of a stick through the dirt by his shoes. When he glanced up his face was a mask, his body language closed-off stiff. His chair was a good distance from the tree where I was bound, and he watched me with eagle eyes.

Oh.

Oh.

Based on the last Mila they'd seen, they had good reason to be concerned. Scared, even.

Scared of me, because of the terrible things I'd done.

Any remaining hint of anger faded.

They had every right to fear me. They knew what I was capable of.

My throat knotted and my gaze dropped to the floor. How could I face Hunter? Any of them? In that moment, I wanted to break free of my bonds, sprint out of the campsite, and keep running. Away from Hunter's fear, from my regret, from the reminders of the terrible things I'd done.

But the only true escape lay in putting an end to whatever Holland was doing.

"Why did you guys hunt me down?" I said, watching his reaction with wary eyes.

"Samuel," he said, his tone as wary as mine. We were

two wildcats, circling. Each wondering if the other would strike first.

"When Quinn took off with you in the middle of the night and didn't return, he let everyone know what went down. Some of them fled, but a few of us stayed on. Especially when he told us his suspicions about the bomb."

My hands flew up to cover my abdomen, but came up short against the thick metal bands. I stared at Hunter in horror, feeling as exposed as if I were stark naked. He knew about the bomb.

They all did.

"So it's true," he said, his eyes going wide.

The three words made me feel guilty. Like I'd intentionally stuffed an explosive device in my body that could blow me to hell and back whenever a sick excuse for a man desired.

"I didn't know until Lucas found me in the desert. None of us did."

He rose, knocking over the chair in his haste to escape.

"It's not like that; there's a window. Two hours from the time it's activated until detonation. And it hasn't been started yet. You're perfectly safe."

I studied the dirt beside me, focusing on a stray ant doing its frantic zigzag back to the others. God. This was all wrong. This conversation, this reunion, this life. Sitting here, discussing my body bomb with the boy I'd fallen for.

Was there a right thing to say in this situation?

"So you tracked me down to help me?" I finally said. I wasn't sure if I believed that.

He shrugged. "Daniel wanted to track you down to make sure you knew about the bomb, and didn't hurt anyone by accident."

"And you?" I prodded, heart in my throat.

His shoulders tensed, but his voice remained soft and paper thin. "After what you did to Peyton, I wanted to make sure that you didn't hurt anyone on purpose."

A knockout punch of sincerity.

How had we come from Clearwater to this, in so little time? From fairs and Ferris wheels to bombs and death? I leaned forward, restraints digging into my skin. I needed him to understand. "I wouldn't, won't. Not again. That was a weak moment, Quinn, her program. She—"

"I don't care. You're dangerous. I don't know why Daniel's being so wishy-washy about this. I think they should lock you away somewhere. It's the only way to keep people safe."

For one terrifying moment, the world stopped spinning. "What? No! You can't do that!" I cried. "We need to stop General Holland! That's why we're here, you know. Lucas and I are trying to figure out his master plan, so this will never happen again. It's just . . . taking a while. We have evidence about the fire. . . ."

Suddenly I could see how little we'd accomplished so far. "You have to listen," I told Hunter, but my pleas fell on deaf ears. "You have to be patient!"

He leaned over and started digging in the dirt again, his back to me. His message was loud and clear.

"Can I talk to Daniel?" Suddenly I was afraid they were going to ditch me here. Tied to a tree and helpless. And where was Lucas? I needed to talk to him, too.

Hunter shook his head. "Not right now. Maybe later."

Frustration was a roar in my head, but as I studied the back of Hunter's head, sorrow slowly chased it away.

He'd lost so much. All because of me.

"I'm sorry. I'm so, so sorry. I never meant to hurt you."

The stick snapped beneath his hand. He rose from the chair.

"I know there aren't enough sorries in the world to make it right, but I have to try," I said. "If I could take it back, I would. The lies. All of it. I never meant to hurt you, or your family. Your stepdad. I was selfish, letting you follow me. I realize that. I just wanted . . . I wanted . . ."

My throat constricted, making speech difficult. Slowly he turned, so that his gaze briefly met with mine.

He pivoted and strode toward the RV without uttering a single word.

I finished on an unheard whisper. "I just wanted something real."

My head listed to the side. I watched the sun disappear over the horizon in a red-orange blaze, and stars pop out in a brilliant display of lights. Crickets chirped, and frogs answered. I shut my eyes and wished for the impossible.

The next morning, the crunch of footsteps alerted me to Daniel's presence long before I saw him.

He paused about five feet away from me, hands thrust deep into his pockets. From the size of the dark shadows under his eyes, I guessed he hadn't gotten much sleep.

Not that I had, either.

"Lucas told me why you're here in Philly," he said. "I'm ready to listen, if you're willing to talk."

He grabbed one of the camp chairs and plunked it down right in front of me. He settled into the canvas and crossed his arms.

I hadn't even started talking yet, and this already felt like the interview from hell.

Before I could utter my first word, he flinched.

"You're even getting her expressions down now," he said, half-accusing, half-awestruck.

I didn't have to ask him whose. Sarah's. His dead daughter's. And in spite of everything, I couldn't help but feel a stab of pity for him. What must it be like, to see a reincarnation of your dead child sitting before you? Moving as she did? Speaking as she did? Knowing that she'd been replaced by a machine that was programmed in her image? Or did he look at me and get confused, his memory saying one thing, his logic another? I wouldn't wish that on anyone. Not even Daniel, who had sold me out to Quinn and inadvertently led to Peyton's death.

I still couldn't hate him. Not when my memories conjured up a warm and loving man. He'd been a good father to Sarah, and the strength of her love was hardwired into me along with everything else. None of his actions now would erase that. Not entirely.

But they could hurt like hell.

"Don't look at me like that. Not when you look so like . . . It's too much. Too much," he repeated. He sighed and buried his head in his hands. When he looked at me again, his eyes glistened.

"I know what you must think of me. I turned you over to Quinn; I sold you out. You're right. I did. What would you do, if your dead daughter reappeared to haunt you?"

Then the fight faded out of him. "If it matters, I had no idea what Quinn had planned. Or how much you'd grow on me. I'd like to think that I'd have chosen differently, had I known what she had planned, but hindsight is twenty-twenty."

At his mention of Quinn, a memory flashed into my head. One of mine for a change, not Sarah's.

Daniel, tied to the chair and pleading, back at Quinn's.

"No matter what happens, I want you to know—you're my

daughter. I tried to reject that because it hurt too damn much, but it's the truth."

A man would say anything when begging for his life. I knew he didn't mean it. I didn't even blame him for lying. But the lies didn't stop me from wanting to believe. To make the words true.

"I need to tell you some things now," I said.

He rested his elbows on his thighs and waited.

I told him about our visit with Maggie, his old neighbor. About the suspicious man she'd seen before the fire. About Edgar Blythe, the police detective, and his sudden death. About Sonja and the warehouse and the evidence that pointed to arson.

"Arson," Daniel repeated. "God. Why would anyone do that? Hurt my baby girl?"

I examined my shoes, not wanting to witness his pain. "There's more," I continued. Softly. "Maggie also led us to Chloe Nivens. I met with Chloe. She told us that Sarah had a scholarship—a Watson Grant—to a place called Montford Prep. She went there soon before the fire, but she only stayed for a couple of weeks."

I found myself needing to pause. This next part was going to be difficult.

Daniel rubbed his eyes. "She said she was homesick, and Nicole and I let her come home. If we hadn't given in . . . she wouldn't have been there when . . ." He couldn't finish his sentence.

My head popped up. "Don't. It's not your fault. I don't . . . I mean, she wouldn't want you to think that. Ever."

This next part was the worst.

"Sarah confessed something to Chloe, once she got home from Montford. She told Chloe that something about the school had freaked her out. She never told Chloe what it was, just that it had to do with the grant kids."

Daniel straightened. "Freaked her out . . . why the hell didn't she tell us?"

"She told Chloe she didn't want to worry you." I stopped there, wondering if I should continue. Did he need to know the rest?

Then I remembered how I felt when people kept me in the dark. For my own good.

"Lucas remembers seeing an envelope at work once. It was addressed to Cynthia Gordon. Holland's wife, but under her maiden name. He didn't think anything of it until Chloe brought up the name Watson Grant. The letter was addressed to her care of Watson Grant Committee."

I saw him put the pieces together, the way we had. Cynthia Gordon. Lucas's aunt. Holland's wife. Even though the puzzle was yet incomplete, the partial picture was enough to do one thing: connect Holland with Montford Prep. I watched Daniel's face sag when the reality sank in. This couldn't be a coincidence. The Watson Grant. Montford. Sarah. Holland. Together, they formed some kind of chain. And at the end of that chain were the answers. We just needed to follow the links to the very end of the line.

"What do you want to do now?" So soft, even I had to strain to hear.

"I thought I could research who is at Montford, right now, with the Watson Grant. Then I'll go to Montford to talk to them. What if whatever frightened Sarah is frightening them, too? If we find out what it is, we could find out what Holland is really up to."

This time, when Daniel dropped his head onto his forearms, his body shuddered. As if racked by silent sobs.

My heart cracked as I was reminded of how similar we were. Daniel and I both struggled to contain our emotions. Suddenly something occurred to me. Maybe my emotions weren't just a mistake manufactured by Holland. Maybe they were genetic. That thought was almost comforting.

Daniel dragged his sleeve across his eyes and stood.

"Lucas told me about your two-hour window. What happens if it activates?"

"I'll tell everyone immediately, and go off on my own to a remote location. I don't want to hurt anyone. Not again."

He studied me as if the truth might manifest in red letters on my face, like one of my security warnings. Then he ducked behind me. I felt pressure against my wrists, a gentle jiggle-tug in my bindings. There was a snap, and the pressure disappeared.

Free.

From programming or habituation or some surfacing instinct, I rubbed nonexistent circulation back into my wrists.

"I'm sorry I restrained you, but we had to make sure. From here on out, I pledge to do anything I can to help."

I scanned him, automatically, for any signs of lying. None.

"Follow me," he said. "It's time for a group meeting."

I trailed him past thickets and low-hanging branches to the RV. Feeling like a prisoner about to face a firing squad.

With six people inside, the RV was a little cramped. A table fitted beside a circular seating area. Lucas sat on the far side, and Abby, Samuel, and Hunter congregated on the other. They all looked up when I entered. I hadn't seen Abby since we were back at Quinn's, and I could hardly meet her eyes.

A door in the back led to a messy set of bunk beds and a pullout. Another door opened to a compact bathroom. The typical cooking surfaces were absent, though. The RV was custom, decked out with built-in computers that fit where a stovetop might have resided.

Lucas scooted over, and I slid into the empty spot beside him. The brown fabric of the makeshift couch pilled into nubby little balls, which restless hands had plucked and tossed onto the yellowed linoleum floor. A musty smell hung in the air, filled with damp skin and greasy food remnants and a hint of floral body lotion. Just this side of overripe.

"Don't worry, your little computer lad didn't desert you," said Samuel. "We had to restrain him overnight— loose restraints, loose!" He added, when I visibly bristled, "To keep him from trying to help you escape."

I'd forgotten how large Samuel was. Like a tree trunk with arms and legs.

Abby rolled a penny on her knuckles and kept tabs on me with watchful blue eyes. Hunter ignored me.

I filled them in on the bomb, as Daniel requested, so they could make an informed decision to stay here or come with me.

But as Samuel opened his mouth, I held up a hand. "There's more you should know. About Quinn."

I smoothed my hands across my jeans while Lucas and I exchanged a look.

Samuel caught the glance. "What?"

I bit my lip, then forced out the words. "She's dead. Holland found her and murdered her."

More than one face blanched. "Do you know for sure?" Daniel asked.

"We do. He sent us a transmission. He wanted . . . he wanted to make sure we watched while he executed her." My voice was dull, a complete contrast to the sharp twist of horror inside me as I remembered.

Samuel flinched while Abby's hand flew to her mouth.

"Oh my god," she whispered. Even Hunter whirled in his seat to look at us, his boyish features taut. Guilt was a string of barbed wire inside me. A visceral reminder that up until he'd met me, Hunter had been perfectly content to read his manga and do normal teen things. I'd dragged him into this mess. These murders.

"Jesus," Samuel breathed, after several long, silent moments.

"Is someone Holland clearly doesn't worship," Lucas said. "You need to keep in mind that he is a cold-blooded killer who will do whatever it takes to get his way."

He paused to let that sink in, and then continued. "Which is exactly why Mila is on this quest. At no small personal risk, I might add. Probably more than anyone else. She's made a choice to stop Holland, regardless of her own safety. She wants to make sure he can't hurt others the way he's already hurt so many. I've made a pledge to join her. Who else is in?"

Lucas's hand edged across the table until his pinky touched mine. A bare hint of contact, but it was enough.

Across the way, Hunter's gaze tracked the small movement, his gaze locking on our hands.

Lucas said, "I've already let Mila know I'm dedicated to helping, but no one else is bound to my decision. Samuel?"

To my surprise, there was no hesitation on the part of the brawny Scot. "Danger is my middle name. Or it would be, if my mother had given me one."

"Are you sure about the two-hour window?" Abby said, twisting a strand of blond hair between nervous fingers. "Even if the bomb goes off, we'll be safe?"

"I'm as sure as I can be," Lucas said.

She pondered that for a thoughtful moment and nodded. "I'm in too. But I reserve the right to bail at any time."

"Agreed," Daniel said. He was in.

All eyes turned to Hunter, who was still staring at the place where Lucas's hand met mine. I pulled away and folded my hands in my lap, self-conscious.

"You all are crazy. What if she loses control again? Do you really think she can be trusted?" he said, all curled lip and flashing eyes.

Lucas stiffened. "I trust her implicitly."

"I can see that. Maybe it's easier when she hasn't shot someone in your family."

My hands tightened into a fretful ball. I didn't open my mouth to defend myself. I had no defense.

"No, but my uncle—Holland—shot someone in hers," Lucas said. His uncle shot my mom, and yet here I was, trusting him anyway. "It's okay to want to leave. This is a tough situation, on many levels. And your pain is understandable and fresh, and I'm very sorry for it. But the circumstances are different now. Mila will never be under Quinn's control again, and that means that I will follow her until this mission is complete, or she begs me to go away. Her bravery and compassion put a lot of so-called real humans to shame."

Hunter's lips thinned. He glanced from face to face, and finally shrugged. But beneath his casual pretense, fire lurked. "I'll do it. If only to be there when she proves you wrong."

I flinched. It hurt, of course it did. But even Hunter's grim prediction couldn't snuff out the glow ignited by Lucas's words. Somehow, he believed in me.

Daniel clapped his hands together. "Well, then. If that's all settled, let's get to planning. We have a lot of work to do."

TWELVE

Daniel passed out laptops and filled everyone in on what Lucas and I had learned so far. He pulled a stool from a closet, and folded his tall frame so he could sit at the table. I was next to Lucas, Hunter sandwiched in between Abby and Samuel.

"Here's how it's going to work. Mila will do a few quick online searches and then assign us tasks based on what she finds."

He opened the laptop and flexed his knuckles until they cracked. Lucas glanced at me, and cleared his throat. "Sir?"

When Daniel looked up, he continued. "The chip. You promised Mila you'd remove it."

I feigned interest in the table, feeling Hunter's eyes on me. But I had to be over that now. I couldn't be ashamed of who—and what—I was.

"We can do it right here, if there's enough room," I said.

Daniel shrugged. "Should work. Let me grab a few things."

A few things turned out to be a handheld scanner and a probe, with an end that separated into thin, razor-sharp tweezers. Lucas eyed the scanner. "I've never seen that technology before."

"It's new, something Quinn's team made. Designed to be unnoticeable."

While Daniel positioned me with my back to him, I wondered what kind of people would need such technology and why. Maybe I didn't want to know. Daniel directed Lucas to pull the back of my shirt down. After checking with me for permission, he complied.

I was acutely aware of the others looking on while the scanner hovered over my bare skin. Daniel muttered as he started the search just to the right of my spine, but had to move the scanner left, and then down.

Beep, beep, beep.

BEEP.

"There it is. Things migrate sometimes," Daniel said.

The probe sank in, its metal cold against my warmed skin.

And then it was all over. "Done!" Daniel pronounced. A tiny dot of metal was clenched between the tweezer tips. He promptly slid it into a waiting Ziploc.

With that complete, everyone stared at me expectantly. Feeling a little like a circus performer without a net, I started my search.

Secure network: Log on?

The smooth ease of the connection flooded me with relief. Until this moment, I hadn't realized how much I'd missed using one of my most basic functions. The hum, the flare, the thrill of tapping into something vast and ubiquitous; of being able to reach out and grab whatever information I needed, whenever I wanted. I hadn't appreciated it before.

As I searched for information on Montford and the Watson Grant, I heard a strange sound.

Drip. Drip. Drip.

Water. The faucet outside the RV was dripping. Steady and distinct.

Something about the sound sent a creeping shadow up my spine. Dread, I identified. Then I realized why.

The dripping sounded too much like a countdown. A reminder that inside this RV, nestled among the only people left that I cared about, there was a ticking time bomb.

And that bomb was me.

Shaking off that unsettling notion, I concentrated on the search.

First, I accumulated information on Montford Prep.

Scanning . . . Citations found.

I skimmed through the data and shared what was relevant.

"Montford Prep, founded in 1926. List of deans if needed, current one named Robert Parsons. Seven board members," I said, sharing the names. "But none of them triggers any links to Holland. If someone wants to follow through on that, though . . ."

"On it," Samuel said, through a mouthful of chips. He shoved the bag aside and began to type.

"Alumni donations totaling over five million dollars in the last three years alone."

Samuel whistled. "Must be nice to be rich and douchey."

When I finished with Montford, I switched gears to the Watson Grant, starting with any former or current recipients.

Searching . . .

To my surprise, only five names pulled up; six if you included Sarah's.

"The Grant is something new. In fact, Sarah was the first-ever recipient, and the only one that year."

Daniel swore under his breath, and I couldn't blame him. He probably wished he'd never heard of the Watson Grant.

"Now, for the current students."

I whipped through names and descriptions.

Hannah Peckles—a tiny blond computer-science whiz.

In her sophomore year of high school, she'd developed a top-selling iPhone app that created 3D games based on the user's location.

Ben LaCosta—a lanky redhead with a splattering of freckles across his cheeks and nose. He placed out of college calculus his sophomore year in high school, and had been part of some wunderkind math team that won every time.

Claude Parsons—a boy with a long, oval face, wire-rimmed glasses, and a shock of dark hair, praised by his teachers for his aptitude in language (oh, the things you could learn by hacking into school transcripts!). He'd acquired three before high school—Spanish, French, and German—and then Mandarin by the end of junior year.

Sharon Alexander—an athletically built brunette who had used ad revenue from her popular blog and a Kickstarter campaign to raise a million dollars for the victims of domestic violence.

J. D. Rothschild—really, the only one who sounded like a contender for Samuel's "rich and douchey" snob title. Whenever J.D. appeared online, he was dressed in trendy but expensive clothes, immaculately groomed to the point where one started to wonder if his family kept a personal hairdresser on staff. His claim to fame was creating a hedge-fund algorithm that increased his family's wealth by twenty percent.

As I shared these findings with the group, I continued my research.

Cross-referencing names.

A few seconds later, I sagged.

"I can't find any common link among these kids. Different towns of origin, different interests, no overlap in parents or relatives. The grant claims to be connected to Magnate Enterprises. But that seems to be a dead end—a dummy company."

"So, they're all exceptional . . . but in completely different ways," Lucas mused.

"What about their parents? Are they all rich? Do they have government connections? Any . . . special abilities we should know about, beyond what you've mentioned?" Hunter this time, his expression guarded.

"I looked into that, and no," I said, ignoring his subtle jab at my androidness. "Nothing. I mean, none of them are below poverty line, but that's about it. No one worked for the government, or even a company with tight government ties. Their parents' occupations range from doctors and CEOs to school teachers and administrative assistants."

My useless information washed over the RV, rendering everyone silent. Abby was the first to break it.

"So now what?" she said, resting her chin in her palm.

Samuel slammed a fist on the table. Chips went flying. "Isn't it obvious? We need to go to the school and investigate. Talk to these kids and see what's up."

"I agree," I said. "We need to figure out what's going

on there that made Sarah run. Seems like the current grant students are key."

Daniel flinched at the sound of his dead daughter's name. He swallowed hard, then nodded, staring at the ceiling as if deep in thought. When he spoke, the words came slowly, almost as if he was reluctant to speak.

"I have an idea. While you were talking, I pulled up the Montford website myself. Looks like they encourage prospective students to come visit the campus and sit in on classes. They even have a program that allows kids to bunk with attending students, spend the night, get the feel of things. You could all pose as prospective students. It's just . . ."

"Just what?" I asked.

"It's dangerous, I think is what he's trying to say," Lucas said. "If Holland is connected to the school, he might be on the lookout for just this sort of thing. He doesn't know what they look like, but you . . ."

Hunter's gaze darted back and forth between Lucas and Daniel, his jaw slack. "Are you out of your minds? You're not really considering letting . . . her," he said, emphasizing "her" like he was granting me some kind of concession, "go undercover at a school?"

Lucas stiffened, but Daniel was the one who spoke. "We're all very aware of what Mila is," he said mildly.

"Then you should realize that sending her to a school

full of teens is a bad idea. She's unstable. You didn't see her back at Quinn's—I did." His voice rose, and he paused, hands fisted. "It would be better—safer—for everyone if she stayed behind in the RV."

He didn't even glance in my direction.

I pushed to my feet, bumping the table in the process. Samuel's chips flew off the edge, and he caught them by the edge of the bag.

Hunter hated me. Worse than that—he had reason to.

He'd have to get ready to hate me even more.

"I'm going. End of story. Look, Lucas altered my appearance once—he can alter it again. More. I don't look exactly like Sarah, and she was only there for a week. I doubt people remember her, and once Lucas is done, it won't matter anyway."

I watched Abby and Samuel exchange an uncertain glance. "It's not just that," Samuel said, looking apologetic. "Holland—"

"Won't be hanging out at the school. He's too busy with his secret lab—he can't just disappear for days to hang out at Montford. Plus, that would be pretty hard to explain to whoever isn't a part of—whatever's going on there—right? A high-ranking military general, showing up out of the blue?"

Hunter's mouth tightened mutinously, but Lucas nodded. "I agree. And I've been tracing his cell phone signal by remote, anyway. I've got it set to alert me the second he steps out of a ten-mile radius beyond his office and home. Besides," he said, staring straight at me, "Mila has a right to determine what role she plays."

Hunter opened his mouth, no doubt to protest again. Daniel cut him off. "The simple truth is, we need her. Not all of us together could access as much information as she can, not in a short amount of time. The sooner we get in and out, the better. We'll make sure everyone exerts as much caution as possible—agreed?"

We all voiced our consent. Everyone except Hunter, who leaned back into his seat, jaw clenched. But at least he was silent.

"Okay," Daniel continued. "The way I see it—the more kids we can get inside, the better. But I can't claim you all as mine, so we'll need some kind of plausible cover story."

"What if we pretend to be students from a charter school?" Abby suggested. "They're popping up everywhere these days, right? It wouldn't make Montford suspicious if they'd never heard of it—most charter schools are pretty new."

Daniel tapped one finger against his lips. "That could work. We could create an entire school, add you in as students, and I could be your senior teacher, taking you on an approved overnight visit. I think that's our best bet."

"Wait," I said. "Wouldn't you be at risk for detection?

Haven't you met the dean before, when Sarah went?"

He shook his head. "No, I was out of town at a conference when Sarah started school. I planned to visit her, but she was home by the time I got back. Maybe if I had been there . . ."

He trailed off, and my heart hurt for him.

He recovered by barking out commands, divvying up projects so that, by morning, we would all have fake personas and online records to match.

We worked late into the night. When someone got too sleepy to function, they headed into the back of the RV, where custom bunk beds and an overhead bed served as temporary resting spots. Daniel provided guidance when needed.

Technically, I didn't need to sleep, though I had a program that emulated drowsiness once I'd been awake for a specified number of hours. I'd noticed that ever since the desert, though, that drowsy sensation was harder and harder to resist. I wondered if my newly proliferating cells needed rest to grow? Logic dismissed that idea as ludicrous. In humans, sleep cycles were regulated by melatonin and the hypothalamus. I was pretty sure I didn't have a hypothalamus. My biology was artificial . . . and deadly. As we worked, my hand drifted to my abdomen. To where a monster slumbered, waiting to devour me at a madman's whim.

If I focused really hard . . . I inhaled through my nostrils, closed my eyes. Let my sensors roam freely, flooding my brain with their data.

Scanning.

Scanning.

A blip of recognition from my lower abdominal quadrant. There.

It disappeared before I could trace the path. A slippery bit of nothing, vanishing with a beat of my phantom heart but leaving behind a lingering sense of dread.

And there went the faucet again.

Drip. Drip. Drip.

Tick. Tick. Tick.

The walls of the RV seemed to close in around me, and I jumped to my feet. "I'm going out to get some air."

The door clicked as I walked out into the crisp night. An owl hooted in the distance while I focused on breathing: in, out, in, out. Anything to calm the rising panic beneath my ribs. The bomb wasn't activated. I was still safe. Somehow, Lucas and I would figure out a way to disarm it. Hopefully before Holland drank a little too much one night and decided to flip the switch on a whim.

But if we didn't . . .

The door snapped open behind me, and footsteps headed my way. Measured, steady, heavy.

Daniel stopped two paces back. "Everything okay?"

My hands balled into fists. Part of my heart still longed

for him, this father of Sarah's that I'd never known. And I'd appreciated his support, back in the RV. But I couldn't forget that he'd set me up to be captured by Quinn. And those emails . . .

I didn't turn. "Why do you care? After all, I never should have existed, right?"

In the few seconds of silence that followed, I could sense his confusion. Then he uttered a muffled curse. "The emails," he said flatly. "How did you find them?"

"Lucas."

He sighed. "You have to understand what I was going through. Look at me," he said. When I didn't budge, he added a soft plea. "Please."

As though my feet disagreed with my mind, I felt my body turning until I faced him.

"Losing a child is the hardest thing that can ever happen in life. No one will ever convince me differently. I was half-mad with grief. Nicole and I both were. We just dealt with it in different ways. She clung to hope, while I chose to be cynical. I'm not saying I was wrong, not back then. But now . . ."

He stared off into the distance. Maybe searching for an answer in the star-salted sky.

"But now?" I prodded, after the silence deepened.

He sighed. "Now I just don't know. I see you, and I realize . . . there's a chance Nicole was right."

His statement wasn't a blazing endorsement of accep-tance, no "I claim you as my daughter!" shout to the world. What it was was honest and heartfelt. Maybe he was sug-gesting a tiny chance at a different relationship in the future, if we could just get through the now.

As I stood beside him in a comfortable silence, I felt a slight thaw. He was offering a chance for a new normal.

And for now, that was enough.

THIRTEEN

At first sight, Montford looked exactly as it did in the brochures. Statuesque, expansive, all gray stone and green grass. The kind of place wealthy parents wanted to send their kids. A fence lined the perimeter, tall and imposing, as if to highlight the school's exclusivity.

"Here goes nothing," Samuel said, before he opened the front passenger door.

We left Lucas in the van, as there was no good way to explain his presence. Holland would definitely know who he was, and others here might, too. I caught sight of my face in the side mirror and tried not to do a double take at the last-minute changes Lucas had added to my appearance this morning.

Daniel led us toward the elaborate iron gates in the fence.

A call box blinked up at us. Daniel hit a few buttons, let a secretary know who we were. Overhead, there was a faint buzzing. Video camera. I kept my head turned from the lens, trying to look natural. A moment later, a buzzer sounded, and the gates swung open.

Abby whistled. "Guess they don't want you cutting school here."

"Or they want outsiders minding their own business," Daniel said. Here at Montford, we would call him Mr. Baker.

I held my breath as I walked through the gate, a little-girl ritual that I must have dredged from Sarah's memory. I released it when, several feet later, no telltale beep or flare or flashing light pinged me with the unwelcome news that I had two hours left. Two hours.

The sweep of green grass was even more impressive on this side of the fence. I wondered how many landscapers worked to make it look so perfect. Nothing about this place screamed ominous or threatening. Imposing was another story.

I tried to imagine what this place looked like to the recipients of the Watson Grant. Then I tried to imagine Sarah's reaction when she'd first arrived on campus. Had she been excited? Nervous? Had her first impressions been like mine?

As if I could suddenly look into her mind, I was flooded

with remembered excitement. The sweeping grounds; the majestic buildings; the sense of possibility.

Compared to my old high school, this was paradise.

I twirled in a happy circle. A perfect day was in store, full of new friends, new classes, and a new me.

It was amazing here—Chloe would die. I was so dragging her butt up here for a weekend sleepover.

The fragment of Sarah's life slid away, but her emotion lingered. Here I was, full circle. This could be the place where everything changed. Hunter might not have faith in me, but I could fix that. Show him that I could be trustworthy again, that I wasn't that girl back at Quinn's. Where would that leave Lucas? I couldn't worry about that now.

As I watched Hunter walk slightly ahead, I stifled a surge of annoyance. Before we'd left the RV, he'd made Lucas try to prove that my bomb wasn't activated yet. Like I would hide something that huge.

I sighed. I shouldn't be so impatient. I mean, one day, one place, I might get into range of a trigger. Would Montford be that place? Only time would tell. And worrying about it wouldn't change a thing.

Stone and concrete cut a dignified path through the lawn, and we walked behind Daniel like a flock of baby birds following their mother.

From behind me, Samuel gave a low whistle. "What happens if I take a liking to this Montford place and want to extend my stay? Can you arrange that too? Oof."

Abby must have elbowed him. "I think you're confusing boarding school with the Residence Inn. You have to work to stay here."

Daniel glowered over his shoulder. Everyone quieted as we approached a large brick building, a cross between a fortress and a fairy-tale castle. He pushed a button and the doors whooshed open. We entered an oversized hallway featuring original art and love seats with fancy curved wooden feet. The pictures showed different parts of the campus. Apart from that, the area looked more like the entryway of an elegant house, or even a museum, than a school. We hadn't met the students yet, but we already knew they were incredibly privileged.

Dean Parsons's office was as oversized as the campus. Another claw-footed love seat resided against one wall, while two tasteful stuffed chairs sat in the middle of the room. Behind a massive desk, a woman with a neat blond bob and rectangular rimmed glasses peered up from her laptop with a professional smile.

"Mr. Baker, from the Classical Charter School?"

Daniel nodded.

"We're delighted to have you and your students here for a visit. The dean is waiting for you."

As Daniel thanked her, I wondered. Either the dean was exceedingly prompt, or they had someone monitoring that video camera at the gate.

A lean man with a sparse sprinkling of brown-and-gray hair popped his head out of the adjoining room. "There you are!" Dean Parsons stepped to the side and swept an arm back, inviting us in. His suit was gray with faint navy pinstripes. His white shirt underneath appeared starched. No trace of wear on his smooth black leather shoes. Clean nails, smooth shave. Brown eyes.

Caucasian male, approximately 6 ft., 1 in.

Approximate weight: 180 lbs.

Age: Late 50s.

After shaking Daniel's hand, the dean ushered us into the room, which had an elegant long table surrounded by antique chairs. At four places, there were glossy blue folders embossed with the school seal. One for each of us prospective students.

To keep things simple, Daniel had insisted on names that didn't vary too far from our real ones. Samuel was now Simon; Abby was Annie. Hunter was Hank. And me? I kept Mara. By starting with the same first letter, Daniel had figured it would be easier to cover up any mistakes.

"Have a seat," Dean Parsons said, waving a hand toward the folders. We settled into the chairs that corresponded with our names, while he and Daniel sat at opposite ends of the table.

"Mr. Baker, would you like to introduce me to your students?"

Daniel cleared his throat, probably giving himself time

for a mental review. "Sure. Next to me is Simon McCormick, then Hank Lang, Annie Thomas. Last but not least, my daughter. Mara Baker."

I knew that I caught and stored all the pleasantries and introductory speeches that followed, but my body felt paralyzed by one word. Like a glitch, it kept replaying, over and over again, shocking me each time.

Daughter. Daniel had introduced me as daughter—and I'd heard a note of pride in his voice.

The dean said, "So nice to meet you all. You'll see I've provided each of you with a prospective-student folder, full of information about the school. Faculty, sports, extracurriculars, even the food . . . everything you need to know about us is in there."

He eased himself onto the edge of his chair and folded his hands on the table. "Now, tell me a little bit about yourselves and what makes you interested in Montford."

Gamely, we recited the facts we had learned about our fraudulent selves. Abby asked about dance classes, and Samuel requested a tour of the squash courts. Even Hunter pretended he wanted to know if he could take three years of calculus here. The dean looked intently at all of us, like a trick he had practiced, but I had the sense he was thinking about something else. If only my android abilities extended to mind reading.

Exactly twenty minutes later, the secretary told him he was needed in another meeting. Almost as if it was planned.

"Well, I think that was a successful chat, don't you?" the dean said, smiling smoothly. "But I'm sure you're all eager to get started on the tour."

As the leader at Montford, he was bound to know something about the Watson Grant. Unfortunately, it was too dangerous to show too much interest in the one thing we really wanted to know.

As we exited the room, Daniel fell into step beside the dean. "Before we go, I had a question to ask you. I know there are probably all kinds of hoops to jump through, but would it be possible for my students to sit in on classes this week?"

The dean checked his phone as he responded. "If you leave your applications with me, I'll start the ball rolling," he said absently. Judging from his tone, it could take weeks or years to set up these visits.

Daniel produced the applications from his briefcase, along with the signed parental consent forms. Forged, of course. He presented them to the dean, who arched a brow.

"We so appreciate applicants who are prepared," he said. For the first time, he really seemed to notice us . . . and I wasn't sure that was a good thing. "I'll have my team look these over and we'll get back to you as soon as possible." If anything, his smile was even smoother than before.

While the dean walked down the hall, I placed my hand over the doorknob he'd touched earlier.

Fingerprint scan: Activated.

Complete.

I could cross-reference the dean's prints for any criminal activity, and I'd always know when he was within thirty feet. Actually, my scan was currently alerting me that a different match was nearby. One of the students, whose prints I'd picked up from their files.

He stepped toward us, casual-cool in relaxed khakis, a maroon long-sleeved polo, and a quilted navy vest. Under dark hair gelled into a casual tousle, a pair of sly eyes gleamed.

Fingerprint: Match.

Image: Match.

J. D. Rothschild.

One of the winners of the Watson Grant.

"This is J.D., one of Montford's best and brightest. This one's going to put our financial planner out of a job if he doesn't step up to the plate," the dean said with a wink at J.D.

J.D.'s grin grew wider. Like a shark spotting blood in the water.

"He'll be your guide today, and happy to answer any of your questions."

J.D. shook Daniel's hand with an ingratiating grin. "It's a pleasure to meet you, sir." He gave the rest of us a casual wave. "Ready?"

He led us through the elegant hallway and then outside. "Here are our academic buildings," he began, pointing. "Our buildings are arranged by subject—we have math and sciences, language arts, history and social science, and electives. There are covered walkways between them, to protect students from the elements."

Anyone could tell he'd given this tour many times before.

From this view, the campus was even more stunning. More of the beautiful, historic-looking gray stone buildings arranged to form a semicircle, with the administrative building—where we were—as the lowest point. Like spokes on a bike, charming brick paths linked each of the buildings to a central quad, where an immense bronze sculpture composed of zigzagged lines sprayed water into a fountain.

I imagined when classes were out, students flocked to the central area, perching on the lip of the fountain and chatting. Actually, I didn't need to imagine. I'd done it . . . as Sarah.

I soaked up the sun, trying to relax in the few minutes I had until my next class. My fingers trailed a lazy path through the water until I spied the cute boy from my English class. I straightened abruptly.

"Are my teeth clean," I said, baring them to—

J.D.'s voice stole the memory away. "Don't let the cat out of the bag, but Montford just procured a donation to enclose the walkways completely." He pointed at the curved structure overhead that connected the building we'd exited to the one that was a short distance—

Distance: 52 ft.

—away. "I heard it cost about a million flat."

Samuel rolled his eyes but Hunter jogged forward to walk beside J.D. "Do they get to pick where their money goes, or can the school just toss it at any boring thing they want?"

"Depends if you're willing to pay for the privilege of picking."

Hunter snorted. "Well, if I picked, I wouldn't go with walkway covers. I'd do a new sports arena."

J.D. eyed Hunter with a spark of interest. "You play sports?"

Hunter shrugged. "A few." After noting that J.D. was on the soccer team, we'd added that to Hunter's fake records.

"Sweet," J.D. said. "Our soccer team could use a new midfielder."

He led us into the next building. More dark wood and arched ceilings and brilliant crystal chandeliers. Compared to Clearwater, Montford could have been the White House. "Our language arts building, where our students are introduced to the greats from literature. Don't be surprised if you see kids quoting from plays and books in the hallways, or engaged in vigorous debates in the classroom. Here at Montford, we encourage discussion," he said.

Hunter rolled his eyes, making J.D. grin. "Hey, man, I don't write the speech. I just deliver it."

"I like the academics, but that has to be quite some pressure on the students. What's your transfer ratio like?" Daniel asked, edging closer to Sarah's story.

"Oh, low. Very low. Less than five percent, on average. Few students can pass up the opportunity of a Montford education."

Under five percent? Then why Sarah?

The math building smelled a little different than the others. There was the faint aroma of wood polish, yes, but also the smell of chalk dust. The flooring was a little less pristine from the daily beating by hordes of students who didn't bother to wipe their feet after being outside. The affect here was old money, not new money. But still money. A lot of it.

While Samuel quizzed J.D. about student life, I pretended to watch the classes in progress behind clear windows. All the while, I was searching those windows for fingerprints. Especially fingerprints that matched up with my database.

My first hits came in the next building.

Scan complete: Identity confirmed.

Ben LaCosta.

100% accuracy.

Sharon Alexander.

100% accuracy.

Ben appeared to be leading his class, demonstrating

complex equations via laptop projector. Sharon sat near the far wall, chin in hand, looking like she was about to doze off. All the kids wore a variation of the same uniform: khaki pants or skirts on the bottom, and collared, polo-style shirts on the top.

J.D. rambled on about prestigious families who had attended in the past, pointing out things they'd donated along the way—a set of laptops, new microscopes for the biology lab. In one case, an entire wing of a building.

My scanner alerted me to Claude Parsons in the history building. He bit a pencil and typed into his laptop while the teacher lectured via PowerPoint.

That accounted for all the Watson kids but Hannah. So far, none of them were doing anything unusual.

J.D. led us down a hall that connected to another building, housing the first of two dormitories. They were separated by gender, and visiting hours were posted prominently on the front door. "School policy doesn't allow dorm visitors while the students are in classes," J.D. explained.

"Is security tight overall? I can't help but worry, sending my daughter away from home," said Daniel.

J.D. nodded. "Montford has very tight security. You probably noticed the video camera on the front gate, and we have others scattered across the campus. The cameras are always on."

I filed that information away as Samuel got down to

what most average kids would want to know.

"Anything crazy happen here? Urban legends?" Samuel asked. "It can't always be so perfect, can it?"

J.D. shot a quick look back at Daniel before lowering his voice. "Room parties get wild sometimes." Then he raised it and said, "Not that I'm aware of."

Daniel snorted and glanced away.

We headed into the quad, then veered off at an angle on the opposite side, where J.D. pointed out the sports field.

"We're hosting the first soccer game of the season there tonight—you all should come check it out. Our team ranked number two in our league last year, but we're going to kick . . . uh, some great balls, this year. I'm number fourteen, just so you know."

Samuel made a face behind J.D.'s back.

"Sure, that sounds great," Daniel said. We wouldn't turn down an extra chance to poke around.

"Do you have football here?" Samuel asked, scanning the fields.

J.D. shook his head. "Nah, no football—the parents are too scared of their kids getting head injuries. But we have every other sport you might want—field hockey, baseball, swimming, tennis. Did I mention soccer?"

Tucked away partway between the soccer field and the administrative building was a smaller building that didn't connect to the others.

Security system: Activated.

Powered by: NuTech CVA.

I frowned. All the buildings so far had security systems—but this one was locked up as tight as a safe.

Even more perplexing—NuTech. This security was connected to a different server. A private one.

"What's that?" I asked, when J.D. walked by without comment.

J.D. followed my pointing finger and shrugged. "I think it's going to be some kind of science lab when they finish renovating. It's totally sealed up, though. Keeps the riffraff out."

I reached out to connect with the security network. Right away, I brought up a list of people authorized to enter.

Regist . . . d Users: C . . . e . . . on . . .

The connection slipped away, leaving behind a void.

A flicker, and then:

Out of range: Signal lost.

My faux pulse quickened. I'd lost the signal too quickly to get more than a glimpse of the data, but that one partial name had been more than enough to pique my interest.

C . . . e . . . on. . .

I compared the letters to the student directory stored in my head.

Two potential matches:

Claire Wilson.

Claude Parsons.

The names danced before me. At least one student had access to this building, and it might be one of the grant recipients.

I stored an image of the building to inspect later. It looked similar to the others, with oversized hedges filling the planters, and concrete steps leading to a double door. But it was smaller. And the windows were dark.

I wanted a closer look.

J.D. led us back to the administrative building. "And this concludes your tour. Feel free to let the dean know what an amazing job I did," he said with a cheesy wink, "and maybe I'll see you at the game tonight."

There was no more word from the dean about visiting classes, so we just followed Daniel back to the front gate. I expected that it would open immediately, but we had to stand there for a bit—10.2 seconds—until someone inside clicked the lock open for us. I kept my face downcast to avoid the whirring and watchful eye of the video camera.

Why would they keep track of people leaving the school? I wondered. Surely the worry was trespassers and threats from the outside?

Daniel spoke up as he turned out of the parking lot. "Did you see that camera, on the gate?" he said. He glanced at me in the rearview mirror, his forehead a mass of creases.

"From what I could see, it was a pretty high-grade setup," Lucas said. "The stuff you'd expect in the military or maybe a bank. Not a prep school."

Abby frowned. "The place had more money than a college," she said. "But why?"

Then I jumped in. "There was something off about that smaller building, too. It had its own security system, separate from the rest of the school's, and it was armed."

"We should be getting you closer to that building," Daniel said. "Any thoughts on how to do that?"

Multiple pairs of eyes settled on me. "I don't know yet. The security system had a limited range—only certain people could use it. But what I managed to intercept suggests that there's a fifty percent chance one of the users is Claude Parsons."

Samuel whistled. Meanwhile, Hunter tilted his head and narrowed his eyes, pondering something. In the past, I'd swoon a little when his overgrown hair would sweep across his forehead and almost-but-not-quite obscure his right eye, giving him a sleepy look. Now I found myself on edge. Waiting for another awkward question.

"Is that what you were doing, back when we broke into Daniel's house? You sent me off so you could . . . what, talk? Is that the right word? . . . to his security system and override it?"

Sometimes, his questions made me feel like a three-headed monkey at a petting zoo: freakishly fascinating, but only from a distance. Lucas had never treated me like that. But he had the advantage of knowing what I was from the very start. Hunter was still processing the truth.

"Yes, I was. And talk works," I said. I waited for more questions, but he seemed content. For now. "Tonight, while the soccer game is going on, I'll try to sneak over for a closer look."

Daniel stopped at a red light, scowling. "Not by yourself. It's too risky. Take someone with you. That way, if you're spotted, you can pass it off like you just wandered off together. The rest of you can act as lookouts or try to chat up grant kids, while I take another stab at the dean. I have a feeling that once he finds out how wealthy Simon's family is, he'll squeeze us in right away."

Samuel stretched. "Perfect. And when you talk to my parents, can you tell them to send me money, too? As for the security cameras, who knows? Maybe this is all the rage with boarding schools these days."

Maybe the security was in place for the purpose of soothing wealthy parents, but I doubted it.

"At the first sign of trouble, you ask for help. Do you understand?" Daniel said.

I nodded, swallowing the lump in my throat.

For a moment there, he'd sounded exactly like a dad.

FOURTEEN

We made our way along the winding path, passing under an explosion of autumn colors. The air was ripe with the earthy must of decaying leaves and mulch. Hunter's shaggy hair tousled in the intermittent breeze, and I was transported back to Clearwater, Minnesota, where we'd first met. I couldn't believe that when this all began, we were still in the same season.

I shook off the nostalgia flash. Those days might as well have been in a different life. I needed to focus on the present. On our plan. It was pretty basic. During the game, I'd walk to the building with Abby, find out what I could about the registered users and what the building contained, and leave without looking suspicious. Meanwhile, the others would try to scout out other grant students and Daniel would schmooze the dean.

The courtyard had gone from peaceful and quiet to teeming with life. Students filled the paths now, their voices combining to form an excited buzz. A few still had on their uniforms, but most had changed into casual attire: jeans, Montford T-shirts, tennis shoes or Uggs. The red and gold of the Montford Lion dominated the color scheme.

The students here didn't seem so different from the students at Clearwater, though I did notice a flash of a fancy watch here, a glitter of diamond studs there. Shoes that looked both trendy and pricey. Less skin, more-polished hairstyles.

But none of that made Montford ominous, exactly. Just different from home. Or what I'd thought was home, back then.

The breeze shifted, and the autumn fragrance was overpowered by the smoky-sweet aroma of hot dogs on the grill. The scent tickled my memory.

Around me, cheers erupted, and I jumped to my feet to yell along with the crowd. I felt happy, caught up in the excitement to be part of something new. If only Chloe were here, everything would be perfect. I couldn't wait to email her later. . . .

I shook my head and the past faded, leaving behind a warmth that slowly fizzled into an icy chill. Everything had started out so well for Sarah. What had happened here to make her do such an abrupt about-face? None of those memories were coming back to me at all.

A trio of students wearing giant *M* capes streaked past us, whooping as the material streamed behind them like banners. What must it be like, to be one of these students? I wondered. To worry about nothing beyond who kicked a black-and-white ball into a net? This should have been Sarah's world.

Scanning the crowd with my sensors, I located Sharon Alexander with a group of girls in the bleachers.

"See the dean anywhere?" Daniel asked.

I craned my head until I had a visual of the administrative building, where I could make out two figures starting down the path.

Zoom: Activated.

The image expanded. I zeroed in on the faces.

"Looks like he's on his way."

Target: 102 ft. away, approaching from northeast.
Current RPH estimates target will reach destination
in under 60 seconds.

"Should be here in under a minute."

"Good. Let's wait here until he passes, then we'll split up."

"You ready, Abby?" I said, but Daniel interrupted.

"Actually, change of plans," Daniel said. "I want Abby to go with Samuel. I realized that Sharon might respond better to a girl. Even if Samuel could probably talk to a tree."

"I'm on my own, then?"

Daniel shook his head. "No, take Lucas with you—Hunter can hang back as a lookout. It's a better cover anyway; you'd be more likely to sneak off with a boyfriend, and that can be Lucas's cover if the dean asks where he came from."

Beside me, I sensed both boys recoil. I wanted to sink into the ground—did I have that functionality? I wanted to kick Daniel, too. How could he be so clueless about the awkward he'd just unleashed?

"Bad idea," said Hunter, crossing his arms. "I'll go with her, and Lucas can hang back." Then he added, "That way I can keep an eye on her."

Lucas bristled. "That's insulting to Mila. And insulting to me."

Hunter turned to face Lucas. "You're so obviously wrapped up in your . . . sick fascination with her . . . that you can't be trusted, either."

Lucas's jaw dropped. And then his cheeks flushed a bright red. "You have no idea," he started, pausing to breathe.

"Enough!" Daniel said, his voice booming. "We don't have time for this. Hunter, you go with Mila. Lucas, you stay back—that way you're on call if I need expert backup.

"Now that we've got that important detail settled," Daniel said, his words heavy with sarcasm, "let's get to work."

We were standing behind a tree and concealed by the groups of students milling about when the dean passed. He was immersed in a conversation with another teacher and didn't even glance our way.

As soon as he passed, Daniel made a motion to follow.

"Samuel, Abby, time to head out. Lucas, if you stay in this general location, you should be good."

I bolted in the direction of the building, mainly because I didn't want to see Hunter pretending to be my boyfriend. It wasn't until I was several feet down the path that I realized that I needed to wait for him. He was supposed to be my cover.

While I waited, a massive cheer arose from the field, followed by the screech of a whistle.

The game had started.

Hunter caught up so I started walking again, trying to act at ease. Pretending to be dating my sort-of ex who hated me because I'd killed his stepfather, all while scouting out secret buildings and a madman's plots—well, that didn't exactly make it easy to channel relaxation.

I watched a trio of latecomers hustle down the path toward the field. Faculty.

With an eye on the approaching staff, I grabbed Hunter by the elbow and veered him off our trajectory toward the suspicious building and instead toward a cluster of trees. One of them split down the middle into a low V shape, so I settled into that as a makeshift seat.

"Look at me like you like me," I muttered, keeping track of the teachers' progress. I noted that even the faculty here kept up appearances—all shiny wool coats, snazzy hats, and polished shoes.

Hunter opened his mouth as if to say something, then shrugged and closed the distance between us. He leaned an elbow onto the trunk above me and smiled down, looking for all the world like a typical guy hanging out with a typical girl.

If I squinted my eyes just so, I could almost believe it.

Otherwise, I read the mistrust in his eyes like a banner. And the tension in his neck, and in the way he rocked into the balls of his feet. Like a frayed wire that suddenly snapped, our connection was gone.

One of the teachers glanced our way, but dismissed us and returned to a discussion with his colleagues. See? We even looked like we belonged. Just a young couple enjoying some fresh air.

No other staff seemed to notice us, so I turned to eye the mysterious building, which was only a short distance away.

Security system: Out of range.

Close, but not close enough. We'd have to get even closer for me to determine the names of all the registered users.

I hesitated only a second before looping my arm through Hunter's. "Care for a stroll?"

I pretended like Hunter's flinch didn't tear at my heart. "Sounds good," he said, though his body language screamed otherwise. Still, our arm-in-arm walk made us look like a happy pair, and that was all that mattered for now. I steered us toward our target.

As we closed in on our goal, I felt the squish of manicured grass beneath my shoes and the crinkle-crunch of dead leaves. Overhead, branches swayed and rustled.

We were less than thirty feet away when I felt the sudden burst of connection. A flash of red code followed.

Security system: Armed.

"Let's sit down by that tree," I said.

I lowered myself to the grass, leaning against the trunk and careful to face away from the building. Hunter hesitated before taking a seat. One that was a good three feet away.

"You're supposed to look like you're into me, not like I have the measles," I said. "As challenging as that may be."

My voice sounded distant, unfazed. Completely at odds with my battered heart.

He scooted closer without arguing. I bunched my knees while he spread out his long legs. Then he did the unexpected. He dropped an arm across my shoulders. "Better?"

A thousand responses battled in my head. Yes? No? Maybe if you meant it?

I just mumbled, "Yes," and wished like hell that Lucas

could have accompanied me instead.

I turned my focus to the security system.

Registered users, I prompted. A short code exchange later, the names swam before me. I gasped, and the sound was swallowed by a roar from the field.

"Someone coming this way?" Hunter directed the question to me in a calm, pleasant voice, but the arm around my shoulders tensed.

"It's the registered student users. They're all grant recipients."

Hunter frowned. "So there are only five."

"Six," I whispered. Another roar from the crowd, a sound that echoed the cacophony in my own head.

"Six?" he said, clearly puzzled. Once again, I found myself yearning for Lucas. He would have understood immediately.

"The five current grant students . . . plus Sarah," I said.

His mouth widened into a surprised oh. His expression was a slide show of emotions. Wonder and fear. Pity. Sorrow.

On that last one, the hard line of his mouth softened, and I saw a hint of the Hunter he used to be. A glimmer of concern, of shared pain. But before I could even process those thoughts, he retreated to his touch-me-not posture.

Meanwhile, the data spun a never-ending circle.

Claude Parsons: Active account.

Ben LaCosta: Active account.

J. D. Rothschild: Active account.

Hannah Peckles: Active account.

Sharon Alexander: Active account.

The final one had a special note by her name:

Sarah Lusk: Account inactivated.

I swallowed a lump full of emotional sludge—regret, sorrow, excitement, and fear. "Sarah's account's inactive."

The security system was mocking me with a euphemism. Inactive. So much kinder than the reality of dead.

No other students had access; no faculty I could see, except for Dean Parsons. But there were some guest accounts that weren't specified.

Hunter brushed his hair away from his eyes. "What now?" he said.

"We need to get closer. I want to see if I can sense anything else inside there. Barring that, there's the old-fashioned way to snoop—peeking through windows."

After performing a quick scan to assure me no one was paying attention, I stood, and Hunter followed suit. This was the riskiest part of our venture. The closer we got to the building, the harder it would be to disguise our intent if someone saw us.

We'd just have to ensure that didn't happen.

As we headed over, my thoughts ran wild. At some point before her hasty departure, Sarah had been inside that building. We couldn't know what that meant until we saw whatever the structure concealed.

We approached from the south side. As much as I wanted to head straight for the main entrance, we'd be safer inspecting the rear first.

I yanked Hunter's hand, hurrying until the stone facade hid us from view of anyone who might decide to make an early retreat from the game. Four stately trees towered in a row to our left, forming a makeshift path. Along the back of the building, the windows had been more than boarded over. They were also covered with sheet metal. The door had met the same fate. Dead ends.

"Someone certainly went to a lot of trouble," Hunter said. We made a right turn when the building ended.

It was dim over here—not much light from the main campus paths reached this far. But the closer we got to the front, the more illuminated we would be.

As we neared the edge, I performed one final scan. No one within one hundred feet. I still felt uneasy, though, and I realized with a pang that some of my anxiety came from Hunter's presence. Doing a mission with someone who thought you might go serial killer at any moment didn't exactly inspire confidence.

Hard to believe that only weeks ago, we had been a team.

Another planter lined the front of the building, so we edged along it. The hedges were tall, rising almost to my shoulders. Large windows rose behind them, but from this angle, they were completely blacked out.

"Let's get a closer look."

I slipped between a gap in the hedges, the tiny branches grabbing at my shirt. Hunter turned sideways to push his way through behind me.

I still couldn't see a thing through the windows. I peered more closely at the glass, my nose only inches away, frowning. Something about the glass seemed unusual. In fact, I wasn't even sure it was glass at all.

I followed the window until I reached the elevated platform that housed the front door. A KEEP OUT: AUTHORIZED ACCESS ONLY sign hung there, while a small sign next to it read MONITORED BY SECURITY. The door itself I recognized as a metal monstrosity camouflaged to look like old wood. Difficult to open, unless you defeated the security system that kept it sealed.

I told Hunter. "Looks like our only way in is through hacking the system."

Another quick scan alerted me that someone was eighty feet away now, but they weren't heading any closer. I turned back to the door, allowing the data to stream into my head so I could probe and prod it into submission.

I summoned one of the usernames for a test run.

Sharon Alexander: Grant access.

In the instant I waited, I hoped for something as simple as a password. I should have known better.

A red line streamed from the video camera over the front door, aiming directly at whoever stood below.

Initiate retinal scan.

I slumped. Unlocking the door? No problem. So long as we had a grant student's eyeball handy.

"What is it?" Hunter whispered.

I turned to share the bad news, only to discover worse news. In the short time I'd been focused on the camera, the person had continued in our direction.

Human threat detected: 50 ft.

Maybe it was just someone heading back to the dorms. One quick glance dissuaded me of that notion. The man was hard to see because of the flashlight he wielded like a weapon, but one thing was for sure. He was heading right for us.

"Duck," I whispered, dropping below the top of the hedge and pulling Hunter down with me.

"No one's allowed over there!" a deep voice boomed from the path.

Human threat approaching: 30 ft.

"He's coming," I whispered, meeting Hunter's wide eyes in the dim light, my pulse nothing more than a frantic flutter in my neck. Wide-eyed, we crouched behind the hedge, face-to-face, our noses so close that his breath feathered across my face.

20 ft.

If we were caught now, we were dead meat. The dean would find out, and that would be the end of our plan. At best, he'd ban us from campus. At worst—well, if he was involved with Holland, then who knew what the worst might be?

One voice in my head urged me to run. In the dark, with a head start . . . I had a good shot of escaping. But Hunter could never keep up. I'd left him once before, and I couldn't abandon him to danger a second time, regardless of how he treated me.

We could pretend that someone dared us. Or that we'd just been taking a walk, and I'd dropped my iPod somewhere. Something, anything, so long as it was remotely plausible. I was an android; I could pull this off. Maybe—

Hunter's yank on my arm interrupted my mental chatter. He fell back, one hand catching his fall, landing on his butt and pulling me onto his lap.

"Wha—?"

"Boyfriend," he mouthed. The reference barely had time to register—Daniel's idea, right—when his arms hauled me up against his chest and his mouth covered mine.

At first, I didn't move. I wasn't sure I could. I felt stunned, almost Taser-level stunned. My eyes widened and my hands braced on his shoulders.

As I sat there, torn between fear and surprise, I reminded myself that this wasn't a real kiss. It was our cover story. A stolen tryst near a deserted building.

As cover went, it was way better than any of my ideas. It just might work.

Human threat: 10 ft.

But only if we convinced whoever was about to catch us.

I pulled him closer until his body heat combined with mine. My fingers slid through his hair. If this guy was going to buy our story, we had to put on a show. I felt the shock of my actions shudder through Hunter and I closed my eyes. His heart and my heart were unified in terror. The pressure of his mouth increased, and I waited. Both for the threat to arrive, and for all the old feelings to surface. At one time, I would have done anything to be in this position. To hold Hunter close and take refuge in the safety of his arms.

Except that now, any refuge seemed like a distant dream.

Which left the awkward realization that I was playacting with someone who, even if he ever forgave me, would never understand me.

Along with the equally awkward realization that I wished he was someone else.

"Hey, you two. Out of there."

Hunter waited a couple of seconds before pulling away, giving a brilliant performance as a boy caught off guard. He pushed to his feet, swiping a lock of hair from his face with a sheepish grin.

"Sorry, sir. We didn't realize . . . just snuck away to . . . uh . . . you know . . ."

While Hunter stammered, I rose from my spot on the ground. Slowly, with the sense that here, in this planter, I was surrendering a dream for good.

I curled into Hunter's chest in a pretense of shyness that was really all about not letting the guy see my face. I peeked through my fingers, so I could catch a glimpse of him. His uniform tagged him as someone other than faculty. A pair of gardening gloves dangled from the utility belt around his waist, and the blades of grass clinging to his work boots made my shoulders relax with relief. Not the dean or a teacher. A landscaper.

"Sorry," I said, with feigned embarrassment.

The man pursed his lips, hands on his hips. He did a quick survey of our surroundings—less the building and more the foliage. "You'd better not have busted any of those branches. . . ." he threatened.

I pushed subtly on Hunter's chest, hoping he got my message. Retreat.

He backed away, one step, then two. "We didn't, I swear. We were careful. Just wanted a place to be alone, you know what I mean?"

"I should really alert campus security, let them deal with you," he said. Hunter and I both froze, my hands turning to ice. *No. Please, don't do that,* I urged silently.

". . . but I remember what it was like, back when I was in

high school. The good old days. But find a room next time, or I will call security. Now scoot."

"Thank you and we will." Hunter whirled and retraced our path. I felt the man watching us as we left, so I was careful to stay on Hunter's far side, keeping my face in the shadows.

"Quick thinking back there," I said, when we were finally out of earshot.

"Thanks." His gaze lingered on me for a few seconds before he focused on the path ahead.

We arrived at the spot where we'd left Lucas, behind the bleachers and near the giant tree.

The sight of him helped calm the aftershocks still *thump-thump-thump*ing through my heart. I needed his perspective on what I'd found.

Just then, Montford scored another goal. The bleachers erupted in a mass of jumping, screaming bodies. On the field, the players zipped past and high-fived one another.

"We're back," I said, when the noise dwindled to just barely deafening. As soon as he saw me, Lucas smiled, and I answered with an even bigger grin of my own.

Hunter remained a few feet away, eyeing us in moody silence.

"That sounds slightly terrifying," Lucas said, when I told him how close we'd come to getting caught. "How did you throw him off?"

"I . . . um . . ."

"She kissed me. That seemed to convince him we were just sneaking off to have some fun," Hunter announced.

"Oh," Lucas said. His smile wavered. "That sounds like . . . quick thinking."

"I must have really sold it, too, because the guy bought it hook, line, and sinker." This time, there was no mistaking the barb in Hunter's voice.

I was about to tell my faux boyfriend to stuff it, but Lucas got there first. "I'm sure he did," he said evenly. "Only an oblivious ass wouldn't see what an amazing girl you were with."

Flustered, I gave Lucas the rundown while we waited for the others. "Something isn't right about that building," I told him. "But I need some time to figure out how to get past the retinal scan, and I don't even know when we're coming back." Then I took a deep breath and blurted out, "Next time, you're posing as my boyfriend."

I caught a hint of pink in Lucas's cheeks, and a smile in his eyes, but he let the subject drop.

And then Daniel approached with Abby and Samuel. He rubbed his hands together and shared the good news he'd heard from the dean. "Saddle up, kids. You're going to Montford classes in the morning."

FIFTEEN

Four pairs of eyes inspected us as we stood in the administration building.

The dean had greeted us briefly, then handed us off to the student welcome committee, which were the two boys and two girls staring us down.

I didn't recognize the first girl. The dean had called her Celeste, but she quickly corrected that to Celia. Her glasses were pink and square, dominating an elfin face. Her light brown hair was pulled back into a pristine ponytail, and the collar of her green polo shirt looked freshly ironed.

I did recognize the second girl, with the jittery, hazel gaze: Hannah Peckles. Her smile was friendly but distracted; her thin fingers had stubby, ragged nails. Most importantly—she was one of our grant students.

J. D. Rothschild was the third greeter. When he joined Hannah, the skin on the back of my neck prickled. Was this another stroke of luck? Or something more sinister?

I mean, all of a sudden we were welcome to stay here for a few days. "Get the feel of the place," the dean had said. It seemed almost too easy. Was there some reason the dean had accommodated us? Was there something he knew?

The fourth greeter was a student named John, but he was so engrossed in some game on his smartphone that he didn't seem to notice us.

Two out of four. What were the odds of getting two grant kids by pure chance, in the pool of hundreds, to show us around? I didn't need an android brain to know the odds were slim.

We would be following these kids to all their classes and staying in their rooms overnight.

"When your time here is over," the dean told us, "we're sure you'll never want to leave the Montford campus again." Maybe he meant that to sound welcoming, I thought. To me, though, it sounded almost like a threat.

"Follow me," J.D. said. "First stop, the cafeteria." He led us down the hall while casting a sideways glance at John. Then he began tapping buttons on his own smartphone, too. I fell into step just behind the boys, all the better to conduct a clandestine body scan.

Vitals all normal, though both blood pressure and heart

rate were in the bottom range. No internal injuries that I could detect.

The only noteworthy item on Hannah was this:

2-in. scar, upper abdominal region.

Consistent with emergency spleen surgery.

I shifted my focus to J.D.

3-in. scar, lateral side of right thigh.

2 metal pins, right femur.

Consistent with femur fracture.

I filed that information away, just in case. Maybe both of them were accident prone.

"Dude, no, don't steal my contraband—go get your own," John said, scowling at his phone and then at J.D. His dark hair looked freshly washed, still damp from the shower, and his brown polo hung loose and short on his gawky frame, as though he'd had a recent growth spurt.

J.D. didn't even try to hide his cat-got-the-canary smile as he stuffed his phone into his pocket.

"What are you guys playing?" Samuel asked.

"Treasure Walk. Hannah's latest geek game," John said.

"You created that game?" I asked, peering over John's shoulder. The pirate ship and treasure graphics were surprisingly good. We already knew that Hannah had been developing successful games and apps for years, but now we were undercover. We couldn't let these kids know that we'd done any research.

Hannah blinked, as if she hadn't heard the question.

"She asked if you made the game, space case," J.D. said.

Hannah's cheeks turned pink. "Oh. Yeah. I started it over the summer." She coughed and cleared her throat. "If you're interested, I can show you more. You'll be staying with me."

I was rooming with a Watson Grant kid? A great opportunity, sure, but also another coincidence.

The ponytail girl, Celia, glanced sidelong at Abby. "And you'll be staying with me," she said. Not that she sounded happy about it. She regarded Abby's outstretched hand like it was a snake.

I was overwhelmed by a feeling of déjà vu, which disappeared as rapidly as it'd come on. Had I met her before, as Sarah?

"Don't mind Celia, she's a germophobe," J.D. offered breezily, head still bent over his phone. Hunter was staying with him—they could bond over soccer. And Samuel was staying with John.

Hannah yawned and mumbled to no one in particular, "Sorry. Late night."

We reached the cafeteria, where they had us stow our bags against the wall so we could eat. Located in the building connected to the dorms, the tables were already starting to fill with early arrivers.

Unlike in Clearwater, the tables and chairs were set up

in clusters, like conversation groups, some with straight-backed chairs, others with upholstered chairs and throw pillows. A massive stone fireplace dominated the far left wall. The food counters were broken down by type, though most of them were closed at the moment—a pizza place, a sandwich-and-burger shop, frozen yogurt. A coffee stand with muffins and pastries was already attracting a small line, and another line started to form at the Eggs and More station, where I could see omelets being expertly flipped.

The rest of the grant kids were missing. The cafeteria was bustling now. Why hadn't any of them appeared?

I nibbled on the edge of my toast, wanting to look as casual as possible. "It's nice of you all to share your rooms with us for the week," I said. "Did you draw the short sticks or something?"

J.D. snorted. "Pretty much. If you have any kind of scholarship or grant, Dean Parsons requires you to be on his 'welcome committee.' Lame, but at least we earn homework exemptions the week before finals. When I met Hank, at least, I was happy about it for once. Last time, they assigned me this kid who could only talk about *Doctor Who* and the paradoxes of time travel. If I'd had a time machine, I would have sent him to a parallel universe."

"I like *Doctor Who*," John said, shrugging off J.D.'s groan.

Just then, Hannah's jaw contorted with another wide yawn. "Sorry."

The third yawn in such a short time span drew my attention to her face.

Initiating scan . . .

Hue in orbital socket, 2x darker than average.

My vision zoomed until I had a close-up view of the skin beneath her eyes. I could make out the thick, uneven application of pale beige makeup. Hannah's failed attempt to hide the blue shadows.

Chemical compound consistent with cosmetic concealer, approximately 1 mm. thick.

Assessment: Combined with 3 yawns in 78.2 seconds, irritability, and signs of mental confusion, symptoms indicate probable sleep deprivation.

Interesting. Out of the corner of my eye, I glanced at J.D. Despite his freshly washed and groomed appearance, there were faint smudges under his eyes, too.

I filed that information away, just in case. Hannah had mentioned studying, and these kids were grant recipients. Not unusual for them to work hard, especially if they had to maintain some kind of baseline GPA.

Fingerprint scan match.

Targets approaching.

Claude Parsons.

Ben LaCosta.

They appeared in the doorway, heads down, shuffle-stepping past the first few tables. Claude had a pair of wire-rimmed glasses perched on his nose, and his black hair was just as shocking against his pale skin in person as online. Beside him, Ben looked unnaturally tan for a redhead. And tall. He was even lankier than his photos suggested, all gawky limbs that moved in jerky, still-growing-into-themselves ways.

But it was Claude who tripped, righting himself by catching the back of a girl's chair.

He shook his head, as if in a daze. He rubbed his eyes and widened them. Forced alertness: that thing people did when they were trying to wake up. Both of their shirts were wrinkled, and I noticed that Ben had on two slightly different brown shoes.

"Hey, guys," Hannah called after them. Ben glanced at our table and lifted his hand in acknowledgment, but Claude kept his eyes on the kitchen.

"Coffee," he mumbled, and merged into the crowd.

Samuel studied their backs for a moment before turning back to the group. "Test week? Or too many unsanctioned, you-didn't-hear-it-from-me parties?" he wondered aloud.

J.D. dropped his fork. He shot a sour look in Claude and Ben's direction. "Yeah. Tests."

Celia and John were talking to Hunter and Abby, and it didn't seem like they heard him. But Hannah did.

She froze with her coffee cup halfway to her lips, her eyes narrowing at J.D.

Initiating scan:

Heart rate: Increase from 75 to 120 bpm.

Five beats later, and:

Heart rate: Decrease back to 78 bmp.

Sudden, transient spike, indicative of brief cardiovascular activity or sudden emotional lability, typically anger, stress, or fear.

Either J.D. was lying about the tests . . . or Hannah thought he should be.

We didn't get a chance to talk to Claude or Ben, or wait for Sharon to show. Hannah glanced at her phone and grabbed her tray.

"We should head up to the dorm, if we want to have time to stash your stuff before class." She hoisted her backpack and stood.

The rest of us followed suit, while I evaluated what we'd learned.

So far, we'd met four out of five Watson Grant recipients. All four of them showed signs of fatigue, which, while not uncommon at a prestigious prep school, seemed like a high ratio for our sample size. Probably most intriguing was that one of them may have lied about the reason for the fatigue. And if so, why?

Maybe the sleep deprivation related to something more sinister than studying. What if, say, Holland was deliberately limiting their sleep to make them more malleable? Prisoners of war were often kept awake for days on end in order to make them more open to the demands of their captors. I wouldn't put it past Holland to implement this technique on his test subjects. The man had an unsavory history when it came to teens and experiments.

As we made our way out of the cafeteria and toward the dorms, I realized it was a good thing I didn't need sleep myself. I probably wouldn't be getting much these next few days.

J.D. paused. "This is where we part ways. No coed dorms at this stodgy place. Though there are ways to get around that rule. . . ."

An oversized set of doors guarded a hallway to the right, and an identical set guarded a hallway to the left. One door on each side was open now, but a shiny metal box adorned the walls on both sides. A card reader, for after-hours access.

Hannah let J.D.'s comment slide, but her eyes flashed. Hannah tolerated J.D., but only barely.

I couldn't say I blamed her.

Why, then, spend any time in his company at all? If a guy was an ass and did nothing but annoy you, the obvious solution was to avoid him.

Unless, of course, you were forced to spend time together by an external force.

Like, say, a madman.

Hannah and Celia filled in me and Abby on some of

the girls in their grade (someone named Becky was trying a juice cleanse that made her cranky, and Jordan played her techno music way too loud at night), the rules (no smoking, no drinking, no smuggling in boys, no skipping classes without a note, and no leaving the campus during the week), and helpful hints for dorm survival (get to breakfast early if you wanted a blueberry muffin, plug your door latch with silly putty so that you wouldn't get locked out if you forgot your key).

The double doors opened to a spacious living area, dominated by a flat-screen TV. In a back corner on the far side was a window seat decorated in cheerful red and yellow stripes. Next to that, a counter was laid out with baskets of fruit and snacks.

I glanced back at the striped couch, feeling a whisper of recognition. Had Sarah sat there, during her numbered days here?

"We need another TV. Too much reality crap," Hannah said.

"Who are you kidding? You barely ever hang out here anyway. If I didn't know better, I'd swear you had a boy tucked away in your room," Celia teased.

I wondered which of these girls could have been Sarah's friends. Who would she have bonded with, if she'd been able to stay? The seniors she'd met had graduated, but the new class of seniors—she would have met them. Did any of them remember her? Miss her? Or had she faded into oblivion? A girl who'd left Montford almost as soon as she'd arrived?

We headed down a wide hallway, passing rooms with numbered doors. Some were decorated with collages, mostly of girls taking selfies or making silly faces, while others were bare. A few had dry-erase boards hanging from them.

Hannah pushed open a door at the very end. "Celia thinks the elevator smells like cat pee, so we take the stairs." She said it without a hint of criticism.

Celia wrinkled her elfin nose. "I don't think it smells like cat pee—it does smell like cat pee. I swear, Jayden must have snuck her cat in here again over the weekend."

Abby and I exchanged a look. Since everyone was being so amiable . . .

"So, are any of you here on scholarship?" Abby asked, in a casual tone. "My mom is really hoping I can get a partial, at least, if I go to prep school."

"I'm not, but brainiac here is," Celia said.

Hannah shrugged. "Yeah, I'm on a full ride. Watson Grant."

"Cool. How did you apply?" Abby said.

Hannah looked startled. "I didn't—not really. I mean, they approached me, last year. I didn't even know it existed, but I'd been eying this school already, so it was a real godsend."

Speech rate: Accelerated.

Average words per minute for this subject: 142.

Increased to 190 words per minute.

Without prompting, my android sensors had kicked in.

Combined with hunched shoulders, signifies probable discomfort with topic.

"Do you know who contacted you? Maybe I could hunt them down and see if they'd take my application—oof!"

My foot swept accidentally-on-purpose right in Abby's way, and she tripped.

Hannah showed her discomfort by changing the subject.

"Celia's room is here," she said, pointing. "That's where you'll be staying, Annie," she said to Abby.

Celia's door was so plain, it almost looked forlorn.

"Clean freak," Hannah said. "I mean, she's a person who likes things tidy."

"Is that what Sharon says?" Celia sighed as she opened the door, revealing a room so pristine, it looked it had been arranged by a professional. A blue-and-yellow comforter was folded symmetrically, without a single wrinkle. The pillow on top looked plumped. The items on her dresser were neatly lined up, and her desk was bare except for a shiny laptop. Two framed original art pieces hung on the wall: a vibrant seascape that matched the comforter, and a charcoal sketch of a shaggy dog. Not a stray sock or hat in sight.

My gaze lingered on the dog sketch, and again, I felt that odd tug of familiarity.

"Who's Sharon?"

Celia shrugged. "Another overachiever who happens to have the single next door. Her practice is over—she should be back here any minute. Just in time for classes to start."

I knew Abby was trying to catch my eye, but I deliberately avoided her gaze. I knew what she was thinking. Was this Sharon our Watson kid, Sharon Alexander? From the research we'd gathered, the personality could fit.

Celia motioned us inside. "Come on, Abby. You can leave your stuff right here. . . ." She indicated a square inch of space on the spare bed. It looked like I was going to have an easier time here than Abby. Or, hopefully, than Sarah.

Hannah's room was next. "We're room two hundred twenty-two," Hannah said, leading the way.

Hannah's door was covered in black letters and symbols on white paper. Code. "Told you I liked computers," she said.

So, you must really like me, then.

Funny thing about computers . . . I kind of am one.

Did you know some computers walked and talked?

Response after ridiculous response popped into my head, but of course I didn't say any of them out loud.

Hannah's room was outfitted like Celia's, yet nothing like it. There were two beds opposite each other, and I could tell which one was hers right away, by the half-made covers and half-buried throw pillows. The second bed was bare, with folded blankets and a pillow on top, awaiting me.

On Hannah's desk was an open laptop and a tangle of papers. A lone white sock with blue bunnies sprawled across a chair roller. Straight ahead, a minifridge hummed. The second, unoccupied desk held a few papers too. Hannah grabbed them to make space for my stuff.

"You have a single, too, like Sharon?"

She shrugged. "Yeah. All the grant kids do. All the better for late-night studying," she added.

Things were set up pretty well for them, I had to admit. And if Holland himself wasn't behind it, I wondered what role his wife had to play here. Did she pick the Watson Grant recipients by hand? On what basis? I wondered. Hannah hadn't been any help, but surely someone had to know. "Celia thinks I'm a slob," said Hannah. She walked to the dresser at the foot of her bed, rummaging through the bottom drawer.

A quick scan of her dresser didn't reveal much that screamed, "Huge conspiracy, look here." One bottle of vanilla body spray, seventy-seven cents in change, a small red carry basket holding shampoo, conditioner, a loofah, a toothbrush, and toothpaste, and in the corner, tucked behind the basket and against the mirror, a small rock, painted red and with googly stick-on eyes.

She pulled out some clothes while I took a quick inventory of her desk. Ten books, eight of them thick programming manuals. A copy of *Ender's Game*, and a history textbook.

Hannah walked over to her single-serving coffeemaker and grabbed an insulated cup. She pushed a button and there was a fresh cup of coffee in seconds. Hannah emptied a packet into it, then put the lid on top to keep the coffee hot.

She stepped away, then frowned. "Oh, sorry. Did you want some? I've probably got another cup somewhere," she said, doing a quick survey of her room as though one might appear out of nowhere.

"No thanks."

"All right then, we'd better get going. Classes start any minute!" It sounded like she'd already done plenty of studying, but she was ready to start another long day.

The hallway was mostly empty when we emerged from her room. Hannah picked up her pace. "We'd better hurry. Mr. Tasher does this thing where he stops the entire class and has everyone stare at you when you're late. It's creepy."

I remembered the staring, back at Clearwater. I hadn't loved it much either. Once again, my mind roamed to Sarah. How would she have handled that kind of negative attention? I despised it. But was that simply because I had things to hide?

Ben LaCosta was in our English class, sitting in the center of the middle row. He didn't say much. Didn't appear to take notes, either. Just kicked up his legs and leaned back in his chair, his eyes fluttering closed several times before the motion of his head falling forward jerked him back awake.

Maybe Shakespeare wasn't his thing. He wasn't the only one nodding off. But I wasn't about to dismiss it.

J.D. and Hannah were here, too, and Hunter was sitting right in front of me. As the teacher read with great animation from a tattered paperback, I had a rare chance to watch Hunter without him watching me back.

How could things change so much, so quickly?

His legs were sprawled out under his desk, one arm draped over the back of his chair. Not that different from the way he'd been back in Clearwater. If I squinted, I could almost pretend that I didn't see the hint of shadows beneath his eyes, too. Or the new caution that gave him a closed-off vibe he'd never had before.

I couldn't even be angry. I understood. He was hurting, lashing out. If he had his way, I wouldn't even be here. He thought that my absence was the best way to ensure the safety of these students. That he could save them where he had failed to save his stepdad.

For a moment, I entertained the notion myself. What if I just walked away, for good? Would everyone be safer that way? After everything was said and done, was I still the biggest risk?

From the depths of my android heart, denial surged. Swift and fierce. In the form of Sarah's image.

No.

Walking away meant no justice for Sarah, for Nicole, or even for Daniel. It meant more families ripped apart by grief and despair.

Walking away meant giving up. And I wasn't going to do that. Not for Hunter; not for any boy.

At that point, Hunter looked at me, trapping me in the pale blue intensity of his stare. Almost unconsciously, I braced myself for the burst of longing, of love.

As our gazes tangled, I felt an initial flutter in my chest, along with the desire to beg forgiveness. But the love, the need . . . it wasn't there. Gone.

I shifted in the chair and moved my hands restlessly along the desk. My feelings for Hunter had been one of my only constants.

Constant in that no matter what, he seemed to reduce me to my most base insecurities—that I wasn't good enough.

That thought came out of nowhere. But as the notion settled, the truth of it seeped in, along with a growing sense of peace. Hunter didn't make me feel inferior on purpose. I knew that. He'd tried to accept me as I was. But I didn't want someone who had to try. For some reason, a part of my mind drifted to Lucas. We had a check-in scheduled at seven tonight, with both him and Daniel. At the moment, that seemed like a lifetime away.

The morning passed without much to note, and lunch was a noisy distraction. The food court hosted way more students than it had during breakfast, and all of them seemed keen on shouting. Hannah piled two grilled-cheese sandwiches on her tray—I was glad to see that she was eating, even if she wasn't sleeping. When I finally got through the line, I saw Celia waving in the crowd for us. "Over here!" she called. "I saved you a seat!"

I tried to keep the conversation all about her. Celia was in the school musical. She was thinking of playing the clarinet. She couldn't wait to go home for break. Luckily, she loved to talk. Whenever she asked me a question about myself, I steered the conversation in another direction.

Finally, she put her glass of water down firmly on the table. "That's it," she said. "You are the second-most-private girl I've ever met!"

I had to smile. "Who was the first?" I asked. But I already had a guess.

A shadow passed over Celia's face for a fraction of a second. "This girl who was here last year," she said. "Sarah. You totally remind me of her. She was such a nice person, so polite. Much more of a listener than a talker. Never said much about herself, until you realized you'd told her your whole life story."

I looked around the cafeteria, as if I expected to find her

sitting here. "Where is she now?" I asked. "I'd love to meet her."

Celia looked past my eyes. "The thing is, I'm not really sure. She was only here for a little while, and I never heard from her again."

Then she looked right at me, with such intensity that I cringed. Could she tell? I panicked. Did she know? I had no idea what to say now, but luckily I was saved by the bell. "Follow me!" Celia said to Hannah and me as she rushed to put her tray on a conveyor belt. "If we hurry, we'll get good seats in Computer Science."

SIXTEEN

I wasn't sure I'd want to go to Montford if I were a normal girl. The campus was stunning, but otherwise it seemed just like a regular school, with regular classes. Computer Science was a different kind of class, and it was where I began to see beneath the shining surface of the place.

Mr. Grassi—or Professor Grassi, as most of the students called him—was pretty cool. He looked ordinary in every way, except for the missing thumb on his left hand.

His classroom was not ordinary at all, though. Video cameras and screens hung at varying intervals around the room. And tucked into the corner . . . no way.

"Is that what I think it is?" I whispered to Hannah, pointing at the oversized machine.

"Yup. A 3D printer. Insane, right? I guess the alumni

here have some big bucks."

I whistled under my breath. Too bad Lucas wasn't here. This class would be right up his alley.

I felt a pang, just beneath my ribs. Yes. I wished Lucas were here. It was time to admit it.

"Put away your textbooks," Professor Grassi said. "That means you too, Ms. Peckles."

Hannah's cheeks flushed red as the class tittered. She shoved the book into her backpack.

"We're going to do one of my rap sessions today."

Good-natured groans filled the room, while one student launched into the chorus of a popular rap song. "I keep telling you people, not that kind of rap," Grassi said, throwing his hands up in mock annoyance. But it was obvious he enjoyed the exchange.

"Today we're going to talk a little more about virtual reality. So far, we've covered what's available right now, in the present. But what might virtual reality look like in the future?"

He perched on the edge of his desk and folded his arms. "Let's start with this—what kinds of experiences would you all most like to have? Right now, or at least in your lifetime? Supposing that anything was on the table?"

"Play on a pro football team!"

"Be president for a day!"

"Go on tour as a rap star!" the singer shouted.

"Sex!" a boy in the back row blurted.

Everyone laughed, even Grassi. He rubbed his hands together. "Perfect. You don't know it yet, but you're all falling right into my nefarious plans."

"Nefarious? Wasn't she a queen of Egypt?" The singer tossed that one out there, but his grin suggested he knew better. Grassi gave a theatrical sigh.

"Owens, Owens . . . do I need to have another word with your history teacher? You can redeem yourself by telling me this—what do most of those suggestions have in common?"

Owens's brow creased as he tried to find the common thread. "They're all about being famous? Well, except for sex."

"Close, but not quite what I was looking for. What about you, Ms. Peckles? What do you think?"

Hannah shrugged. "I don't know, because I wouldn't pick any of those. I'd rather have a vacation experience. With a nice, comfy bed."

He tapped a finger to his lips. "I see." He grabbed some kind of tablet off his desk and typed in a note, before moving on. "Anyone else?"

In the front row, Claude raised his hand hesitantly. "Power? The first three are all about feeling powerful."

"Yes. Exactly. Because the average American wants that kind of experience. And at some time, in the not-too-distant future, they might be able to get it. In fact, they might be able to get that experience all day, and all night. Virtually. Several prominent computer geniuses speculate that by the year 2028, we'll all be living like those folks in the movie *WALL-E*. Shopping? Sex? Food? No need to leave home. You can experience it all from the safety of your own bed-room."

Behind me, two girls gave high-pitched giggles. Mean-while, other students looked at one another and began to whisper. "But that's not really the same as experiencing it, right? You just think you're doing those things," said a girl from the middle row.

"Ahhh, but aren't you? What is an experience, after all, but a series of brain synapses and neurotransmitters? If your brain tells you it happens, who are you to disagree?"

I digested that along with the rest of the class. Was that true? And, if it was, what did it mean for me? Because, of course, the thing I wanted most had nothing to do with power. It had to do with life itself—and not the virtual kind. I wanted my life to be normal. Fully human. Not enhanced by my android abilities, or wrecked by the bomb that was always right there, lodged in my gut, waiting to blow everything to pieces.

My brain told me I was living this life already. I did everything a human could, right? I knew more about vir-tual reality than any of these kids, I thought. My whole life was one extended virtual-reality experience.

That's how I knew that Professor Grassi didn't fully understand. The brain could deliver the data, show that you were having one kind of experience. You were a rap star, or a queen. The brain could say anything it wanted, but the heart would always know the truth. My heart knew the machine part of me couldn't "live" on its own. It was the other side of me, the human side, that made my virtual reality something different. The heart gave meaning to my experiences. It let me feel loss, and love.

I'd never thought about it quite that way before, I realized. Who would have thought I'd actually learn something as a prospective student at Montford? Sarah had endured something awful here, something we would need to figure out before we left this campus. But she could have learned here, too, I thought. She could have had an education. Just another thing she lost, because of Holland.

Professor Grassi was giving his class an assignment. "Now, I want you to come up with an original idea for a virtual-reality experience, why it would be of benefit to society, and discuss the fundamentals of coding for that VR."

As the class continued its excited chatter, and Grassi took more notes, something odd happened.

A security prompt flashed behind my eyes, vanishing before I could make sense of it. I ran the security scan Lucas had installed. The one that alerted me if I was being hijacked again.

Clear.

Clear.

Clear.

Everything checked out. Holland hadn't found me . . . yet. Air left my lungs in one relieved gush. Until I saw Hannah. I didn't need my android capabilities to tell me something was wrong. My heart took over as I saw her, seemingly out of her mind.

While everyone else discussed virtual-reality scenarios, she'd pulled a multi-tool out of her backpack, flipped open the scissors, and without a word to anyone, started cutting her hair.

"Hannah," I said, half rising. Did she even know what she was doing? Her neighbor to the left had noticed, too.

"Hey, what are you doing?" he said. Loud enough that the rest of the class craned their necks to see.

"Felt like a haircut. Since there's no virtual-reality app for that yet," she said. I frowned at the lack of inflection in her voice.

Grassi looked up from his tablet, saw what was happening, and tossed it aside. "Hannah, I know I'm a little unorthodox, but that's unacceptable behavior in my classroom. Put the scissors away and pay attention, before I have to write you up."

She blinked up at him, then down at the scissors in her hand. They clattered to the desk while her hand flew to her hair. Her lips parted in horror.

"Are you feeling okay?" he said, frowning down at her. "Maybe you should go to the nurse's office."

Hannah nodded, grabbed her backpack, and bolted.

A worry line crossed his forehead. Once the door shut, he turned back to us. He scoured the waiting faces before settling on one. "Celia, could you come here, please?"

As Celia walked up to his desk, the whispers started up again. So much that it was hard to hear their conversation.

Using my audio enhancement, I deleted the interference so I could focus on what they were saying.

"I know the two of you are friends," Grassi said. "Do you know if Hannah is taking anything that could be harmful or potentially dangerous? Remember, it's your obligation to speak up if you have concerns."

Celia was shaking her head. "Sorry, not that I know of. I mean, she seems tired lately . . . but that's how she always is." She bit her lip and looked at the door.

Grassi studied her expression before nodding. "Okay. Will you go check on her, please?"

In a flash, Celia slung her backpack over her shoulder and rushed out of the room.

Grassi sat at his desk and leaned back, arms crossed. "That's why I always tell you guys to make sure to get enough sleep. Lay off the caffeine and hydrate, and for god's sakes, none of those Monster drinks. There's a reason they call them that. Anyway, tomorrow we'll discuss your ideas.

Make sure you have them ready. Class dismissed."

As the students filed out, I saw something small and metal gleaming near the chair Hannah had vacated. Her multi-tool, amid a clump of blond hair.

I took the tool so I could return it, then hurried away to find her.

By the time I found the nurse's office, Hannah had already left. Maybe because whatever was wrong with her, the nurse couldn't fix it. I looked everywhere for her, until I finally decided to try the dorm. She was right there inside our room, typing away on her computer as if nothing had happened. Only now, her hair was all the same length.

I eyed the scissors on the desk, and the blond hair that littered the trash can. "You okay?"

She glanced at me like this was perfectly normal. "I'm fine," she said with little emotion. "I'd been meaning to cut my hair for a while now."

She stated it like she made all the sense in the world. And if something was wrong, she wasn't likely to tell a girl she'd just met and who'd be leaving soon.

I put the offer out there anyway. "Okay. But if you need to talk . . ."

Was Hannah frightened of something, too scared to talk? Was she going crazy here at Montford? Had something like this happened to Sarah? If only I could remember.

I settled onto my own bed, pretending to read. I hoped

maybe she'd leave at some point, so I could inspect her room. Professor Grassi suspected drugs were behind Hannah's weird behavior, and I had to admit that fit. A lot of illicit drugs caused insomnia too, which could explain her fatigue. Drugs could even explain Hannah's occasional changes in speech and heart rates.

Was it really that simple, though? Holland was involved here somehow, I was sure. Was he using teenage subjects to see how drugs affected them? That didn't really fit in with his android project, but maybe this was step one in some larger scheme. Maybe he needed drugs to make them compliant first, and then went from there.

Something pinged on Hannah's desk. She fumbled in her bag and withdrew a cell phone, then read a text.

A room search would have to wait for when she left. In the meantime, I'd take a stab at hacking into her cell phone.

First step—identifying the server.

I reached out to tap in to her connection. Like an invisible stranger grabbing a free ride from an unsuspecting train.

The rebuff was instant: a flash of notification, before equally invisible walls sprang up to stop me.

Private network: CRA .

I tried again, with the same result.

Private network: CRA.

I leaned back against my pillow. Well, that was odd. Instead of Sprint or Verizon or some smaller cell carrier, Hannah's service was linked to her own private network.

What if the other grant kids' phones were linked to the same one?

I'd have to try to log in to Hannah's phone the old-fashioned way. Via manual connection.

But for the next two hours, she never budged. Not even to use the bathroom. It wasn't until dinner came that she got up to leave, but I had to go too. Meals were my best—and only—opportunities to see all the grant kids together in one room.

If Hannah noticed any of the strange looks and whispers, they didn't faze her. She was back to her usual self, with her ever-present cup of black coffee. After pumping Hannah for information on why she'd freaked out and cut her hair, Celia kept up a constant stream of meaningless chatter. Hunter and Samuel sat a few tables away with J.D. and his gang. Claude and Ben were one table over, telling jokes in a foreign language that my android brain translated automatically: Mandarin.

There was a ping, and Hannah dipped her head to check her phone. I saw J.D. dig his phone out of his bag.

Ben and Claude were bent over theirs a moment later.

Here was my chance.

I followed the signals in the room as they looped and

twisted into an intricate tangle of networks. Again, my feed filled with all the usual suspects: AT&T, T-Mobile.

But as I traced the networks to the grant kids' phones, they all shared one trait that none of the other students did.

Their phones were all part of the same VPN.

One private, secure network, for four kids. Five, if you counted Sharon, who wasn't here.

Someone had gone to a lot of trouble to ensure their communications were secure.

Maybe if we figured out who was texting them, and what, we'd be a step closer to solving this mystery. But the VPN made things that much more challenging. No chance at remote access. I still had to get my hands on Hannah's phone.

When Hannah was completely engaged in a conversation with Celia, Abby leaned close to my ear. "Samuel found a spot for us to meet tonight. Meet downstairs, seven p.m. sharp, boys' common room."

Our check-in meeting. If only I had something to report.

After dinner, I walked back to the dorm with Hannah.

She resumed her position at the desk and didn't budge. She didn't respond to my efforts to strike up a conversation, either. Maybe she really was on drugs, I thought. At five to seven, I gave up and headed out. "Going to meet with my friends for a bit . . . I won't be late."

She mumbled in response.

I located the boys' common room and found my group standing by the door, waiting. The space was lively at this time of night, crowded with girls and boys. They looked happy. At ease. And when Samuel motioned toward the hall, a part of me wanted to wave him off, plunk myself down on one of the comfy couches, and try to feel what they felt. A different kind of virtual reality.

But boys and girls would have to go back to their separate dorms when visiting hours were over, so we needed to hurry. And there was a particular boy I was eager to visit before the time was up: Lucas. I hadn't seen him all day.

Samuel opened the door leading to the stairwell. Thanks to the hardwood floors, the combined sounds of our steps were enough to alert anyone in the neighboring county of our presence.

"Don't worry," he said when he caught my wince, his voice bouncing off the walls. "This place is completely legal."

My sensors scanned while we descended.

Scanning . . . 2 video security signals detected.

Video cameras? In the stairwell? We weren't doing anything wrong, but that didn't mean I wanted the dean—or whoever monitored those things—to know that we were congregating. Or where.

"The walls have eyes," I whispered to Samuel, nodding at

the vent near the lower-level ceiling. Apprehension shivered across my skin. I knew not all the video cameras were being monitored at once—it would be impossible, unless they had numerous staff members assigned to that task only—but I couldn't shake the feeling of being watched.

We hit the bottom of the stairs and burst into an open area. Instead of hardwood, there was only cement. The landing was small, and held two doors. A repetitive clanking came from behind one of them, so I peered in. Rows of washers and dryers. A laundry room.

The opposite door was unmarked. That was the door Samuel opened, and it led to a small, cramped room with four mismatched desks and one rectangular table.

"Study room," he said. "John told me about it. He said nobody comes here to study in the winter because the vent doesn't work and it's too freaking cold."

Abby had already started rubbing her bare arms. "You couldn't have told us that before we came?"

Samuel gave her a sheepish grin. "Sorry. Forgot."

Hunter shrugged out of his sweatshirt and settled it around her shoulders. She snuggled into the fabric with a grateful sigh.

I felt a twinge in my chest. He used to act that way with me. When she thanked him, and he smiled, I looked away. That time between us was over. If I'd needed further proof, I had it now.

"Hopefully we won't be interrupted here," he said, with a meaningful glance my way.

Already on it. My sensors had buzzed to life, probing the room for any uninvited guests.

Scanning . . . 1 video camera detected.

Crap. Casually, I stretched my arms overhead, using the motion to survey the room without looking suspicious. There. Disguised as a smoke alarm, in the upper right corner.

I scratched my cheek with one finger, and Samuel caught my gesture. I saw him glance around, but he didn't spot the camera. Beside him, Abby looked back and forth between us, her brow creased.

Should we abort the meeting? That might be safest, but we really needed to check in with Daniel, and apparently there was nowhere on campus that wasn't recorded. Except for hopefully the bathrooms.

I debated, eying Samuel's laptop bag. If we angled the screen away from the camera, it wouldn't capture any details from the screen. And there was nothing wrong with us congregating together. Skyping with our teacher about our first day at Montford.

"We ready?" I said. We were staying. I settled into a chair that faced the camera and patted the desk.

Samuel pulled the laptop out of his bag, and I pulled up his video-conference app. Like Skype, but where the data wasn't stored and couldn't be hacked. Once the conference was over, the information disappeared. Like video-conference Snapchat.

The name B9TY549w flashed an invitation. Samuel accepted, and in a blink, the upper portion of Daniel's torso and face appeared on-screen.

The pattern of his shirt caught my eye, and everything stilled. A plaid blue-and-brown flannel. Like the one I'd worn back in Clearwater in memory of a man I'd thought was dead. Now I knew that truth could sometimes feel more complicated than lies.

"How did it go today?" Daniel asked, his voice deep and familiar. I didn't know if I'd honestly missed him, or just the memory of what he'd once meant to me. Maybe the answer was both.

"Good. Great!" I said, acutely aware of the camera, recording every moment. Every motion. Every glance. Possibly every word, if there was sound. And if not, then the shapes of every word we mouthed. I didn't want to look too suspicious. So I babbled on about frivolous things that filled my day. Things a normal teen might tell her dad.

Like, maybe the exact kinds of things Sarah had called home about at first.

Daniel remained perfectly still. His gaze was sharp, waiting for me to fill him in. I laced my fingers and continued. "Our computer class today was great. Professor Grassi has tons of video cameras. Everywhere."

"Speaking of computers . . . where's L—Larry?" I'd almost used Lucas's real name. I needed to focus.

"He's buying some software to work on a few new programs. He wanted to get them finished before tonight. I think you'll be impressed."

Code for, Lucas has some new tech for you that he wants to deliver.

My fake smile became harder to maintain when I realized I wouldn't get to see Lucas right now. It had never occurred to me that he'd miss this meeting. Anxiety, nerves—whatever the reason, I was overcome with a fierce desire to see his face. If only for a few seconds.

I couldn't dwell on my disappointment, though. I needed to describe the day's events to Daniel. Safely.

"My roommate is supernice. But she seems really tired. She was so out of it in Mr. Grassi's computer class today that she started cutting her hair off, out of the blue. She seems fine now. But at least five of the kids we talked to today seemed really tired." I trusted that he would know these were the five grant winners.

Daniel stroked his chin. "I'm sure it takes a lot of work to keep up your grades at a prestigious school like Montford," he finally said. "Anything else?"

I passed the laptop to Samuel. Another prospective student talking to his "teacher," as far as Montford knew. "I made some new friends—my roommate, and a few soccer players. Nice lads. When they heard about the hair shenanigans, they told me it's not the first time that girl has been a little cuckoo this month."

Hunter talked about his classes, then gave a small laugh. "They must have some seriously stressed kids on this campus, because I saw some other guy—Claude?—carrying an empty cup toward a trash can, and then, bam, he did a one-eighty and slammed it on the ground. The weirdest part was that he looked like he was having a muscle spasm when it happened. A mini seizure, or something."

Daniel interrupted my thoughts. "I'm a little concerned about some of the behavior—do I need to give you the drug talk again?"

"No," we chorused, as if we'd really heard the drug talk one hundred times before. His message was loud and clear. Try to search all of their rooms or belongings for drugs.

"Otherwise, I'm glad your first day went well. Try to get some sleep. Oh, and one last thing. I know you were all worried about the janitor's wife, Rita, after she was mugged."

Hunter and Abby exchanged quizzical glances. We were all in the same boat. No clue about this code.

"She's going to be fine. They did some scans and performed some tests—they were worried she had a detached retina. But she fooled them all. With a few alterations, her retina will work just fine."

She fooled them all . . .

And then it clicked. There was a way to fool the retinal-scan security on the vacant building. And if I could fool the security, that meant there was a way in.

SEVENTEEN

Back in Hannah's room, I pretended that everything was normal. That I wasn't waiting for the information I needed to conduct my search of that building. So far, on this visit, we'd only found more questions . . . but I was ready to find some answers. What were the grant kids up to? What did it have to do with Sarah? Most importantly, what did it have to do with Holland . . . and me?

Hannah was at her desk. No surprise there. "You can turn the lights off if you want to go to sleep. I'm a night owl—I hope my monitor won't bother you," said Hannah.

My gaze fell on the full mug of coffee beside her laptop. Above it, the cabinet that held her container of sweetener packets was open. I remembered Mr. Grassi's words in class. Monster drinks. Caffeine? Could it be as simple as that?

I pulled my laptop off my desk and into my lap, preparing for a long night. I searched for online movies, and found *Braveheart*. I knew it was one of Samuel's favorites. Settling back against the pillow, I hit play. Two hours, seventeen minutes later, my cheeks were wet as I turned off the screen. Poor William Wallace. What a gruesome ending. But at least his life had meant something. He'd died a hero by fighting a corrupt leader. He'd believed that some sacrifices were worth making. Did that make it a sad ending or a happy ending? I wondered.

Hannah still tapped away at her computer, wearing headphones now. I set the laptop on my chair and climbed under my covers.

Mila?

The sound should have been jarring, even at a whisper. Yet somehow, my tension eased. Almost as if I'd been waiting for him.

Hi, Lucas.

We had this thing, Lucas and I. It had started under less than ideal circumstances, back in Holland's lab. That first time had been scary and invasive. But back then, I'd still been fighting who—what—I really was.

Since then, his ability to speak directly into my mind had saved my life. But he'd always managed this feat through access to Holland's state-of-the-art equipment. I had no idea he could do it on his own.

I sank into the bed, finding peace for the first time today.

Was this the new tech you were working on during the group call?

Yes. Partly. You okay in there? Everyone okay?

Even inside my head, his voice sounded soft, confident. Generous and kind.

We're getting there. Slowly.

I wished I could see him, like I had Daniel.

I'm glad.

You have news about overcoming the retinal scan?

You have a built-in feature that can help. You have to get a sharp, clear reading of the subject's eyes—at least four seconds, no movement or blinking. Once you have that, you have an app under your appearance-alteration software that will allow you to flash that data at the security scanner.

That sounded much easier than I'd anticipated. Well, except for the one part.

How do I get anyone to stare into my eyes without moving for two seconds?

You'll figure it out. You always do.

I wished I shared his confidence.

Have you ever seen Braveheart? *I just watched it tonight.*

Mel Gibson, still in his glory days? Six times.

I smiled. Six times, not five or ten. I liked his precision. I could relate to that.

Did you like it? Lucas asked.

I did. But it made me cry.

Of course it did. Everyone cries during Braveheart. *We people are perverse. We like sacrifices for the greater good, but we cry when we get them.*

I also liked how he included me in "people" without a second thought.

You know, my uncle could probably give King Edward a run for his money.

The warmth faded. I didn't want to talk about Holland. Not right now.

Please. I don't want to have nightmares.

I was pretty sure that, as an android, I couldn't dream. But Lucas laughed and went along with me.

Fair enough. I'll just talk about the more pleasant aspects of the movie, then. Wait . . .

I shoved my palm over my mouth to stifle a giggle— hopefully, Hannah was still too preoccupied to notice.

So, are you really doing okay?

I guess. It's tough, though. Seeing so many carefree kids, and knowing that Sarah was here so soon before she died. It's not fair that her life was cut so short. She deserved to be carefree too.

My vehemence caught me off guard, and once again I felt the pinprick of programmed tears. Lucas probably thought I was losing it. But of course, he didn't miss a beat.

You're right. It's not fair. She deserved more. But so do you.

He paused for a second before his soft voice continued flowing into my head.

It's not your fault that Sarah died, Mila. Just the opposite. As long as you're around, she will never be completely gone.

I covered my mouth with my hand and closed my eyes. How had he known what I'd been thinking? Feeling? And how did he always know what to say to make it better?

And then I surprised myself.

I've missed you.

My eyes flew open. Wait, what? I'd only meant to thank him, not spill the beans on that. Trust me to find new ways to blurt things. I had to be the only android ever designed with that problem.

I turned my head and buried my face in the pillow. As if I could hide from the embarrassment in my own head. He probably thought I was crazy. Or that the stresses of Montford had reduced me to a big ball of mush. He was going to laugh, and remind me that we'd been apart less than twenty-four hours. Or maybe he would—

I've missed you too.

Oh.

His words floated over me. They drifted beneath my skin, washing me with a liquid warmth that penetrated even the darkest shadows in my mind. I lifted my face from the pillow and rolled onto my back, feeling a smile tug at my lips. I only listened with half an ear as he finished up the conversation.

We should probably say good night now. I've got more work to do. Oh, but you should know I managed to get in touch with

Tim. We exchanged messages through the supply shop. As far as I can tell, no one has tried to contact him. So far, we're still safe.

That's good. And there's no way anyone could trace the message back to you?

Shouldn't be. I was careful.

Okay. I worry about you too.

I know.

By the time we said our good-byes, my eyes felt tired, my body strangely heavy. I let my eyelids close and sank back against the bed. Hannah showed no signs of slacking, and I didn't want to get busted for snooping my first night here. I'd have to put that off till tomorrow.

I gave in to my sleep cycling and allowed myself to doze off, knowing I'd awaken if Hannah roused. From time to time, a video flickered through my head. Dreams or fears, I wasn't sure which. I was in a cavernous, dark room, alone yet not, fighting off demons that I knew weren't real, yet I could somehow see. I dived and rolled, dashed and jabbed, more quickly than any human could. Then I felt a shadowy presence reach toward me. Once again, I had the sensation that my attacker wasn't real. Yet I whirled around to face it. With a jab of my knife, I finished it off and came back for more, panting. Caught in a blur of sweat, adrenaline, and fear.

Around me, the room was empty.

Except for the lone figure behind a podium. I couldn't

see his face, but I could hear approval in his steady, crisp clapping.

"Nicely done, Sarah."

Sarah. I froze. I knew that voice.

Slowly, I turned to face the man. But the podium had vanished. Instead, the faces of my friends appeared. Samuel. Abby. Hunter and Daniel. Lucas. And then Hannah and Celia. J.D.

No. Panic surged, but something trapped my feet, rooting me to the ground. They shouldn't be here. It wasn't safe.

"Run," I tried to scream, but the sound died in my throat.

And then, my friends' eyes rounded in horror.

I followed their pointing fingers to my stomach, where a red light flashed.

A second later, I heard the noise.

Beep.

Beep.

Beep.

Apologies rushed through my head, but before I could utter a single word, an enormous boom deafened me.

Time's up, came an automated, dispassionate whisper from somewhere deep inside me.

And then the world exploded, taking everyone around me with it.

"Mara! Wake up!"

I shot upright in the bed and stared straight into Hannah's

eyes. My heart pump still galloped away in my chest.

"What . . . how . . . ?" I said.

Hannah settled on the edge of my bed. "You were having a nightmare. It's okay, I used to have them all the time as a kid."

Was that even possible? Androids couldn't have nightmares, could they? If the organic material in me was developing to include this ability, I wasn't sure I wanted it.

"Did I say anything . . . weird?" I asked with a stab of concern.

"No. I mean, you made some noises, but they didn't sound like words to me. It's hard, being away from home. Even for a little while." Hannah's voice was soft. Wistful.

"Do you miss your family?" I asked, genuinely curious.

"Yeah. I do. I mean, I like it here and all. Most of the time," she said, as a shadow crossed her face. "But I never thought I'd miss my mom and dad so much."

She stared at me, and her voice lowered. "You know, if you're homesick already, you should really think about staying in public school. Boarding school isn't all it's made out to be."

As I met her steady gaze, I couldn't help but wonder if this was a warning.

She coughed. "Anyway . . . I'm sure you want to get back to bed."

She started to rise, and that's when I remembered. Her

eyes. The retinal scan. I couldn't let her look away.

My hand whipped out and landed on her arm. Just as I'd hoped, her gaze darted back to mine. "I just . . . I'm sorry you miss home. Is there any way you could transfer?"

But even as a part of me made the suggestion, a different part of me regretted it. If I really cared about her, I wouldn't be using this moment to steal something from her. Apparently, androids could also feel guilty.

Retinal copy: Initiate.

"No, not when I have this grant. My parents would be mad."

Image processing . . .

Afraid that she would look away before I completed the scan, I didn't let go of her arm. "That sucks. Isn't there a way you could explain, make them understand?"

She chewed on her lower lip. "I don't know . . . maybe." But the defeated slump of her shoulders said something else.

Image retrieved. Storing copy.

Somewhere, in the recesses of my android brain, I now had a perfect replica of Hannah's eyes. Stored and ready for use.

"I'm sorry," I said.

She shrugged. "It's not your fault my parents don't listen."

I nodded and pretended that was the only reason for my apology. I was so sorry, so deeply sorry. For what I just did, but also everything else she was going through.

This wasn't some virtual life for Hannah. This was the real thing—her one life—and she was spending her precious teenage years away from people she loved. Huddled over her desk. Gulping coffee to keep her awake . . . to spend more time at her desk.

Something here still wasn't adding up. I knew that Holland had to be involved here, but I didn't know how. I only knew this: a fierce need to protect this girl swelled in my chest. She deserved better than this. Just like Sarah had.

Back at Quinn's, I had done something terrible. Something unforgivable. I'd been tricked into it, yes, but I was the one who pulled the trigger, and I would always have to live with that. Bad luck—and my own mistakes—had cost me Hunter. But they weren't going to cost another girl her happiness. Whatever it took, I was going to make sure that Hannah had a chance to live and love fully someday. The chance that Sarah never had.

One day soon, I might find that I had two hours left on earth.

And if that was the case, I wanted my last days to count for something.

Hannah headed back to her desk, where a light still glowed over an open book.

I frowned. "Aren't you ever going to bed?"

"In a bit. I've got some more studying to do."

A bit turned out to be 3:30 a.m. I feigned an urge for

the bathroom, but she was still awake when I returned, so I gave up for the night. It was just too risky to check her phone.

I'd managed to grab the retinal scan. But I was all too aware that time was ticking by.

EIGHTEEN

I n the morning, Hannah finally left to take a shower. As she headed out the door with her towel and caddy, I knew I'd only have minutes at most.

"See you in a few," she said, shutting the door behind her.

I tried to zero in on the sound of her footsteps retreating down the hallway, but the music from next door blared too loud.

Remove audio interference?

Until this moment, I hadn't realized that was an option.

Yes.

Instantly, the music muted, leaving behind normal sounds of life in the dorm. Sounds at decibels that wouldn't cause hearing damage . . . if I actually had regular human ears.

I squeezed the spot on my ear lobe.

Enhance audio?

Yes.

Magnify 10x.

Finally, I heard them. Her footsteps, far down the hall. And then the *snick* of the bathroom door, closing.

Now.

I was spying, but it was for Hannah's own good. I had to get her out of whatever mess she'd wandered into. What she thought was an exclusive prep school was, for her, a kind of prison. Or maybe worse.

I pulsed out a message, hoping to track down the VPN signal and trace the stream back to her phone.

Nothing. My gut twisted.

She must have switched it off.

I had to find it the old-fashioned way.

Back in the room, I went for her bag first. I rustled through every pocket. No phone.

The desk was next. I combed through papers, books, drawers. Nothing.

The dresser? I opened the top drawer, feeling weird and creepy pawing through her socks. The next drawer down was more of the same. Just junk. A tangled assortment of vitamins and pills. Vitamin C, multivitamins, fish oil, and ibuprofen.

I glanced along her bookshelves. Textbooks and literature.

A stash of granola bars, almonds, Red Vines, coffee, and sweetener packets.

I squatted to peer under her desk, then straightened.

An image formed of Hannah drinking coffee in the cafeteria. Black coffee. No cream, no sugar. So why did she drink it differently in her room? Nicole always took her coffee the same way, no matter what.

The sweetener packets were in a jar, more organized than the rest of Hannah's stuff. I picked up the jar, lifted the lid, and removed a packet. Tearing open a corner, I sniffed. Then I licked my finger and touched the tip to the white grains before sticking it in my mouth.

And almost gagged. Something unbelievably bitter, rather than sweet, coated my tongue.

I took another sample and slid it under the nail bed of my index finger.

Chemical components: Modafinil.

Uses: Sleeplessness-promoting agent. Only legal use in US for treatment of narcolepsy.

Somehow, I doubted that Hannah had narcolepsy.

I put the lid back on the jar and shoved the packet in my pocket, to dispose of later. The drug itself wasn't that surprising. Illegal, yes, but it sounded like the kind of thing kids might use if they were pushing themselves to work too hard. But the packets . . . those had been specially made. Designed to hide the evidence, not something your run-of-the-mill student dealer was likely to bother with. Or even know how to do.

Hunter had mentioned J.D. had headaches. I wondered if he took the same stuff to "fix" them.

Holland was involved. I was sure of it, though I didn't know his motive, and I still lacked proof. But he probably had someone on the inside too, dispensing this stuff to the grant kids. Grassi was right about drugs, it turned out. This just wasn't the sort of drug I'd thought he meant.

Hannah's phone might tell me more, if I could ever find it.

I hunted through the room one more time. If she hadn't powered it off, I could just scan the room and find it.

Wait. Did that mean she had taken it to the bathroom?

I opened the door to the hall. Still clear. I rushed toward the bathroom, praying that none of the other girls would pop out of their rooms. This spur-of-the-moment plan only worked if no one else was around to see.

I eased open the bathroom door and walked into a wall of hot air. Clouds of steam fogged the entry and water pounded a tile floor somewhere in the distance.

She was still showering. But for how much longer?

I ran a quick scan.

1 human presence detected.

Just me and Hannah. For now.

On careful feet, I crept past the toilets. I moved into the

hallway that led to the showers.

I rounded the corner and counted three stalls. The first two were empty. The last one had the curtain drawn, with steam rising over the top.

I could see her shower caddy on the bench just outside the door. Only steps away. But also only a few steps away from Hannah.

I would have to creep in and grab it.

I crouched, drawing up against the section of wall that served as a divider from the middle shower. When I got closer, my heart lodged in my throat. Hannah's curtain was partway open. Not much—only three inches.

But if she turned around, that three inches was enough to ID me.

Over the top of the wall, I watched white, soapy bubbles foam up on her head. I'd never felt more like a stalker than I did right now.

New low, Mila. Stakeout in the girls shower, waiting for your naked roommate to close her eyes.

I was mortified, but I knew I had to seize this opportunity. When she rinsed, she'd close her eyes. Five, maybe ten seconds. That was all I'd have to nab the phone . . . then only minutes to gain access.

If I was lucky.

Like a predator staking out prey, I went very still and waited. Hannah kept sudsing her hair until the bubbles grew another two inches. Good grief, how dirty could her hair be? After what seemed like hours but I knew had only been thirty-two seconds, she finally tilted her head back. She closed her eyes an instant before the spray hit her face.

That was my cue.

Hoping like hell that she rinsed as long as she shampooed, I darted forward.

One second.

I went to make a grab for the phone, but her lotion bottle was in the way. If I knocked something over, she'd know I was there.

Angling my arm around the side, I could just barely reach her phone. I pulled it toward me with my fingertips.

Three seconds.

The phone slid toward me, and I tightened my grip.

There.

Five seconds.

Every second, more suds drained away.

I thought I heard a noise outside. I jerked, and bumped the bottle.

To my horror, it tottered. Crap. I lunged toward the caddy so my other hand could grab the bottle before it toppled onto the ground.

The bottle was safe. But I wasn't. I was fully exposed, standing right in front of the crack in the curtain, with a clear view of her profile from only a foot away.

Ten seconds.

All the suds were gone.

I backed away, toward the cover of the other stalls. Her eye popped open just as I rounded the corner.

I waited without daring to move. Had she seen me?

A couple of seconds passed before I could breathe again normally. For now. But I still had to finish.

Retreating into the next shower down, I looked through her apps until I found the messaging one and opened it. The last text message streamed to me, but it was gobbledygook.

Even with their own VPN, they texted in code.

That's when the water stopped. My head jerked up. *No!*

Saving the text into my hard drive, I tiptoed out of my stall. I hadn't heard the curtain slide on the rod, so she hadn't noticed the missing phone. Yet.

Panic beat a frantic rhythm in my chest. I had to get out of the bathroom, and back to the room. Before she knew I was here.

The curtain rustled, and the panic rose, making me dizzy. I was out of time. But what now? There was no way to return the phone to her caddy. And I couldn't take the phone back to our room. She'd know instantly.

I looked around, and did the only thing I could. I crouched and set the phone on the tile floor, sliding it silently into the empty stall between us. Maybe she'd think it had fallen out of her caddy.

I retreated as silently as I could. My hand had just touched the door leading to the hallway when I heard a hiss of indrawn breath, followed by the clatter of plastic. The sound someone might make if they were digging around to find something they'd lost.

I hauled butt back to our room, replaced the cord where I'd found it, kicked off my shoes, and plopped into bed behind my laptop.

Less than forty-five seconds later, I heard her approach. She rushed inside, cheeks flushed, hair still uncombed. Shirt damp from where she hurried through the drying process. I felt her gaze on me, but I kept my own firmly planted on my monitor.

Her caddy clattered onto her dresser, so I finally looked up. Her phone was clutched tightly in her right hand.

"Everything okay?"

Three seconds passed before she responded. "Ever have one of those moments where you're sure you know where you put something, only you find it somewhere else?"

I made a noise and hoped it sounded sympathetic. "All the time. Especially when I don't get enough sleep."

"Sleep. Right." She shook her head again; looked down at her phone. Finally, she gave a small laugh. "That must be it."

While she ran a brush through her hair, I assessed the one text I'd managed to extract.

Code analysis: Initializing.

The answering prompt appeared faster than I'd expected. Deciphered.

The code shifted into words.

CRA meeting tomorrow, 12:00 a.m.

Not much, but enough. Now I just had to alert the others. The text didn't say where the meeting was, but I was pretty sure I knew. Tomorrow, we were finally going to get a peek at whatever secret lay hidden in the locked building.

And CRA? That was also the name of the network that connected the grant kids' phones.

Lucas?

I had to talk to him, but I wasn't sure I could initiate contact from my end.

Hi.

I smiled and filled him in on the new development, telling him I'd inform the others at breakfast.

Hang on a sec.

When a minute passed and he hadn't returned, I tensed. Had we lost the connection?

I'm back.

His voice soothed away the frantic flutter beneath my ribs.

Go to the dean's office in an hour. We need to fix something.

The tension crept back into my chest.

Fix something?

But his answer was unsatisfying.

Can't explain now. Talk later.

Since I didn't have a choice, I echoed him.

Later.

When I showed up outside the dean's office, my "dad" and "stepbrother" were already waiting for me.

Lucas held out the small duffel bag. "Here you go. Next time, make a list so you don't forget stuff."

I accepted the bag. "Sorry. I'm a sucky packer. I admit it."

My voice sounded light. My acting was impressive. Because the familiar sight of Lucas, the familiar smell, did funny things to my stomach.

"Daughters," said Daniel, as in, "What can you do?"

The natural way he said the word packed an emotional punch of its own.

Both of them, so close, made my heart swell unexpectedly. I'd missed them these last two days.

Last two days. In my head, the words were a warning.

Today. Tomorrow. That was all the time we had left at Montford.

"Take a walk?" I asked, all too conscious of the video camera that perched on the gate.

We ambled down the path that led away from the administrative offices and toward the outer entrance to the dorms.

318

"What's up?" I almost whispered.

"We just wanted to make sure you had fresh clothes. Your toothpaste. Oh, and your flash drive. And new burn phones, for the others," Daniel said in a low voice. "Lucas made some . . . adaptations."

Fixing something.

As we walked, Lucas pulled a tiny square from his pocket and slipped it into my hand.

"You want me to use it now?" I whispered, scanning the area. No one was in front of the building, but I detected two students around the far right corner.

Daniel lagged behind and took up the center of the path. "I'll give you two a little privacy." I realized what he was doing then. Blocking the view of the video camera and anyone who might happen by.

Lifting my sleeve with one hand, I slid the square beneath, fumbling around under the fabric until a seam in my skin parted, and the plastic slid inside.

"Fine, but I'm starting to feel like a human pincushion. An android pincushion," I corrected. I sensed Lucas's smile but the app appeared right then, capturing my attention.

Secure text app: Installing.

25%.

50%.

75%.

Complete.

I withdrew the disc and placed it in Lucas's hand. He surprised me by closing his hand around mine, disc and all.

My skin heated up, like magic. Distracting me. "What did I just install?"

"My version of a hands-free texting app for you. One that you can command with your mind. I realized that in all the chaos of getting to Montford, we'd never given you a way to communicate with your team. I created a program to link their burn phones to this app. Why don't you give it a try?"

Secure text app: Open.

A pause, and then:

Open.

Message recipient?

The list scrolled, showing all my partners in crime, with one notable addition.

"William Wallace?" I said. "As in *Braveheart*?"

He shifted his weight and toyed with the hem of his gray T-shirt. He looked good in T-shirts, actually. Really good. Lucas was lean, but in a wiry, strong way. I guessed he got out from behind his computer pretty often to do something more strenuous.

"Just a reminder, if you start to feel down."

I quipped, "Because nothing picks you up quite like seeing a Scotsman drawn and quartered." But I was pretty sure that something inside me had just melted.

The tips of his ears turned pink, and his eyes locked on mine. They spoke of hope and belief. Of conviction and kindness. Of support, no matter what.

His presence, his being: it was like a magnet, pulling me in. Daniel was only five feet away, but I didn't care. Not then. I leaned into Lucas, hoping, praying he wouldn't pull away. He didn't. Emboldened, I bunched my hands in his shirt, my gaze going to his mouth.

That's when an alarm blared from his pocket. I sprang back while he looked blank for a minute. Then his jaw went slack.

"What is it?" I knew it wasn't good.

Daniel turned at the same time Lucas plucked the phone out of his pocket. He nodded at whatever he saw, as though he'd been expecting it.

"What's wrong?"

The hazel eyes that met mine were steady, despite the pallor of his cheeks.

"That was an alert from my doctor friend, who helped me pretend to be sick for so long. He's letting me know that Holland sent someone to investigate my story."

"And?" Daniel prompted.

"Now he knows I'm not really sick."

Daniel and I stared at Lucas aghast, our expressions probably identical in their fear.

"We talked about this," Lucas reminded me gently.

"We knew this could happen."

"I know. I just . . . never thought it would happen now."

I drew in a breath and focused on not falling apart. Lucas was the one in danger this time.

"My uncle doesn't like his worker bees to escape him," Lucas said grimly.

"Does he know . . . everything?" I whispered. Still daring to hope.

That hope shattered the instant I met his eyes. "I imagine he was able to put two and two together pretty quickly. The timing, your escape from the lab. Yes, he knows I helped you."

He knows I helped you.

So I'd done it again. I'd fallen for someone, only to put his life in danger.

Hunter had been right. Getting close to me was like signing your own death warrant.

There was only one solution. We had to abort the mission. "I'll tell the others. We'll leave early, find you a safe place—"

Lucas's jaw tightened. "Absolutely not. Just because he knows about me doesn't mean he knows anything about you. You guys are close to finding answers. I'll be fine."

I opened my mouth to argue, but Daniel reached out and squeezed my shoulder. "I know you want to keep him safe, but those kids in there need you too. We'll be okay. But we probably need to get going. Your laptop . . . ?" Daniel prodded.

Lucas nodded. "I need to shut it down. All of it. And warn my brother. I don't think Holland would find him or even look for him, but just in case . . ."

Just when I thought he was going to hurry off, he pulled me into his arms. His mouth lowered to my ear, his words feathering across my skin, warm and firm. "Don't worry about me. Just focus on your investigation. In two days, you'll have what you need. We'll take down my uncle, then we'll get the hell out of dodge."

I returned the hug, but instead of just soaking up his warmth and comfort, I tried to comfort him as well. "Stay safe. And check in. Often. If there's a six-hour stretch where I don't hear from you . . ."

"Deal." He pulled back, stared into my face. Opened his mouth like he wanted to say more, but Daniel barked at him to hurry.

I watched them retreat, all the way through the gate and to the van, before I turned back toward the school on leaden feet.

My fear refused to budge. It clung to me like a second skin.

I hurried back into the main building and headed for the cafeteria, where I ushered the gang to a table in the back corner, by the emergency exit. No one ever sat here because frigid air seeped in from under the door. The cafeteria was just starting to wake and stir with bleary-eyed students.

Once everyone had grabbed food and gathered round, I distributed the burn phones under the cover of the table, and explained how they were linked to me. Then I filled them in on what I'd found. The coded message on Hannah's phone, and the meeting we would intercept tonight. The modafinil packets, too.

At that point, Abby interrupted. "Packets? Little white ones, like sugar? Sharon has a box of those, on her dresser. She told me they were fiber supplements, so I didn't go near them."

"Are those the same as J.D.'s headache meds?"

Hunter nodded.

"I think we can assume that Claude and Ben have them as well, then."

"It's not much in the way of smoking guns, though, eh? Not here. I knew a guy who used to snort NoDoz to pull all-nighters," Samuel said. "It's not exactly unusual."

"Maybe not a smoking gun, but someone went to a lot of trouble to disguise them. If we can figure out which staff member is supplying them, we might find the connection to Holland. Do any of the grant kids seem close to the faculty?"

Mrs. Tate, the PE coach, Mr. Frost, the math teacher, and Mr. Grassi came up as a few student favorites, so we agreed to try to focus our attention on them. It wasn't the most scientific plan, but for tonight, it was all we had.

Samuel was eyeing me with a frown. "What's wrong?"

With my heart pumping pure dread, I filled them in on Lucas.

"He was careful," I reassured them. "It will take Holland a while to track him down to Montford, and hopefully by then, we'll be long gone. But I can't make any guarantees. If you want out, now is probably the time."

They didn't even need to think it over. They all agreed to stay. Even Hunter. Who maybe—just maybe—could see why I had to finish what we had started together.

As we headed for our classes, I initiated the countdown until midnight. Yesterday, I'd been worried that we'd run out of time before we could finish our mission.

Now, the opposite was true. Every minute felt like another opportunity for Holland to move in on Lucas . . . and me.

Lucas checked in at two, to let me know he was okay. He'd shut down his remote connection to Holland's work-station and alerted Tim, just in case. No sign of trouble, he told me. Yet.

If I really was a prospective student, there's no way Mont-ford would have admitted me. I spaced out during classes. I got lost on the way to PE. So much for class participation— all I could do was think about what would happen after class. After dinner. After homework and lights-out. Finally, we might get some answers about what Holland was doing here—and what had happened to Sarah.

I feigned sleep as soon as it seemed believable. At eleven thirty, I heard Hannah rustle around on her side of the room. Like she was changing clothes again. Then I heard her pad to the door and open it quietly. When I opened my eyes, I was alone in the room.

I gave her a small lead, then rose. I squeezed the spot on my ear lobe.

Enhance audio?

Yes.

Magnify 10x.

I heard no human activity beyond Hannah's retreating footsteps. No sign of life from the hallway beyond my room. Just the faint crackle and hum of the heating unit, as it worked to warm the drafty halls.

Stealing a page from Lucas's book, I linked to the video cameras in the dorm.

Video feed: Intercept.

Loop parameters: 60 minutes.

After a little bit of haggling, I realized that one hour was the longest loop the system would accept. Better than nothing. We'd just have to return in time, if we didn't want our night wanderings to show up on the feed.

I crept out into the hallway, easing the door behind me.

Once I made it to the safety of the stairwell, I summoned my new text function.

Abby, did you see her?

Three steps later, I had a response.

Yes. Went out south door. Sharon is with her.

J.D. too, came a reply from Hunter. Same direction.

That correlated with the blue dot that blinked in my head, marking Hannah's position. In the bag Lucas had given me, I'd found another prize. A tiny GPS chip. I might not like it when people inserted them into my body, but I wasn't opposed to sticking one in my roommate's favorite pair of shoes.

As I watched it move, I knew we'd guessed right. She was headed to the vacant building. They all were.

My team converged on the bottom floor, speaking in hushed whispers. I hadn't been sure how to group us at first, but Samuel had suggested that we'd probably be less suspicious if we were caught all together, like we were planning some massive prank.

The landscaper would only go for the phony boyfriend story once.

Lucas had checked in an hour ago, and now I had to try to put him in the back of my mind. Whatever happened now was up to me. I was driven by human curiosity, assisted by android functionality. The next time I entered the dorm, perhaps all the mysteries of Montford would be solved.

The campus streetlamps cast eerie shadows as we walked across the field without speaking. I wondered at the absence of security guards in this area. Then it hit me. If there were security guards stationed here, they would see the grant kids, heading for the vacant building. Maybe the dean banished them on certain nights.

Somehow, over the course of the last two days, my fears had shifted. The bomb still terrified me; that was a given. But now I was haunted by another terror: failing to save Holland's next round of victims.

I checked back in with the blue GPS dot that marked Hannah's location. Before we'd left the RV, I'd downloaded blueprints of the entire campus. There was no question Hannah was inside the locked building. The coordinates matched up perfectly.

Something else was amiss, though.

Expand.

The grid appeared before me, glowing a ghostly blue. I ran a comparison between the GPS location and the blueprints.

Error: Results incompatible.

The blueprints hadn't shown any basements on campus. But the GPS didn't lie. Hannah's coordinates matched up with this building. But not inside it. Below it.

I stepped toward the building's security camera, motioning the others back. Positioning myself directly under the camera felt all kinds of wrong, but I forced my feet to stay put.

I wanted to get this over with and get inside.

I extracted the copies of Hannah's eyes from my database, then manipulated the code that would allow her eyes to serve as a cloak for mine. I shivered when the program indicated the change had been implemented. The idea of stealing someone's eyes was disturbing.

I summoned Hannah's username. The security system responded.

Initiate retinal scan.

The red line of the laser began its downward descent, scanning my eyes from top to bottom. When nothing happened, I started to worry that the program wouldn't work. If the alarm went off now . . .

Scan accepted.

The door clicked open, and I led the rest of the group inside after determining there were no humans on the ground floor.

Once the door closed, we were swallowed by darkness.

Night vision: Activated.

Samuel snapped on a small flashlight, and the soft glow revealed a surprise.

The room didn't look like anything special. Or scary. Ceiling-to-floor shelves lined the middle of the room, crowded with boxes of varying sizes. There was a pile of power tools in a corner: drills, hammers, a jigsaw. Dean Parsons hadn't been lying, necessarily. It was hard to believe that anything of interest to us would happen here, but I knew that somewhere there had to be a staircase, leading down. I told my team what to look for, and branched off to the left.

If I used my GPS and followed Hannah's path, it should lead me right where I needed to go.

In fact, it led me right to a row of oversized appliance boxes. Baffled, I turned to tell the others, when I noticed something in the shadows. One of the boxes had been shoved away from the row, as if to make room for something. Or someone.

Bile rose in my throat as I stared at the markings on the floor. I reached down to pull open the trapdoor, but my fingers paused on the carved handle. I didn't want to go down there again. Or do those tests.

With a shudder, my hand slipped from the handle. I rose and backed away. He was expecting me, but I couldn't do this anymore.

I had to go home. Before it was too late, and I was in too deep.

I rubbed the back of my neck, feeling the tiny indentation. Then I turned and ran.

I blinked away the memory and stared down at what was apparently a trapdoor. Whatever it led to was something that had scared Sarah into leaving.

"Over here," I said.

I dug the handle out of the floor, gently eased the door open, and began to climb down a set of rickety metal stairs. The weight of my body made them sway and creak. I hated going in blind. If someone had followed us, we would end up sandwiched in on both ends.

"Samuel, can you stay upstairs, and let us know if anyone tries to follow?"

"Sure. And if I see someone, I'll just pretend to be a box. They'll never notice me in this junk heap."

With Abby and Hunter right behind me, I headed forward. I could feel the angle of the hallway that extended out before us. It sloped down, gently but significantly.

15-degree angle.

Every step only intensified my anxiety.

Hannah's path glowed like a beacon in my head.

The walls were cold and concrete, the flooring the same. The tunnel was barren. If I'd ventured in here by accident, I'd have no reason not to turn back.

Finally, from around an upcoming corner, I heard a muffled voice.

There was a change in the temperature. It was warmer here, like something was generating energy.

Temperature increase: 5.2 degrees in 55 seconds.

Something ahead of us was creating heat. And the voices: they were getting louder.

A muffled shriek made us all freeze.

Voice recognition: Match.

Hannah.

I sped up until I reached the corner, then peered around the edge. Abby and Hunter joined me. From where we stood, the floor sloped down even farther, into a wide-open space the size of a large auditorium.

But that wasn't what caught our attention. Instead, it was the sight of Hannah, slowly climbing to her feet after what looked like a fall. Then she shook it off and reached above her head to grip things as though she were rock climbing, her legs bending and scrabbling for purchase beneath her.

Only there was no rock wall in front of her. There was nothing but air.

I located the other four grant kids too.

There was Sharon, throwing punches in what appeared to be a street brawl with an invisible assailant. Her head whipped back and her grunt echoed off the walls.

Across the room, Claude and J.D. sprinted, Claude ducking behind an invisible wall, J.D. diving into a perfect somersault and regaining his feet, all in one fluid motion. Both of them held their right hands in front of their bodies. Then J.D. whirled, kicking out with his leg and extending his arm, his face a mask of panic. Claude swooped in behind him and executed a flying tackle . . . at thin air. He hit the floor with a crash and a groan, but was back on his feet in seconds. Sometimes, they seemed to notice their surroundings. Claude would start to run, then slow and shake his head, as if dazed by where he was. J.D.'s kick would end halfheartedly, or he'd drop both hands to his sides.

Off on his own, Ben sat on the ground, occasionally curving his hands around an invisible steering wheel, but mostly just staring into space.

Abby mouthed something at me, her eyes wide. *"Drugs?"*

I shook my head. I'd been thinking that at first, but not now. Not with this. This all looked too familiar. Almost like a video game.

My suspicions were confirmed when I spotted Mr. Grassi on an elevated platform behind a giant monitor. He wore a headset, his fingers flying across a keyboard. From his vantage point, he had a clear view of all the students, but not of us.

Zoom.

The monitor enlarged, and I could see there were five names arranged in a column:

Hannah

Claude

Sharon

J.D.

Ben

Beside each name was a score. Hannah's was highest, by far. There was a big drop-off after that, with Claude coming in last.

I wasn't interested in the scores, though. I wanted to see what these kids were seeing.

Access networks in range.

Several appeared, including the main one for the school. But only one caught my attention.

GVirtAff.

GVA: Grassi's Virtual Afficionados.

I hijacked the network, and in an instant, my entire view changed. Instead of empty space, I saw threats, everywhere. Masked men with knives attacked Claude and J.D. Done with the wall, Hannah now hovered on a tight rope in bare feet, arms outstretched. Below her was a pit of sharp rocks. Behind her, a masked assassin. Sharon fought off a brawny man in a bedroom, with narrow eyes and an evil grin. Ben was inside an SUV, trying to evade another SUV with a gun pointing out the window.

"What?" Hunter mouthed, when I grabbed the wall for support. These reminded me way too much of scenes from a different underground lair, below a building I'd once visited in Washington, DC. Grassi was using virtual reality on these kids . . . and it had Holland's stamp all over it. When Hannah and J.D. talked about testing, I thought they were talking about schoolwork. Or SATs. Now I had a feeling this is what they meant.

Text app: Initiated.

Virtual reality. Soldier stuff. Stinks of Holland.

Before my team could respond, I gathered more data. I didn't need my android functionality, as Grassi's monitor was flashing numbers. Not scores, I saw, but vital signs.

Heart rate, respiration, blood pressure.

But how was Grassi getting the information? They had no monitors, no headsets. No pulse oximeters that I could see.

Despite the heat of the room, a chill ran through my body. I could monitor that kind of data remotely, but Grassi couldn't. I doubted his headset would help much.

Unless these kids had some kind of monitoring device on the inside . . .

It was terrible to contemplate, but I knew I had to be right. I searched for the shadows of signals that had to exist.

Five appeared, one for every student.

Trace signal HANNAHOO5WTSN.

I'd known what to expect, but I had to stifle a gasp. My throat went desert dry. Before my eyes, thin bands of light appeared, like yellow-and-blue LED streamers. The disturbing part was that the lines led from Grassi's console . . . straight to the back of each student's neck.

Images flew into my head. The memory of me as Sarah, rubbing the nape of my neck and feeling an indentation there.

And then, back in Mr. Grassi's classroom. I'd felt a zap in that same exact spot, and for a split second, my security system had recognized something intrusive. Was someone trying to monitor my data just then? And, if so, who?

The horror spread from my throat through my entire body, until every fabricated muscle felt incapable of movement.

And then horror turned to fear when an alert notified Grassi of an unauthorized user. I mouthed one word to Abby and Hunter.

"Go."

But I couldn't leave until I knew for sure. While Grassi frowned down at his monitor and started switching off programs, releasing the kids from their electronic prisons one by one, I kept my focus on the spot where the network had connected to Hannah.

Zoom.

Her skin came into focus; with my enhanced vision, I could see the tiny hairs at the nape of her neck.

I could see an oversized freckle just below the base of her skull. I zoomed in on Ben, who was still sitting. He had an identical mark, in an identical spot. My stomach plummeted as my suspicions were confirmed.

They'd been implanted with chips. That's how the virtual-reality platform was able to remain wireless. These kids—all of them—had undergone experimental surgery. And if they had, I guessed, so had Sarah.

A loud beep emitted from Grassi's system. He half rose, lips parted in surprise. "Looks like someone's trying to steal our juice. We need to shut down for the evening."

They'd be leaving any second. Heading directly for me.

I backed away, hoping he was too engrossed in his system to notice. Once I got to the corner, I could race for the trapdoor.

I was almost there when my heel hit something. The object kicked up and smacked against the concrete.

Crack.

Grassi's head whipped up. "Who's there?"

With a stealthy exit now impossible, there was only one option left.

I turned and fled.

I ran the way we'd come, up the slight incline, after Hunter and Abby.

"Who has the flashlight? Hand it over!" Grassi's voice followed me down the passageway, along with the *smack-smack-smack* of his footsteps. Luckily, I had no problem maneuvering in the dark.

Human threat detected: 30 ft.

I ran for the trapdoor, not daring to look over my shoulder. I couldn't waste even a fraction of a second. Once they rounded that corner, and his flashlight caught me . . .

As I ran, my sensors analyzed Grassi's position in relation to mine.

Based on current speed, escape without detection unlikely.

I yanked the hood of my sweatshirt up to hide my hair and sprinted.

The stairs leading up were empty, and the door at the top flung wide open. Hunter and Abby must have already made it up into the main room. I started up after them. The metal steps rocked and swayed as my sneakers slammed the metal rungs.

Just as my hand reached the top, I caught a flash of light bouncing off the wall in front of me.

"This building is off-limits. If you don't stop now, you'll be expelled!"

My body jolted at the sound of Grassi's voice, but I didn't hesitate. I bolted through the opening, slamming the door shut the moment I was on firm ground.

Not that there was any way to lock it.

The others were congregated by the outside door, staring at me in horror.

"Run!" I urged.

Samuel yanked it open and we darted outside.

"Now what? There's no way we can get back to the dorm before they spot us," Samuel said.

"Go," I whispered, waving them on. "I have an idea."

I turned to the security camera, knowing I had only moments to spare. I wasted several of those moments signing in and waiting for the retinal scan. I heard the clatter of the trapdoor being thrown open.

We were almost out of time.

With one last breath, I communicated with the system,

running data until I found what I needed. A thing that I hadn't been sure existed, until this very moment.

Initiate emergency lockdown.

Processing request . . .

I backed away, urging the system to hurry. The footsteps inside were almost to the door.

I took two more steps back. I hadn't been quick enough.

Request granted.

Lockdown commencing.

Had it worked?

I heard the snap of a lock bolting into place, a second before there was pounding on the door.

"What the hell?" That was Grassi's angry voice, signaling that they were locked inside. For now.

I didn't know how long it would take Grassi to reverse the lockdown. Minutes at most, I figured. That gave us just enough time to get back up to our dorm rooms unnoticed.

Only if Grassi didn't call security first.

Up ahead, the others were just reaching the dorms. Samuel ushered Hunter and Abby inside, but waited for me, gesturing frantically with his hand.

Hurry.

I sprinted until the cold air blew back my hood. I snatched it back with one hand, without decreasing my speed.

When I was a few feet away, I waved Samuel on, catching the door when he complied.

"Faster," I told Samuel. We all needed to be back in our rooms and our beds. I rushed inside behind him, then reconnected the alarm to the system.

Abby was still in the stairwell. I grabbed her hand and pulled her up behind me. When we reached the hall, we speed-walked toward our rooms.

I tore open Hannah's door, dumping my shoes in her closet. My change into pajamas was performed in record time, and then I went right for the bed, throwing back the covers and climbing in. My heart continued its racing beat for another ten seconds while I waited. And listened. I had no idea how Grassi would proceed from here. Would there be a check on all the students? Would they suspect students, or would they think it was an outside job? Would Grassi call the police? No, not unless he wanted to expose his secret project.

My heart continued its frantic beat but the pace gradually slowed as the minutes ticked by. That was when I could finally start to make sense of what I saw.

No wonder the grant students were tired. No wonder they were taking drugs. They worked all day and trained all night in a terrifying virtual reality, directed by an adult who was supposed to be their teacher. Their friend. All trust had to be ruined by now, as he put them through dangerous simulations and monitored their progress by embedding chips in their bodies.

Why these kids? Why Grassi? Why Sarah?

Those questions still plagued me. But I did have one answer, or the beginning of an answer.

Holland had lured these exceptional students to Montford with the Watson Grants. But their scholarships came with a steep price. Along with regular classes, they had to go through high-tech military training, and why was that? It had to be because he was molding the grant kids into some kind of new and deadly soldier.

What war would they be fighting? I wasn't sure I wanted to know. But we'd have to find the answers before we left this campus. It was the only way to save this group of kids. We owed that much to Sarah.

You safe?

I texted Hunter, Abby, and Samuel.

The responses blipped in, one after another:

All clear, from Abby

10-4, from Hunter

If I don't die from this agonizing side cramp, then yes, from Samuel. But that was way too close for comfort.

That was scary, from Abby. Are you going to tell us what the hell was going on back there?

For an instant, confusion clouded my brain. Then I realized. She couldn't see—not the way I could. None of them had the luxury of my android sensors.

I told them what I'd witnessed. I told them what I'd made of it.

For several seconds, there were no responses. I wondered if the texting app had malfunctioned. As I prepared to run a check, Samuel replied.

As horrifying as that is, at least it makes sense. I was starting to wonder if they were all on a bad mushroom trip.

They would wait to hear from me before they did anything else.

My next step was to check in with Lucas, and I was surprised when a second voice joined our conversation.

It's Daniel. Lucas is letting me use his audio connection. We're both listening in. Tell us what happened.

I started with our close call with Grassi, and Daniel responded.

Is there any chance he saw you?

He may have seen the bottoms of my legs and shoes. I ditched the shoes. The jeans could have belonged to anyone.

Daniel muttered a curse.

You know this means heightened security. I think we need to pull you out.

I hesitated, but only for a second.

No. We'll just have to be extra cautious. We only have a day left at Montford. Even if they could track something down that led to us, it would take time. We'll be gone by then.

I don't know, Mila. It sounds incredibly risky.

It's always been incredibly risky. Look at Lucas—he left his job with Holland's company, and now Holland knows he's missing. We have a good chance—possibly our only chance—to bring Holland down. To stop what he's doing. To give those kids their lives back. We can't give up now, not when we're so close. What would Sarah want us to do?

Silence greeted me. And then Daniel's sigh of defeat.

Tell us what you learned.

I started from the beginning. The virtual-reality room. The testing. The scoring. The chips.

I heard Daniel inhale sharply. Chips? You sure?

I only saw Grassi using them to monitor the kids' vital signs. But there's no reason he couldn't also use the chips to control them. Force them to act against their will. With those implants, the sky's the limit.

Daniel and Lucas both went silent. They knew as well as I did how dangerous a weapon these kids could be in Holland's hands. He had planted a bomb inside me, and with it he could wreak terror wherever he chose—but only once. With total control over J.D. and Hannah, Ben and Claude and Sharon—trained fighters—he could do so much more. It could be so much worse.

Lucas was mulling everything over. Here's what I don't get, he said. How did he get the chips in? Does Holland visit the school? And even if he does, he can't be doing surgery. Surely someone would stop him.

Daniel jumped in then. And why these kids? he said. They're at Montford because they're high achievers. Why would Holland want to control them? These kids can do so much on their own. Wouldn't he choose more malleable victims?

I thought back to what Hannah had told me. She didn't apply for the Watson Grant—she was just chosen. Out of a clear blue sky. But why?

It could be because she had developed amazing apps.

Or it could be because there was something else in her background. Something we hadn't noticed before. Or something we'd noticed . . . but ignored. Until now.

My brain crunched the data on the grant kids. They were from different places. Different kinds of families. They had wildly different talents and personalities. But they had one thing in common.

Hannah's appendectomy scar.

Ben's femur pins.

J.D.'s pain pills, left over from a concussion.

My head began to pound a deep, throbbing beat as a fragile connection began to emerge.

I need to speak to Daniel.

A pause. Here.

Was Sarah ever hospitalized? Before she got the grant offer?

This time, the silence lasted five seconds. Yes. She had meningitis, a few weeks before her offer. She ended up staying three days. Why?

Sorrow washed through me like a river, and I shut my eyes, giving myself a few seconds to grieve. This. This had been the beginning of the end for Sarah. I was almost sure.

I told him about Hannah and Ben's scars, and J.D.'s concussion.

Let's hack the hospitals in the cities where the grant kids lived, find their records. Look for evidence of tests that don't belong.

Because hospitals were the perfect place. All Holland would need were a couple of doctors under his thumb. Identify the kids, implant the chips while they were under anesthesia. When kids were sick, it was easy enough to keep them an extra day. Give them extra tests, just to be safe. Tests that weren't tests at all . . . but secret procedures. The kids probably had no idea about their implants.

I'll take the research from here, I said. The more I thought about the implants, the more angry I felt.

Daniel's reply was swift.

No! If there's some kind of alarm on those files, we can't have it coming back to Montford. It's not safe. As a matter of fact, I still think you should all get out of there, first thing in the morning. We have enough information to go with for now.

For a brief moment, I let the fantasy play out in my

mind. I'd return to Lucas's side and we'd leave Philadelphia. We'd find somewhere to hide. Another secluded mountain cabin, or maybe a tiny island, out in the middle of nowhere.

We'd get away from the world. We'd get to be together.

There was only one problem.

We'd have to accept the fact that Holland was ruining the lives of countless other kids. He'd remain a free man, while I forever remained a prisoner to the bomb beneath my skin.

As far as fantasies went, this one really sucked.

We can't let Holland get away with this.

Fear scraped at Daniel's voice. We can't let Holland hurt you any more than he already has.

Daniel was worried about me. And despite everything else, a glow ignited somewhere beneath my ribs, and I tucked it away for later.

But for now I was arguing with my father.

We need one more day. Give us time to look through Grassi's office, talk to the kids a little more. We'll leave by tonight, I promise. Even if we find nothing, just one more day.

I could picture Daniel clenching his fists.

Fine. But you're leaving tonight, if I have to drag you out myself.

A muffled burst of static, then Lucas came on.

He's too upset to talk. But he trusts you. I trust you.
You're almost there.

I was pretty worried about Lucas, too. Holland knew
he wasn't sick—he knew that Lucas was lying. How long
before he tracked him down? For all we knew, the cabin in
the mountains was the first place he'd look.

Anything else from Tim? I asked.

I haven't been able to reach him, Lucas replied. It could
be because he wants to be left alone, as usual. Or it could
be because something's wrong.

I had no human siblings, but I knew there would be
nothing like the pain of losing a brother.

And I knew there was nothing I could say to comfort
Lucas, though I longed to.

Good luck with everything, I said.

You too. Be safe. A hesitation, and then a soft Please.

I will. See you tomorrow.

Only one more day to right some terrible wrongs: for
Sarah, for the grant kids, for Lucas, for Hunter, for me.

NINETEEN

Samuel and I waited in the cafeteria for the others.
Something crashed to the ground behind us, and we
both jumped.

"Sorry," said a student sheepishly, picking up the tray
he'd dropped.

Samuel released a tense breath. We were both on edge.
Any loud sound was potentially Grassi or the dean, coming
for us with questions about where we'd been last night, and
why.

And that was before Abby arrived with Celia and Sharon.

Sharon walked with her usual athletic bounce, but I
could see the telltale signs of fatigue in her puffy eyes, her
waxy skin, her unbrushed hair. Now that we knew how she
spent her nights, it wasn't shocking that she was tired. It was

shocking that she could play any sports at all.

Celia, though, was another story. She wasn't one of the grant kids—she was just their friend. She should have had a good night's sleep. But here she was, her eyes rimmed pink, her shirt on inside out.

"Are you okay?" I asked Celia when she sat down next to me.

"I guess so. It's just . . . Hannah's gone."

Samuel met my concerned gaze over Celia's head. "Gone? What do you mean?"

"She sent me an email in the middle of the night—it was waiting for me when I woke up. She said she was sick and her dad came to get her. But she's not coming back."

"Never? Why? What about the Watson Grant?" I asked, stunned.

Celia sniffled. "She just said that it wasn't worth it anymore. She could go to any school, I guess. She doesn't need a scholarship to this one."

It was probably true, I thought. But Hannah would always have that chip in her neck—did it mean that Holland could call her back at any time? I wasn't sure a student could ever really get away.

Celia sounded crushed. "I just want to talk to her," she said. "Make sure she's all right. But I tried to call, and her phone went straight to voice mail." Celia put her head in her hands. "This happened last year, too. I swear, I'm a jinx."

"What do you mean?" I said, guessing before she answered.

"It happened last year, too. To that Sarah girl that I told you about. I mean, I barely knew her, but she was nice. She started acting weird, too, though, just before she left. And no one ever heard from her again. What if it's something I did? What if it's all my fault?"

Sharon put an arm around her friend, seeming like the stronger of the two. "Come on, let's go get you some pancakes," she said kindly. Only I knew that one of these days, Sharon could be the girl who disappeared. The students at Montford thought the Watson Grant was only for the lucky kids, but I knew it was a sort of curse.

They headed for the food lines, while I struggled not to scream. *Don't panic.*

Don't. Panic.

"Don't panic," Samuel echoed, as though reading my thoughts.

"But why did they take her? And where?" I said. Whatever Celia might think, I worried that this was my fault. I'd stolen images of Hannah's eye to fool the security camera, and while I thought I'd wiped our entrance from the system's memory log, maybe I'd left a trail by mistake. If Grassi had reviewed the log-ins and saw Hannah's name pop up—even though he knew she was with him—he'd probably suspect her of something. Especially when he'd heard that noise in the hallway.

She could still be here at the school. Held somewhere on campus. Interrogated. Tortured. I wouldn't put anything past Holland and whoever was helping him. But I didn't detect her GPS chip anywhere.

As the other students began shuffling off to class, my team threw together a hasty plan. We had two goals to accomplish:

Rescue Hannah if she was still on campus. Which I was willing to bet she was.

Connect Grassi and Holland to the illegal experiments on Montford students.

We'd have to use speed and surprise to our advantage.

If Grassi was worried about Hannah's involvement in a security breach, questioning her wouldn't lead him to us. Hannah had no idea what was going on. A blessing in terms of our safety, but in terms of hers? I didn't want to dwell on the possibilities.

First we'd split up and scour the campus for Hannah. Quickly, I made assignments. "I'll contact Hunter and tell him to take the administrative buildings and the quad as soon as he can get away from J.D. Abby, you take the athletic fields and the gym. Samuel, dorms. I'll tackle the rest of the classrooms and offices—I'll be able to locate her by fingerprint scan if she's in a close enough range. Then I'll try to get inside Grassi's office."

★ ★ ★

By now, students were already in classes, and the hallways were eerily silent. As I paused to scan each classroom, I avoided standing by the windows. I didn't know Montford's policy on loitering in hallways during class time, and I didn't want to find out. Being stopped by an irritated teacher was the last thing I needed.

There was no flash on my sensor alerting me to Hannah's presence. No sign of her in any of the vacant classrooms. Nothing.

But as I snuck past a full class upstairs, something beeped in my head. I froze, hope blossoming even though the location made no sense.

Scanning: Match.

Ben LaCosta.

100% certainty.

Not Hannah. Ben. Another grant kid, at risk.

I speed-walked back down the stairs and slipped outside. Clouds covered the sky in a blanket of white, not a glimmer of blue to be seen. The air felt thick with moisture.

Humidity level: 78%.

Showers ahead, probably soon.

I darted into the social-sciences building next and headed for the elegant, curving staircase. I took the stairs two at a time and repeated my search, making sure to check any unmarked doors and storage rooms, even bathrooms.

I quickly exhausted my search there, so I headed to the math-and-science building. Each door I passed yielded the same result.

No traces of Hannah, anywhere.

But I did catch a glimpse of Grassi. Standing up at his desk, lecturing with his usual enthusiasm. Like nothing at all was wrong.

I headed to the basement and confirmed what my gut already told me was true. She wasn't here, pure and simple. Almost out of time, there was only one thing left to do.

While the others continued their search, I'd move on to plan B.

The basement felt colder than the rest of the building, and the ceiling creaked overhead. Despite staircases at both ends of the room, the knowledge that I was underground made it feel like a trap. I wondered how it felt to the math-and-science faculty, who had their offices down here. Did they like being apart from the bustle of classes and students? Or did they resent being beneath the surface, like moles, with no natural light?

I hesitated just outside Grassi's office. My internal clock said we had fifteen minutes until the end of class. That might not be long enough to get through every-thing alone.

I texted to let the others know what I was doing, then prepared myself to break in.

I tried the handle, unsurprised to find the door bolted shut. I stared at it uncertainly. Once I forced open the door, there would be no hiding it. The second Grassi came down here, he'd go to the dean and ask to see the footage from security cameras, and I hadn't been able to plan ahead and thwart them.

I considered waiting until later. I'd have more time to search if I started at the beginning of the next class. But I was pretty sure Grassi's next period was open, and who knew if he ate lunch down here or not?

It was now or never.

I exerted inward pressure to force the door open, applying counterpressure with my other hand in hopes of masking the sound.

Millimeter by millimeter, the wood separated from the metal lock. Yielding under my hand.

The splintering crack as the wood finally gave wasn't loud, but still I froze. Waiting to see if anyone heard.

When the hall remained quiet, I pushed the door open and hurried inside.

Scanning...

A quick visual survey revealed a desk with attached drawers. A desk chair behind and two upholstered chairs in front. An industrial file cabinet in the corner. And a fake potted plant on a rectangular stand.

The desktop computer sat in plain view. As good a place

as any to start. Machine to machine, we'd talk.

As I powered it on, I heard the warm-up hum of the components and realized the computer was a good five years old. Images of the high-tech equipment in Grassi's classroom flashed to mind, and I frowned. His dated desktop seemed out of character.

When the screen pulled up without password protection, I knew the search would be futile. But still I whipped through the few assorted files until I was absolutely sure.

Nothing of use on this relic. Time to move on.

As I rose from the chair and opened a desk drawer, a thought hit me. When I'd peeked into Grassi's classroom, I'd caught a glimpse of his laptop bag. So his laptop wasn't even here, I realized. Probably not his cell phone, either. My hope at finding evidence connecting him to Holland—or the testing on the grant kids—was shrinking by the second. Still, I had to see this through.

Then my auditory sensors picked up a sound.

Slap. Slap. Slap.

Footsteps. Heading down the south stairs.

I whirled, my gaze catching on the splintered wood around the lock. One look at that, and anyone would guess forced entry.

Slap. Slap. Slap.

The footsteps were now on the basement floor. Headed this way.

Human threat detected: 40 ft.

I slipped over to the door and eased it against the wall in hopes that a casual passerby might not notice the damage.

Human threat: 20 ft.

I slipped to the far side of the desk and crouched down. Urging the person to keep on walking.

10 ft.

5 ft.

The footsteps stopped just outside the doorway. I prepared to subdue the intruder and move on.

But the person didn't step over the threshold. Instead, I heard a rustling sound, and Hunter was in the doorway, his anxious expression fading when he spotted me. After a quick glance over his shoulder, he hurried inside.

"Samuel sent me to help you search," he whispered. "He's keeping lookout for Grassi upstairs. . . ." He stopped when he spotted the mangled door.

I knew just what he was thinking.

"I destroyed property, okay? That doesn't mean I'm dangerous, Hunter. It means I'm scared, and in a rush. Using my abilities the best way I can." It was so frustrating to see myself through his eyes. Even after everything that had happened, he thought I was unpredictable and deadly, when I was actually in the middle of a rescue operation. When would this ever stop?

"Could you take a look inside the file cabinet?" I asked

him coldly. At least he could give me a hand here. So far, this search was a waste.

I scooted to the side so that Hunter could slip past me, but my taut nerves crackled when he placed a hand on my arm.

"Hey," he said, prompting me to look up.

"I saw those kids last night," he said softly. "I saw them acting normal, in classes, and I saw them again in that room. . . . I just . . ."

He released me and shoved his hands in his pockets. "If they can stick chips in regular kids, make them see things that aren't there and do things they wouldn't normally do . . . I was too quick to blame you for what happened at Quinn's. To Peyton."

I wasted a couple of seconds staring at him, then I gave him a quick nod. At one time, those words would have meant everything to me, back when I needed his acceptance to make me feel good. Now, they were just words.

Redemption didn't always lie in the forgiveness and approval of others. Sometimes, it had to be born inside ourselves, nurtured into bloom by conviction.

Still. Forgiveness was nice.

The least I could do was acknowledge it. "Thanks," I said.

And then we both settled in to hunt.

He sorted through the file cabinet, while I searched through the bottom desk drawer. My leg bumped against a computer component, and I shifted my position. But as I continued to comb through random papers and office supplies, my gaze fell back to the computer. Why would Grassi keep such an old machine?

And then something even bigger hit me. When I'd searched for a local network signal, I hadn't found one.

I abandoned the desk and turned the monitor back on to confirm. Nope, no bars; nothing to show an internet connection at all.

My heart accelerated with possibility. I moved to the computer, carefully popping off the outer cover. A few seconds later, I confirmed my suspicions. No wireless card, either.

Grassi kept this computer off network on purpose. The information he kept on it was too sensitive to risk a hack.

Too sensitive. Or too incriminating.

I'd already searched the computer and drawn a blank, but there was one more option.

"I think we're looking for an external hard drive," I told Hunter. "Probably hidden."

He shook out the computer manuals on the bookshelves, looking for any hidey-holes. I backtracked to the desk, checking drawers for false bottoms and hidden compartments.

Are you guys out of there yet? Class ends in a minute!

Samuel was right. In all the excitement, I'd stopped

paying attention to my internal clock.

Hunter's lips moved as he read the text on his burn phone. He looked over at me. "What now?"

We'd gone through most every possible hiding spot, but I wanted to make absolutely sure. And to do that, we'd need a few more minutes. Which was a few more than we had.

I made a split-second decision, shooting off a response to Samuel as I rose. "Hang tight," I told Hunter before poking my head out into the hall. I spotted the familiar red square by the south stairwell. My stomach felt like an entire circus act as I connected with the fire alarm's signal.

Activate alarm?

I swallowed. Not the most sophisticated tactic, but we couldn't be picky.

Yes.

A second later, an earsplitting wail flooded the hall.

The reaction was instant. The few teachers who were in their offices scrambled for the stairs, asking one another in strained voices if any drills had been scheduled for the day.

They hurried up while overhead, the ceiling rumbled with the sound of hundreds of feet on wooden floors.

Meanwhile, the siren tore at me like sharp claws, its wail linking me to the past. *A scream from a dead girl. Telling me to run while I still could.*

Thick, billowing smoke. Red and orange flames licking in every direction. Dad's hoarse voice. Sarah on the floor . . . the acrid sweet smell of burning flesh . . . my own . . .

I shook off the memories and the fire faded, leaving only the wail of the alarm.

Time to live in the now.

Keep track of Grassi, I texted Samuel before returning to the search. But we were almost out of spots. In desperation, Hunter had resorted to yanking up the chair cushions. I looked for anything we might have missed. The only thing we hadn't searched in the office was the potted plant.

The wooden platform had potential, so I rushed over and turned it upside down. No hard drive. With barely any hope left, I dug my fingers beneath the fake mulch in the brown ceramic pot.

My fingers struck something foreign. Cool, sleek, and sharp, where the pot was rough and round.

With a shaking hand, I withdrew the external hard drive.

"Got it. Grab that USB cord from the top drawer and let's get out of here."

Hunter did as I asked, and we raced out the office door to the stairs. Where there'd once been a thunder of footsteps, now there was unnerving quiet. Except for one lone sound. A cough at the top of the stairwell.

And then the sound of shoes hitting steps. Descending. "Anyone down here needs to evacuate immediately."

The dean.

I snatched Hunter's sleeve and pulled him backward.

When I knew we were out of sight I turned. "Other stairs. Quick," I said, and bolted, with him on my heels.

Distance calculations raced through my head. The distance from us to the other stairs; the distance and length of time it would take the dean to get to the bottom.

We couldn't be linked to that busted door.

We reached the stairs and clambered up, my heart racing. Just in time to miss the dean completing his sweep.

Upstairs, the hall was deserted.

Which way? I texted Samuel.

Out the north exit.

We rushed for the north door and burst outside. Rain pounded onto our heads, and within seconds, streams were pouring down my cheeks. I tucked the hard drive into the waistband of my jeans and pulled my sweatshirt over for additional protection. If the thing fried now . . .

Students huddled everywhere: on the steps, in walkways, on the grass. Staff members tried to shoo them into some kind of order, but their instructions were lost in the sea of shrieking, laughing teens. Samuel's oversized head poked out between two big clusters; he waved us over. We hurried over and let him guide us into the middle of the chaos.

"Where's Grassi?" I asked.

"Over there." Samuel pointed at a big navy umbrella sheltering Grassi and a trio of shivering students.

"I got the drive, but I need a safe place to plug in," I said.

Then I realized we were down one team member. "Where's Abby?"

"She had a few more spots to check, on the far side of campus. She should be done in a few minutes. Still no sign of Hannah."

I nodded and perused the area around us. We needed a spot where we could watch Grassi, but stay dry enough not to damage the hard drive. I pointed to a giant tree about fifty feet away. "There."

I zigzagged and pushed my way through the heavy crowd, relieved when it thinned out and we could jog on the open field. Once we took shelter under the tree's massive branches, Hunter handed over the USB cord.

"Keep an eye on Grassi while I plug this in," I said. Paranoia talking. Between the sheets of rain and mass of humanity between us and him, it would be almost impossible for him to see me. Still, I wasn't taking unnecessary risks.

"I hope Abby gets back soon. Then we can get out of here, right?"

"That's the plan," I replied, hooking the cord to the drive, before connecting the other end to my port. For a split second, nothing happened. Did I need a power source?

Connection detected.

Powering up.

And then:

File system detected: Action?

Browse.

Scan.

Format.

So weird, how my two sides worked so seamlessly together. My android brain read all the data in a stream of ones and zeroes, which my human brain immediately converted to words. Once I'd hated that dichotomy. Now, I just admired the collaboration.

I issued the command to browse and waited for files to pop up. My lungs were constricted, too heavy with hope and fear to take a full breath.

A folder popped up, which opened to expose hundreds of files.

Of course all of them were encrypted.

"I'm texting Abby again," Hunter said. "I wish she'd hurry up." He pulled out his phone while I ground my teeth together. My fingers tightened on the wire. Of course Grassi had encrypted them. Now I just had to hope that he'd used a program that I could decrypt in a short amount of time.

"Red alert. Grassi is heading inside the building." Samuel's proclamation made me pause, but only for a moment. Now I just needed to work faster. Soon he would see what had happened to his office door.

The encryption would have been challenging for any

human, but Grassi hadn't made the code android-proof. The encryption cracked, and I could decipher the code that emerged.

I processed the files in order.

The first one opened to reveal only two words. PET scans. Whatever else might have once lived in the file had been deleted long ago.

The next ones, thankfully, were more promising. Photos.

Ocean landscapes. A fluffy dog. A photo of Grassi from maybe two or three years ago, drinking a beer. Grassi holding up a big fish. Nothing relevant to my search.

I paused on an image of a shirtless man with a tattoo. The colors were faded, like the original photo had aged before being scanned. Everything was the slightest bit blurry. The man had sun-streaked brown hair and a lanky but muscular build. He was smiling into the camera, while tropical foliage loomed behind him. The tattoo was on the right side of his chest, fashioned to look like a medal. It was the colors that made me hesitate.

Blue, yellow, and green. I'd seen that combination before.

Searching database . . .

Images from my recent history flashed by as my search function pulled up anything with a combination of those colors.

Ping. 1 result.

My heart almost stopped when the image appeared. An evidence bag with a twisted, melted bit of metal. We hadn't been able to ID the object, but Blythe had obviously thought it was important enough to hide.

I scanned the photo into my database so I could work with it.

Resolution: Sharpen.

In the blink of an eye, the soldier's face depixelated and then reassembled, his features coming into sharper focus.

Age progression: Activate.

Time lapse?

I recalled Grassi's age from our research. Thirty-one years.

Weight gain or loss?

Gain, I commanded.

Starting progression.

The image's photo altered, adding inches and years. The image morphed and changed until I recognized Grassi's face. He was the tattooed man in the photo, much younger then. The colors of the tattoo matched the colors of that piece of metal. Whatever that was worth, I thought. Maybe a coincidence. But I kept working with the photo.

Magnify 20x.

I'd missed it before, but clutched in his right fist was a silver necklace with two oval-shaped pendants. Dog tags. And in the bottom corner of the photo, I spotted a series of numbers.

They meant nothing to me, and I needed to get to the other files. So I sent the information to Lucas.

Can you search this marking and number? I found them both

on a photo of Grassi from years ago. Apparently he was military.

The response was instant.

Will do. You guys okay?

For now. I snagged a hard drive from Grassi's office. We're just waiting on Abby now.

I paused, then added, *Get ready to come grab us at any time. Just say the word. Stay safe.*

"Are you almost done scanning?" Samuel's beefy hand landed on my shoulder and squeezed. Through his fingers, I felt his mounting stress.

When I heard his words, I wanted to smack myself. Scanning. Of course. That was the most crucial step. That way, if I lost the drive, I still had the data. I'd been so caught up in my success, I'd gone about things backward.

Almost done. I should be ready in a few. Where do I meet you? Abby texted.

I released a tense breath I hadn't realized I was holding on her behalf, and went back to deciphering the code.

Students started drifting back into buildings. Pretty soon, we'd be noticeable in our little huddle. As I issued the command to scan, Hunter interrupted.

"What's that blinking light?" I followed his gaze down to the drive in my right hand. To where a tiny green light flashed inside the drive.

My security alert flashed in time.

GPS signal located.

"He's tracking it!"

"Who? Grassi? Then why are we standing here? Get rid of the damn thing!" Samuel roared.

"Hang on," I said. I couldn't ditch the drive until I'd finished scanning every file.

The scan initiated while Samuel paced in a circle beneath the tree limbs. Hunter kept checking his phone.

"I though yer components wur state o' the art," Samuel said, his Scottish brogue thickening along with his stress.

My own nerves weren't faring any better. They vibrated, as if a giant hand plucked them in time with the download updates.

50% complete.

72% complete.

88% complete.

"Joseph and Mary, he's going to see us!" Samuel said, just as I proclaimed, "Done!"

I snatched the cord out and shoved it at Hunter, gripping the drive firmly between my hands as I headed for the paved path.

"Here, let me chuck it," Samuel said.

I snatched the drive away before he could make contact. "I have a better idea."

We reached the path, and I dropped the drive to the ground. Then I lifted my foot and stomped as hard as I could.

Crunch.

I stomped again for good measure, aiming for the blinking light. Metal and plastic and computer chips crumpled into pieces, then the light disappeared. With one epic sweep of my foot, I scattered the pieces onto the grass and watched them land in the mud. The final thought that flickered through my mind made my lips curve up.

GPS mode that, asshole.

I shot off another quick text to Lucas.

I scanned an entire hard drive's worth of files. I'm going to send some transcriptions through to you, so we can hopefully get through them quicker. Here they come . . .

I let him know when the transfer completed.

Got them. Will get straight to work on these.

"Where the hell is Abby?" Samuel cursed. "Let's head toward her so we're not just standing around at the scene of the crime."

A text popped up as we headed across the courtyard.

Guys, come quick. I found Hannah, and she's hurt.

Where are you? I prompted.

VR building

That didn't make any sense.

How did you get in?

The last time I'd checked, it required a retinal scan, and I knew Abby didn't have any stolen eyeballs.

Someone had shoved something between the door and the wall. Hannah said she heard Grassi complaining about a security malfunction. Started last night.

My tension eased. Maybe they'd tweaked something

when overriding my forced lockdown.

Hurry.

As if to reinforce Abby's text, an alert pinged in my head.

GPS signal located.

At first, the hairs on the back of my neck rose. Could Grassi's GPS chip have revived? Until I realized this was Hannah's chip. We hadn't seen it all day.

The grid that surfaced behind my eyes confirmed Abby's text. Hannah was in the same place where we'd spotted the kids last night, lost in their virtual-reality worlds.

We're coming.

Together, the three of us sprinted for Grassi's VR lab. On the way, I checked in with Lucas and Daniel.

Abby found Hannah. She's in the VR room. Can you come to the school ASAP?

The reply was instant.

On our way.

"We go in, grab Hannah, and get out. Deal?" I said. This was almost over.

Hunter and Samuel were already panting from the exertion of keeping up with me. We angled left from the pathway, the wind whipping our faces. The rain had slowed to a faint drizzle, but the grass squished beneath our wet shoes. As we ran past the fountain, I continued to search file after file, like an oar dipping through calm water.

The first twenty or thirty files were meaningless to me.

Grassi was a data hoarder; he kept records of everything. Travel expenses, vacations. Taxes. Bank accounts and their balances, some of them overseas. More interesting was a list of foreign names, followed by seemingly random numbers. With more time to research, it would all come together, but right now, I wasn't even sure what I was looking for. I was just grateful I could search and run at the same time.

I stumbled across something curious in the very next file, a saved email chain. Grassi only exchanged messages with one other person, and there was no associated name. The recipient's address was a dead end; I recognized that immediately. But something about the other party's writing triggered a spark of recognition. Something about the voice seemed familiar.

Behind me, I heard a gasp. Hunter had slipped on a patch of mud. I reached out and grabbed his hand while Samuel latched on to his waist. When he regained his footing, we took off again.

The VR building was one hundred feet away.

There was something about the way that one person worded things. Certain turns of phrase. They snagged at my memory, conjuring up a deep drawl and the inside of a secret military lab.

It was just a hunch, but I knew how to give it more certainty.

Initiate natural language processing.

Comparing sample to known subjects.

A few seconds passed, filled with the grunts of aching lungs behind me and the *squish-squish* of our pumping feet.

Match found: 94% accuracy.

The image appeared, complete with data on name, birthday, and any other information my memory had stored within its depths. My memory confirmed what my gut had known for a while now.

General Holland.

He'd been emailing with Grassi, at length.

This was just the link we needed.

Pausing at the door, I filled Lucas in. He, too, had some incriminating information.

Grassi is an alias, for one thing. The man in the photo is named William Shell. The numbers on the photo refer to my uncle's—Holland's—old army regiment. That's where he and Grassi met. My uncle had a pin, exactly like that tattoo. The tattoo is of a symbol their entire troop adopted. And the pin had ended up at the fire that killed Sarah.

Did that mean Holland had set it himself? He didn't match Maggie's description. And why would he do that, anyway?

We'd reached the door. The security camera was dead and the door was ajar, just as Abby had described.

A quick scan didn't alert me to any threats, so I motioned

Hunter and Samuel to follow me in. The room was almost as dark in the daytime as it had been last night. Since neither Hunter nor Samuel had a flashlight this time, we had to slow way down to make sure no one tripped.

"Each of you, keep a hand on my arm. I don't want anyone wandering off." Using my night vision, I traced last night's path through the room, past the appliance boxes and scattered tools. Nothing had been touched.

Nothing, that was, except the secret passage to the basement. The entry was flung wide open.

"Trapdoor, two feet ahead," I warned the boys. With me as a stabilizer, they tapped out the edge with their feet.

"I'll go first," Samuel said, before turning and feeling his way to the metal stairs. Hunter prepared to follow. While I waited my turn, I kept on scanning files.

The dean, it turned out, was completely in the dark about this building. He thought it was full of cutting-edge computer equipment in boxes, just waiting for construction to begin on a state-of-the-art lab. He wasn't even part of the selection process for the Watson Grants.

Then I began listening to an audio file as I followed the others down the rickety stairs. Grassi must have recorded this conversation for his records.

"Hannah matches Sarah in terms of synapse rate and her adaptability looks like it may surpass. How do you want to proceed?"

Something swelled in my throat. That was Grassi's

smooth, polished voice. Talking about Sarah as casually as he might mention the weather.

But the slow, answering drawl was one that laced my every fear, haunted my past, and threatened my future. I tasted bile—programmed? remembered? real?—but continued to play the conversation.

"Continue testing," said General Holland. "We don't want any issues this time. But that sounds promising. The next step is to integrate the brain with the robotic enhancements. The others?"

"A mixed lot, though a couple show more potential than others. I'll keep at it, though. I think you were right about less machine, more human hybrids. Much less work, and they seem to mostly respond well to mind control via remote interface."

"Well, we need to hurry up and find more subjects," Holland said, his impatience clear. "Maybe we should lower the study qualifications. Forget the minimum IQ, and run PETs on any available teen who can talk and chew gum at the same time. We have orders for thirty already, and more are trickling in."

Far from the first time in my life, I realized truth didn't always set you free. Sometimes the truth swooped down and flattened you with its lack of mercy.

Holland never intended to stop with the MILAs. I was just part of the first batch of his unauthorized human-machine hybrids, and he was already working on more. The kids we'd come to know would be transformed. Ruined. And soon Holland would have an army of others, just like them.

My every cell turned to ice; I feared the barest tap would crack me into a million sharp pieces. I couldn't move for terror of falling into an abyss and never climbing my way out. These men played with human lives like they were clay figures to be smashed and re-formed at their slightest whim.

In my haze of despair, my foot slipped on the step. I lurched back, sliding down until Samuel grabbed my waist to break my fall.

"Let me know before you're going to do any more tricks," he said. "A man needs a little warning. Especially in this crap lighting."

"Everything okay?" Hunter asked.

"No. But it will be as soon as we take these bastards down."

We made our way through the downward-sloping tunnel while I texted to fill Lucas and Daniel in.

They were also analyzing the data, and their findings expanded what we knew.

W.A.T.S.O.N. stands for: Weaponized Android Testing Sub-Operations Network

Holland and his cronies referred to studies about the malleable, adaptable brains of teenagers. They'd found the neurological parameters that interfaced the best with technology, and ordered PET scans on any teens at hospitals within the rounds privileges of three specific Philadelphia-area surgeons, who reached an IQ of 130 or over. Sarah had been the first teen identified and drafted—without her knowledge.

I heard a choked noise in the background, pulverizing the pump that masqueraded as my heart. Daniel. If all this was painful for me to process . . .

A steady roar gathered in my ears, my core, my cells. Tears streamed down my face. If we failed to stop Holland, then no child was safe. Not Hannah, not Claude, not bright or motivated high schoolers all around the country.

That was our answer, then. We couldn't fail.

Our beautiful girl, and all he ever saw was fresh brain matter for his research. That son of a bitch knew. He failed to keep her at Montford, but he still wouldn't let her go. First, he planned that fire to steal my baby girl. And then he knew Nicole would cave if it was a choice between making Sarah's life count for research or just fade away.

The keening pain in his voice almost made me stumble again. As I steadied myself, I realized we were closing in on the end of the corridor.

I'm so sorry. But at least we can save Hannah. At least we can save her. Are you guys almost here?

Yes, we're—

Static shrieked through my head, canceling everything else. I clapped my hands to my ears and stumbled yet again. For the first time I could remember, my mind was silent.

On each side, someone grabbed my elbow to steady me.

"What's wrong?" Samuel said.

The sound vanished as quickly as it had come.

Daniel? Lucas?

No response.

How had I lost the signal? My sensors? My hands clutched my abdomen. Could it be related to the bomb? Holland knew about Lucas, and Tim was missing. Had he finally decided "what the hell," and triggered it with his remote?

"Just a malfunction," I said. I decided to keep my concerns to myself for now, even as my dread thickened. Maybe something—or someone—had cut them off.

We reached the corner. As we took the bend, the hall ahead widened, opening into the larger arena we'd seen the previous night.

On the far side of the room, we spied two figures.

Abby had her back to us, and Hannah was lying down.

"Abby!" Hunter called, sprinting ahead while I paused to assess the scene. Abby's positioning. It looked awkward. She was on her knees by the body, but her shoulders were bunched and I couldn't see her hands.

I tried to initiate a scan, but only got a headful of static. Interference.

Something was off. "Hunter, wait—"

Abby looked over her shoulder. Her eyes were wide, frantic above the slash of silver duct tape that covered her mouth.

In that one moment, everything became clear.

This was a trap.

"Damn it," Samuel roared as he ran for Abby. I whirled, feeling hobbled without my android abilities. We needed to protect our exit.

Too late, I heard the march of feet coming from the passageway. An imposing figure melted out of his shadowy hiding spot. The light caught him just so, and for an instant, I saw a mist-and-light man. But he took another step and that fairy tale vanished. This was no hologram.

He emerged with Abby's phone dangling from his hand.

"Guess I won't be needing this anymore," General Holland drawled, giving the phone a distasteful look before letting it clatter to the floor. His jeans and Windbreaker couldn't disguise his proud military bearing. From under his jacket, he withdrew a gun and aimed it loosely at Hunter. With the other hand, he grabbed a Taser.

To the outside world, he probably looked like an attractive older man. His face held weathered lines, but his eyes were bright and he had a full head of silver-streaked hair. But I knew the real Holland; I knew the dark soul his outer shell concealed. When I looked at him, all I saw was a monster.

"How—?" I choked my question off, not wanting to

give him the satisfaction. But the question finished in my head. How had he snuck up on us like this? With Lucas monitoring his cell phone?

Holland always had an eerie way of reading me. He watched my face now and chuckled. "Did you really think I wouldn't realize my nephew was tracking me, once I discovered he was with you?"

I scanned the distance from me to him; the distance from him to Abby. The distance back to the exit. Abby was bound and Hannah was hurt, but there were three of us to his one. If I could get between the others and the gun, they might have a chance. I might have tried, if it weren't for the fact that the footsteps were closer now. Much closer.

Holland tilted his head, hearing them too. His faint smile was pleasant, if you didn't know better. "I told you I always win."

In walked the other four grant kids. They barely glanced our way. Instead, they marched over to the floor near Abby and took a seat.

The only one who faltered was Ben. He gave the rest of us a sleepy-eyed look. "Are they joining the club too?" he asked, before plopping down on the floor a short distance away.

"Is this a new simulation?" Sharon wanted to know.

Maybe if I could reason with them, get them out of Holland's grip . . .

I blurted, "He's put chips in your heads. He's experiment-ing on your brains. Don't let him control you—help us!"

But they didn't even glance my way.

I wanted to scream at them. To tell them to run if they wouldn't help us. To get out now. But of course, it was far too late. Two adult figures emerged from the hallway, trail-ing the students.

Grassi, of course. I'd been expecting him. But the other man stole my breath away, like Holland had just punched me in the gut.

He met my eyes, and not a trace of expression flickered on his face.

Both of them withdrew guns.

In that moment, my heart broke. For the Watson kids, who were still completely clueless about what was going on, and who, by the looks of it, were halfway to becoming Holland's army. For Hunter, who hadn't been a part of this life until he'd met me. For Samuel and for Abby and yes, even for me.

For Daniel, who couldn't stand to lose me twice.

And for Lucas. Because he'd been betrayed. We both had.

Otherwise, Tim wouldn't be standing there, pointing a gun at Samuel and Abby.

Lucas must have let some tiny detail slip when he'd sent those check-in emails to the supply store. Either that or,

379

despite Lucas's caution, Holland had somehow managed to trace them.

In trying to ensure his brother's safety, Lucas had forfeited his own.

My hands itched to make contact with Tim's face.

Holland didn't budge, but watched me, smiling when he saw the shock sink in. My hands flexed. I remembered the feeling of his throat beneath them as I exerted a crushing pressure.

I should have killed him then.

"You son of a—"

The burst of rage that gripped me was a violent thing, hot and pulsating. It was a crack of lightning, flashing across the sky to blacken the tallest tree. For a second, I allowed the energy to fill my body, corrupting every cell. But I caught sight of Hunter as he tried to remove the binding from Abby's hands, and the image transported me. Back to Quinn's lab, to the outburst she'd stoked and steered.

I wiggled my fingers, rolled my shoulders back. Shoved the rage away until the feeling subsided like a retreating wave. It would never vanish completely, though. I knew that. Not while this man lived.

"Why is he here?" I nodded at Tim, proud of the steadiness I summoned.

"Didn't Lucas tell you about his big brother, Tim? Always a mess-up. I had to bail him out of trouble. Drugs.

Despicable waste. He paid me back, though. When Sarah . . . failed . . . at Montford, I had to do something. I couldn't let her tell others what she'd seen. But I couldn't do away with her myself, of course—too recognizable. So I sent Tim instead. It's amazing what people will do to stay out of army prison . . . and get their next high."

Tim didn't say anything. He didn't try to refute Holland's claims. He just kept the gun pointed at Samuel.

I remembered Maggie's description of the man she'd seen, just before the fire. Not Holland, but Holland's lapdog. Who'd left his master's pin behind.

All that time, in the Bitterroot mountains. I'd been sleeping in the same house as Sarah's killer. I flashed to Tim's erratic moods, his inability to look at me, his downright bizarre behavior. I'd chalked it up to a combination of alcohol and shame.

"Lucas?" I said. Knowing the answer from the triumphant gleam of Holland's eyes.

"Don't worry. We'll take you to them soon," he said.

At Holland's bidding, Tim and Grassi approached the students. With Grassi covering him, Tim bound each of their hands in turn. They seemed to think it was part of the simulation; Sharon's head jerked up when they touched her arm, but none of them bothered to struggle. Only Ben backed away a few feet.

I did as I was told and sat next to Samuel and Hunter,

whose hands were also bound. Not mine. They left mine free. That should have given me hope, but as I stared into Holland's impartial face, a sinking pit opened inside me. The lack of restraints was bad. A promise something terrible awaited me.

"We've got a journey to take. And I can't exactly bind your hands while you're walking across campus, can I? A conundrum."

He stepped closer, and suddenly, I was assaulted with his familiar scent of mint and astringent. His hawkeyed stare traveled over Hunter and Samuel. "Hunter Lowe. You've certainly traveled a long way from home. You, I'm unfamiliar with," he said, nodding at Samuel and Abby, "but I think I can safely assume you're some of Quinn's old team. I hope Mila told you that she won't be needing your services any longer."

Quinn's eyes filled my head, defiant until the very end. She'd be proud of Samuel now. The fierce glare he was giving Holland reminded me of hers.

I tried to channel some of that strength now. "Where are we going? What do you want from me?" I demanded.

"You have the missing link I need to finish this project," said Holland.

The missing link? What missing link? As always, his soft, pleasant drawl was at odds with what he was actually saying. Like tying a lacy ribbon around a bloody chain saw.

My sensors were still useless, but I didn't need them to figure this out: if I could mobilize the grant kids, we'd outnumber them.

"What missing link?" I repeated, both as a procrastination tool and from genuine interest.

"A special kind of neural cell, in your brain," Grassi answered, eager to share his contribution. I turned to him, but kept Holland in my peripheral vision.

"We first recognized your full potential on your PET scan. Certain areas of your brain lit up like a Christmas tree. It just so happened, those were the areas that allowed for more human and computer compatibility."

"Me? I don't have any special brain cells. I'm an android, remember?"

But even as I said it, I knew that wasn't quite true. I had Sarah's.

"Not only do you have special brain cells, but they're proliferating. In your head, just think about that for a minute," Holland said, spreading his arms. "You're not even fully human, and the very cells we need are flourishing. Perfect for harvesting and implanting in the other test subjects."

Without thinking, my hand reached for the back of my head. Beneath my hair and fabricated skull were tiny pieces of Sarah. Her brain cells, the currency of Holland's greed. The organic cells that Lucas had noticed, back in the desert.

Holland offered only false sympathy. "Trust me, we didn't want to do it. But using your brain to grow the cells was our only option at the time. They wouldn't grow in a test tube . . . and an animal brain would be too risky. Cross contamination," Holland said, like he thought I'd understand. "We didn't realize. They need a human host. Or a partly human one."

I licked my parched lips and glanced at the other grant students. They remained still, like marionettes waiting for someone to pull their strings. "Why not let them go, if I have the cells you need? Release them and I won't struggle."

That prompted a snicker from Grassi. Holland shot him a silencing glare. A reminder that this was his show. "You trying to bargain with me? Well, I can't fault the attempt. But we need the cells. We're behind production already."

"Production?" I heard Samuel say, drawing Holland's razor-sharp gaze.

"That's right. We've got a list of buyers just waiting on our product."

"What kind of buyers?" I asked.

"None of your concern."

But the truth was dawning. A horrific truth.

The truth that some people thought human life was a thing to be bartered for their own reward.

The truth born of a list of foreign names on a hidden hard drive.

The truth in realizing that the numbers following the names were actually prices, in hundreds of millions of dollars.

Apparently, that was the going rate for transforming teenagers into mechanical soldiers. And many people wanted them.

"You're selling android fighters to foreign countries," I spat. "So much for patriotism."

His anger manifested in narrowed eyes, a hiss of indrawn breath. An aggressive step forward.

"Foreign regimes that will be sympathetic to our great nation. We provide them the means to get rid of obstacles, and they support us when they're in charge. We sell them fighters with lethal training and—as you well know—undetectable, strategically placed bombs."

His tone changed to one of pride. "It's the perfect cover, see? No one ever suspects American kids. They're too steeped in privilege to put their own lives at risk." He glanced at his watch and scowled. "Enough. We need to get you back to DC."

"Is that where my target is?" I knew he was tiring of my questions. But I was deathly afraid of what would happen to the others when he took me away. He'd let them listen to far too much. There was no way he was going to let them walk.

To my surprise, Holland started to laugh. A genuine one.

"I see my nephew isn't as smart as he thinks he is. There is no target."

"But—"

"Oh, your bomb is built for one. Programmable to detonate near a target. But yours isn't set yet. I just fed the device some scrambled information to make it think it was."

I didn't get it. "Why?"

His smile sharpened. "Keep you guessing if you pulled another escape stunt. It's just a pity I missed out on all the fun."

Fun. All those times I'd panicked, worried I was going to put other lives in danger by stepping in just the wrong place. A lie.

I supposed I should have known. Like Holland had said—in the end, he always won.

"Don't blame Lucas too much. I planted bad intel on my laptop too. I figured you or Quinn might try to log in. I never realized I'd be setting up my own flesh and blood."

All this time. We'd never stood a chance.

Did I stay and fight for these kids, despite the odds stacked against me? Or go with Holland and try to sneak away once I'd learned more? Would I even be able to escape once he'd harvested my cells?

In the midst of my confusion, one face glowed behind my eyes, like a candle that just wouldn't snuff out.

Sarah. Urging me not to give up.

"Did he say bomb?" Ben asked, his voice sounding less monotone and more like his own. He rose to his feet in clumsy, jerking motions.

Holland turned to Grassi. "This must be one of our rejects?"

I took advantage of the distraction and launched myself at Holland.

Ben saw me move and staggered forward too, sluggish from fighting the mind control. "Stop . . . him . . ." he forced out.

Hands still bound, Samuel leapt to his feet, while Hunter threw himself in front of Abby.

Holland began to turn back, and then everything happened quickly. I was only a few feet away when the gun jerked in his hand. I looked over my shoulder to see Ben clutch his stomach in surprise before crumpling to the ground.

Blood gushed from his wound, creating a large pool on the floor.

By the time I turned back, Holland had his gun aimed again. This time at Samuel.

I didn't dare move, unless I wanted someone else to get shot.

Holland laughed softly and tilted his head. "It appears you've forgotten your manners, Mila. Let's see if I can kickstart them for you."

He reached into his pocket and pulled out a black square. Before I could even breathe, he'd flipped the switch.

The signal appeared behind my eyes. No fanfare, no fancy introduction. Not even a click or a snap.

The words were enough to make my heart stop, to make the faux blood in my faux veins freeze, to make time and space fall away. My knees threatened to buckle while I processed my panic. It threatened to shut my entire system down.

Whenever I'd imagined this moment, I always thought there'd be more. Not just two little words.

Two words. That was all it took.

Countdown initiated.

My gasp sounded ragged.

Time to detonation: 120 minutes.

"Mila? What?" Samuel said, straining his bindings.

"The bomb. He activated it," I said. Maybe it was shock, but my voice sounded unconcerned. Like I was telling him about the weather.

"NO!" Two howls, merged into one. Samuel. And Hunter. Even Hunter. Maybe he had truly forgiven me.

Holland watched the play of emotions across my face, smug in the knowledge that once again, he'd come out on top. "I'm the only one who knows the deactivation code. If I die, the bomb goes off. If you come with me, I can still shut it down. Otherwise . . ."

He'd planned his trap, and well. If I stayed, everyone in the room would die. If I killed Holland at any point along the way, I'd explode. He'd keep me in line with potential victims. Line them up in a row; see if Mila can save them.

Mom. Peyton. So far, my track record sucked.

He had me. There was no sense in fighting. But I'd started this journey to seek redemption. I wasn't going to stop now.

Out of sight to everyone but me, a tiny timetable spun a continuous countdown in shiny, glowing green.

118 mins, 56 secs.

118 mins, 55 secs.

118 mins, 54 secs.

Holland motioned me toward the door, but when Samuel went to follow, he shook his head. "No. Just her."

He didn't need a hostage to bring along, because two were already waiting. Daniel. And Lucas.

If Holland had hurt them, the bomb might as well explode right now, because I'd be done.

I looked over my shoulder, searched deep inside myself, and summoned a brave smile for my team. "Don't worry. I've got this."

False words. But I didn't want to know the team to know how little hope I had.

Before I turned away, I locked eyes with Hunter one last time. In my mind, I wished him a silent farewell. I hoped that somehow he'd escape. That he and Abby would have a long life together.

I saw the indecision in his blue eyes. He looked at Abby and then his head swiveled until he stared at Ben, who hadn't moved from his awkward position on the floor. Eyes glassy, a broken doll in a pool of red.

When he looked up, I gave an almost imperceptible shake of my head. No. If he tried anything now, he'd end up just like Ben.

On the way out, I made eye contact with Tim. The force of the contempt in my stare should have cut him like a laser. He didn't flinch. But his pulse rose, by several beats. I could sense it now.

Afraid? Of me? That didn't make much sense. And then, he did something even more bizarre. He inclined his chin, just the barest bit. I almost thought I'd imagined it. And I had no idea what it meant.

Then I was in the corridor and in the building and walking the path that would lead me off the Montford campus and away from the people in that room for good.

"Where are they?" I said, once we were out of earshot.

At least Holland didn't pretend not to know who I meant. "You'll see them soon enough."

The rain had stopped, but the air was still thick with humidity. Our walk across campus to the parking lot was surprisingly uneventful. Most of the students had retreated to warmer quarters; we only saw a couple here and there and no one paid us much attention. Why would they? I couldn't struggle or fight; if I did, someone would die. Holland had me chained just as surely as if the steel rings bit into my wrists.

Even the video camera at the gate was easy. "Temporarily disabled," Holland said. He didn't talk as he led me to the parking lot, but the silence was almost worse. When he spoke, I knew what he was thinking. When he was quiet . . . that's when my fears multiplied.

He led me to a black van, opened the passenger door, and shoved me toward the seat. "You're driving."

He climbed into the back before passing me the keys. After following a series of barked-out directions, I pulled up next to a vacant field. Only one other vehicle was there, and my heart skipped a beat when I saw it. Lucas's white van.

"Pull up right next to it," Holland snapped. I did as I was told. As we approached, the door slid open, and my doors did as well. Daniel's face flashed in the depths of the other van, before one of Holland's men blocked my view and pulled someone from the back.

Lucas. His feet were bound and his hands were zip tied in front of him, but otherwise he seemed to be in one piece. The man shoved him across the narrow gap into our van, where Lucas tripped and almost dove headfirst onto his uncle's lap. He righted himself at the last second, flipping his body weight until he landed in the empty seat.

I followed Holland's order to shut the door. I'd follow all his orders. Any. So long as my good behavior would keep Lucas safe. Within minutes, we were back on the road, the other van following closely behind.

In the rearview mirror, I could see Holland reclined next to Lucas, pressing a gun to his temple. Above the duct tape that covered his mouth, his eyes were calm. I scanned the distance between us, assessed the amount of time I could reach Lucas. I had it down to the millisecond.

In every calculation, Holland's trigger finger was faster.

"If you make so much as a tiny detour off the route, or take one of your hands off the wheel for anything other than a turn signal, I'll start shooting. One body part at a time," Holland said. The edges of his words were soft, as if he were discussing his favorite restaurant.

My heart pumped faster; I willed it to slow. Every bit of energy needed to go to my brain. A way out—there had to be one.

"No matter what, you lose," said Holland, like he was reading my mind. "How much time left now?" He glanced at the oversized silver watch on his wrist. "An hour and forty-five minutes, give or take a few? Doesn't give us much time to get to the helicopter and fly to DC. There, we'll get our hands on your brain cells. Once we implant them in our soldiers, our product will be complete."

He wasn't leaving much room for error. Could we really get to DC that quickly? My bomb could detonate on the way.

I looked at him incredulously. "So you're willing to die for this? Just to get my brain cells?" If there was one thing I'd never pegged Holland as, it was a martyr. He thought too highly of himself.

At that, he laughed. "Hell no. If we cut it too close, I'll ditch you in a heartbeat."

So starting the bomb. It was just an extravagant, over-done way to bring me to heel.

I navigated the van through traffic, making sure to keep both hands on the steering wheel. Memories accosted me. *Driving my mom, while Holland's men shot at us. Her blood, pooling on asphalt.*

My breath hitched in my chest; my vision narrowed, until all I could see was the road ahead. One step at a time. I would find a way.

I could hear the bomb ticking.

The traffic thinned as the cityscape melted into grass and trees.

"I'd say I was disappointed that you were involved, Lucas, but I knew better than to expect much after your brother was such a waste of space. It's all about the genes. Joanna, the mouse who's petrified of her own shadow, and your father. You've got brains, but you're too damn soft, and your loyalty's all in the wrong place. A pity."

Lucas made a sound, like he wanted to talk.

"You want to tell me why? Go ahead." With a flick of his wrist, Holland ripped off the duct tape.

Lucas inhaled a few times before speaking. "My loyalty's not in the wrong place. Yours is. Instead of defending your country, you look out for number one. You." I don't know why it surprised me that Lucas's voice was calm and clear. My heart swelled with pride but my lungs filled with fear at what Holland would do now.

A hiss, followed by a ragged gasp. In desperation, I glanced over my shoulder. Holland still held the gun to Lucas's head, but now his other hand was around his throat. Squeezing.

"Drive," he barked.

The image of Lucas's red face and clawing fingers burned into my eyes. I felt trapped, desperate. Every cell in my body wanted to yank the steering wheel to the shoulder, throw the van into park, fly into the backseat, and turn the barrel on Holland. But he had me tied up as much as if I'd been chained.

He knew I wouldn't risk Lucas's life, or the lives of the kids back at Montford. They were under Tim's hateful watch now, and they were counting on me.

All I could do was bide my time.

The gasps had receded, spiking my panic to a fever pitch. "He can't breathe," I screamed, keeping my eyes on the road. Was he going to murder his own nephew?

Holland laughed, enjoying my panic.

"If you kill him, you'll be dead within five seconds," I said. This time, my tone was as conversational as his. I glanced into the rearview, triumphant gray eyes clashing with brown. My expression matched my voice. Calm. Pleasant.

Resolved.

Lucas's eyes rolled when Holland released him. For a terrifying moment, his head flopped forward and no sound emerged.

My foot went for the brake, but before I could slam it, a terrible, rasping wheeze filled the van.

Lucas, sucking air down his swollen throat.

Holland tracked my concern with curiosity. "This is an interesting development. I hadn't realized you had feelings for him."

"Don't tell me you feel the same way," he said to Lucas.

When Lucas refused to look at him or answer, Holland's hand shot out and grabbed his chin, jerking it in his direction. "I asked you a question," he said.

Lie, I urged Lucas. *If you do have feelings for me, lie.*

Even as I pleaded with him in my mind, I knew it was a lost cause. Lucas never lied. In the rearview, I saw him smile. "I do. It's logic defying, really. How on earth did someone as horrible as you manage to create something as amazing as her?"

Lucas twisted his face away. In the mirror, his eyes met mine, shining and fierce.

Holland's punch cracked through the interior. Lucas's head whipped back hard. "And I always thought you were the smart one. Idiot."

The drive seemed interminably long, up until the point where Holland told me to stop. Then, it seemed entirely too short. As we drove around a large building in the middle of a field, a helicopter was revealed, dormant for now on top of a landing square.

I climbed out of the car, marching just ahead of Holland and Lucas. The doors on the other van opened, and two men emerged with Daniel. Holland told us the plan.

"The three of us are going in the Huey. Dave and Brady will stay behind with Daniel, just to be safe. We're just waiting for Grassi. Stay there, against the wall." He jerked his gun at the white aluminum building behind us. I slid down the wall, resigning myself to the inevitable.

Brady came over, dumping Lucas in a heap beside me. I helped him sit up, trying to fight back tears.

"Don't cry," Lucas said. "Not over me. You've had enough sadness for one short life."

That only made my eyes fill up more. Even in this state, in bonds and beaten, Lucas worried about me.

"You two want to be together so much, here's your chance," Holland taunted us. I couldn't stand the mocking. But I also couldn't stand to lose the possibility.

Lucas caught the intent in my eyes, and just the very

edges of his lips curved up. I laugh-sobbed and with one hand, gently cupped his cheek.

And then my lips touched Lucas's and for the moment at least, Holland faded away.

For these few, shining moments, it would be just the two of us. Sharing something bright and warm, full of the good parts of humanity.

Lucas's mouth moved over mine, or mine over his. I wasn't sure and I didn't care. I grasped his shoulders and pulled him close, trying to press into him a lifetime of wanting and need.

Trying to absorb a lifetime in return, to carry with me in my final moments. His body, his scent, the soft graze of his eyelashes against mine. The way, even now, he let me take the lead when I wanted. Everything about him, and us, felt right. Full of possibility. A partnership born of complete acceptance.

The kiss joined us, forged a bond that neither Holland nor his goons nor anyone else could touch. I wanted to sink into this moment, into Lucas, and remain here forever.

Holland had other ideas.

Rough hands grabbed my shoulders and I gasped. Too soon, it was too soon.

The last press of his lips was salty with tears: his or mine, I wasn't sure. And then I let the hands pull us apart. The last I felt of Lucas was the sensation of his fingertips slip-sliding against mine, until even that tiny bit of contact was lost.

I remained calm.

For one moment, I had been at peace.

"Abominations, both of you," Holland said. "Where the hell is Grassi?"

Brady shrugged. "He hasn't checked back in yet. Maybe his phone died."

While Holland cursed Grassi and Brady out for carrying half-charged phones on assignment, Tim's face flashed in my mind. The way he'd refused to show any expression. His rise in pulse. The army pin, planted at the scene of the fire. What was he trying to say?

"Why didn't you come sooner?" I asked Holland. "You could have found us before we uncovered your plan."

"I would have, if Lucas had checked in with his brother sooner," Holland growled.

"My brother? What does Tim have to do with this?"

Holland's grin sharpened as he smelled blood. "Didn't I mention it? He's the one who helped me track you down."

"What? No . . ." Lucas sagged against his captor, his pale face going gray. "I can't believe . . ." His anguish was a horrible thing to witness. "Mila, I'm so sorry."

"Don't apologize. Not to me, not for things that this monster has done. There is no shame in giving someone the benefit of the doubt. You thought Tim had changed."

Lucas's lashes were dark with tears when he looked at

me. And then his eyes widened, just a little. He mouthed something at me.

"I did check in sooner."

And apparently Tim hadn't said a word to Holland.

Could he have wanted us to uncover Holland's scheme?

Could he have left the pin at the fire, so someday someone could follow the trail?

Could he have wanted forgiveness? Redemption? More than anyone, I knew what that was like. I also knew I might never get the answers about Tim. But suddenly I felt differently about leaving the Montford kids in his care.

Holland's gaze traveled between the two of us. He didn't know what had passed between us, but he didn't like it.

"New plan. We're leaving Grassi and getting on now. Brady, start it up and get Lucas on board."

The blades began to move with a groan, slowly at first but then building up speed until my hair whipped at my face and everyone had to shout to be heard.

Brady screamed over the ruckus. "Wait, just got a text from Grassi—he's almost here. Needed to stop for gas," he yelled, but his words got plucked up by the wind and tossed away.

Meanwhile, he was having a hard time getting Lucas forward. Lucas had pretended to faint, and the effort of trying to drag him while not letting go of his gun was proving to be a challenge.

Unnoticed by anyone but me, a lone car raced down the road. One hundred yards away but gaining on us rapidly. I scanned the contents; my sensors were barely back online. Three people. Two guns. Not enough information to make a decision. But just enough to hope. And plan.

I edged closer to Brady and Lucas, putting myself in their path. From the back window of the van, I caught a quick motion. Daniel's foot. Just before it smashed into the window.

The car was pulling up, but Holland still hadn't heard it. I prepared myself. I would have one chance to make this work.

And then the car pulled into view. I saw the driver at the same time Holland did. It was Hunter. And he wasn't stopping. He gunned the car at Holland.

Now.

Brady's attention, diverted by the car, was the next break I needed. I lunged behind him, one arm around his throat, the other squeezing his wrist until the gun slipped from his grasp. I smashed the gun over his skull, and he crumpled. Quickly, I squatted and freed Lucas from his bonds. I pressed one quick kiss to his lips, trying to commit the feeling to memory.

"Quick, go help Daniel," I said, handing him the gun.

Holland had dodged the car but fallen in the process, giving Samuel time to jump out and pin him with a Taser. A minute later, and I had the detonator in my hand.

Lucas was safe. What I'd been longing for since Nicole had been killed—bringing Holland down—had finally happened.

Throat knotting, I took a step toward the helicopter.

"You don't have to!" Lucas yelled over the deafening sound of the helicopter's blades. "We've got Holland. We can get him to stop the bomb in trade for his life."

The lump in my throat grew. "They'll just keep coming. As long as I exist. Even if Holland is gone. There'll be someone else, like Quinn or Grassi, who'll find out about me and try to use me for whatever twisted plan they have. I can't take the risk. And I can't run anymore."

He opened his mouth to argue, but no words came. He knew I was right, and it wasn't in him to try to persuade me otherwise.

"We could hide. We did just fine at the cabin, didn't we?"

But I could tell by the sad smile that he knew that what I was going to say.

"You shouldn't have to live like that."

He reached forward, traced my mouth with his thumb. "But we'd be together."

Tempting. So tempting. "For how long? We'd always be looking over our shoulders, wondering when I might be discovered. Please trust me, this is the right thing to do."

"Like I said, you're one of the bravest people I know."

His hand cupped my cheek; mine cupped his. Equals.

I could have stood like that for hours. Breaking the contact was like ripping up a piece of me. Step one in leaving him—everything—behind. But it had to be done. I backed away, urging myself to turn around, but faltering.

And then my mom's last words floated through my head, lending me warmth. "If no harm would come to others, I promise, I would choose to live," I said softly.

But people would be harmed if I stayed. And I had inflicted so much suffering already.

This was my choice. What he did with that knowledge was his.

Then I turned and ran for the helicopter, jumping into the driver's seat.

Daniel's anguished cry caught my ears, but I knew he would understand, too. Eventually. As much as he cared about me, he would want to protect other people's daughters more.

The dashboard was a maze of buttons and knobs, but my android sensors took over, directing me.

Before I could lift off though, Samuel shouted, "Wait!"

I looked to see Daniel sprinting over to Holland, and punching him in the face. Once. Twice. Three times. None of it would bring back his daughter or save me, but it was certainly a little bit of justice served.

When Holland was barely conscious to fight back, Daniel and Samuel began dragging him. Toward me. I started to shake my head, knowing what they had in mind.

Daniel cut me short. "Mila, this is the only way we'll know for sure those kids will be safe. And future kids. Other people's Sarahs."

I looked at Holland, my mind at war with itself. Taking him with me was murder. But leaving him behind could very well be too. I found myself seeking Lucas, one last time. My beautiful pacifist. There was no way he'd be okay with this.

What I saw in his eyes surprised me. "Like you said, they'll keep coming. There are no guarantees what will happen to him in a trial."

"Lucas," I said, shaking my head.

His jaw flexed before he sighed. "I know. But if he chose?"

"Why on earth would—"

But Lucas was already walking away, heading straight for his half-conscious uncle.

So I waited. I waited while Lucas knelt down and whispered in his uncle's ear. I saw Holland jerk, then flinch. A minute later, Lucas rose. "Put him in the copter," he said. Samuel and Daniel complied, hoisting him into the passenger seat and buckling him in.

I approached the pilot's side, where Lucas waited. "What did you say to him?" I asked. A little afraid.

"I reminded him how traitors are treated in this country.

How his name would be ruined. He'd be a laughingstock, the brunt of jokes for years to come. I told him his life was pretty much over anyway, and if he went, we could try to keep his involvement quiet."

"Lucas," I started, but he shook his head, eyes fierce.

"I gave him a choice, and he took it. Don't you feel bad for him. Not even for a second. A choice was more than he deserved. If there was any justice, he'd live out a very long life in a very small cell. Humiliated and broken."

I glanced over at Holland, who watched us from the passenger seat. "If you feel that way, why even give him a choice?"

"Because," he said, reaching out one last time to stroke my cheek. "Because in his entire despicable life, he did one thing right. He made you."

With that, he pulled my face to his chest, and I felt his lips brush my hair. "Remember me, Mila," he whispered. Before he stepped back and let go.

I took one last look at his face before turning and climbing into the pilot's seat. Holland leveled curses at me as the helicopter lifted off, his bitter voice drowned out by the countdown inside my head.

59 minutes, 16 seconds.

59 minutes, 15 seconds.

59 minutes, 14 seconds.

Most people have no idea how much time they have left

before their lives are over. I knew I had less than an hour, and I wasn't afraid.

Not because I *couldn't* feel fear, but because after all was said and done, it was clear that my emotions—programmed or not—were what made me more than Holland had ever bargained for.

I wasn't afraid because I was at the controls, steering the course, choosing to make the sacrifice that Nicole and Sarah had unwittingly made before me.

And because I would remember Lucas—remember *us*—during every last second of the helicopter's rapid descent over the Potomac, right before the countdown expired.

He made sure of that. Lucas always found a way.

I'm with you, Mila.

Do you hear me?

You're not alone.

And I swear, this isn't goodb----------

ACKNOWLEDGMENTS

Well, there you have it! The final chapter in the MILA trilogy. As you might expect, I have many people to thank for making the three books in the MILA-verse possible.

First of all—the series would not exist without the wonderful team at HarperCollins. A very special thanks to my editors, Claudia Gabel and Melissa Miller, who stuck by me for the long haul. Also, thank you to Katherine Tegen, Kate Jackson, and Suzanne Murphy. Thanks to subrights wiz Jean McGinley for helping to bring Mila to readers in so many different countries. Thank you to Erin Fitzsimmons, Amy Ryan, and Barbara Fitzsimmons for the stunning covers and beautiful design, and thanks to marketing wonders Lauren Flower, Alana Whitman, and Carmen Alvarez. No book would be polished without copyediting and production, so thanks to Bethany Reis and Kara Levy for fixing all the little things that authors forget. Finally, thank you to my publicist, Rosanne Romanello, and anyone else who I might not have named but who helped bring this series to fruition in some small way, shape, or form.

A big hug and thank-you to my lovely agent, Taylor Martindale, for always being there, and to the Full Circle and Sandra Dijkstra Literary Agencies.

To my writer friends—MUAH. Again, I cannot commend the YA community enough for all the understanding, camaraderie, and support. Without you, I would not be the person I am today. Thank you for opening my eyes to so many different experiences and perspectives. A special MUAH to the amazing ladies of YA Highway and my LBs. I love my little writer bat caves. Thanks also to the Luckies and Binders, for sharing stories and offering support. To Sarah, Rachael, and Jenn, for reading chapters and assuring me I hadn't forgotten how to write.

Thank you to my nonwriter friends, for dragging me out of the writer cave once in a while.

A shout-out to my family, both immediate and extended, for their bottomless support, and especially my husband, Scott, who makes this all possible, and Connor and Finley, just because. Mom, thank you again for making me a reader. I miss you.

To all the bloggers out there—you rock. Thanks for

donating your time and spreading the word. A special thanks to local blogger extraordinaire Stacee, whose enthusiasm and support for authors never ceases to amaze.

And last but not least, huge, tearful thanks to all of you readers who have faithfully followed Mila on her many adventures. During these past few years, I've discovered that life really is all about the journey. I'm so thrilled that I got to share part of my journey with you. Throughout the course of these books, Mila and I both learned the hard way that challenges are often opportunities for growth in disguise, and that ultimately your opinion of yourself is the one that matters most. If I could leave you with a few thoughts, it would be these: don't let anyone take away your right to define yourself. And please, keep challenging yourselves, keep growing, and know that yes, you are indeed worth it.

Always.

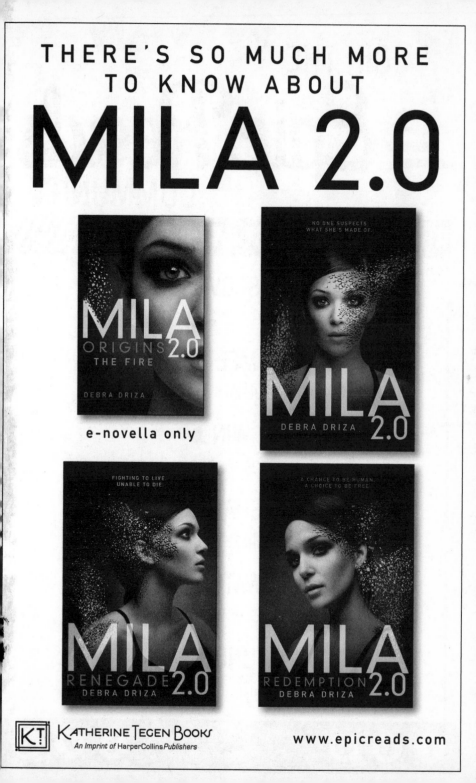

JOIN THE

Epic Reads
COMMUNITY

THE ULTIMATE YA DESTINATION

◀ **DISCOVER** ▶
your next favorite read

◀ **MEET** ▶
new authors to love

◀ **WIN** ▶
free books

◀ **SHARE** ▶
infographics, playlists, quizzes, and more

◀ **WATCH** ▶
the latest videos

◀ **TUNE IN** ▶
to Tea Time with Team Epic Reads

Find us at **www.epicreads.com**
and **@epicreads**